W9-AJO-486

The Great Days

Other books by John Dos Passos:

Three Soldiers
Manhattan Transfer
U.S.A.
District of Columbia
Chosen Country
The Most Likely to Succeed

John Dos Passos

NEW YORK
SAGAMORE PRESS INC.

The Great Days

Although many of the events described in this novel actually happened the people who are described as taking part in them were all made up in the author's head. Any resemblances to actual men and women living or dead are accidental and unintended.

The Great Days

Published simultaneously in Canada
by McClelland & Stewart Ltd.
Library of Congress Card Number: 58-6966
Manufactured in the United States of America
Designers: Ernst Reichl Associates

1

The man in the belted raincoat stands hesitant at the top of the gangway. His ears roar. Blinking, he looks out across the colorless dazzle of the airfield towards the row of nondescript sheds and barracks that throw wan shadows in the early light.

This is not what he was remembering. As the press of passengers behind him forces him down the rubberlined steps he is telling himself (you damn fool) that what he was remembering was the old seaplane base and the blue and umber globe in the middle of the bright hall and the glitter of brass and the names of southerly cities: Camaguey, Paramaribo, Belem, Porto Alegre; the sunlight pouring through; and sunscorched friends to meet him: "God it's good to see you, Ro," and the hard grasp of their hands and their eyes admiring and their quizzical words, "Roly the rolling stone," and drinks and sitting easy at tables on the edge of the sunlight in the briny wind off the Gulf Stream and looking out past their laughing faces at the purple shoal water and the horizon capped with cumulus clouds and under the clouds the deep swell of the ocean and the knowledge of islands in the wind's eye.

With his ticket in his hand the man in the belted raincoat shuffles in the queue waiting at the baggage counter. He looks up at the clock on the wall. An hour and forty-five minutes before her plane arrives. Time to pull himself together. He finds himself staring at two suitcases of scuffed English pigskin. They have an alien look but they must be his. There's his name: Roland Lancaster; *Hotel Lafayette* on the smeared tags. God he's sick of seeing that name on a byline.

Not the only one to be sick of it, says a little spiteful inner voice. They are tearing down the old hotel; every time he publishes anything the critics tear down his poor old name. He hears the spite in his own voice when he asks the attendant about rechecking his bags. Lay off, it's not that guy's fault. The misery he planned to leave behind rises in him like bile. Forlorn. Even five years ago there would have been someone to meet him, the sour face of an aging old crony twisted into a reminiscent smile, or a kid reporter who had gotten up early to ask his slant on the morning's news.

The English raincoat with its heavy lining. Stifling him. That's the trouble. It was snowing last night at La Guardia.

Breakfast. Eat some breakfast and forget it. Breakfast will put the lid on all the old leftover gloom. This is the first breakfast on his trip.

The man in the belted raincoat buys a morning paper

and sits down at the lunchcounter and orders fried eggs and bacon from a fagged waitress. When he opens the paper he half expects from the force of old habit to see his name. Hell nobody knows he's here. Wouldn't mean anything to them anymore if they did know.

Easy now . . . Hasn't he always entertained the dream of boxing up his old wornout life and sending it to dead storage? And changing his name and moving to another country. A new life from today henceforward. Well? The new girl is flying to meet him. Not doing too badly . . . A man can start again at fiftynine, if he's man enough.

Roland Lancaster grins into his coffee cup. He can see Elsa the way she must look right now sitting with her eyes closed in the seat of the humming stratoliner with that sullen puzzled expression he saw on her face under the mop of her red hair when she slept that night on the train.

He drinks down his orange juice.

He is relishing his coffee.

The headlines in the paper fade in his mind as fast as he reads them. For the third time he starts to read the column on a grand jury's indictment of the district attorney for taking money from a syndicate of gamblers.

Half way down the page the print fades . . . Is he in love with Elsa or isn't he? She's a strange girl. Too young for him, of course, but so much has happened to her: her hapless marriage has aged her up. Forlorn. She needs him as much as he needs her.

More.

It is not only a question of money. It is his confidence she needs, the ability to put on the dog, that sort of thing. He'll make plenty of money once he gets his grip on the world again. He has always made money. But he will have to tell her how close he is sailing to the wind right now. She isn't a girl who kids herself. The figures $49.50 pop up in his head like the total on a cash register. That's his bank balance. $49.50 was his bank balance after he paid the plane fares and drew out the cash for his trip. At least he isn't overdrawn.

He feels the sour grin spreading across his face. In the old days he was always overdrawn. Didn't matter in the old days with all that money coming in. All his life he'd found ways to make money when he needed it. Would again, but he'd have to be careful. Elsa wasn't extravagant. Still he was a fool to carry his money in cash. Ought to have bought express checks instead of toting that great wad of cash. Buy express checks in Havana, he admonishes himself sagely. He lets his hand slip back to his back trousers pocket to make sure his wallet is still there.

As he sips the last of his coffee his eyes follow the waitress while she limps around behind the saggy counter with a rag in her hand. Her frizzy hair has grown out since it was bleached so that the dark ends show against her head. Bags under her eyes. Crowsfeet. Saggy granulated skin. Fagged. Up too late last night. Middleaged. Forlorn.

Elsa is young and strong, but that's the sort of job she would be taking if she got stranded someplace. That waitress and Elsa they live in the same world.

A gamble, this trip is a gamble for both of them. Maybe he and Elsa will get stranded together.

What would the waitress think if she knew he was sitting there sipping her lousy coffee with three thousand smackers in his pocket? A gamble. Elsa now, Elsa was the kind of girl who'd love a gambling man.

He has to admit to himself he doesn't know too much what kind of a girl she is, not with those kids always around. The old woman who lived in a shoe, he'd teased her about that. Those twins never would go to bed. How did that damned jive artist ever manage to support them all?

. . . Now for me, the man in the belted raincoat thinks,

for me money never was a problem. I never had any trouble supporting Grace or paying Chips' or Louie's college bills for that matter up to the time they flunked out. The trouble was somewhere else, hadn't raised them right, poor little devils. Oh well, the army and navy had taken them over. The Korean war. It was up to Uncle Sam to turn boys into men . . .

The waitress is scrutinizing him with a bleary eye. "Another cup of coffee?" she asks. He doesn't answer.

. . . And Grace's face pale and taut in the hospital bed, her hair a muss on the pillow. "It's because of us, Ro. If we'd turned out right, they would . . ."

It was the day before she died.

He winces from the pain. These are the things he went to all this trouble to stop thinking about.

The waitress has her eye on him. She piles his knife and fork and cup and saucer on his eggy plate and brushes the crumbs off the counter with his crumpled paper napkin.

"You sick?" she asks.

He shakes his head.

"I don't mind telling you I am," she says with a sigh.

To get her inquisitive eyes off his face he orders another cup of coffee.

He must keep his mind on Elsa.

He begins to think meticulously back over the last months. They'd never really been alone except that night on the Pennsylvania train in the drawing room when they drank so much whiskey. He was on his way to do the big Chicago article. What a flop that article had been. Damn good article too.

He has finished the coffee.

For the fourth time he tries to read the grand jury's indictment of the district attorney.

He feels too damn miserable.

It would have been so simple just to have died the day the Japs shot up that observation plane over Manila . . .

. . . The black oil from the conked out motor welling over the wing beside me and the thoughtful way the P.R.O. in the next seat kept licking his lips and how quiet we all sat as we passed the heavy belts of ammo back to the gunner who was dropping them out through the bombbay. "I guess they'll throw out the correspondents next," I shouted and somebody repeated it over the intercom and the guys looked grateful to me for breaking up the tension.

God how alive we felt when we tumbled out of the plane onto the steel mesh of Lingayen airstrip and how we laughed in the faces of the men with the fire extinguishers and the ambulance waiting. Alive enough to live a thousand years.

It was after I came home that the misery began . . .

The man in the belted raincoat is staring up at the "on time" on the blackboard against the number of the incoming Chicago plane. He has been waiting patiently, hardly anxious at all, but now he is in a dither to see her.

Half afraid, too.

The attendants in their white jumpers are pushing the gangway up against the plane's trembling silver flank while he stands batting his eyes as he leans against the railing looking into the sun.

The door opens. The stewardess smiles at somebody. Inconsequential people come tumbling out, pallid, wintry-looking; Elsa among them, tall and frowsty with her hair over her shoulders. Her hair shines cruelly red in the flailing sun. She is still wearing those canvas sneakers that always look runover. She walks well all the same. A calm even stride.

"Well," she says and puts her hand on his arm. "I didn't sleep a wink. Did you?"

He kisses her but her mouth slips away from his.

"Had any breakfast?"

She puckers her lips.

"An airplane breakfast. I'd just gotten to sleep when a stewardess shoved it under my nose. When do we take off?"

"Ten thirty. Rancho Boyeros in about an hour. Lunch at that place at the beginning of Obispo I keep forgetting the name of."

"Las Delicias?" she asks with a childish pleased smile. He is surprised how well she pronounces the Spanish. "That's where we met Mortimer Price." Her tongue starts rattling. "The great man was very nice to us. Asked us over to his table and everything. Everybody said he'd bite our heads off."

"He likes up and coming young guys."

"Up and coming phew."

She faces him with eyes hard as pebbles. Then quickly she smiles. "And next day we met you. We sure were excited about meeting all the celebrities."

"You were coming out of the elevator in the old Spanish hotel."

He's remembering the skin pink behind the white embroidery of her blouse, the heavy auburn of her hair, the pale brown eyes round like an astonished schoolboy's, the frank "How do you do," the delighted "Imagine meeting you here," the plain handshake like a man's. "Gov said you were staying in the same hotel but I didn't believe him."

Even a year ago she didn't look young; forlorn, rather, Ro's remembering. Behind her came shambling that sallow short young man, with extraordinarily large dark eyes that he kept blinking. Gouverneur Haines. Ro remembers how his first thought was that the guy must be a bloody bore, these young New York characters that get successful too soon.

"This time we'll make the world our oyster." The boom of Ro's voice jars on his own ears as he settles Elsa at a table in the lunchroom. He catches a disapproving smirk on the fagged face of the waitress behind the counter. The waitress's mouth is all pursed up. "Old enough to be her father," that's what the waitress is thinking; and suddenly he sees himself through the waitress's eyes, a sick old fool doddering over a young woman.

"You drink the coffee while I check us in at the counter," he says to Elsa in a tone more peremptory than he intends. "A cup of coffee, please," he tells the waitress defiantly. "For the young lady."

He feels like a travel agent as he strides across the waitingroom ruffling the edges of the tickets through his fingers. He is good at that sort of thing, Lord knows he has had enough practice.

When he sees her two oldfashioned suitcases leaning pathetically together on the scales, the tenderness clutchs at his heart like a hand. They must have belonged to her mother. Not a golddigger's suitcases, not by a long shot. They are the suitcases a Swedish servant girl would land with at Ellis Island.

His eyes are still moist when he starts back towards her. He is thinking about how to tell her about that comic wartime flight with Mortimer to Lisbon, and the old seaplane base, and the Dorchester during the bombings, and wartime Washington, the diagnostic finger on the pulse of power; the days when Key West was still an island and there were all the fish in the sea to catch, all the whiskey in all the pubs to drink, all the grand guys in the world to be friends with. He must kindle that feeling in her, the feeling of great days.

"Gate four in ten minutes," he tells her. His pulse flutters a little with the old giddiness of departure.

She looks up at him with crinkled brows as he leans across the table to pick up the check. "Ro," she asks, "what color was your hair before it turned gray?"

He feels a tenseness in his hands. "You ought to know by this time, kind of reddish." He finds he is snapping his fingers.

"I wish it hadn't been. My husband was a redhead too. Redheads should never take up with each other."

"How about Gov? His hair is black."

Her eyes are those pebbles again. Suddenly there is no light in them. "You needn't have brought that up," she says pouting.

"But Elsa," he starts in a reasoning fatherly tone, "we'll both have to retrace our lives a little. Havana will be full of old footsteps to me. Even for you. After all that was where we first met last year. You were stepping out of that decrepit openwork elevator."

"Thought I looked decrepit, did you?" She's kidding him now. They both begin to laugh. The loudspeaker voice is rattling off the departure of their plane. Arm in arm they hurry out into the sunlight.

The tenderness wells up in him again when he leans over her to fasten her seatbelt. He feels as if tears might come to his eyes. "We've got so much to catch up on," he whispers with his lips against her ear. She doesn't use any perfume. His nostrils fill with the tang of her red hair. He can feel the warmth of her body through the tips of his fingers.

The plane has begun to taxi off across the airfield; she can't hear what he is saying anyway. He grins at her reassuringly. She grins back. There is something quieting and strengthening about the feel of her thigh against his. He needs a woman so. He lays his hand over hers where it lies in her lap. She grasps his hand with her long fingers. It has been years since he has felt happy like this. They are both of them looking out expectantly along the bright surface of the wing.

The motors roar to warm up. The plane shakes. The motors are throttled down. The plane starts to race down the runway into the wind. They are airborne.

For an instant Miami spreads out beyond the end of the wing in pink and white cubes, then flattens to a map on the wall; soon the wing is sweeping the bay sprinkled with toy boats and the fancy architecture of the ranked hotels and the long stretch of beach blurred where the surf is. Then they are levelling off over rippled sea so blue it is purple and looking down on the steamy clouds over the Gulf Stream.

It all crowds back so fast into his head he can't find the place to begin. I must tell her about everything. He must even tell her about Thurloe, Thurloe and Grace; and Mortimer Price. What he doesn't know about Mortimer.

"Remind me to tell you a story about Mortimer," Ro shouts into Elsa's ear. The tangle of her red hair tickles his nose as she turns her face towards his with an uncomprehending smile. She hardly seems to know who he is. She too is deep in some reverie. "No use trying to talk," he goes on lamely, "just jangles your vocal chords."

A couple of minutes later, he is the travel agent again. He points past her short nose towards the curved reach of mottled land and water, colored like the contours in a geography book, white and yellow and muddy green with streaks of bright green darkening to blue where the channels are. "Those are the Florida Keys," he shouts.

It is like falling, like falling deep in a dream, the way the words open a pit of memory as he speaks them: the Florida Keys . . .

. . . Grace and I had hardly been married a year. I remember us sitting in the sun with the top down in that Ford roadster we bought in Miami. How we loved that old Model A. We were navigating the rough old road south of Homestead. It was Grace's stint at the wheel. I couldn't keep my eyes off her she looked so cute and plump and selfpossessed with her curls that were so blonde in those days all tied up in a blue bandanna. When it turned out that we were late and had to race to catch the ferry the tiny tip of a pink tongue showed between her lips as she drove.

It was our first trip south. We kept arguing as we raced for the ferry over whether we had crossed the Tropic yet. She kept insisting that we had. I kept explaining that we hadn't. "But I can *feel* the tropics, Ro," she was saying as we jounced over the gangway onto the old rattletrap ferry boat. As an asthmatic motor pushed us out from the shore we stood in the bow looking down into the still opal water that reflected the sky where drifting cotton clouds were light green underneath from the sheen off the sea. We watched the black man-of-war birds coasting overhead and the pelicans that fly in single file and the booby gulls teetering on stakes and the white herons taking off from the shallows. We were so happy we could hardly bear it.

The crossing seemed to take all day.

The air was briny and incredibly mellow.

We ate our lunch out of a basket as we sat in the car.

We hated to leave that ferry. When we did we were back on the white coral road through the Keys between groves of stunted limes overgrown with brush. Then there was another ferry that chugged along beside the stately arches of Flagler's railroad causeway which scalloped the horizon.

A shorter ride this time, bluer water.

Then the coral road again and a late afternoon drive into a lost town of sunbleached frame houses on that westernmost key that smelt pungently of rotting coral and of sponges laid out to dry.

I stopped the car by a broken fence under a coconut palm that rustled overhead in the seawind to ask a colored man the way to George Elbert Warner's house. Of course he didn't know. The next man was a Cuban and didn't speak English. Every minute Grace made me stop to look at some flowering plant or other. At last we found the house behind a hibiscus hedge fronting a forgotten back bay where old skiffs and scows and broken sailboats lay tipped and derelict on the marly flats.

It was a white frame house with an upstairs gallery. There was a noisy crowd there, drinking and whooping.

How glad we all were to see each other in those days. Mortimer was there, very preachy, very much the long-faced young Columbia instructor but he hadn't yet lost that disarming middlewestern look of being still a little wet behind the ears. He was still living with his first wife, Lou, a big blowzy girl in eyeglasses. George Elbert's Maria had bright black eyes and hair black and shiny like jet. And Jug Wells, a local boy who ran a marine supply store had brought his goodlooking Mrs. Wells whose first name was Alzira. Then there was stately Alicia Thurloe.

Before Mortimer left to drive over to Casa Marina to fetch the Thurloes George Elbert had been scornfully describing Roger Thurloe as a customers' man, and Mortimer had been apologetic about Thurloe's being so rich. Mortimer was always apologizing in those days. Of course that was years before Thurloe got to be a figure in the Administration. At that time he hadn't a thought of Washington. He was working for a New York bank. Mortimer always did have a nose for sniffing out influential people even before they became influential. The Thurloes had come down from Hobe Sound on somebody's yacht. They had taken a fancy to Key West and decided to stay a few days. We all took a liking to them and Alicia Thurloe was just so stunning to look at nobody cared whether she was rich or poor.

I was feeling fine that evening because Grace hit it off so well with George Elbert and Maria. It was the first time she had met them and I guess I'd been talking pretty big about my friends. It was a pleasure to find them all with such a youthful husky outdoor look. What pretty wives we all had in those days and how well we all talked. We never seemed to get to the end of the things there were to talk about.

The Warners asked everybody to stay to supper. They had a tall lightbronze woman named Lottie cooking for them. She smiled round the table with a flock of white teeth as she brought each dish out of the kitchen. We were eating supper in a hurry at a deal table on the concrete cistern out back of the house under a passionflower vine. Grace kept exclaiming over the deepsea taste of the first red snapper she ever ate. It was baked and basted with lime juice and salt, old sour they called it down there. We washed it down with a dark Spanish wine George Elbert bought by the gallon from an Asturian who got it off the Havana car ferry. The tomatoes were local: Alicia Thurloe declared she had never tasted such tomatoes in her life. Grace kept kicking me under the table to let me know what a good time she was having.

We'd hardly cleaned the last homemade guava paste out of our plates before George Elbert was roaring, "Let's go." Jug Wells was taking us all out tarpon fishing in his motor boat. I drove the whole crowd in installments down to the dock. Mortimer's car had turned out to be low on gas and the Warners didn't have a car in those days.

George Elbert was carrying on high about how Mortimer and Roger Thurloe were such landlubbers he couldn't trust them with the good rods. As soon as he got a little wine in him he had started to ride Thurloe. He made him carry the bait bucket, mullets bedded down in cracked ice with a bottle of champagne tucked in between them. Whenever he could get me off in a corner he would hiss into my ear, "That merchant's too bloody rich."

George Elbert was in one of his grouches by this time. He kept growling that we had lost the best of the tide by sitting so long over supper. Once we got out in the channel we were all having such fun in the chugging boat breathing the soursweet tropical breeze that nobody cared about anybody's grouch. Jug Wells was pointing out the old paddlewheel steamer stranded on the flats in the hurricane years ago. Her ancient pilothouse was picked out in bright lavender by the light of the rising moon against the last saffron streak in the West. Grace and I held hands shamelessly like schoolkids, and whenever we were out of George Elbert's earshot we giggled and nuzzled each other's ears and whispered it was being out in the boat we enjoyed, we didn't care whether we caught a fish or not.

As it turned out Grace was holding the rod that got the first strike.

She let out a shriek when she saw the great fish heave his silver scales up into the moonlight from out of the boat's wake. Poor Grace did the best she could—she was such a spunky little thing—but she couldn't reel in fast enough. When George Elbert grabbed the rod out of her hand it was already too late. The fish had torn loose.

George Elbert was fit to be tied; and it didn't make

his temper any better to have Roger Thurloe, whom he'd been razzing for an ignorant dude from Hobe Sound whose fingers were all thumbs, get the next strike and play his tarpon very competently and bring it up to the side of the boat.

We hung in a breathless huddle over the rail looking down at the spent fish looming pale in the milky moonlit water. George Elbert lunged with the gaff and missed and spat out a four letter word as the fish's tail flashed and it flopped over and vanished leaving Thurloe holding a broken end of line.

George Elbert caught sight of the bleeding streak at the base of Thurloe's thumb.

"Never take the line in your hands!" he yelled. "What do you think the rod's for?"

Maria broke up what might have turned into an argument by crying out that now was the time for the champagne, and the girls gathered round Thurloe to bandage his hand. Grace and I couldn't help liking the modest humorous way he laughed the whole thing off. The first thing we had noticed about him was that look of amused astonishment he wore. It made us like him in spite of the small sharp jaw and the tight mouth.

Grace cried out that seeing those tarpon jump was the most exciting moment in her life. Alzira chimed in that she hated to catch them because they weren't good to eat. The real show was seeing them jump.

Even George Elbert forgot his disappointment in the beauty of the night. The beauty of the night quieted everybody down. The sea was milk under the moon. We sat silent in a row on the boat's rail in the tepid shore breeze, breathing the scorched oilsmell of the motor coughing at our feet, drinking champagne out of tin cups with the moonlight about us while the baits dragged astern.

There weren't any more strikes that night. Jug Wells

said the tide had turned. When we got tired of chugging up and down the channel he ran the boat into the dock again. George Elbert was fussy about taking home all his fishing equipment right at once; but after we got back to the house, as the sky blazed every moment brighter with moonlight, nobody wanted to go to bed.

I drove them all downtown again in the Model A and George Elbert routed out his redfaced Asturian who sold the wine. We sat at a long table under a single electric light bulb behind a screen in the back of his dark tiled restaurant while he brought out bottle after bottle of his Spanish wine, and bread and anchovies and cheese.

While we sat drinking and munching and talking, I was staring across the wide room at the shadow an awkward old model of a singlestacked steamboat cast on the plaster wall opposite. I was enjoying the feeling of remoteness, and my sunburn from the drive over the Keys in the open roadster, and the seasalt on my lips, and the round tart taste of the wine, and the feeling that I'd never in my life sat at a table with men who talked so well.

Grace perched beside me plump and neat as a little pigeon. She had a way of bubbling over suddenly with a crack that threw something somebody else was saying into a comical light. I'd never loved her so much. George Elbert told about rumrunners through the Keys and Cuban fishermen smuggling chinks. Jug Wells who usually never said a word, loosened up about turtle crawls and crocodiles swimming clear across the Gulf from Belize and how he had once caught a rattler five miles out at sea.

It was in the year of the stockmarket crash. The beginning of the end of capitalism, Mortimer was calling it. He held forth magnificently about planning an economy of abundance. In his quiet unassuming way Roger Thurloe led Mortimer on, as cooly as he'd played the tarpon, until he caught him in a dead end.

"But just suppose Mortimer, for the sake of the argument, you fellows who handle the controls don't do a good job?"

"But we've got to do a good job."

"Who's to tell? . . . With a business concern you can tell right away by whether it's making money or not."

"The business of the economy as a whole is to produce goods and services."

"But what'll your yardstick be if it isn't the figures on the balance sheet? Who'll decide whether you are doing your work efficiently or not?"

"The public will decide. Money making isn't the only thing in the world."

"But how can the public decide without checking the figures?"

Mortimer was stumped, for the moment at least. Thurloe laughed himself out of the argument as if the joke were on him instead of on Mortimer.

The Thurloes were obviously enjoying themselves. Maybe Alicia did show her wine a little. She had a rather brassy laugh and the tall Gainsborough look of a titled Englishwoman. She kept up a spoofing air towards the intellectuals. Maybe she had just a little bit the feeling that she was slumming.

It was George Elbert who shut up Mortimer just as he was getting going again on a planned economy. George Elbert shouted in his savage way that all government was a gyp, always had been since the beginning of time, government was a racket chiefly concerned with who got the rakeoff from ginmills and whorehouses. "Ask the Asturian, he'll tell you about government."

But the Asturian only smiled and kneaded his hands over his green baize apron and said he was sorry señores he'd have to close up.

We all rose to our feet without interrupting the conversation. We must have had the feeling that there were still things of the highest importance to be said. None of us wanted to break up the evening. George Elbert and Mortimer were still at it hammer and tongs on the street outside as to whether you could describe all government as a racket.

Segments of moonlight poured through the dark bronzy leaves of a tree overhead and gleamed underfoot like handfuls of new quarters poured out on the pavement. George Elbert announced that he was going to find Manolo the onelegged accordion player who played in the fishermen's bar; this was the night for dancing.

"You take the car," I heard myself saying in a lordly way. "Grace and I want to walk. We'll follow on foot."

All I wanted was a short private moment to pick the little thing up and kiss her behind the ears, but Grace took it oddly. "But it's our car," she spluttered, "they've taken our car."

For the longest time I thought it was an act. She was such a little tease. It wasn't until she burst into tears that I understood how peeved she was. I tried to distract her by pointing out the old lighthouse potbellied in the moonlight. "But it's an island," I was trying idiotically to explain. "They can't take the car off the island."

It was late. We had been driving and ferrying all day. Grace was tired. She was never the most reasonable girl in the world. All at once we noticed that we weren't alone. Roger Thurloe had stayed behind with us when the others crowded into the car. He must have felt embarrassed to find himself in the middle of a lovers' tiff. What he did was to vault neatly over the nearest picket fence and to pick Grace a handful of very fragrant white flowers.

Dama de noche, lady of the night, they called them there.

His spryness surprised us. He must have been in his

Capria

early forties then. He wore the same quiet unassuming smile when he came back with the flowers. Afterwards when I knew the Thurloes better I decided it must have been years of smiling off Alicia's vagaries that trained him so in tact. Grace gave a little chortle of pleasure and the three of us went hopscotching down the street towards the fishermen's bar . . .

The man in the belted raincoat can't remember any more. Dark faces. A crowded room. A glimpse of them all dancing. His recollections become tiny distant little pictures seen through the wrong end of a telescope, tinier and further away until they fade altogether. God that was long ago.

With a start he remembers where he is.

How many lives does a man have to live before he dies?

Elsa has fallen asleep with her head against the buff-colored shade. Her mouth is a little open. Her teeth aren't too good, but she has beautifully moulded lips.

Beyond her ruddy fringe of hair he can see puffed clouds white as marshmallow in the sun and their shadows dark on the foamstreaked ultramarine beneath. It is a relief not to have to talk to her right now. It gives him a chance to arrange in his head the things he wants to tell her about.

To make her feel it's all part of me, everything I've ever been through, everything I've told the world about, the voice inside his head is saying, that's what I must make her feel. She is quite well read. She has a real taste for writing. She will understand.

He looks down at her affectionately. She is still asleep. He notices that her eyelashes are much darker than her hair.

He squeezes her hand very gently to wake her. The sign

has just come on: *Fasten your seatbelts. No smoking.*

She opens her eyes with a start. "Cuba," he whispers.

She nods frowning.

Cloud is scudding past the window. The air hisses in the ventilators. The plane bounces a little in the turbulence of a small rainstorm.

Then they are out in the sunlight again looking down at rocks ringed with surf and matted mangroves and crescent beaches and right away they are flying low over the short Cuban hills stately with the white stalks of the royal palms.

Elsa is smiling now.

Everything looks very gay when they step out at Rancho Boyeros. The runways are wet from the recent shower. There are flowerbeds. The grass is very green. Their baggage comes quickly. The customs men are deft and polite. An immigration official who is wearing a most immaculate white uniform takes off his hat.

"Mr. Lancaster eet is an honor. Allow me to introduce myself. José Garcia Cisneros." He hands Ro his visiting card. "In the name of Cuban journalism allow me to welcome you . . . I read your articles with admiration. Yours is a great name in my country."

"That was several years ago." Ro catches the peevish tone in his own voice and covers it with a laugh. He makes a pretense of trying to find a visiting card in his wallet. "I seem to have run out," he says.

"A name like yours. No need," says the immigration official. His voice is warm oil. "Your series on Latin America is still remembered . . . Magneeficent. Your countrymen do not take enough interest in Latin America. You come to write our poleetical situation?" He clicks his tongue and makes a little deprecatory gesture with one hand. "Let us off easy please," he smiles and rolls his eyes ingratiatingly, "in the name of 'emispheric solidarity."

"This time I have no commitments," says Ro.

He notices that the immigration official's rolling eyes are taking in Elsa with a quick comprehending stare. "Ah, a vacation," the immigration official says smiling confidentially. "Well, happy days."

They shake hands again and the immigration official in the most immaculate uniform details another immigration official in a slightly less immaculate uniform to see that the porter doesn't overcharge them for carrying their bags and that they don't have to wait too long for a taxi.

"Well," says Elsa, "that's what it's like to travel with a celebrity. Last time it took us an hour."

Elsa has the look of treading on air. She links her arm tightly in his. They are too busy to talk looking out from the window of the car at the colors and shapes and the sunny sights of the city.

2

Ro dabs with a brush at his wiry gray hair. He glances around at the familiar furnishings of the old Spanish hotel, a dresser, a wardrobe and two chairs gaunt against the high plaster walls. Then he hurries after Elsa. Her room is next door to his.

He finds her with her elbows on the windowsill looking out across the roofs of rusty tiles at the clustered chimney pots and the stone flourishes that frame the façade of the cathedral, and the masts and the stacks and the white superstructure of steamships along the wharves beyond, and the gleaming streak of the harbor, and the old fortresses on the other side that lie gaunt and gray athwart the blazing sky.

Elsa doesn't turn her head when he leans out beside her.

The midday city beneath them stirs and grumbles under the sun. From the shadowed street under their chins rises blue smoke of roasting coffee and a sound of honking and shouts of newsboys and yelps of vendors of lottery tickets. The tradewind, clean off the sea, freshens their faces.

When he slides his arm across her shoulders he fancies he can feel her back stiffen. He pulls her into the room impatiently and tries to draw her body to his and to cover her lips with his mouth.

"Not yet," she says breathing hard through clenched teeth. "Can't you see?" Her voice is a whisper. "It's got to be right for us . . . before we . . ."

Her arms are surprisingly muscular. As she pushes him away from her he catches a glimpse of himself in the chevalglass beside the bureau: an elderly gangling man with a long knobby skinned-looking raddled old face, wrestling awkwardly with an untidy redhead.

"Don't let's be ridiculous," he says.

He holds her by the shoulders and tries to get her to look at him so that he can make her laugh at the thought that has come into his head: here he is still thinking of himself as the lean longstriding scornful young reporter, not handsome but striking looking and irresistible to women. In that glass just now he saw himself as others see him. He wants her to see the grim joke, to feel sorry for him maybe.

"You must let me enjoy it this time," she is already explaining in her emphatic drawl. "You don't know how exciting it is just to be here. It's the greatest thrill in my twentyeight year old life." She looks into his face, with the level frank look in her eyes that he likes so. "Last time I didn't get a chance. Imagine being in a place like this as the fiancée of a heel."

"The fiancée of a heel—," he laughs raucously, "that's a title for *True Confessions*."

The hard glaze comes over her eyes again; her lips pout.

"I'm starving. Aren't we going some place for lunch?"

"It's not far, let's walk," he says. All at once he feels cheerful again. Lunch will be fun. "I always used to love walking up Obispo."

He glances down at her feet while they stand waiting for the elevator. "Haven't you any heavier shoes? Those sneakers look thin for walking."

"They are the only kind that don't hurt my feet." She gives him a defiant look.

"Maybe we can pick you up a pair . . . I thought we might walk around the town a little after lunch. It's the best way to see it."

"Let's go," she says. "I'm going to love it all."

When they step out into the scorching band of heat on the narrow pavement crowded by the mudguards of cars all glinting with sunlight that pass in an endless file, she starts to blink.

"I love it but it hurts my eyes," she is muttering. "It's a nuisance being a redhead in the tropics."

They are walking past a small shop window crowded with dark glasses of every conceivable color. "Suppose I set you up to some." He makes a flourish with his hand.

"That's big of you."

She takes the longest time to pick out a pair. She tries green and amber and blue in plastic and glass. She tries black frames and white frames. "They none of them fit my funny little nose," she keeps complaining. He has trouble getting her away from some huge tortoiseshell frames set with rhinestones. With each new pair the man brings out she rushes out the door to try it in the sun.

"Don't I have fun?" she's laughing.

"I thought you were hungry, young woman."

"I am, starving, especially for a daiquiri," she cries and

suddenly saunters out with a green pair, green frames, green glass.

It takes him a little time to get his change, so that he has to run to catch up.

With her hair all fiery from the sun he finds her skipping along in her billowy skirt kicking out her toes in their light canvas sneakers without looking to the right or left. Every man on the street is staring at her.

Ro is out of breath when he catches her.

He puts his arm round her waist and walks alongside holding her tight.

"Elsa act your age," he whispers fiercely. "Don't forget that in a Latin country you mustn't stimulate the pinching reflex. I've known girls who came home with their little bottoms black and blue."

"You've known girls . . . I bet they were tarts every one of them." She throws back her head.

"I was thinking of my wife," he says seriously. "Grace. She used to get so mad."

Elsa suddenly squeezes his arm with her elbow. "Poor Roland," she whispers, "to the dark tower came."

He remembered Obispo as full of variegated overdressed people; tortoise shell and jet in jewellers' windows, embroidery work and alligator skins, lace mantillas; racks of books a man would want to look at in the bookstores; fruitstands, a continual temptation of mangoes and mameyes and soursaps and pineapples; today the street seems long and empty with only the endless lines of cars grinding past. The window displays have a flyspecked look.

They are both of them tired and sweating when they slip past the darkleaved evergreens that shade the entrance into the restaurant.

"A strenuous sightseer," she gasps as she drops into a chair at the nearest table. "I hadn't planned for that."

"I know a better table," he starts to say. All the way up

the hot stony street he has been deciding to try for the table in the last window embrasure in back where there is always a breeze and the noise of the traffic isn't so deafening.

"Can't move a step." She purses in her lips under her nose. "Get me a frozen daiquiri quick before I go down for the third time."

Ro vaguely remembers the old waiter's blackjowled frowning countenance but the old waiter doesn't recognize him. Ro orders in Spanish and is answered in English.

While the waiter waddles off on his flat feet to the bar to fetch their cocktails, Ro studies the menu carefully. The look of the type brings up old times.

He wants this to be a bang up lunch.

The smell of the rum and limes and of fresh bread and starched linen brings back recollections of other meals years ago, with Grace and her brother Joe and his wife when they all had their kids along, and the table became a shambles, but the kids were so comical even if the waiters were furious. Then there'd been long talkative dinners with George Elbert and Mortimer and Maria and Lou and Sanchez Herrero and the Basques, oh Lord the Basques, and difficult luncheons with Cuban politicos he'd be trying to induce to tell what they knew for some story or other.

"With Gov we always ate lobster and hearts of palm salad," Elsa is saying.

"Moro crab is much better," Ro answers complacently, "but Elsa,"—he tries to stifle the little whine of irritation in his voice—"please take those blinders off so that I can see whom I'm lunching with."

As soon as the waiter comes with the cocktails she orders another.

When he brings it she pulls off the dark glasses and folds them into her handbag. "Now I feel strong enough," she says and smiles quickly into Ro's face in a way he has come to find particularly attractive.

She lights a cigarette and sits puffing contentedly while she watches him from across the table.

Meanwhile Ro is ordering fruta bomba with a squeeze of lime—but be sure they are thoroughly ripe he cautions the waiter—and then cangrejos moros con mayonaisa and a little rice on the side.

"And hearts of palm salad," she pipes up again.

"We will if you want," he says, "but they always taste like wood to me. How about wine?"

She shakes her head.

"The local beer's excellent."

". . . And me from Milwaukee . . . I hate beer," she says. "Dad works in a brewery . . . Only daiquiris," she adds, giving Ro a mischievous look, "processions of daiquiris."

She doesn't pay much attention to the papaya, though he tries to interest her in it by explaining that in Cuba you have to ask for fruta bomba because papaya is a four letter word.

"I must remember that," she laughs.

The daiquiris have already put them in accord, so that when one laughs the other laughs. When the third daiquiri comes Ro gets his face ready to open up with the funny story about what Mortimer called his doomed man's luck at that casino outside of Lisbon, on their way to London during the bombings, but already Elsa is leaning across the table and embarking on the same tale of her unhappy childhood she began that night on the Pennsylvania train before they fell to pulling each other's clothes off.

Once she is launched there is no stopping her: it all comes in a torrent.

She loved school, probably because she hated it so at

home. Her mother had been just too selfish to let her go to college. She could have, Dad made perfectly good money but her mother still had all the ideas she had brought from the old country thirty years ago. You didn't educate girls, you just set 'em to do housework. Elsa hated housework. She wanted to write: the English teacher always read her stories to the class and she'd made a hit as Juliet in the junior play and when the dramatic club wrote its own musical show senior year, she'd been the star. They would have done anything for her in the English department. She knew she could get a scholarship but her mother said No and Dad didn't have the spirit of a louse. Her mother had said "Elsa get a job" and so she damn well went and got a job, the kind of job that would make her mother maddest, dancing in St. Louis at the Silver Room.

She hated it at the Silver Room, but she hated home worse.

She pauses while the waiter takes away the rinds of the papayas.

"I didn't have such a bad time in that period of my life," Ro has broken in hastily.

All these reminiscences make him feel like talking about himself. His life all at once appears visibly behind him like the road unreeling behind the rear window of a car.

"Worked my way through college, worked my head off. But people were always ready to pitch in and help a hard-working young fellow in the small town I came from . . . I really got a good many breaks. Oh Lord the ups and downs," he hears himself say. "The last five years now, they've been horrible."

He feels the misery rise in him.

It's all been horrible, she interrupts. She has the floor again now. The only one who ever gave her a break she is hastening to declare was Rube Mothershead who ran the Silver Room. Maybe you'd call him an old procurer but he certainly had treated her white. He came from Milwaukee himself and he still read the hometown papers. He'd seen the writeup about how good she was in the Drat Club show so when she walked into his office he was delighted. Arranged for her to live in his divorced wife's apartment. Treated her like a father; honestly, no rough stuff. He was a specialist in young girls' careers, he wanted her to marry a millionaire at least.

It almost broke Rube's heart when she married Al . . .

. . . Elsa is busy with her recitation. Her eyes are shining. She seems to enjoy the sense of injury. When the waiter comes she stops talking suddenly. Her mouth is open but no sound comes out.

Puffing and wheezing the waiter presents a large white-metal platter crowned with great red and black crab claws and edged with mayonnaise and lettuce leaves. From the crab comes a cool whiff of coral reefs and of iodine off the deep rocks and of sliced lime and beaten up olive oil.

"In my opinion," Ro begins with an introductory wave of the hand, "moro crab is one of the best things you can eat in the world."

"Looks good enough for another daiquiri," she says giving the waiter a habitué's wink. She's perfectly at her ease now.

While she gobbles her crab she goes on talking without a pause. Ro is thinking he must get her to stop talking with her mouth full . . .

. . . Al played the Silver Room two weeks and when he moved on she went with him. He was a promising young bandleader then, with his own band. All the hep-cats were mad for him. It was more like brother and sister than being in love. He was a redhead and so was she. Kind of incestuous, she guessed that had been the trouble with it. He'd never had any breaks as a kid nor had she. He could have been a great musician if his folks had let him have the proper lessons. Both of them sore as hell at everybody. That was what had brought them together, and she couldn't think of anything but getting out of that Silver Room. It wasn't her idea of life to spend her nights sticking out her tummy for a lot of weary salesmen.

She leans across the table chewing as she talks: "I wanted to read and write poetry and I was crazy about having a baby . . . I learned about that the hard way . . . Al didn't do so good after we got married. I kind of took his mind off his bandleading I guess and the big operators hired his gang away from him so that he had to go back to his crooning in another guy's orchestra, and we were always driving in the middle of the night from one godforsaken middlewestern town to another and me with the baby coming and the nausea every morning. They drove so fast . . . just to scare me. They were devils, those guys, hopped up with dope most of the time. What I could write about being a swing musician's wife. Al just lived on aspirin and benzedrine. I wasn't twenty yet. If he hadn't been a heel he'd have taken better care of me. They wrecked the car one night out near Amarillo Texas. I thought I was going to have the baby then and there. I went to a nice woman doctor for a checkup the next morning. She said I was physically all right but I was a mass of nerves. Do you know what she did? She called my mother on the telephone right from her office and she told her that if she didn't want a dead girl she'd better wire me money to go home. My mother did that. It meant a lot of trouble and she didn't like it too well but she took care of me till Alma was born and then Al turned up while I was still in the hospital, saying he was in the chips and had an engagement for the whole winter in Chi and wouldn't I go back to him? I did like a ninny."

Elsa has stopped eating and taken to smoking again.

Ro is sipping his drink and watching her. He wishes she wouldn't smoke so much. He has given up trying to explain himself. That will have to come later, after they have settled down together. Now he must just enjoy the relaxation of a foreign country. He must let himself drift contentedly down a river of daiquiris, savoring the flavor of the crab and the rice and the mayonnaise and the crisp romaine and the fresh bread, cheered by the neverceasing rattle of Spanish in his ears. Drift, he tells himself.

He sits back in his chair and watches her. She is a very handsome girl. Even if she does talk with her mouth full she is a very handsome girl. There isn't a man in the room who can keep his eyes off her. She's going to be a handful all right.

He is drinking in little sips what he promises himself will be his final daiquiri. In the light that flows in level streaks full of motes off the glary street and filters through the dark leaves of the plants in the windows into spiralled crinkling tobacco smoke over the tables he lets his eyes roam, deliberately as a Cuban's would, over her poised breasts and the neat outlines of her lips unspoiled by lipstick, and round the contours of her transparent cheeks under that uncontrollable hair.

The waiter hovers over them with the traditional cream cheese and guava paste.

Ro straightens up and orders himself a cigar.

. . . At home it was just too horrible, she is declaring. Whenever her mother caught her reading a book her mother found some housework for her to do. My it was a relief to move to Chicago with Al into a nice apartment with a maid to tend the baby girl part time. She ought to have been happy then but she wasn't. Alma was already toddling about and into everything and the twins were on their way. Of course she hadn't known it was twins. She would have jumped in the lake if she had. The morning sickness was awful. She never was any good at housekeeping. Her mother never had taught her. She guess she'd been pretty extravagant and Al never had two nickels to rub together the morning after he got paid.

Then Al had to get into a row with the management and they terminated the engagement. It was up to her of course to go around with him to see Rube. And her big as a house with the twins. Rube was nice as could be. He got Al another month in St. Louis. After the twins she never could feel the same about Al. No twins in her family. Al was a heel.

"How about coffee?" Ro interrupts at her first pause for breath.

She nods with a pleasant crinkling of the skin round her eyes. "And B and B?"

"Sure. This is our bang up day."

Let yourself drift, he keeps telling himself; stop worrying about money and magazine articles and the state of the nation; just do what she does, let yourself drift.

"It was Gov started me on B and B," she is saying. "There were things I learned from him. Honest Ro I did everything in the world to make a go of it." She looks him straight in the eye. "It wasn't my fault."

Ro leans back in his chair when he has lit his cigar. Their eyes meet cozily.

"I like being with an older man smoking a cigar," she says in a low purring voice. "Well," she hurries on in the same breath for fear he might interrupt her story again. "We sure would have been in a mess if it hadn't been for

Rube. He even ended by paying for the hospital when the twins were born, and for the nurse afterwards and everything . . . I had a tough time." She screws up her face. "Rube couldn't have been more understanding. He kept telling me that if I'd stop having babies I could be one of the most successful women in America. He even thought he could build up Al for a while but then he got discouraged and when Al went to St. Louis for that engagement Rube began bringing Gouverneur Haines around. Rube was interested in Gov because he was a Milwaukee boy who'd made a big success but he was worried about his sex life . . . He'd had a nervous breakdown. Rube felt he needed a nice wholesome girl. I'd known Gov a little bit in high school though I'd never had a crush on him or anything like that. The lad kind of left me cold to tell the truth. All I could think of then was I wanted to write a novel but of course the kids never gave me time."

She lights a fresh cigarette.

"I bet they are making my mother's life a hell right now." She laughs. "Maybe they'll pay her back for some of the things she did to me."

She lays her cigarette down on the edge of her plate and takes a sip of her liqueur. "What I was dreaming about," she drawls, looking up through a puff of smoke towards the ceiling, "was being a female Orpen Molloy."

Ro reaches over, rescues her cigarette out of the cream cheese, and puts it between her fingers.

"But there was one," says Ro. "I knew her well. She ended in a sanitarium."

"Maybe I'll end up in one too . . . Tell me about her. Of course the way it turned out instead of writing a novel I became Gov Haines' fiancée. We were waiting till I could get a divorce from Al, of course."

She holds up her empty glass and twists it meditatively over the table cloth. Ro waves for the waiter. She smiles gratefully. "Now I'll shut up. You tell me everything."

"Nobody's life," he begins, "is all beer and skittles . . . I guess I was successful too young. It's an American disease. That's why I have a certain fellow feeling for your friend Gov. He must be a bright little fellow."

"You don't know him . . . It sure was a surprise to find that the little piefaced kid I'd known in school had come out of the army and made himself a pile."

"He was phenomenally successful." Ro can't help the twinge of envy when he says it. "He must have hornswoggled a lot of Texans."

"What does that prove?"

"It still takes brains for a man to make a million in oil leases before he is thirty."

"Doesn't help a girl if the guy's a heel," she says. With pouting lips she seems to be studying Ro's face through the amber liquid in her brandy glass.

"He looked a little halfbaked maybe," Ro admits with an embarrassed laugh. That hard look in her eyes bothers him. Again he is remembering the sallow short young man with huge dark eyes that kept blinking. "Of course I didn't really get a chance to talk to him but his face stuck in my mind. I suppose he was pretty boring but he left me with the feeling I'd like to have heard what he had to say . . . a little of it maybe."

She is not listening.

To keep her entertained Ro starts rattling off about how he'd been in a hurry that evening when he first met her at the hotel because he had an appointment at the Nacional with Mortimer Price. Mortimer had a story he wanted to inspire. Mortimer was quite miffed, Ro adds laughing, when they couldn't get it printed. Mortimer was getting to be Washington's chief specialist on Caribbean affairs. "I never could understand why." Ro arches his eyebrows. "You know he never could learn Spanish.

All he ever knew was what George Elbert and I used to tell him."

Ro catches himself giggling like a schoolgirl.

Elsa has thrown back her head and opened her mouth. Her eyes take on that round luminous admiring look that pleases him so.

"Imagine having lived with celebrities all your life . . . Expatriate in the twenties," she is declaiming. "War correspondent on every front . . . an intimate friend of the great Roger Thurloe. Knowing Mortimer Price and George Elbert Warner and the Molloys. Mr. Price was full of funny stories about the Thurloes that night we met him right here in this restaurant . . . He wasn't a bit impressed by the guy even if he was dead and he said his wife was a rummy. I wish I'd been there all the time. Don't you think I'd make a good secretary for a celebrity?"

Ro doesn't quite like the way she says the word 'celebrity', still he is laughing.

"Make your application," he shouts, "in triplicate!"

They are both laughing at the same time. Eating and drinking and poking fun, Ro is telling himself, that they have in common.

He calls for the check.

"Suppose we nose around the town for a while, it's so long since I've been on the loose."

He tots up the bill more carefully than usual on account of all those daiquiris. The total seems correct. Damned expensive, but what the hell, he thinks as he piles his greenbacks on the waiter's little silver tray. One good whopping article will set things to rights. In New York he was too damned discouraged to write. Just one unhappy thing after another.

This is adventure. This will start him off. A man needs the feeling of being at the helm of his destiny.

"Wasn't that crab good?" he adds reminiscently as he

reaches for her arm. He is a little afraid she may stagger.

"Crab made Gov desperately sick," she hisses spitefully in his ear. "Everything he ate made him sick . . . Of course I'm grateful to him for bringing me over and buying me all those nice dresses and introducing me to Joe Herkimer—you must know him, the famous athlete. He's retired now—and the nonobjective painter Pinillo and . . ." a sort of hush comes into her voice . . . "Paco Cortes."

They are standing in the doorway feeling the ovenblast of the afternoon sun in their faces, ignoring the clamor of bootblacks and taximen on the sidewalk outside.

"We'll meet them."

She stands with her hand on his wrist talking fast: "I wrote Joe I was coming . . . He won't know about Paco. Paco's not his dish. We'll go to Paco's tonight for the rhumba. You can talk Spanish to him and get him to tell you all about the comparsas."

"You mean in the carnival?"

"Of course." Her hand grips his wrist hard. She looks into his face with shining eyes. "There are things even you don't know about this town."

"I didn't think it was anything. In Rio now . . ."

"It's one of the things I know about. It's going on now. Sunday nights in Lent. Gov said it bored him . . . Let's take that cab."

As she strides out across the pavement she has to stop suddenly to avoid a little Negro with a shaven head who shakes a string of lottery tickets under her nose. Ro hurrying after her steps on her heel. The canvas sneaker shoots off her foot. Ro picks it up amid the titters of the bootblacks and the sidewalk loafers.

The door of a royalblue touring car is being held open for them by a smiling yellowfaced young man in a buff tunic. Elsa lets herself drop into the seat and reaches for the sneaker. Before she pulls it on she shows Ro the black on the sole of her bare foot. She is laughing.

"I guess we'll have to go to the beach after all," she says. "I could go for a new bathing suit," she adds in a whisper as the car starts. Her hand clutches his wrist again. "And tell him to drive slowly," she goes on whispering in a frail little peevish voice. "The man this morning, he drove too fast. Ever since that time in Amarillo fast driving upsets me."

"First we'll go buy you a decent pair of shoes," Ro is announcing to Elsa.

Her leg that has been snuggling against his since he slipped into the seat beside her pulls away from him a little. "A bathing suit," she says.

"La Primavera," Ro calls out in a firm voice to the taximan. "And slow."

3

It is a hot afternoon. The streets roar with traffic. Ro has no feeling of being himself sitting beside the new girl in the brightly polished Havana cab. The man's leg that touches her woman's leg seems hardly his, nor is the hand that holds her narrow hand. His real self is so many years ago, before all that business in Washington, before Grace died . . .

. . . It was the fall we rented Miss Nanny's little house on a back street in Alexandria. Miss Nancy Carter. Cyarter she called it. Grace just loved her. Grace said Miss Nanny reminded her of a pressed flower you would find in an old family album. It would have been an album of the Lee family. Of course it was Grace who rented the house. I couldn't help acting a little stuffy when I found that Miss Nanny came along with the house. I had heard her mumble something about wanting to keep one room separate to store her old family things, but we hadn't expected Miss Nanny to be stored along with them. She was supposed to have a separate entrance but she took to making sudden appearances in our part of the house. Grace used to say she came through the walls like ectoplasm. The boys were home that year. We had managed to get them into the Episcopal High School. Eleven and thirteen. Naturally whenever one of them so much as looked at an antique chair or a table a leg fell off and there would be Miss Nanny hovering over it with that crushed pansy look on her face mumbling through her gums about the old Cyarter pieces, or the Ludwells or the Lees. She had confided in us first thing that she couldn't abide her dentures. Repairing Miss Nanny's heirlooms kept us broke all that season and we ended by chipping in on new dentures. Miss Nanny acted so helpless when the plumbing went out of order we just couldn't bear to suggest that it was the landlord's business to put it in shape. Grace used to claim it was George Washington himself who had installed Miss Nanny's plumbing.

Miss Nanny's troubles and the continuous rain of soot in the garden and the boys' flunking out of school wove a background of private dismay for Grace and me behind all that year's public excitements.

It was on account of Miss Nanny we really got to know the Thurloes. The poor soul didn't have a cent in the world and her house was up for sale, but she was asking such an enormous price for it that nobody would buy. It was late one October afternoon during the lovely slow Virginia fall that we were sitting out in Miss Nanny's garden among the chrysanthemums while the boys did their home work in the living room. It was the autumn after the fall of France and Dunkerque and the bombing of London. The papers were full of the Willkie-Roosevelt campaign. I was just getting ready to break the news to Grace that I had signed up with Parkman's Magazine to do some articles about England under the bombings when who should appear at the garden gate but Roger and Alicia Thurloe. Roger was already high up in the Administration and had been appointed to a new post just under cabinet rank. They had finally come to admit they were in Washington for the duration and they were househunting. We hadn't seen them since Key West and it took us a minute before we knew who they were. We all had a good laugh about how they were getting ready to buy the house out from under us.

Roger and Grace hit it off again immediately. Grace looked desperately pretty that afternoon even if she did have a smudge of soot on her cute little nose. She was wearing an immensely becoming summer dress with big polka dots that nobody else could have worn. We went inside to get out of the falling soot and set the Thurloes up to drinks while they waited for Miss Nanny. In fact Alicia had a great many drinks and carried on about what fun it was to do something unpremeditated. For six months they hadn't had a free evening to themselves. For once Miss Nanny was out. She never did turn up. The Thurloes were having such a good time that when Grace asked them to stay to supper they jumped at the invitation.

It was a pleasant evening. Roger talked to the boys about their schoolwork and football and Babe Ruth in that straight from the shoulder way he had, so they thought he was wonderful. Grace hung on his every word. When it came out that I was going to England for six or eight weeks he was very much interested. He wanted a first hand private report on how the English were holding out. "In the long run it's the ordinary citizen who wins a war." He was trying to get Mortimer Price to make the trip but Mortimer didn't seem any too eager. I was intrigued by that remark because I'd eaten lunch with Mortimer that very day and he hadn't said a word about any trip to England. "Anyway Mortimer never will report anything but the inside dope," Roger said. "I want to know how the outsiders feel." Roger liked Mortimer but he was on to him all right. Mortimer's foibles got to be a private joke between us . . . So it really was on account of Miss Nanny that I found myself with that little private mission for the Administration on top of my public mission for the magazine.

Mortimer's nose sure was out of joint when he found out that Roger and I were calling each other by our first names. Of course everybody in Washington called everybody else by his first name anyway, at least behind his back, so it didn't mean a thing. But Mortimer had come to think of Roger Thurloe as his personal property, his own private pipeline into the Administration. I found out afterwards that in spite of the fact that we were the best of friends in those days Mortimer had gone to considerable trouble to keep Grace and me from meeting the Thurloes.

He never did get used to the idea that we were closer to the Thurloes than he was. Too close. If it hadn't been for Roger Thurloe, tense, brilliant, tragic, marvelous, miserable Roger, everything might have been different.

When Mortimer found out I was going to England for Roger Thurloe Mortimer had to go along if it killed him.

He sure did have to nerve himself up for that trip. I didn't think he would actually make it until I found him aboard the clipper at Miami. There we were the two of us sitting over scotch and soda in the lounge of the clipper in the humming quiet of ten thousand feet and Mortimer shoving his furrowed black brows across the little table into my face and hissing into my ear that he carried a $75,000 life insurance and that he never expected to come back from England alive, not with those bombings getting worse every day.

I never will forget the look of infantile joy that came over Mortimer's long lantern face when the steward told us we would have to put in to Bermuda to fix a leaky fuel pipe. It was a wonderful break. Like landing in paradise when you expected to go to hell. Only I kept thinking how wonderful if I'd only had Grace along instead of Mortimer. Still we did enjoy that twentyfour hours: the halcyon quiet of the empty English hotel; and Mortimer and me both of us unusually tall and lanky and awkward and a bit pot bellied, me ruddy and Mortimer dark and sallow faced, plunging and swimming like two schoolkids in the silky blue water off the hotel dock; and the pretty English girls with intriguing smiles who turned up after lunch to take us sailing in their knockabout between the islands. It was be-kind-to-Americans week all over the empire, I guess. Those girls gave us the feeling that just to be Americans was somehow divine.

The whole flight was pure pleasure, jolly meals and scotch and soda skimming in the sun above the alabaster clouds; the sight of cloudcapped Pico; and the sea indigo between the green Azores.

It was when the clipper finally settled without a jar on the littered Tagus and I was craning my neck to look out through the porthole at Lisbon's crowded hills and the domes and the murky baroque facades hemmed by heaving yellow tile roofs that I noticed that Mortimer really did have the wind up.

He had begun to talk dolefully about how a man ought to use the last days of his life to the best possible advantage. We drank a great deal of wine at dinner in Lisbon that night. After dinner Mortimer said he couldn't think of going to bed so we spent the night gambling desperately with depreciated escudos at the casino at Cascaes. Mortimer kept winning. "It's the luck of a doomed man," he would groan as he shovelled the grimy banknotes into his pockets.

We were both horribly sleepy driving out to Coimbra in the morning. I never was one to worry too much about my own skin, but Mortimer's terror was contagious. I sure did have cold feet when we climbed aboard the Dutch plane to fly to England. The pallid squarefaced Swiss behind the desk at the hotel had been whispering to us that the Nazis had shot down one of these same Dutch planes over the Bay of Biscay only last week. He shook his head portentously. "Carrying very important personages," he moaned.

That was the first time I'd heard of V.I.Ps. Something about the sound of the words "very important personages" set Mortimer up no end. He squared his shoulders and squared his jaw as if to say, "That's me."

Mortimer was a changed man.

I was thinking as I buckled myself into my seat that this was the first time in my life I had understood how literal the phrase was about getting cold feet. Not even the level blue eyes and the dapper look of the apt young Hollanders who flew the plane made me feel easy. My hands and feet were icy all the way to Bristol, but Mortimer seemed fine.

That was the first time I understood that Mortimer had become a real stuffed shirt. He didn't mind dying so much if he could die as a V.I.P. Lord how peeved Mortimer was when the man with the briefcase from the Foreign Office who met us at the airport turned out to be a reader of my articles. Instead of paying attention to Mortimer he kept asking me eager questions about what he called the science of rapportage all the way into London on the tiny train that had, I kept imagining, a sinister look, like a train in a Conan Doyle story.

As we sat on the edges of our seats in the reserved compartment shuttling through the spinachy greens of the English countryside in the rainy twilight, our eyes peeled expectantly for the first signs of war damage, I could feel Mortimer puffing out with selfimportance on the seat beside me. At last Mortimer couldn't stand the Foreign Office man's disquisitions on the American genius for rapportage any more and let drop a remark that began: "Just as I was leaving the President's office."

"Oh I say," the Foreign Office man interrupted blandly, "we never speak of that sort of thing."

Mortimer got his revenge when we arrived in London and he was whisked off in state to the Dorchester in a government car because his mission was semiofficial, while I was left stumbling about in the dim blue light of the station to find my way alone across the city in the blackout to the old Savoy.

The poetry of the London blackout. The beauty of the dim crowded streets where you walked with all your senses sharpened by the knowledge that a ton of bricks might drop on your head any moment. The tiny blue crosses of the traffic lights. The way faces bloomed out at the striking of a match.

Funny that I never was actually in an air raid. I travelled all over England without actually seeing one, though blocks of houses were still burning in Bristol when we drove in and when I went to Great Yarmouth the blitz had been the night before.

Heroism; I had never understood the meaning of the word not even in France in the old war until I went to England. Those stodgy stubbly Britishers. Civil defense; their dogged selfeffacement as they went about their grim chores.

That redfaced firewarden at the beach resort who was a

newsvendor in private life: I found him poking around in the back end of his tiny house. The house had been knocked about a bit, so he put it, in the blitz the day before. His wife was climbing out on all fours up a slide of broken brickbats from the basement apologizing for looking like a chimneysweep. She held a pet duck dusty but undamaged in her arms.

"We like a bit of poultry for Christmas," the newsvendor explained. Then he excused himself, and murmuring that he couldn't remember when he'd last had a real sleep, went off on his night's vigil.

And the absurd little curate of that Queen Anne church in the East End. The church was only four black walls and one corner of a steeple. He bustled up and down on the steps in front of the vanished façade to marshal the wives and children of his parishioners to be taken out to the country to safer lodgings in buses with exactly the words and gestures he would have used to get a peacetime Sundayschool picnic on the road. He even checked on the babies' bottles. "Are you sure you've got your sandwiches, Mrs. Grigg?"

And the cinema director and his friends from Mayfair trundling a pushcart miles through ravaged streets to take hot tea and sandwiches to some bombedout families on Tottenham Court Road everyone else had forgotten about, and pointing out the chiarascuro so like Piranese in the ruins on the way.

And the boy at Covent Garden market who boasted in twanging cockney about putting out an incendiary bomb with a bag of Brussels sprouts.

And the grimy men with bucket pumps, waiting for fire bombs on the roof of St. Paul's.

And the hands swollen with cold and the feet wet in soggy boots in the sooty drizzle, and everywhere the smell of burning rags.

And me sitting at my little Swiss aluminum typewriter amid the antiquated damask hangings of the Savoy. The musty smell and me always hungry because all you could get for breakfast was a slice of broiled tomato and some chips of soggy toast, and smoking straw cigarettes and searching for the words that would make people feel they too had smelt disaster in the air and seen the smouldering ruins of the great warehouses along the Thames and felt the emptiness of the gutted city beyond St. Paul's and the anachronism of an occasional green tree and the fireweed blooming on the new ruins.

Though I knew it would take some of the bloom off the articles I was getting up for the magazine, I had to tell every word of it to Roger Thurloe at Miss Nanny's the night I got home. I had hardly time to give Grace a squeeze and a hug and say hello to the boys when he was on the phone asking if we would mind if he came over.

He came alone. "Not well," he said curtly when we asked about Alicia. He looked pale and lonely.

He questioned me endlessly. He was greedy for details. He made me repeat everything that happened from the moment I got off the Dutch plane at that airport in the west of England nobody would tell the name of. He was pleased with the duck and the newsvendor at Great Yarmouth and the boy putting the incendiary bomb out with a bag of Brussels sprouts and the cinema director with his pushcart but what he liked best was my meeting with H. G. Wells.

His eyes absolutely popped when I told him I had seen H. G. Wells. Roger had been crazy about Wells when he was a boy. So was I, I told him. He sat there absolutely breathless while I described the three times I'd seen the grand old romancer. It wasn't easy to tell because there wasn't too much of it. The first time I met him was just casually. He had been making a little speech, a funny mischievous little speech at a meeting of some literary association. It wasn't that anything particularly interesting had been going on. I kept having to remind Roger and Grace—the boys had long since been packed off to bed—that the fact that a bomb might come through the ceiling at any minute gave a sort of dignity to the most banal proceedings. Right away I got the feeling that old Wells appreciated the irony of his situation. Here he was a sort of sorcerer's apprentice who had survived into an industrial fantasia he had helped imagine. The Battle of Britain was something he might very well have written himself in the days when flying machines were just a crackpot notion in the heads of a few eccentric inventors. Now he had achieved the agreeable irresponsibility of extreme old age. He stood there teasingly at ease letting the crinkled lids droop drowsily over his bright reptilian eyes, like a smart old lizard in a bunch of bumbling flies.

The next time was at a meeting of something called the British Institution. It was a forum on light. The speakers were marvelous. I never did catch their names. They were all very elderly. The ancient lecture theatre was so full I couldn't get a seat. I shouldn't have gotten in at all if it hadn't been for my friend the cinema director who was filming the proceedings and who let me stand beside the camera he was poking in between the red curtains that closed off the aisle. I was looking down through the streaked gray light that came in through the tall Georgian windows into a red upholstered pit ranked with intent gray heads, and imagining I could make out profiles of Darwin and Wallace and Huxley and of all the great departed figures of British nineteenth century science, when I found that the small man wriggling through the curtains beside me was Wells. He smiled and shook hands and asked me to dine with him. Then he hurried down the aisle and walked cockily up to an empty seat on the platform.

"That would never have happened to me," Thurloe cried out bitterly. "When a man takes public office nothing pleasantly accidental happens any more. A man gets to be a goddam waxwork."

"And they love it." Grace gave one of her little shrieks.

I told them about starting out from the Savoy the evening I dined with Wells at the beginning of one of those long English twilights.

In wartime up near the front there come those lulls that give you the feeling of the most intense peace. London was the front lines for sure that summer, but that evening you felt the weird calm of a city under siege when the guns cease firing. I'd felt the same thing in Madrid. When I got out of the tube at Baker Street—Sherlock Holmes' Baker Street—I had the feeling again that I was living in one of Wells' own tales I used to read up in the attic when I was a boy. It wasn't dark yet but at the tube station people were crowding down the round tiled tunnels with their blankets and their mattresses. Some of them had cot beds and thermos bottles. There were whole families, couples, solitary spinsters. They all had a gray dusty look. Everybody seemed to know just where his place was. Everybody carried on with that funny casual air of routine the British manage to give to everything. That is their special type of heroism.

When I came out on the street it was as Wells would have described it. He had a marvelous gift for matter of fact description. The humdrum look of London but empty. Not a soul to be seen. Not a sound of traffic. A few sleepy swallows twittering. Nobody to ask the way. I had to use a map to find the house: it turned out to be in one of those magnificent colonnaded blocks of dwellings Beau Nash promoted for the rich and powerful of his time round the edges of Regent's Park. The occasional houses that had been hit were crumpled up like abandoned stage scenery. The wrought iron fences and the great gates, naturally, had gone for scrap. At last I managed to find the number. When I'd rung the bell I stood looking up at the primrose and lavender sky. A perfect night for an air raid.

Those evenings in London whenever you stopped doing anything you listened for the sound of motors.

Wells came to the door himself. He was alone in the house. Whoever waited on him must have already gone off to the tube station.

The solitude of old age.

The two of us sat at a rubbed mahogany table in the tall old regency dining room eating cold partridge washed down with a bottle of burgundy. Not a sound came through the blackout curtains. There was a sense of quiet leisure, of endless emptiness about us as if we two were the last survivors on a ravaged planet.

I wasn't quite as easy as I tried to seem. I couldn't help straining an ear from time to time to catch that first warning rumble of planes overhead.

Wells seemed completely comfortable as he munched on the partridge and the crisp roll and drank little sips of his burgundy. We each had a pat of real butter which was a surprise in wartime England. As he ate he talked in a leisurely way methodically assessing the world he knew he was soon to leave.

He was essentially a political minded man. It was Western civilization that had been the love of his life. He used to think of it as Progress. Ever since he had worked on the *Outline of History,* he explained wryly, he had been a little doubtful about progress, but there had been something, there still was something. The British at their best had had more of it than most people. The Russians had a bit of it but not enough. They were ruining everything by the abysmal barbarism of their methods. But, now who would carry on? Civilization had to be led. The battle for the English skies was won, but it was Britain's last effort . . .

"But what did he say? Tell me exactly what he said." Thurloe jumped to his feet impatiently.

"It was something like this." I was straining to remember. "If you Americans can't find some way of carrying the burden of empire we are sunk, all of us, sunk!"

Thurloe's eyes sparkled. He set his small jaw. His face wore that look of almost comical determination he sometimes showed in his photographs. "We must," he said.

With an unexpectedly affectionate gesture he grabbed my hand with his left and Grace's hand with his right. "Good night my dears," he said and hurried out to his waiting car.

"My ears and whiskers said the rabbit, I'm late already," was what Grace exploded with after he'd gone. She was laughing but her eyes were moist. "Still he is quite a dear," she added as an afterthought . . .

4

Up on the fourth floor of La Primavera all of a sudden like coming out of a trance Ro finds himself sitting in a wicker armchair beside a papier mâché lighthouse. He is staring listlessly at a row of mannequins arrayed in beach togs posed among lifepreservers and striped umbrellas against a blue backdrop lit by neon from below. He is smoking a fresh cigar. A broad catfaced saleslady with tight peroxide curls brings a woman's bathing suit out of its box and dangles it before Ro's eyes. "A bazen suit for ze beautiful daughter," she coos in Parisian English in his ear.

"I'm his mother" hoots Elsa. "la madre . . . la mamá."

She mimicks the Spanish pronunciation remarkably well.

She is still a little high from all those daiquiris at lunch. They both are. Humming *Siboney* Elsa shuffles off to the dressing room with the bathing suit. When she comes back she puts on her professional showgirl walk as if she were modelling the bathing suit for a fashion show.

It is the time of the midafternoon pause. They are the only customers. A few blackeyed salesgirls idle yawning in the background. The place smells stuffily of textiles and dyes and of perfume and singed hair from the nearby hairdressing parlor. The electric light seems dim to Ro's eyes after the brilliance of outofdoors. The daiquiris buzz in his ears. He has the feeling of being smothered in women's underwear.

Ro feels that Elsa is showing her daiquiris more than she should so he tries to quiet her down by telling a story. It seems funny to him. It is about a man he used to know who wrote advertising copy for this very department store. It was the winter that Grace had been sick and they brought the children down and spent several months. Sanchez Herrera was an exile from South America. The dictator of his country at that period had chased his family out and he had been stranded in Havana with big ideas and very little money. He made about twentyfive dollars a week. Poor Sanchez had a notion that come what may he had to have American girls. He cultivated them assiduously. Most of them were debutantes on the loose or an occasional little bitch of a journalist. All they cared about was night spots and local color. They kept him broke, and usually held out on him in the end. They drove him to despair. After one unsuccessful venture of this kind he announced he was going to kill himself. It took all evening and a full fish dinner and quarts of rum to argue him out of it. "He called Grace and me his sentimental advisers."

"What's the point of the story?" Elsa asks pouting when she comes back in a fresh bathing suit. "Are you sure you're not trying to put me in my place?"

The story has no point at all, Ro insists still laughing. Coming to this store made him think of it that's all.

"Joe Herkimer knows the manager," Elsa murmurs as she dreamily takes various poses before the pierglass. "He brought Gov and I here. Gov wanted to buy the place out but I wouldn't let him . . . Even more than a bathing suit I need a portable radio to take to the beach . . . I can't live without a radio."

"But we are in bathing suits now," Ro says firmly. She pays no attention. Ro goes back to his story.

Sanchez' chief attraction for his lady friends when everything else failed was a cousin he had who ate straw hats. Juanito was a sappylooking sawed off fat man who made a hobby of it. It took a good deal of rum to get him started but suddenly, when the evening was far enough advanced, he would start breaking off little pieces of the brim of somebody's straw hat and chewing on them and before you knew it the straw hat was gone. The girls were enchanted. Usually they fell into Sanchez' arms on the strength of it. Nobody ever thought of falling into Juanito's arms. He looked too repulsive.

Elsa hasn't been listening.

"How about this one?" She shuffles up in front of him in a green brassière and panties and stands snapping her fingers and undulating to *Siboney*.

"Let's take it," says Ro. "Let's get out in the street. I'm suffocating."

Framed in cigar smoke the whole scene is going dreamy. He is still a little muzzy from the daiquiris. If he could only keep his head from swirling. The catfaced saleslady is making goggle eyes and praising the gentleman's taste, exquisito. She is behaving more and more like the madam in a brothel.

When Elsa shuffles off to change back into her street clothes the floorwalker begins to model something vase-shaped in the air with his hands. He's a repulsive waxy faced man with an eyebrow mustache. "The torso of a marble in the museum," he says in Spanish, and leers lasciviously in the direction of the dressingroom. The fashionable procurer, thinks Ro.

He doesn't like the way the pair of them look at him. Their eyes are going to roll out of their heads. He tries to shake off the illusion that instead of the bathing suit it is the girl he is picking out.

The cigar begins to taste rank in his mouth.

He tries to pull himself together by stiffening his muscles and leaning back with his hands clasped tight on the arms of his wicker chair. He tries to enjoy the feeling of being an elderly rake buying clothes for his kept woman.

Drift, just let yourself drift, he keeps telling himself.

Something about the exhalations of the ladies' hairdressing parlor brings to his mind a ridiculous little tableau that took place in that same department store years ago . . .

I had gone to La Primavera to pick up Grace who had been getting her hair washed to take her out to lunch with the Molloys and Mortimer and a raft of people . . . The fun we used to have at lunch in those days. That trip we always ate at the Valenciana . . .

When Elsa comes back in her street clothes Ro takes her arm and starts to whisper his fresh story in her ear while they wait for the bathing suit to be wrapped: "While she was getting her hair dried Grace had been listening to the life story of the woman next to her who was all trussed up for a permanent. She was one of those characters we used to call Miami blondes. Sloppy Joe's was crawling with them in those days. Grace and the Miami blonde came out together. While I waited I'd been watching an elderly Cuban with big white mustaches and a cigar and a tight bouquet of roses wrapped up in wax paper. He kept sort of pawing the floor with his little pointed feet. Impatient. Of course he wore spats. He looked like the sweet poppa in a French farce. His eyes popped out of his head when they lit on his Miami blonde. She was crying. Her hair had turned green. Grace explained afterwards it was some kind of hair dye that the heat affected, but green it was. Grace made a funny story of it and had everybody laughing about it the whole weekend. Of course Grace was a natural blonde."

Elsa isn't listening. She stands staring in Ro's face wiggling her hips to *Siboney*. Ro shouts at her to make her see the point. "The old man hadn't known her hair was dyed, see? It came over him that he was being played for a sucker. You could see it in his face . . . She began to shriek and he began to shout for the manager. Both at once. It was like a duet from grand opera."

Elsa interrupts him. "Is my hair green?" she asks, putting her face close to his with her eyes like hard pebbles again.

"Absolutely not," Ro stammers.

"Then you've got a big white mustache."

5

. . . We got to seeing more and more of the Thurloes but it wasn't until the afternoon we heard the news of Pearl Harbor that Grace and I found ourselves right in the middle of their lives. It was during the summer when Hitler was making his onslaught on the Russians that we made our move to Georgetown. Miss Nanny had finally found a buyer for the Alexandria house and besides Grace had been wanting right along to move on account of the soot. One afternoon she discovered a little narrow brick house on Dumbarton Avenue with an ironwork balcony hidden under wistaria. There was a 'For Sale' sign on it. It turned out to have marble mantels and a flagged terrace under a grapevine in the back yard. We bought it next day though it cost more than we could afford. It wasn't until we recorded the deed that we found that we were in the same block with the great handsome corner mansion with panelled rooms and a federal style fanlight over the front door which the Thurloes had finally settled on as their Washington residence.

When we first heard the Pearl Harbor news we were driving back from a place out in Virginia where we had been lunching with Mortimer and his new wife. Gertrude Ann owned a farm and saddle horses and a kennel full of boxer dogs halfway to Winchester. She was a widow with several grown children. She was a nice tweedy grayhaired woman with flat heels and a sensible outofdoors look. She must have been a little older than Mortimer. On the way home Grace said Gertrude Ann had taken on Mortimer the way she might have taken on a new jumping horse. She intended to show him and if possible to win some blue ribbons with him.

We ate on a side porch overlooking a garden stuffed with overgrown boxbushes. It was a crisp bright early winter Sunday. We really had a very nice lunch. Mortimer was relaxed and amusing and nothing hush hush came up to bring out that stuffy official side of him. In fact we sat there for two hours without mentioning the war or the President or lend-lease or any of the usual topics. Mortimer and I talked about Thackeray and Dickens. Grace and Gertrude Ann got into a friendly little feminine argument about Jane Austen's heroines. Gertrude Ann thought they were spineless little creatures but Grace said she just loved them, because they really ran everything in their mouselike fashion. We came away feeling that we'd had a very good time and planning to see a lot more of the Mortimers.

On the way home I stopped in a drugstore in Falls Church to make a phone call and there was the news pouring out over a portable radio somebody had set up on the counter. I knew something of the sort was going to happen but I certainly wasn't prepared for the shame and dismay of the way it did happen. I guess my first thought was Thank God the boys aren't old enough to be drafted.

The minute I told Grace she knew what I'd been thinking. "The boys are too young and you are too old, Ro," she said.

I couldn't help being a little nettled at that. "We'll see," I answered huffily.

"There'll be plenty for everybody to do." Grace let her eyes close wearily. "Ro I hate it all so," she said in a tiny beaten voice. "At least we don't have to decide tonight." Then she exploded all at once in that spunky little bantam way she had. "Why the little yellow bastards!"

We could hear the phone ringing as we stopped under the big maple tree in front of the door. Grace ran in to answer while I was locking up the car. "It's Roger. Talk to him." She gave me a frightened look as she handed me the receiver. Roger's voice was very tense. He was clipping his words short. "Roland," he said, "walk around the block to see how Alicia is. I might not be home for two or three days. There's no one else I can trust. She's not been well for some time you understand, not well in the head. Keep her quieted down. See that she gets some dinner . . . All right"—I heard his voice perfectly calm and relaxed as he turned to some secretary—"I'm ready for that next call."

We found the front door of the Thurloes' house wide open. Nobody answered the bell. It took us some time to find Alicia. We called and called. At last we found her in a little back room on the third floor. It must have been a sewing room because there was one of those false torsos in black bombazine women use to fit dresses on standing in the corner. The floor was full of spools of thread spilt out of some drawer. Alicia was wearing a wadded dressing gown. Her tawny hair was in a tangle and her fingers were stained with ink but she still had her stately Gainsborough look.

"I'm so glad you finally came," she said as if she had been expecting us all along. She put her hand to her forehead in a dazed sort of way. "Something keeps me from making up my mind about all these things." She swept her hand distractedly around the room. She started to stride back and forth between a wicker chair piled with evening dresses and another batch heaped helterskelter on a cot. She kicked the tangled spools of thread out of the way with the pointed toes of her small gold slippers as she strode. "Have a drink," she said pointing to a bottle of Gordon's gin that stood on the dresser. "Don't you like the label? I always thought it was stylish."

I didn't know what to say or do but Grace fell into the mood perfectly. "Alicia," she said, "we have Gordon's gin too . . . Why don't we go around to our house for a drink and an early supper and then we'll all go to bed and get a good rest? I feel absolutely worn out at the thought of all the decisions we've got to make."

"It's the cook's day off. I sent the maid home because she was staring at me so." Her face crinkled suspiciously. "Don't you stare at me. You are sure that Roger didn't tell you to come and stare at me?"

"My dear," Grace was saying, "it's this dreadful news that's got everybody upset. Let's not make any more decisions tonight."

"I'll cook you dinner right here. You didn't know I took a course at the Cordon Bleu school in Paris, I bet you never thought of that." Alicia gave her head a toss.

"But I've got some lovely cold beef," Grace was pleading. "All I need to do is fix a salad."

"Wartime. Nobody's going to dress." Alicia suddenly turned her back on us and snatched up a nilegreen evening gown off one of the piles. "I better pitch all these things out of the window."

"Alicia, I bet you can't make us a supreme de volaille," said Grace with considerable presence of mind.

"Of course I can . . . Roland you go down and fix us a cocktail. You'll find everything in the little pantry back of the dining room."

That was a good excuse for me to get hold of the gin bottle, and to walk off downstairs with it. I felt absolutely limp. I had come to feel real affection and admiration for Alicia. She was a strange awkward woman for all her stately bearing, but there was nothing small about her. What could be the trouble? She had certainly been drinking but this was not exactly drunkenness. I tried to think of the name of a psychiatrist. This was the worst possible time to try to get hold of a doctor. When the two women came downstairs Alicia caught me poring over the phone book in the hall. Grace had gotten her tidied up a bit. She had put on a flowered green and lavender dress. She seemed much less distracted.

"No Roland," she said in her peremptory way. "I don't want anybody coming around here this evening . . . Roger might come home and I want him to feel free to talk. Of course he couldn't if there were strangers here . . . Roger's been planning for this." We were following her down the stairs into the kitchen. "Roger's a deep one," she was mumbling; "too deep for his own good."

The two women started poking around in the big basement kitchen, peering into the icebox, reaching for canned goods from the shelves. Alicia was on her knees with her arms around a nest of mixing bowls she was dragging out of a cupboard. She looked up at me sharply: "What about that cocktail, barman. You are the worst barman I ever saw."

I tried to make the martinis extra weak. When I came down with three little glasses on a tray Alicia reached for one and tasted it. "Puddle water!" she cried and poured it into the sink. "Try again barman," she said in a tone so taunting I had to struggle to keep my temper. "Five to one and some zest of lemon," she bawled after me as I started up the corkscrew iron stairway that led to the butler's pantry above.

By the time I got back with three really honest martini cocktails the kitchen was in an uproar. A pan of butter was burning on the electric stove. Alicia had spilt flour down the front of her dress and over most of the tiled floor. Poor Grace who, though she hated housework, was a neat competent little cook, was running around after her trying to clean up. Grace was muffled in a white apron much too big for her. She looked so funny I couldn't help laughing. "There must be some tarragon . . . I can't move a step without tarragon," Alicia was wailing in a loud hysterical voice. "Do you suppose those damn servants have stolen my tarragon?" The shelves were littered with condiments and halfopen packages of dried herbs. Onions were everywhere. There was a huge pile of chopped parsley. Alicia was brandishing an eggbeater dripping with beaten up egg as she strode about the kitchen.

Grace, who was always a tiny drinker, was so rattled she tossed off her martini at a gulp.

"That's better, Roland," said Alicia condescendingly, "just for a sample. Now make us a shaker full."

There was no way of arguing with her. I went back up the stairs and took as long as I could over the next batch. I packed in all the ice the shaker would hold and even sneaked a glass of water into it. At last I began to be scared for Grace if I stayed too long. When I tiptoed down the stairs with my shaker I found Alicia sitting at the table poring with pursed lips and frowning brows over a French cookbook. Grace was leaning over patting her gently on the shoulder and whining pleadingly in her ear, "Please Alicia, let's not do any more cooking tonight." There were tears in her eyes. "Please Alicia, I'm so tired. I want to go home to bed."

At that moment there were footsteps in the entrance hall above. The door to the lower hall opened and Roger's face poked into the kitchen. It was calm collected completely impersonal. He pushed the door open further. Behind him was a doctor looking man with a black bag and a trained nurse. I stepped over towards him trying not to show how relieved I felt. "When your phone didn't answer," he said in a low voice, "I knew you and Grace would be here." He was smiling. "No use trying to explain how much I thank you. Alicia will too one of these days," he whispered hurriedly. "Dr. Glendinning and Miss Sargeant are here to take over . . . I'm picking up a couple of shirts and a toothbrush and going back to the office."

"Anything I could do for you right now?"

He shook his head.

Alicia didn't seem to notice that Roger had come home.

It turned out that Dr. Glendinning was quite a gourmet himself. He wanted to know all about Alicia's course at the Cordon Bleu. Miss Sargeant was interested too. Alicia let us all kiss her good night like a sleepy little girl who had been playing too hard. When we left they were trying to help her find the tarragon.

Roger followed us out of the front door onto the sidewalk. He kissed Grace lightly on the cheek. "This is for both of you, my dears," he said. Then he added in a tone of strange unconcern: "It's going to be darned interesting to see what the people of this country can do when we are put on our mettle . . . Maybe it's about time."

We walked home around the block and each drank a glass of milk in the kitchen and tumbled into bed. We were too tired to eat. We fell right asleep. It was always so happy when Grace and I were in bed, alone in that little narrow house on Dumbarton Avenue . . .

6

Back in the car Elsa has slid way over to her side and is nursing on her knees the new portable pigskin radio. She lets Ro hold her hand which lies slender on the seat between them. The taximan, the smile frozen under the narrow mustache on his face yellow as jaundice is driving them slowly round the Malecon. In rasping English he describes the points of interest, talking through his smile like through a mask.

The tradewind has freshened and spray from an occasional wave splatters over the seawall. A smell of warm brine and urine rises from the rocks below. Ro is drowsy. The afternoon is beginning to sag. He sits up with a start when Elsa points out the apartment house where the nonobjective painter Pinillo lives, but too late to see it. By the time they reach the Maine monument, Elsa has begun to talk about needing another drink.

Ro argues feebly between yawns that they would enjoy a drink more after a dip in the ocean. He tries to keep Elsa distracted by pointing out the hibiscus hedges and the roses and the balconies bowered in jasmine out through the Vedado. She keeps insisting that sightseeing makes her thirsty. At the Almendares bridge she takes matters in her own hands. She taps the driver on the shoulder and makes him stop at what looks like a soft drink stand equipped with rickety painted tables set in a clump of rustling coconut palms.

"I bet Gov never brought you here," Ro grumbles.

"Gov would never do anything," Elsa says pettishly. "I want to look at the river."

Sure enough a narrow river ripples in the sunshine at their feet. There are motorboats at anchor. A knockabout is tacking in to a mooring.White skiffs lie off from plank landings. The breeze reeks of the open sea. Overhead the long dry fronds of the coconut palms rustle against the sky.

They are the only customers. A radio blares from a loudspeaker in the stand behind them. The frayed waiter who comes out to dab with a dirty rag at the table seems to be looking them over curiously. Ro catches the sarcastic sidelong look he tosses over their heads at the taxidriver who lolls eternally smiling behind the wheel of his car.

To get back a feeling of consequence Ro begins to marshal his story about how he and Mortimer Price flew into England on that little Dutch plane during the bombings.

Elsa has drunk her first Scotch down in a hurry. She interrupts him to order a second. As Ro sits talking, he is seeing himself as the waiter and the taxidriver must be seeing him, a tall grayhaired skinned-looking man making sweet talk across the table to a pretty redhead. They don't know she's really interested, he thinks as he talks: she has a very active mind.

She's interrupting him again. "I love to drink in the afternoon," she is saying in a musing drawl.

He turns to see where she is looking. Together they watch a white motorboat nose up to a small wharf under the fringe of palms across the river. The river is the color of washing blue with a sheen of gold on it. The boats are golden white in the slanting sun. Terns fly overhead. They are looking at the same things, feeling the same things.

"Time and space seem suspended," she says. She taps a fresh cigarette on the edge of the table. "Go on about England, Ro," she looks him straight in the eye with one of her quick grins. "I love to hear people reminisce."

The radio roars out a rhumba so loud Ro can't remember what he has started to say. He jumps to his feet and strides scowling back to the stand. The frayed waiter gives him a frightened look out of tiny black eyes. "Turn it off," Ro shouts. Then he pulls out a dollar bill and shakes it under the man's cringing nose. "Just a few minutes," he adds in coaxing Spanish. "Then we'll go to Marianao to bathe in the surf."

Now Ro can hear clearly again the rustling of the coconut palms as their long fronds stream out in the tradewind overhead. His spine stiff with satisfaction from his overcoming of the radio and the waiter, he towers over Elsa and fixes an eye of authority on her face. Her eyes are wide with admiration. Her hair shines like copper wire. The great metal leaves of a seagrape creak faintly behind her as they stir in the breeze. Ro is swaying a little.

Elsa looks up at him vaguely as if she were trying to remember what they had been talking about.

"You said you met George Bernard Shaw over there?"

Ro has the feeling he is trying to make conversation at a party. He looks her hard in the face. "You mean H. G. Wells," he corrects her.

She nods obediently. She is paying attention now.

Searching for terms she will understand he falls to watching the sunlight dribbling in streaks through the deepscalloped leaves of the seagrape behind her. It fills her hair with little coppery sparks. She has taken off those wretched sunglasses. She is a remarkably handsome girl, intelligent too, only he must find the terms she understands. He slides his hands over her hands as they clutch the edge of the sticky table.

"H. G. Wells," he repeats, "was the great admiration of my life. When I was a kid I used to read his stories in a stack of old Strand magazines I found in the attic in our house in Columbus. My dad taught at the university there. It was an English magazine. Lord knows how it got there. I used to creep up the dusty stairs with a candle after my light was supposed to be out. As I read I used to finger the soft warm wax under the candleflame. Candlegrease stings when you get it under your fingernails. Once I almost set my hair on fire. I had quite a time explaining the singed place to the family at breakfast in the morning."

"Never read him," whines Elsa complainingly. "I was born too late," she adds with a sigh.

Suddenly she thinks of something: "After Gov got to be such a heel I couldn't stand it anymore. I played with some of the off Broadway fellows in New York for a while. They said I'd never need to read Wells or Shaw either." There's a teasing look in her pale brown eyes. She grins. "Purely suburban, they said."

Ro raises his voice. "It's a whole lot easier to act superior like the boys around Greenwich Village. Our society happens to be suburban. Wells took the trouble to think. He foresaw the new technology, the new social systems. That was his great gift. Giving fantastic things that kind of suburban reality. It gave me a hint of what I wanted to do in the world . . . a certain kind of journalism."

Ro makes a wide gesture with his arms. He can't help it. He is on the lecture platform.

The gesture has given the frayed waiter the idea that Ro is ordering another drink. All at once the man is standing over them, obsequiously piling fresh ice into their glasses, while Elsa smiles approvingly up into his face.

"The kind of journalism," Ro is saying, "that's between history and prophecy."

The waiter nods eagerly as if he understood exactly what Ro is talking about. He is having trouble getting the seal off the fresh bottle of Black and White. Elsa has taken to fiddling with the dials of her radio. A scrap of tune bursts out. She gives Ro a quick apologetic grin as she chokes it off.

Ro can't remember what he's talking about any more. He jumps to his feet. "Let's get out of this dump. We've got to go to Marianao."

"A stirrup cup," Elsa whoops cheerfully. "Bottoms up."

He has to help her to her feet. "My legs got stiff." She makes a face. "It's that hard stool."

"Señor," the man breaks out in Spanish when he trots back panting with the change. "The señores will find the water somewhat cold at this hour." He smiles obsequiously as if to apologize for his boldness. "There is danger of taking a chill. For us it is still winter." He gives his hands a chilly little shake.

Ro hears himself declaiming in a loud stately voice. "I bathe at Marianao at all seasons."

The frayed waiter smiles and shrugs as his fingers close over his tip.

Ro helps Elsa into the back seat of the royalblue touring car with elaborate courtliness. "To Marianao," he announces to the never unsmiling taxidriver, "and fast."

Elsa puts her arm round his shoulder and snuggles up against him. She nestles her head against his neck and whispers, "Ro please, not too fast."

"Slowly," Ro hears his stern voice admonishing the driver. As they ride he picks up the thread of his discourse again.

He is telling about his talk with Roger Thurloe three weeks after Pearl Harbor . . .

. . . We hadn't seen the Thurloes since that night. Everything had been happening so fast I had lost count of the days. Then late one evening when Grace and I were walking up and down in our bathrobes in the little back study, arguing about whether I ought to stay on in Washington covering the war effort for Parkman's or whether I ought to try to get into uniform the way all my friends seemed to be doing, all at once Roger was in the room. He had a fresh well exercised look as if he had just played a game of tennis and taken a shower. He walked in almost jauntily, apologizing for not having called us up. Alicia was doing quite nicely in a sanitarium. She had gone back to her painting. He was sorry about the sanitarium but he had to choose between that and his job. Right at that moment his job was more important. Their son Joe had enlisted. He was already out on the Coast training for the PT boats and happy as a clam at high tide.

"Ro's worrying himself sick because he's not in uniform," Grace broke in. "You know the inside story Roger. Tell him what he ought to do."

"Go on doing what you are doing. Tell the story, as much as it can be told, as it goes along. The American people are going to need some independent observers, Ro. Lord man I shudder to think of the propaganda we are going to dish out. Take me in my job . . . if I can't get somebody to give me an appraisal from the outside I'll start believing it myself."

"Isn't that just what I was saying?" Grace broke in again.

"Darling let Roger talk. He's only got a minute."

"You are wrong," said Roger. "I've got fifteen minutes." He plunked himself solemnly down in a chair.

"Well I had two things on my chest when I came in and then I'll shut up and listen. I'm a better listener than you think," said Roger laughing. "The first one's about the armed forces. We are going to win this war. I know right now things don't look too hot . . . but up there in my office I'm surprised every hour . . . overwhelmed sometimes, at evidences of selfless patriotism on the part of the old time army and navy men. I knew I'd find it in the civilians. It's been the civilians who have always fought our wars for us. But the command has got to come from the men trained for the job. We've got the leadership . . . We've got the military brains. Here's the second thing. Up there in the office I get everything through channels. I need some guys like you and Grace to keep me informed: How does it all look to the ordinary citizen? That's why I want you to keep out of uniform, Ro. And don't you go hush hush on me like Mortimer. Mortimer won't even tell me what he hears when he goes to the White House for a press conference."

We couldn't help tittering at that, Grace and I. We'd seen Mortimer's long authoritative strides as he walked back across Lafayette Square from the White House.

"Now suppose we sit around for ten minutes and drink just one comfortable scotch and stretch our arms and legs and then I'll let you kids go to bed. I have a rollaway cot in my office and I'm planning to get five delicious hours of sleep before all hell breaks loose again."

"Thanks," he said with a sort of schoolboy gratefulness when I brought him a drink. He sipped it thoughtfully. Obviously there were more things he wanted to say, but in spite of himself, his small tense jaw was locked tight. "It's going to be a long war," he blurted out before he left. "It's up to us to last out the duration. . . ."

. . . A burst of *Siboney* interrupts Ro's tale. Elsa's fingers have been fiddling with her radio again. She chokes it down with a giggle. "Go on," she says. "I like your voice against the music."

Ro has forgotten what he's trying to say. The palms and villas of Marianao flit past. The car has turned into a drive round the casino and come to a stop behind the bathhouses.

"Joe Herkimer took us there," says Elsa, cocking her head in the direction of the casino. "Gov lost some money and it added to his depression."

"I need a swim in the ocean," Ro is still insisting as he climbs out of the car.

He hurries out onto the beach.

Of course it is too late. The sun has set. The beach has a wan forsaken look. The ocean is gray. The bathhouses are closed. Years ago he would have found a lonely spot and gone in anyway, but now it seems too much trouble.

When Ro comes forlornly back to the car Elsa is nowhere to be seen. Smiling expressionlessly under his narrow mustache the taxidriver points to a neon sign that has just come on. *Bar* it reads. Ro stalks under it in a fluster. He is telling himself that at this time of the evening they ought to be in Central Park or walking on the Prado.

"I ordered you a scotch." She looks up at him archly from her seat on a high stool. Elsa always looks thoroughly at home on a high stool against a bar. She seems to enjoy the flood of neon light that has sucked all the brilliance out of the gloaming. Except for two young Cubans in Waikiki shirts the place is empty.

"Gov always used to catch cold when he went in swimming . . ." Her voice trails off.

Ro stares straight ahead at the row of brilliantly lit Bacardi bottles in front of him. "I was trying to tell you something," he begins, "something I have been trying to do. It's something like bringing that Wellsian world up to date. Science fiction isn't the answer . . . Thurloe used to like to quote what old Wells told me that night in London. 'If you Americans can't find some way of carrying the burden of empire we are sunk, all of us, sunk' . . ."

Elsa isn't paying attention.

"Ro," she nudges him and whispers in his ear, "those boys are pansies. One wears a bracelet. I want to hear what they are saying. Look they are holding hands."

"They may understand English," Ro grumbles.

He feels unbelievably lonely.

The neon lights have turned the twilight into ink. Long tired rollers crunch on the empty beach outside. The metal brightness of the bar cuts into his eyes. The cooing and chirruping of the two young men is immeasurably depressing.

Ro finds the disgust he feels mirrored in the face of the barman, a ruddy barrelshaped man about Ro's age, a Spaniard undoubtedly.

"It's out of season. The bathhouses are closed. Nothing to it but to go back to town," Ro explains confidentially in Spanish.

The barman smiles approval. He looks pleased to see a man of his own age helling around with such a goodlooking girl.

"Carnival," says the barman. His eyes glitter. "They are all dancing." He snaps his fingers.

"Are you from Asturias?" Ro asks.

"Almost." The man shows even white teeth when he smiles. "From the Mountain of Santander."

"There are good people there. They speak the most beautiful Castilian."

The barman smiles again. "A drink on the house? You know . . . carnival."

"We are in the hands of friends," Ro pushes the new drink toward Elsa. Damn it, he is saying to himself, if she wants to drink so much, let's drink.

Elsa is absorbed in watching the two young men. When she sees the fresh drink she looks gratefully up in Ro's face. "You have friends everywhere," she says making her eyes very round.

Ro shakes hands with the Spanish barman amid an elaborate exchange of good wishes when they get ready to leave.

Elsa is hanging on Ro's arm as they walk back to the car. "I bet the taxidriver's one too," she giggles. "That's why he acts so superior . . . It's funny because back home pansies are attracted to me . . . I can't get them out of my hair."

"There are plenty of people attracted to you." Ro squares his shoulders as they start back to town. He kisses her brazenly on the mouth. "And they are not all pansies either."

She has tuned in on a sobbing tango on her radio. Driving home she lets Ro dandle her, radio and all, in his arms. Her body is lovely to touch. Inside the city the streets are packed with traffic. They lie back in the seat arm in arm and look out at the crowding cars full of dark-eyed women in bright dresses; and families jammed into long limousines, the children all in fancy clothes; and sports cars full of darkfaced men. Horns honk, claxons bleat, tires hiss. On every face Ro can trace a glassy sort of public smile, like the taxidriver's smile. Everyone is on his way somewhere, avidly on his way toward some public pleasure.

"I've often thought," Ro drones in a tender whisper with his lips touching her ear, "that Havana would be a horrible place to be alone in."

"I don't think I'd be lonesome," she says, "not with all the music."

"We'll go back to the hotel and take a shower," the words purr caressingly from his lips.

"Together?" she grins at him teasingly.

"Why not?" The thought makes him blush and then he adds hurriedly, to cover his embarrassment, "We'll go across the street to the old restaurant and eat a little bite . . . after all this scotch."

"We've got to do something to pass the time," she says in a practical tone. "Paco Cortes doesn't open till ten. It's midnight before they really warm up."

"But we don't need to go tonight." Ro hates night clubs. "There'll be plenty of nights for dancing the rhumba."

She pulls herself away from him and sits up stiffly on the edge of the seat. "Don't you understand?" she says emphasizing each syllable. "It's terribly important . . . for us."

Ro can't imagine what she means. Hell, women have to do these things in their own way; let yourself drift, he tells himself. At least she said "us." She is thinking of us.

They are driving in a slow line of cars down a narrow street where the headlights make moving bright stains on the stucco flanks of the buildings. Elsa still sits bolt upright, taught as a fiddlestring. In the flicker of the streetlights Ro sees a tense look of listening in her face. From somewhere comes the sound of drums.

"Stop right here," she cries. "Pay him Ro. Stop," she shouts.

Ro is nettled by being ordered around this way, but he does as he's told. They have run up a thumping bill with the taxidriver. Ro thinks he'll never stop pulling the greenbacks off the wad he has in his pocket. The driver's smile never varies. "Tonight," he says in the confidential tone that so irritates Ro, "you go to the Club Paco."

Ro doesn't answer. He isn't going to let this damned taxidriver in on his most intimate affairs. Even after he's driven away Ro fancies he can pick out his same icy smile under the narrow mustache on the faces of men who brush past him on the street.

He stands on the curb looking up and down the sidewalk for Elsa. Elsa has disappeared again. Impatiently snapping his fingers he follows the sound of the lame dragging drumbeat. He hears voices singing. In a square to one side from the traffic people are dancing. Many of them are Negroes, some are mulattos, some are white. Some dance barefooted on the stone pavings. They wear oldfashioned costumes. Some of the men are in threecornered hats. Some carry lighted carriage lanterns on tall poles. The women wear bustles in bright colors and gypsylooking shawls. They sing in unison as they circle humbly through the crowd shuffling to the beat of the drums in the lame rhumba rhythm.

"It's the comparsas." Elsa has bobbed up from somewhere out of the crowd. Her hips are swaying. "Let's go along with them." She can't seem to stop the urgent swaying of her hips. "It's the comparsas, I told you."

Ro links his arm in hers and turns her resolutely around. "We're quite near the hotel," he says firmly. "They might not want us. We're not members of the club."

She walks along limply with her head against his shoulder. "I don't know why it's so exciting," she is almost sobbing.

The minute she gets up to her room she turns on the

radio. She works the dials until she finds a mambo orchestra. She kicks off her sneakers and shuffles round her room to the music. When Ro tries to put his arms round her she slips away from him with a twist of her shoulders without looking him in the face. Dancing round the room with halfclosed eyes she pulls off her clothes. She pays no attention to him when he walks toward her.

There is something so casual about the way she stands there stark naked in front of the door of her shower stuffing her hair into a bathing cap that Ro has the feeling of being in a strait jacket. He wants to reach for her but he can't.

His shoulders rise in a violent shrug. He turns on his heel and, being very careful to close her door tight behind him, strides into his own room. In his eyes there lingers an after image of the tall white figure and the flash of auburn between the thighs . . .

7

. . . Grace and I were particularly happy together that summer though in other ways I remember it as a difficult time. The boys' school reports were depressing. They had both been unsettled enough even before Pearl Harbor. Now their heads spun like a couple of little tops. We had packed them off to a summer camp in desperation. It was one of those miseries that we faced side by side; somehow it drew us together even more than our mutual pleasures did.

The June weather was exceptionally muggy even for Washington. The weekly I was doing an article for had an airconditioned office downtown. They had loaned me a desk there and I had fallen into the habit of leaving the house about seven and walking downtown before it was too hot. One morning as I passed the Thurloes' front door who should pop out of it but Roger.

We were genuinely pleased to see each other. It was months since we had met. It was a little embarrassing too because I knew that Roger must know that I had been trying to get him on the phone for three days. His secretary had been most apologetic but she had said she just couldn't imagine any way he could be reached. We both hemmed and hawed a little at first. Neither of us was much on small talk. Then Roger muttered something about how his job left him no time for his tennis so, to get a speck of exercise, he had taken to walking to the office in the morning. I said so had I.

Roger was a small man but he had a remarkably fast bouncy stride. I found it hard to keep up with him. We chatted in a desultory way as we walked. The conversation, I felt, was as frustrating to him as to me. We couldn't mention the things we really wanted to talk about. The Coral Sea. Midway. The Prime Minister's arrival in town. I was eaten up inside with questions I knew Roger had the answers to. What were the President and Prime Minister talking about upstairs at 1600 Pennsylvania Avenue? Were they really planning a second front in Europe? Were the Russians really making a comeback? I knew through the press club scuttlebutt that most of the high brass from the combined British and American command was gathered in the new staff room rigged up on the White House grounds. It was a horrible temptation to put leading questions. Roger had been a little tense when we started our walk but as soon as he discovered I wasn't going to smuggle any questions into our conversation he let himself relax. In fact he seemed almost embarrassingly grateful.

I was telling him my worries about Chips and Louie. Roger had been through it all with his boy until Joe had walked out of college and enlisted. "I would have done the same thing at his age." But what were you going to do if they were too young? Chips was only fourteen. "Children were much happier in our fathers' time," Roger said musingly. "Everything was either black or white then and nobody asked them to make any decisions and there were plenty of chores to be done. The way we live now we have to make up work for them and they resent it."

I started to try to explain that I thought the boys were upset by my own restlessness. Wartime was so unsettling unless you were in it up to the hilt. I had been happier during the last little unpleasantness when I was a buck private in the rear rank.

"I operated a seaplane," said Roger. "I remember it as a supremely happy time . . . My lord Ro the way it is now a man feels so helpless . . . if I had time to think I'd probably blow my brains out . . . But I won't," he added grinning impishly, "not for the duration. I won't have a minute. I'm too busy breaking up bottlenecks."

We had reached the corner of Pennsylvania Avenue opposite the old War and State Building. "You must excuse me," he said. "I've got to cross the street." He turned back after he had left me. "By the way Ro, some of us are going to drop in on the Prices this evening to congratulate Mortimer on his appointment. They've just moved into a house on Kalorama Road."

He was studying my face. When he saw I was doubtful he added curtly. "Please come, Ro. Alicia is coming. We decided we ought to be seen together once in a while."

"All right we'll try to make it."

He had already started off across the street. As I walked on towards Lafayette Square I could see Roger out of the corner of my eye showing his pass to the sentry who guarded the entrance to the piece of street that had been fenced off between the War Department and the White

House grounds. There was something youthful and ingratiating about the set of Roger's back and the tilt of his head, a small boy trying to talk his way into a ball park.

They never would make a stuffed shirt out of Roger, I was telling myself: but Mortimer, poor old Mortimer had been stuffing his own shirt for years. Mortimer dishing out war information. I was an old friend and I was fond of him and I respected his ability but he sure was going to be stuffy to deal with. I could hear him already booming something about not letting his private feelings stand in the way of the public service. Mortimer wouldn't be worrying so much about information getting into the hands of the enemy, as about information getting into the hands of the wrong people at home, isolationists, critics of the New Deal and such. I very much suspected Mortimer knew me well enough to class me with the wrong people. He had an extraordinary knack for uncovering the tiniest mustard seed of unbelief. He would find it his painful duty to keep me in the outer dark.

Maybe my feelings were all envy, I was telling myself as I walked down the empty street. Mortimer was making a successful career of wartime Washington. Mortimer was on the inside. All I seemed to be accomplishing was to fret myself to death.

It was cool in the early morning office building. It was pleasant to go up alone in the elevator and to let myself into the empty office and to settle down at my desk and to slip a fresh sheet of yellow foolscap into my typewriter.

That was as far as I got that morning. I had it all ready in my head going up in the elevator but when I put my fingers to the keys I couldn't find the words.

All I could imagine was the Prime Minister's cigar and the President's wheelchair or perhaps his long cigarette holder jutting jauntily out from his jaw. I sensed a certain exultation about them. These gentlemen were enjoying themselves. Both men had zest. Of course they sat up late and had themselves awakened early. They rolled in their beds in an agony of decision. They puckered their brows and strained their eyes over stubborn and adverse facts grouped under the rubric of unfamiliar names their aides spelled out on the great maps; Murmansk, Tobruk, Kiska, Attu.

Responsibility was a weight but it was a tonic too. What was the special pleasure the helmsman felt? The helmsman knew his job. This was something different. This was the gambler's delight in hazarding fleets and cities full of tiny crawling men and sorefooted armies on the march. An island here. A continent there. The whole wide world at stake.

And beyond the curve of the wobbling world I could imagine their opposite numbers; the cartoon gesticulations, the Austrian paperhanger hissing and spluttering into the microphone: the swart sawedoff bandit from the Caucasus mum behind his mustache. Signing deathwarrants was their daily treat; they ground millions into dust. Yet they uplifted the hearts of men. For them bleeding partisans hurried off to die on frozen rivercrossings. Tank crews suffocated at their command as they plowed the snows or the sterile sands of the Sahara. The will to kill. These were pleasures few men had tasted to the uttermost since the Roman three bestrode the ancient world.

I could not expect to understand those others. I wrote them off as outrageous monsters. But ours, the familiar superiority of Groton, the indifference of Harvard, the small boat sailing, the vacationing down East, the being bored with the law, the fad for public service, the intoxication with politics, the nineteenth century furnishings he grew up in at Hyde Park: these were all things I knew: the friendly fireside voice. Yet when the time came to run up a butcher's bill our Hudson River gentleman would sit there drinking blood with the best of them. Not a word against the President.

There was no way of writing what I was thinking and even if there were it wouldn't be just what I meant; but wasn't it maybe this blood giddiness that made the kings of men a little careless with their plans for the lives and deaths of the rest of us?

Though the sheet was still blank I pulled it out of the typewriter and crumpled it in the wastebasket. This was no time to write about the kings of men. But how about the seconds in command, the men who knew how, the skillful fellows with finance or production who made all this madness possible? The breakers of bottlenecks. What was Roger trying to tell me when he cried out that he'd blow his brains out if he had time to think? . . . Roger himself . . . But what a job to write up Roger. A man who wouldn't even answer the questionnaire from Who's Who. Even if you managed to get the story cleared for security it would take a derrick to get anything about his own work out of that modest guy.

I sat there a couple of hours outlining the project in pencil on a scratchpad. Then I suddenly felt all in, horribly depressed. The depression of ignorance, the depression of impotence. I needed to talk to Grace. I dialed our number.

Thank God she was home.

Of course we would go to Mortimers'. Might as well help him enjoy his moment. In six months he would be the most hated man in America. "Poor Mortimer. He's too innocent to know what he's facing . . . he thinks he's so wonderful. It's right pathetic. You know he loves so to be liked. You can't guess who I'm taking out to lunch." Grace gave a little shriek of laughter. "Miss Nanny. Come along Ro, you sound depressed. We'll take her to the Mayflower. I'll reserve a table. Miss Nanny among the dollar a year men.

She'll put them in their place. I may run her for Congress."

When I found them amid the rattle and the jabber and the appraising glances from table to table—who's lunching with whom?—of the crowded hotel diningroom, Miss Nanny certainly was responding to the environment, and to a glass of sherry wine.

The tiny little creature had quite a dashing look in a lavender lace dress and a little porkpie hat with multicolored clusters of flowers and fruit around the brim. Her eyes flashed in her little faded pansy face and she tossed her head from side to side as she talked. "I drink to confusion," she said lifting her glass as I sat down. "That was Brother Randolph's toast . . . The sweetest boy you ever knew with such a brilliant future; it was the war set him on the path to perdition . . . I declare, Grace dear," she suddenly squealed and grabbed Grace's hand across the table, "maybe it's not too late for me to follow in his footsteps . . . Did I ever tell you about Deacon Worthington? I bet I did. You just stop the old lady if she rambles on too much. Deacon Worthington was a friend of dear Papa's in Richmond before the war. He was the most straightlaced sober man and highly censorious of others, you understand, until his seventyfirst birthday. On that day he was induced to take a sip of liquor. My dear he never stopped drinking till the day he died. And it wasn't only the bottle. It was every sort of scandal. Don't ask me to describe them." Miss Nanny put her hand over her eyes. Her hat had slipped over to a rakish angle.

Miss Nanny was off. Neither Grace not I could get in a word. "Warbabies they call them. I know all about them," chortled Miss Nanny shaking the flowers and fruit on her hat, "because I was a warbaby myself. I came into the world in wartime and it looks very much as if I'd go out of it the same way."

She had a funny headlong way of talking, like a soda

water bottle suddenly uncorked. "I bet you never knew I was born the day the Virginia Convention voted secession. Dear Mama used to remind me of it often. We packed up when I was still a tiny creature in a bassinet to get away from the marauding Federal troops and left our poor house to its fate. Things happened in Alexandria that poor Mr. Lincoln never knew about. These days I think so often about Mr. Lincoln. If only God had spared him. The young people don't understand how we felt about Mr. Lincoln in the South during the war. My adored Papa always spoke of him so respectfully as a worthy opponent. My dear,"—she grabbed Grace's hand again—"I can remember the way the news came to us, I know I can. Of course I was very little but times of war and privation make children so precocious. Cousin Bessie used to say that I just remembered it because dear Mama told me about it, but I always told her 'Shut your mouth Bessie I can see it now just as it happened.' . . . We had moved to Montgomery. On account of my adored Papa's high official position—he was virtually a member of the cabinet during those last dreadful days—he got the news even before it came out in the newspapers. We were just sitting down to dinner when the orderly came with a slip of paper. I don't know what we had. It couldn't have been much. We were always hungry in those days. My dear, people go around complaining about rationing. The trouble in Montgomery was there wasn't anything to ration. This day the cook had fricasseed a skinny old fowl. I remember how hungry it made us children just to smell it simmering. Aunt Esther, she'd been my Mammy, she couldn't abide those Alabama darkies. Aunt Esther came of a long line of house servants tenderly reared in dear Mama's family. She was crying when she brought in that fowl. 'Marse John hit's tough as an old shoe,' she was saying. Papa said 'Never mind Esther, next week we shall verily be stewing up old shoes.' I know Papa was hungry but when he'd read off that slip of paper the news that had come over the telegraph he couldn't eat a bite. 'My darling,' he told Mama, 'Mr. Lincoln is dead . . . This is perhaps the must shattering blow of all . . .' And so it turned out. It was the humiliation. Reconstruction killed my adored Papa."

All the little clusters of flowers and fruit vibrated round Miss Nanny's hat as she shook her head to dislodge a tear that was running down her straight little nose. Grace and I were almost crying ourselves. Grace tried to get her to eat. "Not yet my dear, I'm not quite talked out," Miss Nanny said firmly. "It's terrible to be too old to be useful. Little as I was I helped dear Mama tear bandages, and we made up boxes of small comforts for the soldiers. When that war came over in Europe I worked with the Red Cross. In fact I headed the Red Cross chapter in Alexandria. I declare I know you are wondering how I did it knowing how feckless I am about money matters. Well, I did."

She gave her small head another toss and all the little clusters of flowers and fruit shook perilously, "But now I'm just an extra mouth to feed, a useless old hag I used to tell myself until my dear, I started to pray . . . I know people have given up praying in these days. Oldfashioned or not I have to be the way I am. When I pray I always pray the same thing, that the dear God will allow the spirit of Mr. Lincoln to watch over us in this our hour of need, that the spirit of Mr. Lincoln will be permitted to inspire the present occupant of the White House with a decent 'umbleness before man and before God."

"If Lincoln were alive today," I began, but I couldn't get a word in, Miss Nanny wouldn't stop talking even for a minute. The words were tumbling helterskelter out of her mouth. "My dear, I don't have anything else to do since I allowed myself to be prevailed upon to part with the old Cyarter place but read and listen to the wireless. In everything I hear I find pride and vainglory. Mr. Lincoln was an 'umble man. Every night I pray that some of Mr. Lincoln's 'umbleness will make its way into the councils of our reunited nation. We all know that pride cometh before a fall."

Miss Nanny wiped her eyes and sneezed. "Now you children do the talking," she said and patted her face all over with her little lace handkerchief, and fell to eating her creamed chicken patty with right good will.

Poor Miss Nanny, that must have been about the last time she came out, with us at least. Grace and I were so happy afterwards that we had spent that hour with her. Grace particularly had become absolutely devoted to Miss Nanny. Grace went to see her every day she could after Miss Nanny took to her bed although it was a slow trip over to Alexandria on the bus after the gasoline rationing had cut down on the use of the car. A few months later she was dead.

That evening we hadn't been long at the Prices' before Grace came up to me and made a little pansy face and mimicked Miss Nanny with great tenderness. "Pride my dear," she whispered. "Cometh before a fall," I finished the quotation. If anybody heard us they must have thought we were crazy.

Then Grace pulled me into a corner and whispered in my ear: "It's like trying to swim against the tide, through weeds, great clammy clinging waterweeds." She wanted to go home right then, but I insisted on waiting till the Thurloes arrived.

It was a most uncomfortable evening. More than half the men were in uniform. That meant that almost everybody was outranked by somebody. The field officers couldn't be easy because there were general officers there and the general officers couldn't unbend in the presence of the lower ranks.

It was about the same with the civilians. The Secretary of State was surrounded by a hushed throng in one corner of the big living room, while a Supreme Court Justice conducted his sibilant monologue in another. Meanwhile Herman Boggs "the most cantankerous cabinet member" was competing for attention among the potted plants on the glassed in porch by letting off a string of the sour remarks he was famous for. Grace said he reminded her of a small boy setting off firecrackers behind Grandpa's chair.

Poor Gertrude Ann, who was new to Washington parties, was in a tizzy, bustling from one group to the other followed by two great boxer dogs that kept tripping people up. She seemed so anxious not to be seen giving the less important people the same welcome as the more important people that the result was that everybody felt neglected.

When the Thurloes arrived it was late and they were both in evening dress. That in wartime Washington could mean only one thing. They'd been dining with the Prime Minister. In spite of anything either Mortimer, who had the look of a lost birddog when he was preoccupied, or busy Gertrude Ann could do to keep the conversation general, their guests began to crowd about the Thurloes.

It was the longest time before we could get within hailing distance of them. I found Alicia looking haggard but selfpossessed in a silvery yellow gown with a lot of black lace thrown over it. She had a huge Spanish comb in her hair that made her look eight feet tall. Roger's face wore the expression of patient resignation it always did at social gatherings. He was counting the minutes that would have to pass before he could get home and go to bed. We none of us could find a word to say to each other.

A heavy thunderstorm had come up. This seemed to

Grace a good excuse so she started working her way through the crush towards the door. The crashing of thunder and the driving of rain on the windowpanes and the cool air that filtered into the house had by that time distracted people enough from their social preoccupations so that Grace could produce a few smiles with some of her shrill little cracks as she went.

Mortimer followed us out into the hall. He seemed relieved to see us leave. He'd probably been afraid all evening that one of us would say something indiscreet. Still he couldn't approve of our leaving first.

"Isn't it a little early?" he asked, meaning that it wasn't the thing for us unimportant people to leave before the high brass left. We mumbled something about early rising. He shrugged his sloping shoulders. If we insisted on going he would see to it that we left as inconspicuously as possible.

Mortimer's heavy brows drew together in a frown when he saw Roger Thurloe extricate himself neatly from the crush and follow us into the hall. Roger grinned at Grace and tapped me briskly on the arm. "How about it Ro? Seven in front of my house?"

I said great I'd be there on the dot. He nodded and grinned again and, with that look of exaggerated resignation on his face, melted back into the crowd.

Mortimer was grudgingly helping us into our raincoats. Grace had begun to murmur that since we hadn't our car maybe we ought to phone for a cab.

Mortimer made as if he hadn't heard. He squared his shoulders to block our way back into the house. When we opened the front door we were confronted by a dense curtain of rain. Rain fell in sheets over the row of black towncars along the curb. "Can't we use the phone?" whined Grace.

"Connecticut Avenue is full of cabs," said Mortimer firmly. "You can run between the drops."

Before we knew what had happened the door had closed behind us and there we were splashing our way through the downpour. We were soaked to the skin and half mad and half laughing before we managed to slog our way into a phonebooth in a drugstore.

"Well Mortimer certainly put us in our place," hooted Grace as we tore off our wet clothes in the quiet privacy of our bedroom on Dumbarton Avenue.

We poured ourselves out a drink and sat in our nightclothes on the bed listening to the rain on the leaves of the vine outside of the open window. Grace had decided to take it all as a joke. "They sure do draw the line in this town," she said "between the insiders and the outsiders." Then she burst out: "I always thought like Miss Nanny I was better than anybody." We both got to laughing. "How did we ever get to be outsiders?" Grace giggled. "Miss Nanny was right," she shouted with that little shriek she gave when she found something particularly amusing. "It's the pride."

"The question is whose fall it cometh before," I said.

I put my arms around her. Lord it was cosy just the two of us that night against the world in the little Georgetown house with the rain pounding outside . . .

8

All the while he is stripping off his clammy clothes and freshening himself up in the shower Ro keeps struggling with the feeling he has that he is really somebody else. He isn't Roland Lancaster any more. What a drunken old goat he's somehow swapped lives with! The cold water sobers him a little but still he has trouble keeping his face together when he looks at it in the mirror. His features keep sliding all over the place like in a Picasso portrait. At least he isn't staggering. Trying to hold on to the sense of dignity that comes from the freshness of his clean palmbeach suit, he knocks on Elsa's door. Is he sure he has the right room? Suppose it's some woman he doesn't know.

It is a woman he does not know. Of course it's Elsa but she is so insistent. "I'm starving," she cries as she pulls open the door to let him in. "Let's go out on the town. This is a real bender."

"A goodtime Charley," cries Ro. "If my friends could see me now."

In the shabby old highceilinged restaurant at dinner she continually bubbles with a tinny sort of amusement. She grins at everything he says and now and then bursts out laughing. Even when he talks seriously, too too seriously, she listens with parted lips.

"It was when I tried to explain to people the contrast between our achievements in a technical way and our failures in international politics that I got into difficulties. Nobody wanted to listen."

"I'm listening," she says.

"Wells never had that difficulty, everybody always read everything he wrote."

"I didn't," says Elsa.

She brandishes a bone from the fried yellowtail accusingly and lays it on the side of her plate. "I thought these were boneless . . . Of course I never read anything but *The Waste Land* and things like that."

"Somebody's got to take an interest in the fate of our country . . . It's the fate of all of us," Ro hears himself intoning. "My that's a flat sounding remark," he adds.

She nods vigorously. "It's only how you write that matters." She lays down her knife and fork and looks him straight in the eye. She has her mouth full of fried potatoes. "Honestly I believe in art. I don't believe in current events."

"I wish I didn't," says Ro. He fills her glass with the iced white wine again.

"This wine'll be the ruination of me," she giggles.

"Let's be ruinated . . . Let's go to hell in a hack."

He orders coffee and Fundador and then more Fundador. The waiter leaves the bottle.

When they come out of the restaurant hours later the taxidriver with the yellow smile is waiting in the royal-blue touring car at the head of the line of cabs. "No avoiding our fate," mumbles Ro. No need to tell the driver where to take them. The driver already knows.

Paco's place turns out to be a very long way from town. The roads are empty. A northerly breeze has come in so cool they have to hug each other for warmth in the open touring car. At last the driver shoves on his brakes with a rattle of gravel beside a peeling plaster wall under some swaying Australian pines. Behind them clouds scud across the face of a halfmoon soaring high in the sky.

There are three other cars.

Ro feels so lonesome he could howl like a dog.

From somewhere comes barely audible music. The miniscule rattle of the gourds picks out the rhythms the way specks of phosphorescence pick out the heaving waves in a cove off the ocean at night. When she hears the music Ro can feel a shudder go through Elsa beside him. Her hip stirs in rhythm against his as they walk into the nightclub.

The place smells of damp plaster. It is shaped like a coffin with the orchestra on a platform at the narrow end. Blue walls faded and peeling hem in the rows of empty tables. On the dancefloor in front of the band a few dancing couples barely sway. While Ro is getting his number from the hatcheck girl a puffy pallid brown woman stuffed into pink rushes up and throws her arms around Elsa.

"The carrothead," she cries in Spanish. "How could I forget? Last year."

She seizes Ro's wrist and leads him towards a table

with a "reserved" sign on it at the edge of the dancefloor. "Remedios, a sus ordenes," she whispers in a hoarse voice in his ear as she beckons to a waiter with a dimpled hand.

Paco Cortes, she hurries to explain, hasn't come in yet. Very soon he will come. With him will come the crowd from the frontón.

She sits down with them at their table and chatters on. Her Spanish is too fast for Elsa. Ro has to translate. And how is the poor little young man with such a sad face? In New York, Ro answers, gaining much money. And Pinillo, the man without shame? The nonobjective painter Pinillo? They will call on him tomorrow. And the old one who teaches sport? Why have none of them come back?

"I'm the one who liked it," says Elsa. When the woman in pink laughs it is a racking bronchial laugh. "We drink rum here," Elsa whispers to Ro behind her hand. "The other drinks are terrible."

The waiter has already brought three Cuba libres in tall glasses. Ro sits with squared shoulders at the back of the table looking the place over. These joints aren't so bad if you speak the language. He's pleased to discover how well he's holding his liquor. It's years since he's drunk so much. Let yourself drift you goodtime Charley, he tells himself.

The woman in pink moves to another table. In a tense whisper Elsa tells Ro the names of the men in the orchestra. She points out the frantic clarinetist, the greenfaced little man who plays the piano, the big Negro who shuffles the drums, the crosseyed yellow boy who shakes the gourds, the haggard elderly European with deep pockmarks on his face who strums the bass viol. They are the same as last year, she murmurs delightedly.

Elsa tries to teach Ro to mambo. He hasn't got it in him. His feet won't shuffle to the rhythm. When they get back panting to their table he explains that his feet learned the twostep when they were young, can't teach old dogs new tricks.

"Old dogs," he laughs.

She ought to be laughing too but she's looking away from him across the room.

A man in longwaisted tight black trousers and a skimpy jacket comes strolling across the dancefloor. He has the dark skin of a Negro but not the features. Under a highbridged nose blue lips are parted over yellow horse teeth in a long Hapsburg jaw. His eyes are close together. He has powerful shoulders and a narrow torso set in broad hips. As he climbs the steps to the platform with his slow splayfooted gait the musicians come to life. He pushes the pianist gently off the stool and takes his place.

The piano shakes. Immediately the dance tune begins to move. The lame dragging rhythm is on the march. The music moves in slow parade lewd and solemn through the muffled dark. He leaves the piano and smiling snatches up the clarinet. The rhythm is shot through with a violent embroidery of sound. Elsa has grabbed Ro's hand. She squeezes so hard it hurts. She's shaking. "It's Paco Cortes," she says.

After the number, while the applause still clatters from the sprinkling of customers who have appeared at the tables, Ro notices that Remedios is whispering in Paco Cortes' ear, reminding him of something.

Elsa hardly breathes as she watches Paco Cortes walking across the floor towards their table. She jumps to her feet. "Be seated," Paco Cortes says in a deep dignified voice. He greets Ro politely. He consents to drink a rum with them. He looks Elsa up and down with a weary smile. Well, how has she been?

With highflown courtesy he addresses every word to Ro.

His health has been poor. It has been a poor tourist season. Last year was better, eh? He gives Elsa a half mocking half reminiscent smile. The winter has been cold, one norther after another. This is a dog's life when a man's health is poor. He strokes his forehead with his long dark fingers. An unhealthy life, one never gets to bed. The doctors' bills. It's all right if there's a crowd, money coming in, but tonight. Is this worth a man's killing himself for? The doctors told him to beware of tuberculosis, to get plenty of rest. When he does get to bed his cough keeps him awake.

The orchestra has started again, a danzon with odd pauses.

"Do you want to dance daughter?" Paco asks Elsa with a condescending smile. "With your permission sir," he says gravely to Ro. Elsa is up, already swaying with her eyes closed. She kicks off her sneakers and dances barefoot.

Ro reaches down and picks up the wellworn sneakers still warm from her feet. He holds her sneakers in his hand. This can't be me. How did I ever get into this spot? He sits at the empty table with four glasses on it and watches the slow revolution of the couples on the floor. A few more have come, all Cubans, no Americans. Now and then behind the other heads Ro catches sight of Paco Cortes' beaked face abstractedly beetling over Elsa's shoulder. Elsa's face is white, the eyes are slits. Her body is glued against the man's broad swaying hips. She moves in a trance.

When the music stops they turn back towards the table. Elsa has suddenly become blundering drunk. Paco steers her deftly by an elbow.

"The comparsas, ask him about the comparsas," she splutters.

Paco Cortes shrugs politely. "They are humble people.

They practice popular music and once a year they have a chance for a prize. For a tourist it is very typical."

The woman in pink comes up all dimples and smiles. Won't Elsa dance with her? Elsa pushes her away. She holds out her hand towards Paco. "One more," she says. Paco bows gravely to Ro as if in apology before he leads her away.

Ro sits holloweyed nursing the empty sneakers until they have finished their dance. He feels so cold he is beginning to shiver. He has already called for the check. He gets to his feet. He's had enough of this.

When Elsa comes back she is reeling. She stumbles into Ro's arms. He has to hold her tight by the shoulders.

"Take me home," she whispers with her lips against his ear. "Don't wait. Take me now."

It all takes time, waiting for the change, getting his panama from the hatcheck girl, sending for the taxidriver. Even before the royalblue touring car drives up Ro is dreading the driver's ironic smile.

Overhead the Australian pines sway dolefully against a black cloudstreaked sky.

Ro bundles Elsa into the car as best he can. Immediately she fastens her lips to his. She presses her legs to his. They roll knotted together in the back seat. The car tears through the windy night. Her hands roam over his body under his shirt.

At the hotel Ro shoves a handful of bills at the driver without looking at him.

They have to wait for the wheezy old watchman with his flashlight and his bunch of keys to open the outside door of the hotel. The watchman is a gallego with a big tired face all crinkly like a spent balloon. He is old and suspicious and slow. He fixes his small disapproving eyes on Ro's face. He takes an endless time to find the room keys and to search for the right button to press in the elevator. As the ancient elevator slides haltingly up towards their floor Ro is seeing the two of them as the watchman sees them. A goodtime Charley far past his prime, a drunken old goat dragged off to bed by a drunken whore.

9

His sleep splits open as if an axe had split it. As the warm protective coverlet of his sleep falls away from him he lies miserably awake staring up into the dark with every throbbing nerve exposed. His head aches like a stone.

The new girl sleeps quiet on the other side of the bed. The new girl's breathing is even and easy.

Words form in his head. He is talking to himself. Words go on forming in his head. It is not himself it is Elsa he is talking to: "This wasn't how I'd planned it, honest it wasn't. What I'd planned was being together in a bare little house under coconut palms by a beach. Breakfasting quietly together after a swim in the early sun, so that we should get to know each other gradually, to give our poor carcasses time to get into tune. Then we could decide between ourselves whether we ought to marry and have children. You said you wanted another, don't you remember? But before there can be children there must be love. Husband and wife warmly linked in their own double bed. Loving sleep is what they build their lives on. You must have known that happiness, just for a moment, now and then, perhaps."

He feels quieter. His remembering sinks him fast below the floor of pain . . .

. . . The happiest time we ever had in Cuba was after that first scare about Grace's health. We were still living in New York. The boys were so little we thought it wouldn't set them back too much if we took them out of school for one midwinter month. We went down to Havana on the old Ward Line and rented the lower floor of a crumbling stucco villa on the beach near Matanzas. The Cuban we rented from was a sergeant. It always confused us because he spoke of himself as a sergeant in the navy.

In spite of the civil war in Spain and the fighting in China that seemed to go on without end, the world on the whole was at peace. Chamberlain's peace in our time. A peace that meant no good. I had come back from a trip to Europe full of forebodings after a nightmare glimpse of the bloody business in Spain. I needed a rest and a little time to collect my thoughts if I had any. It was a bare gawky old house but it was drenched in unbelievable peace. We were so happy there we were afraid to speak of it even to each other.

This peacefulness seemed to emanate from Sergeant Pacheco and from his stout señora and their two homely daughters. I suppose they had their troubles like everybody else but to us their lives seemed unbelievably serene.

Mornings after Grace and the boys had gone trooping off down to the playa I would settle down at the light mahogany table that was the livingroom's only furniture, scratching with a pen on a pad or copying notes on my ancient Corona portable I had had with me in Madrid and now and then looking up at the redfringed blossoms dangling from among the tattered softgreen leaves of the banana plants outside the window, and hearing the tradewind swish through the stiff palm fronds overhead, and the muffled clucking of the señora's hens, and the unobtrusive rustling of the señora herself and of her two plain daughters going about their household business on the upper floor. There never was such peace.

There was something so effortless about the comings and goings of the sergeant's family that peace seemed to seep out of the very walls. They never hurried. During breakfast we would see the sergeant stroll with dignity in his freshlaundered uniform to the corner of the street to wait for the guagua that took him into Havana where he fulfilled some small routine duty at the arsenal which seemed to furnish him with every conceivable satisfaction. In the evening, while Grace was feeding the boys their supper, he would reappear, his cap jauntily cocked in anticipation of the evening meal; nearly always he would be carrying a bag of fruit or candies for his girls which he had bought for a few cents in the market, or flowers for the señora.

The señora grew goodnaturedly stouter day by day. The daughters didn't seem to mind being plain. None of them could do enough for us. The house was so full of peace that sitting over my papers every morning, I would feel the fretful need to be at work, to accomplish, to excel, ebb and ebb until I would find myself staring up at the banana leaves and letting my thoughts drift at large the way the piled clouds drifted through the enormous blue globular sky over the Gulf Stream.

Sitting over scrambled papers at the table with half-closed eyes I would feel myself soaring into that halcyon blue until I could look down on the swarming lives of men diagrammed on a vast relief map in the brilliant dispassionate light. Here, I would tell myself, pointing with an ethereal pointer, is a new social system forming, a fresh hierarchy of powers arranged in office buildings; here on the farms a few rags and tatters of the old family allegiances; fragments of civic dignity in the smaller towns; here the bloody resurgence of gangs out of the stone age ruled by a boss with a club; here the frail beginnings of the adaptation of selfgovernment to the pyramiding of industrial power. Surely the words could be found to project that instant of clear thought on a screen for all the world to read. First dreamily I'd think and then I would find the words.

Around noon I'd knock off unsatisfied but happy, and put on my bathing trunks and walk along the row of silent candycolored villas under their rustling palms to the beach. The boys would run to meet me kicking and jumping and we would all pitch in together to build sand castles with moats and lagoons to float their toy boats in. We would plunge and screech and splatter in the low breakers of the shallows behind the reef and when the sun began to weigh on us we would crouch in a circle to eat our lunch in the scanty shade of a cluster of coconut palms and go back to the house afterwards to play records and to sprawl and snooze on the beds. Even the boys didn't quarrel, and Grace picked up strength, and we all loved each other . . .

. . . He tries to hold on to that memory lying in the dark beside the new girl in anguish too great to be borne.

"It may be my fault again, Elsa. You thought you'd taken up with a successful man at the height of his career. It took you just one evening to find out you had a failure on your hands."

Memories of happiness are stabbing pain like the nerve in an aching tooth. How can he lie still? He doesn't dare wake her. He's not ready yet to have her speak to him. He gets to his feet and tiptoes to the window.

No air stirs. The breath of the empty pavements is fetid and stale. At intervals, along the deep street under the window, lamps glare malevolent as the unshaded lights in a jail.

A great crowing suddenly shatters the silence. Ro shudders and then grins. Get hold of those nerves. It's only a rooster crowing on the flat roof under the window. The rooster crows again. Not the only one awake in the city thinks Ro. He lies down again carefully on the edge of the bed. He can't bear the thought of waking Elsa, not just yet. He has to get hold of his nerves first.

He tries to think his whole life over carefully and consistently.

"I failed," the word clangs in Ro's head like a cracked bell.

Ro lies motionless on the edge of the bed. His hands are shaking less. He feels stronger. When you have faced failure you are beginning to overcome it. The rooster crows again from the roof below, this time a pleasurable cadenza in the dawn. The sky is beginning to glow round the harsh edges of the fortresses that hem the city in to the southeast. With daylight will come the breeze off the sea. Try to get some sleep. He pillows his head in the crook of his arm.

"We'll have a hangover," he is whispering soundlessly to Elsa, "but today I'll know how to make you happy. We're both of us a couple of poor wrecks. Maybe we can pull each other together. Out of your happiness I'll remake mine . . ."

10

. . . The afternoon Roger got tne news his boy Joe was killed in the Southwest Pacific I was over in Arlington helping Herman Boggs dig sweet potatoes in his war garden. He was inordinately proud of his war garden. The Secretary was a large man with gray hair that bristled around a brown bald head. I found him draped in an enormous suit of blue dungarees, sweating like a fountain as he pushed one of those Planet Junior onewheel plows through the stubborn red dirt. How he got sweet potatoes to grow at all in that clay was a miracle.

"Lend me a hand there Roland," he cried as soon as he saw me come in the gate.

He shoved and grunted. He cursed terribly whenever his little plow cut into one of the soft tubers.

"Careful, there," he would roar at me if I sliced into one with my hoe. "Every time you ruin a sweet potato it will mean just so many calories less in the national larder."

Herman Boggs was well along in his sixties. He was popeyed and purple in the face from the effort. I was afraid he'd have a stroke then and there. It was a relief when he fished his big oldfashioned turnip of a watch out from some pocket under his dungarees and said puffing: "We'll lay off now. Better come to my house for a shower. We'll talk as we drive . . . First I've got to sort these. Bring me two of those gunny sacks."

He put all the whole tubers in one sack and all the damaged ones in the other. "You take those home Roland," he said with a gesture of one of his stubby hands that indicated reckless generosity as he handed me the half filled bag of sliced and mangled sweet potatoes. He let out one of his abrupt cackles of laughter.

We lugged the two sacks of potatoes past a row of half finished war houses to where the black official car was waiting for him. This particular car had *Fish and Wildlife Service* written on the door. Herman had gone striding off ahead of me with his sack on his back. He waited till I caught up with him so that I shouldn't miss the fact that he was sending the government car back to the garage. "You drive me home in your gas buggy," he said in his peremptory way. "That'll save gas . . ."

We set the gunny sacks on the back seat. "This is just an example of what I've been talking about. This is the story I want you to tell. In conservation it's the small things that count. As you know conservation has been my hobby all my life. I ought to know something about it by this time."

Still panting and wheezing he settled himself beside me and stretched out his legs under the hood.

"Now speaking of small things," he cried out suddenly.

"I'm going to ask you an honest question and I want an honest answer. Is that Wells Hartley a friend of yours?"

I answered hesitantly that I could hardly call Wells Hartley a friend. Wells Hartley was an institution. A man couldn't be friends with an institution.

"You can tell him from me that he's the smallest picayunest little peeping Tom I ever heard of in my life."

He soon had me admitting that I had read the offending column. The mere reading of it involved me in Hartley's guilt. When I stopped for a traffic light I glanced around and saw his small suspicious eyes fixed on me. Every time I tried to get around to the subject of wartime conservation as I drove him through town he would come back to what a lowdown rascal Hartley was. That kind of contemptible scuttlebutt came mighty near to sabotage of the war effort. He was sending the column over to the Department of Justice for an opinion.

By that time we had reached Herman's plain suburban-looking house on one of the nondescript streets off Connecticut Avenue beyond the viaduct over Rock Creek. He went blustering off to take a shower. Mrs. Boggs didn't look any too happy about all those sweet potatoes. "I never did care much for sweet potatoes," she muttered.

It was while I was waiting for the Secretary to finish his shower that I got Grace's call.

"What's wrong?" I asked.

"It's about Roger," she said. "Young Joe Thurloe was killed during the first minutes of the Bougainville landing." Grace's words gave me a sensation like dropping in an elevator. The only child. Everything the man loved in the world. "Roger's coming over. I know he'll want to see you."

I found Roger already there when I got home. Grace had made him tea. They sat staring into their teacups on opposite sides of the narrow yellowpapered front parlor.

Roger got to his feet when I walked in.

"It is the problem of how to tell Alicia," Roger announced without looking at me. He spoke in clipped practical tones as if he were discussing some problem of the organization of procurement. "She has been functioning so much better. We don't want to upset that precarious balance."

He walked over and stood with his back to the empty fireplace. All at once he looked me straight in the face. He was biting his lips to keep them from trembling.

"You two must forgive me," he blurted out, "there's nobody else I can talk to . . . You know my sister Jane, she's wonderful about most things, but she's always been so down on Alicia."

Neither Grace nor I could think of anything to say.

He crossed the room and let himself drop wearily into his chair. He took a mechanical swallow out of his teacup as if it had burned him, although the tea was already cold.

After he had set the cup and saucer carefully down out of reach on a table in the corner of the room, he said, "Maybe what I like about being a public servant is that it gives me no time for any private life. It is whittled away and away and away and suddenly it's gone."

Though Grace hardly ever smoked she had lit herself a cigarette. She began to walk up and down blowing the smoke out amateurishly in puffs. As she raised her thin white hand to push the hair off her temple I noticed for the first time that there was a streak of gray in the blonde wave over her little pink ear. The sight caught at my heart.

"Roger, where is she?" Grace was asking distractedly.

"To the best of my belief," Roger answered in the tone he would use in testifying before a congressional committee, "she is over at the house. We are supposed to dine out somewhere, I've forgotten where. Ever since she got back from the sanatorium our relations have been purely formal." Suddenly there was bitter passion in his voice. "I suppose she will never forgive me for that."

As I looked at Roger I saw that the man's face was all screwed up. He was going to cry. "Excuse me," he said and turned sharp on his heel and walked out of the room. He still had that curious bouncy way of walking. We heard the door from the downstairs washroom into the hall close behind him.

"Nobody has a right to have so much selfcontrol," Grace whispered. "It's going to kill him and he's too valuable to lose."

She put her hand on mine in that ingratiating little girl way she had. "I'd better run around the corner to see what's going on . . . Get him to take a drink or something."

There was no sound from the washroom so I settled myself in the wing chair by the floorlamp to check over my notes of the interview with Secretary Boggs.

When Roger came back into the room he didn't seem to notice that Grace had gone. "Ro," he said abruptly as if picking up some previous conversation, "I got a great deal out of that English trip of yours and the articles you wrote were honeys. How about doing the same thing for the Pacific war? A man can get around there now without too much interference from the Jap."

He explained that he could send me around as a VIP but he didn't think I would get as much out of it as if I went as a regular correspondent. He needed a proxy to tell him about the rank and file. "I mustn't get walled in," he exclaimed. He had tried to put himself in those guys' shoes on his last tour out there but there just wasn't time. It wasn't so much on account of seeing only the high brass —they had their feelings and failings just as much as the GIs did—but there just wasn't time in the day. After all his business was bottlenecks. But he needed to know about morale. Morale had a lot to do with bottlenecks.

Just as I was telling him that I was crazy to go, in fact that I'd already taken the matter up with the editors, it was only a couple of family problems that had been holding me back, Grace came into the room again with a wry little smile on her face.

Just as if he were at his desk Roger finished up the business in hand before going on to the next item: "Take it in stages Ro," he said. "A couple of months out and a couple of months home. And let me know the minute there is something I can do." Then he turned with a smile to Grace. "Well?"

"You men ought to know by this time women don't need to be told things," Grace said. Though she was trying to be facetious there was something almost spiteful in her tone of voice. "Of course Alicia knows all about it. She's known all day. She's wondering whether you want to go on with this dinner date. It's with the Chief Justice."

"Did you tell her I was here?" asked Roger getting abruptly to his feet.

Grace flared up. "Can't you understand, Roger? There was no need to tell her anything."

After Roger had gone home Grace sidled up to me and began to stroke my hand in that little affectionate confidential way she had. Poor Alicia, she whispered; she was like a watch that had been wound too tight. The mainspring had broken. Joe's death might really turn out to be a relief to her after the constant anxiety of the last two years. "I kept thinking: suppose it was Chips. Aren't we all selfish brutes . . . ? But I do feel for them."

She snuggled her head against my chest. "Make me feel strong Ro, these are such dreadful times. If I'd known what was coming when the boys were born, honestly I don't think I'd have tried to raise them."

When I put my arms around her she looked up at me with her face all wet with tears. She swallowed a little sob.

"Roger and Alicia are both of them so unbending, no wonder Alicia goes off her rocker now and then. I would too," she went on in a choking voice. "But Ro I love and admire them both so much . . . Alicia looked at me with a sort of frightening exultation in her eyes. She seemed to glory in it somehow . . . in her misery. What she said was 'This completes the circle of hell.' "

I tried that night to tell Grace about my going out to the Pacific for a little tour as a correspondent, but I couldn't quite get round to it. We saw by the paper next morning that Associate Secretary of the Navy and Mrs. Roger Thurloe had appeared at the Chief Justice's dinner. "I don't ever want to be a hero," was what Grace said. "Ro don't you ever be a hero either."

Actually several months went by before I was able to set the trip up. I had committed myself to do a series of articles on the war effort at home which I had to finish first. The few times I saw Roger during that period he did not disguise his disappointment that I was taking so long to get off. Each time he saw me he told me the same thing: "Look here Ro, while we are fighting the war we ought to be laying the foundation for the kind of world we want to have after the peace. It's a subject I can't get anybody interested in in this town . . . but maybe more is being done than we realize . . . up from the grassroots, unconsciously . . . it's your business to find out."

At last the day came for me to fly to San Francisco. Grace drove me across to the airport. I always expected Grace to be such a good sport, but it seemed to me that she was taking it oddly, my going and all that. You would think she would be used to my going off on trips by this time. It was on account of the boys, she said. Chips was fifteen now. He had just flunked out of another boarding school. Lack of discipline. No application to his studies. Grace was going to put him in a summer school she had unearthed and tutor him herself. Her idea was I ought to stay and help. Next winter would make or break him. I told her I thought it would be better if I were away. He'd get the feeling of responsibility that came from being the chief man of the family. We argued about it for weeks without coming to any agreement. Grace was showing a sort of pique that wasn't a bit like her.

Of course when the time came for her to see me off we had forgotten all that. All we thought of was how we loved being together and how we missed each other when we were separated. It was a lovely summer evening and that made us feel worse. Grace was saying with a little toss of her head that maybe she would take a job herself. She was bored with being a Gray Lady.

It turned out that the plane would be an hour late, so we decided she'd better go home to make sure Chips got his supper and didn't get to roaming instead of doing his homework. Instead of her seeing me off, I saw her off. I stood there in my brand new uniform watching her drive away, an erect determined little figure at the wheel of the open convertible with a pert little blue hat at a pert tilt over her graying blonde curls.

I'd never in my life felt a bitterer lump in my throat than I felt as I walked back to the airline counter with my bulky overseas bag nagging at my shins as I carried it.

Then came the pleasure of the long night flight and starting to read *War and Peace* for the third or fourth time, and arriving at San Francisco in the misty morning freshness. I rode on a cable car and scaled Telegraph Hill and ate abalone at the Fisherman's Wharf and walked back up through Chinatown to the Top of the Mark. There I sat alone musing and drinking and looking out at the opal mists melting and clotting over the city and the Golden Gate and the Bay.

I couldn't stand it not having Grace there with me. I called her up long distance to explain to her how much I missed her. I tried to tell her about that special quality the city had that gave a certain flavor to even the most banal tourist attractions. Her voice over the telephone sounded strange and far away. She seemed to resent it a little that I should try to interest her in these distant trivialities of sight and sound and smell. After I hung up I felt infinitely more depressed than I did before I called her.

Drowned fathoms deep in solitude, I took a cab downtown to the building where I was to board the navy bus.

A correspondent really led the life of Riley in that war. Once you were accredited you were the public guest of the armed services. The whole wide world, except for the sections of the globe still occupied by the enemy and the northern slice of the Eurasian land mass which was under the sway of what we liked to call our ally, was yours to roam over for the asking. Except for the drinks in the officers' clubs it was all free. In my case I had a little private boost from Roger who was letting it be known in naval circles that his office was interested in my seeing as much as it was safe to show me. There was a perpetual magic carpet at my command. If the Navy couldn't take you the Army would: if they both failed you would call on the Marines. All my life I had found travelling delightful.

I couldn't help feeling a little dizzy from all the possibilities ahead as I fastened the belt in my comfortable civilian seat on the big fourmotor job that was to take me to Pearl Harbor.

As I sat drowsing through the night over the ocean I carried on two unspoken conversations. One was with

Roger about the foundations he had spoken about, the foundations of the coming peace. The other was with Grace. For Grace I saved all the funny little human oddities, the despatching officer's special intonation when he pronounced the abracadabra word Cincpac as he handed me my travel orders, and the enormous lift I'd felt when the plane clawed its way through the ocean overcast out into the light of the hurrying moon and I caught sight of the plane's shadow skimming the silver white floor of clouds beneath us.

The first day in Honolulu I saw everybody through a drowsy haze. Airplane motors still roared in my ears. Against the background of bright green grass and ferny foliage and the redtiled roofs of white and buffcolored buildings and of jerrybuilt offices packed full of too many typewriters and too many maps and too many bulletin boards, moved an endless variety of faces. The bodies were all uniform in tropical khaki. The same shirts open at the throat. The caps were uniform. The men I saw were of all ranks from general or admiral down to sergeant or petty officer. Young and old and middleaged, they came from all walks of American life. What struck me that first day was the look of puzzled determination they all shared. "How did I ever get into this situation?"

Out of failures and discouragements teams were being put together. A man here and a man there was learning to do his job supremely well. Organizations were beginning to mesh. The look on their faces was the look I had become accustomed to on Roger Thurloe's face when he talked about breaking bottlenecks. The look of the drafters of blueprints. The engineer's look.

War is an industrial enterprise I started to tell myself.

And friends and acquaintances. Everywhere I ran into men I hadn't seen in years: boys I'd known in highschool, fellows I'd gone to college with, the real estate dealer we bought our Georgetown house from, newspaper men I'd run into in the most varied and out of the way places. All America seemed to be converging on Pearl Harbor.

It was inevitable in those surroundings that George Elbert Warner should turn up. He had already become a headliner among war correspondents. Large as life he came charging into the lobby of the little hotel I was billeted in at Waikiki while I was waiting to be shown my room.

He'd grown into a huge thickbarreled man. He was red-faced and sweating. His big bulbous nose was peeling from sunburn. His great girth was exaggerated by the musette bags and spyglasses and automatics in holsters that dangled from him in all directions. He had a roll of tapa cloth under his arm and some kind of savage spear in one hand.

"Ro," he shouted as soon as he set eyes on me. "Why you old son of a bitch. So you decided to drag that fat ass of yours out of your Washington armchair. It's about time . . . have a drink on it."

After a lot of cursing and tugging at the fastenings of one of his musettes he managed to extricate a bottle of whiskey from the tangle of equipment. He pulled the cork with his teeth and handed me the bottle.

"Take a good swig. You look all in. Can't take it any more eh?"

Then he turned and bellowed at the hollowchested little man behind the desk. "I want the biggest room in the house and the biggest bathtub . . . George Elbert Warner, you may have heard the name. I'm in from the Southwest Pacific. Haven't had a bath since Christ was a corporal."

The clerk turned on him pettishly. "All in due time, sir," he snapped. "I've got to show this man his room first."

Nothing could keep George Elbert from following us up the stairs, tripping us up with the shaft of his spear as he babbled on in his high cracked voice about the narrow squeaks he'd had at Lae and Salamau. Fighting in New Guinea was like fighting on the face of the moon. The most inconceivable, unpredictable inhospitable impossible piece of goddam terrain the world had ever seen. No wonder the natives were subhuman. "That island just ain't fit for human habitation."

Just as George Elbert said, I was all in. While I pulled off my clothes and ducked into the shower, George Elbert strode around the room, unpacking his souvenirs, unrolling his tapa cloth, scattering his equipment, reading me scraps of despatches he'd been rowing with the censors about.

"I suppose you came out here to report a war against the Jap." George Elbert stuck his big tousled head into the bathroom where I was wiping myself off after my shower. "Well so did I and what do I find? I find the navy fighting the army. I find the marines fighting MacArthur. Are those leathernecks burned up against Mac? You'd think he was Yamamoto himself. And everybody wrangles with the Aussies. And there's George Elbert Warner's war with the censorship. Which of these fronts do you want to be filled in on first?"

I came out in my bathrobe and told George Elbert firmly that I didn't want to be filled in on anything, not till tomorrow. I hadn't been to bed in two days and I was full up to here with impressions and I was going to take a nap. Why didn't he go make sure he had a room?

"Why hasn't that damn 4F come back?" George Elbert went off roaring and pounding down the corridor. I locked the door after him and lay down on the bed to take a little rest before supper. It was twilight. A lovely fresh mountain-tasting breeze rustled the foliage outside my window. I could hear the myna birds sleepily squawking and whistling in the trees as they settled down. I closed my eyes and immediately fell asleep.

As it turned out I stayed in Honolulu a whole lot longer than I had intended, spending hours in those temporary offices at Pearl Harbor that looked so much like enormous chicken coops ranked on the hills. There I talked to the men who spent their days in expediting the stream of shipping that poured out of every North American port into the Pacific. I watched them diagramming the sea roads of supply over their great blue maps. The course of every LST, every oiler, every wallowing old tub loaded with ammo or foodstuffs had to be plotted ahead. The departures of ships from the Atlantic coast had to be carefully staggered so as not to clog up the Canal. Consumption of oil, consumption of food, the wear and tear on the sailors' socks all had to be calculated, tabulized, reduced to workable averages. The complications of the operation increased in geometric proportion to the distance to be covered. And now that MacArthur's forces were on the move out of Australia, and the navy was probing further and further into the Pacific, the fighting forces were half the watery world away from base.

It was distance that had to be conquered first. Beside the problem of supply the problem of enemy action began to seem almost negligible.

That wasn't what I wrote Roger about. It would be no news to him. He had already thrown his whole life into fostering the production of these rivers of oil and explosives and hardware and canned rations which were eventually to overwhelm the enemy in every remotest theatre of war. He wanted to know about people. I filled my letters to Roger with the people I saw between times.

The Hawaiian islands were a revelation.

Except to shake a deploring head over the exploitations of the sugar and pineapple kings as described in the liberal weeklies I hadn't thought of these green volcanos and these blue bays straight out of paradise since reading Captain Cook's Voyages as a boy. Now I found them become a sort of capital of the Pacific.

It was George Elbert who set me on the track of what I wrote up, specially for Roger's eye, as the "real" story of wartime Hawaii. For all his fluster and bluster George Elbert had an extraordinary nose for scenting out first rate people. The night before he flew off to the theaters again I went to his room for a drink before dinner. As soon as I stepped in the door he introduced a stocky pale brown man with a big head of short cut wiry gray hair. George Elbert introduced him tersely as the greatest living Maori. Sir James Hawkins turned out to be the famous anthropologist. He had come up from some New Zealand University to give a course at the University of Hawaii, and was advising the navy's survival school on the side. He spoke with an Oxford accent but his knowledge of the islanders of the Pacific was far from academic. Before I arrived he had been showing George Elbert how to make fire with a bow and some charred sticks the way the Fiji people did. He spoke all the languages; he knew all the plants and the winds and the ocean currents; he seemed to have been cast away on every atoll.

After a few drinks, in which Sir James, who said with a sly smile that he preferred coconut milk, did not share, we went out on the town.

We dined in a Cantonese restaurant with a Chinese merchant who was a friend of Sir James. There was a young Hawaiian among the company whom Sir James guyed unmercifully partly in English and partly in what seemed to be a succession of Polynesian dialects for forgetting his mother tongue. After dinner we went to call on a Japanese lawyer of Sir James' acquaintance who was a member of the territorial legislature. He was a Harvard law school graduate and knew the States like the palm of his hand. This man talked frankly and simply of the tragedy which had overtaken the Japanese in California hustled off to concentration camps in a fit of hysterics on the part of the governing authorities. He spoke ironically but without bitterness. "We in Hawaii have been more realistic. We have understood that our Japanese population remains loyal and wedded to the American way of life. Stateside," he said with his toothy smile, "the Americans do not know their own strength . . . They do not realize how other peoples crave the opportunity offered by their style of living."

"That," said Sir James, "is what America will have to learn."

Driving across town in an open touring car Sir James launched into a defense of the early American missionaries. Their Christian creed had proved a real liberation to the islanders caught in a straitjacket of superstition and tradition.

"Crackpots, hypocrites," shouted George Elbert. "Give me the village witch doctor, every time."

"But my dear fellow," responded Sir James in his most Oxonian tones, "you don't know them as I do. I am the village witch doctor."

Sir James was taking us to a dance at the University of Hawaii. It wasn't a very large dance but the company was thoroughly mixed. It was in a room hung with tapa cloths with an open wall that opened directly on a patch of green lawn, festooned with strings of Japanese lanterns. Overhead the palms rustled in the night breeze off the mountains. I stood next to Sir James at the edge of the dance floor, watching the tanned couples in their light brightcolored clothes. He took a collector's pleasure in pointing out the various racial characteristics. There was every kind of North of Europe type, blonde and dark and redhaired, a sprinkling of Jews, here and there a Negro or a mulatto. There were a couple of young men who belonged to one of the darkskinned races of India. There were some Portuguese, sons and daughters of the Portuguese laborers and fishermen who still occupied the bottom of the heap socially, so he explained. "The latest come the furthest down . . . That's how it always is," he said with his creaky laugh.

He showed me every sort of mixture of European blood with Chinese and Japanese or both, sometimes with a touch of Polynesian thrown in. "It's the melting pot, much more so than New York, but my dear fellow you Americans don't seem to have the slightest idea of how well you've done it . . . In my opinion out of this melting pot may well come the future of the Pacific."

George Elbert was already tugging at my arm and whispering "For chrissake let's go home for a night cap." He had to be at John Rogers at 5 A.M.

Back at his room heaped with a clutter of half packed equipment he guyed me, over a final snort of whiskey, about all this sociology and economics. What a hell of a way to see a war. Combat was what happened in a war . . . "That's what you can't see any other time, soldiers in combat."

He was already yawning. "What do you bet that lousy 4F of a night clerk forgets to wake me." As I got up to leave he grasped my hand hard and dropped it. "Ro," he said all in a bunch, "if I should manage to get myself bumped off . . . You know I couldn't care less . . . But you and Grace be nice to Maria."

There was real tenderness in his voice.

"Give my regards to the chairborne infantry," he suddenly bellowed and slammed the door after me as I walked away down the hill.

Back in my room I tried to keep awake long enough to sketch out a letter to Roger. This had to do with morale all right but it wasn't military morale. It could be the foundations he'd talked about, the foundations of some orderly Pacific world to come. "Put it in concrete terms"; I could hear Roger's voice impatiently questioning. I was too sleepy. I scratched off a little word for Grace on my pad and crawled into bed.

It was lonely with George Elbert gone. I wrote Grace every day telling about talking mynas and Hawaiian foods and waterfalls and what a tiny little scrunched up beach they boasted so about at Waikiki, and a friend's dog named Hannah and other items that I thought would not invite the censor's shears. Her letters in return were scarce and comical, as usual, but they left me quite in the dark about how she and the boys were getting along. She had a secretarial job in a government office but she didn't say where.

When at last I took off by navy plane westward for newly retaken Guam it was with the feeling that the last cord that bound us was being broken. I might not get any more letters until I came back to Pearl. At least I was promising myself to be home by Christmas.

It was an agreeable flight, in bucket seats this time. We were held over for part of a night on an island I forget the name of, just an airfield and a few yellow clapboard sheds and hangars that might have been in the Middle West somewhere except that instead of being hemmed by prairie we were hemmed on every side by the endless heaving wastes of the Pacific. The night was drowned in moonlight. There was no one on the island but a squad of marines, some Seabees, a few lonesome mechanics and maintenance men. Not a woman in a thousand miles. As I lay on a cot in the dormitory trying to sleep and listening to the strange moaning cry of a curious gull that flocked to the beaches, I thought of Grace. The lack of her was active positive pain like a broken leg. Now I understood what the GI's meant when they talked about being rock happy, and the pathetic pinups of girls they so prized. Only I was due to leave next day. And those boys might be there for the duration.

When I arrived in Guam a young Texan drove me in a jeep from the airstrip through the topsy turvy landscape of a tropical island churned by bombardment. What remained of wrecked thatched huts and mangled groves of papayas and bananas and pitted cornfields was being levelled by the bulldozers and the draglines and the sheepfoot rollers of the Seabees laying out airfields. My driver pointed to a long drab tent on top of a hill as the jeep sloughed up through a rivulet of red mud. "That's where we shack the correspondents," he said. "They shot four Japs back of your hill last night . . . Island's still lousy with them," he added grinning as I scrambled out with my dunnage.

The first thing I heard as I stepped into the shade of the tent from out of the ferocious sunshine that beat you over the head like a baseball bat, was George Elbert Warner's high pitched voice. As soon as I'd piled my dunnage on an empty cot I followed the voice out through the tent flap to where it mingled with the sound of showers. There he was hopping up and down behind a screen of drab cloth set so that all it screened was the middles of the bathers. He was bellowing and spluttering about the bloody Saipan landing to three other men who were soaping themselves under the other showers. "The Battle of the two Smiths is what I'm calling it . . . that little disagreement between the Army and the Marines cost us a thousand casualties."

He came striding out of the shower stark naked waving a muddy little strip of towel in front of his huge bulk. "Gangway!"

He charged into me as I came ducking under the tent flap towards him. "Roly the rolling stone," he cried and grabbed me by the shoulders. "Sorry . . . I had to get in here before those damn nurses at the hospital tent could focus their spy glasses. Well Ro," he backed off and gave me an angry look, "you managed to miss the bloodiest little show since Tarawa . . . I thought I'd seen combat but I hadn't seen nothin' till I saw it on Saipan." He talked as he climbed back into his sweaty khaki. "Better get yourself a shower while the water holds out. This is the first shower we've had in three days . . . You are out in the boondocks now boy . . . You're not at Hibiscus Inn on the beach at Waikiki."

After a shower and a skimpy lunch of heated up C rations which we contested with the flies in the messtent George Elbert and I started out to explore the recently recaptured island. He had somehow managed to get himself a jeep and a rosy cheeked and respectful PRO lieutenant (jg) to drive it. He had slung over his shoulder a Japanese rifle which he'd brought back from Saipan as a souvenir. His pants pockets were full of Jap ammunition. "Just thought I might pick me off a little yellow bastard," he said thoughtfully stroking the barrel of his gun as we started off down the hill.

The afternoon was steamy hot. It had rained while we were eating and it rained again as we sat jouncing in the jeep that slithered through the mud and rubble of what had been an old Spanish town along the ocean front. Rubbish heaps on either side of the road were tangled with galvanized iron roofing twisted and curled as if by giant pliers. Here and there the carefully squared stone of some fragment of old Spanish masonry stood out with an antique dignity. Morning glories bloomed on battered walls. Wherever there was half a house standing or a scrap of roofing to give shelter from the rain a huddle of brown and yellow faces looked out at us. "The goddam Chamorros," snorted George Elbert, "damned if they aren't smiling at us."

"Why shouldn't they? They've considered themselves Americans since the Spanish-American War," piped up the little PRO whom George Elbert insisted on calling Junior.

"Don't get him started on the Chamorros. I want a shot at a Jap," grumbled George Elbert.

In spite of George Elbert's complaints Junior saw to it that we interviewed the military government people and visited a civilian hospital. He introduced us to the parish priest in a leanto chapel made of coconut matting behind the ruins of the cathedral. "What do you think we are, Junior, visiting royalty?" George Elbert asked as we climbed back in the jeep. "You'll have us laying a cornerstone next. Skip the social service Junior for godsake. Take us out to see a Marine patrol. I want to know what it's like to hunt Japs in the jungle. God knows they've hunted us long enough."

Junior promptly drove us to a Marine rest area they were setting up among great groves of coconut palms on the other side of the island. Prefabricated cantonments and quonsets were everywhere being slapped into shape.

There was a baseball game in progress. A row of those amphibian scows with wheels on them we called ducks in those days served as a grandstand. The bleachers were ranks of jeeps and parked trucks. It looked like a good ball game; baseball was action all right but George Elbert said it wasn't the sort of action he was looking for so he bullied Junior into driving off down an old pitted asphalt road that seemed to lead in the direction of the northern end of the island.

Suddenly the countryside was deserted. In war there is usually that empty look before you find the scene of the fighting. The road wound through abandoned taro plantations and weedy groves of bananas. At a sudden turn in the road we came on a Marine patrol. What we saw first was the leaves moving the men had stuck in the netting of their helmets.

They came straggling out of the thorny underbrush at the jungle's edge. They were caked with mud and their faces were gray with fatigue. Their wet shirts clung to their backs. As they reached the hard road the sergeant let his voice out like a whip and they formed into columns. Abreast of our jeep he halted them and gave them at ease. We could see the grim hunter and hunted look of combat already melting off their faces. Their faces all turned inquisitively towards ours. Look at me, I'm still alive, was the look we read on their faces.

George Elbert had unlimbered his rifle and sat with it loaded on his knees. He asked the sergeant eagerly where he could find him a Jap.

"Look out he don't see you first, Pop," shouted a boy from the rear rank.

The sergeant explained patiently that they had been out eight hours and they hadn't seen nutten. Mostly the Nips came out at night to swipe stuff from the ration dumps.

"We caught three the other night tryin' to sit in on our movie," piped up another man.

George Elbert made Junior drive on before some officer might get it into his head to stop us. We drove and drove. We didn't find any Japs, but the worn old road got lonesomer and lonesomer. At last we came out on a village at the head of a beautiful narrow blue bay hemmed in by grassy hills. It was a seedy looking village but there was no trace of shellfire. When we drove in there was no one in sight. Only a scattering of bantam fowls picking among the stones. We came to a stop under a feathery ironwood tree in a little cobbled plaza. At the water's edge in front of us stood a crumbling obelisk. We found it marked the spot where Magellan was supposed to have landed in 1521. The name of the place was Umanac.

While we were trying to make out the rest of the scaling inscription on the pedestal the local inhabitants started gathering around. A sallow frogfaced man in a navy scrim-shirt who spoke considerable English was excited to learn that we were correspondents for stateside newspapers. He immediately invited us into his house and sent some little barelegged boys scampering off after bananas and tuba. "What's that old hulk?" asked George Elbert who had been sweeping the hills with his binoculars hoping for the sight of a Jap.

Anchored right off shore in the still green water clear and smooth as glass lay the rusty hull of an old iron ship. There was something familiar about the ramshaped prow. It must be the dismantled ruin of an early battleship. We both turned inquiringly to Junior. Junior was so embarrassed he blushed red. "I shouldn't have let you come this far. It's the old Oregon and it's classified . . . the classifiedest thing on Guam."

That was all he knew. Probably she was going to be used in some forthcoming operation. He begged us not to mention her to any of the other correspondents.

George Elbert lit up at once. Why were they classifying the only story on the whole damned island? This would be the cause of another battle between George Elbert Warner and the censor. While we sat at a table under the vines at the frogfaced man's front door drinking his tuba and eating his bananas George Elbert tormented Junior with a description of the story he was going to write. *"The last of the Great White Fleet engaged in a mysterious mission . . . Ghosts of blue jackets of another age pace the decks of the grand old relic of the Spanish American war . . . The old Oregon's last encounter . . ."*

George Elbert was pressing Junior hard. "Do you suppose it's really security, or is the navy just scared some congressman will raise a storm about the abuse of a historic relic?"

Junior was peeved almost to tears. "If I did know I wouldn't tell you," he declared.

Poor Junior was too young to remember anything about the Oregon but George Elbert and I gave him an earful of childhood recollections of her famous cruise from Puget Sound and through the Straits of Magellan to Santiago Bay. I found myself rambling on sentimentally about a toy model I'd had of the battleship Oregon as a child that shot real firecrackers out of its cannons. Our host chimed in with stories his father had told him of fighting insurrectos in the Philippines.

The tuba was plentiful and strong. We were highly exhilarated by the time we got up to start back to camp. Our host wouldn't let us leave before he showed us a weathered wooden cupboard full of books under a stucco arch in the plaza. There were several shelves of mouldy American novels, from *Penrod* to Kenneth Roberts. The townspeople had kept them religiously hidden in their houses all through the Japanese occupation. He called it Umanac's pride.

On the way back, about halfway between the Marine encampment and the press tent we were attracted by the strains of *Roll Out the Barrel* coming from under a galvanized roof on a hilltop. It wasn't only a piano, it was a whole band and GI voices singing. Junior resolutely turned off the road and plowed through the black mud up the hill, slithered around the end of a thorny hedge and jammed on his brakes in front of a long table set with a white cloth ornamented with asparagus fern and hibiscus flowers.

It was a wedding. The parish priest presided. A couple of GIs and some local boys provided the music. There was an American style wedding cake. In a little booth hung with paper streamers the bride and groom both very small and very young and very brown and dressed in immaculate white, were patiently wrapping up slices of the cake in paper napkins for the guests to take home.

The parish priest made room for us at the head of the table. As a sort of introduction he proudly announced in his low gentle voice that the island of Guam had raised more than two hundred thousand dollars for the Sixth War Loan.

"We are Americans," another man insisted. "We are not Filipinos."

The local judge chimed in, "We feel like Americans . . . Tell them that stateside . . . But tell them too that the airfields are taking all our farmland. It is a small island. Before the Jap nobody was ever hungry. How can we live if we have no land for crops?"

They plied us with chocolate and Coca-Cola and Spanish rice and barbecued suckling pig. A bottle of tuba came speeding round the table. After a couple of swigs George Elbert and I were promising we'd speak up for them to the authorities in Washington.

Before long we were all Chamorros.

Next thing I knew George Elbert was betting me five dollars I couldn't ride a water buffalo. Our carabao race was something less than a success because neither of us could get the great black shambling beasts out of a walk.

Marines in green fatigues kept joining the party. The band played and played. Everybody danced. All the Americans sang *Dixie*. Then *Sweet Adeline*. As a final attraction George Elbert gave an exhibition of fancy shooting. He shot at tin cans little boys set up for him on distant fences. He shot lying and standing and kneeling and with the rifle held upside down between his legs.

In the end he shot a carabao that poked his head out of the jungle at a thousand yards.

One of the weazened old women sitting in a row of chairs watching the dancing from under the galvanized roof put her dun hand over her mouth to choke a cry. Tears spurted out of her eyes. It was her carabao.

George Elbert pulled a wad of bills out of the back pocket of his fatigues. How much was a carabao? He piled bills in the old woman's lap. She paid no attention but sat there silently crying with her hand over her mouth.

Junior hustled us into the jeep and away. As we left the wedding guests were crowding about the old woman trying to console her. Junior had the last word. "Well," he said stonily, "that's what I call good public relations."

Next day George Elbert and I were both on a cruiser bound for Ulithi. Ulithi was a name that had appeared all at once out of nowhere. It was so heavily classified people spoke it in a whisper. The cruiser's executive officer, a pale square-faced man with closecropped gray hair, told us about Ulithi that night as we sat under an electric fan at a green baize table in his cabin.

As he talked he embroidered a pattern of flowers on an oldfashioned tambour frame he held on his knees. "I'm embroidering some chairbacks for my wife," he explained in a matteroffact way. "This type of work takes your mind off the tension."

He was saying that we'd first found out about Ulithi

when somebody unearthed a chart of the atoll among captured records at the Japanese naval headquarters on Saipan. Those little Nips drew a mean chart. Looked like just the place to establish a floating base for future operations to the westward. Meant bypassing Yap and Truk and the socalled Japanese strong points in the Carolines. Five hundred miles inside of enemy lines, he said with a grin. So we had moved in. There was hardly any land on that atoll but there was eighteen miles of deepwater anchorage. The reefs afforded protection against submarines. It would serve until the next typhoon season. A proper typhoon might well dump the whole outfit in Greasy Creek.

"Sounds like one of the greatest stories of the war," I told the Exec.

"You'll never get clearance." His square pale jaw closed tight.

Long before we saw the islands we could make out a crosshatching of crowded masts and superstructures and radar grids and signal flags and then stacks and gun turrets and blinker lights in busy conversation. As we slowed our speed three fighter planes rolled and tumbled friendly as porpoises over our bow. We were passing the booms and buoys of the submarine net. Ahead we could make out a line of battleships at anchor and beyond them the great barns of aircraft carriers, planes with folded wings crowded close on their decks as bees swarming on a hive. Further on, hulldown to the southward there were tankers, ranks and ranks of destroyers, camouflaged merchant ships, every kind of vessel you ever saw. In the broad lanes between the rows of anchored ships, bluntnosed landing craft, tugs, destroyer escorts, patrol boats, barges, whaleboats staggered through the steep green seas in a churn of white water. It was like steaming into a great port, New York or Liverpool, only there was no land.

George Elbert was in a stew to get to headquarters to start arranging for his flight to the Philippines. Among other things our friend the Exec had told us about the landings just beginning on Leyte and the great successful engagement with the Japanese fleet now petering out in the narrow seas off the Philippines. George Elbert was hopping around the deck officer like a pea on a hot griddle while we waited for a boat to take us ashore.

At last the two of us were tumbled with our dunnage into the stern of a heaving whaleboat. We sprawled landlubberly on the mailbags under an awning as the boat nosed into the warm greasy seas. The first stop was at a landing ship turned into a floating postoffice. With wet behinds and dripping trouser legs we scrambled up the ramp in the open bow.

Inside we found ourselves in an electric lighted tunnel piled high with mailbags on every side. There was a smell of mould and damp planking. Lines of men, all wet and sweating as we were, stood cheerfully in line along worn board tables while the mailclerks, stripped to their blue cotton pants, rummaged among the grimy canvas bags. All eyes were shining at the thought of mail from home. By some miracle I found a packet with my name on it. There was a letter from Grace.

Climbing an iron ladder to the deck to find a quiet less stifling spot to read Grace's letter I found myself standing beside a brown young fellow with tousled curly hair who wore wet khaki pants torn at the knees and a blue denim jacket without any buttons. Beside him stood a small brown dog with a trace of cocker about him. The boy and the dog both had the same brown pop eyes and brown curly hair. "Mail," he said when he saw me open my letter. "You lucky son of a bitch."

He stopped with his mouth open when he noticed that my correspondent's uniform had some faint resemblance to an officer's. He snapped into a salute. "Excuse me sir," he stammered, "I mean you're a very lucky gentleman."

To put him at his ease I told him it would take more than an Act of Congress to turn a correspondent into a gentleman. I asked him how he liked it here.

"Wonderful . . . I've been figuring out from the ships present list that there must be more than two million tons of shipping in this anchorage already . . . We're the only post office for a population of several hundred thousand. A busy corner."

I had started to read my letter. "The reason I spoke as I did sir," he added apologetically, "was we get kinda sore always handin' out other people's mail an' never gettin' any ourselves."

Grace's letter was perplexing. Her office work, she wrote—"imagine me an office manager, can you picture it?"—kept her so busy she had no time for house work. She had rented the Dumbarton Avenue house furnished for a very good price and was living in an apartment she'd subleased downtown on Connecticut Avenue. She included the phone number. The boys liked the arrangement fine. They seemed to be getting along all right at Western High. Half the letter was typed. At the bottom she had written in pencil: "Darling do come home soon. I'm doing the best I can, about *everything*." 'Everything' was underlined. "But I have a feeling sometimes I'm being swept out of my depth, dangerously, afar."

I didn't have time to worry about Grace's letter just then; all I felt was the immensity of the distance between us. The men in the whaleboat were ready to push on for the headquarters islet.

"Bad news?" asked George Elbert when I sat down beside him in the sopping stern sheets. I shook my head.

A few days after Thanksgiving which we had celebrated with the Seabees in style George Elbert took off for the Philippines in a plane full of blood plasma. I stayed on in the little shack set apart for the press on Azor, eating salt tablets and trying to write up a story I was calling The Miracle of Supply. As I collected my notes I had made up my mind that Roger would be the man to find a way of getting enough of it released to give the country an inkling of the marvels that were being accomplished. It was a decision that would have to be made in the higher echelons. A few days in Washington—maybe I could smuggle in Christmas—would give me a chance to catch up on Grace and the boys. I missed her so horribly.

As I lay on my cot about daybreak one morning turning over in my mind the various ways I might wangle a trip home, the island PRO came striding in. "Commodore wants to see you," he said. I shaved in a hurry in a glass of drinking water and dabbled the rest of it on my face.

The commodore, an aggressive rough diamond of a man, was already waiting for me impatiently in his jeep. "I suppose you've heard the phrase enemy action, Mr. Lancaster," he said looking me straight in the eye and clipping off his words as if he blamed me for something that had happened. "I thought you might like to see what it means."

Already we were down at the dock climbing aboard the port director's tug. Nobody spoke as we sped out of the crinkly smooth green water into the blue steep waves that foamed under the lash of the rising tradewind. Among several officers aboard I recognized the thinlipped frowning man who commanded a repair ship. Nobody spoke. Every face was tense. Ten miles or so out in the anchorage we came under the stern of a flattop.

The hull was all right but even before we climbed the swinging ladder up the ship's steelplated flank we could see that the superstructure was blackened and blistered by fire. When we stepped on what was left of the deck we found ourselves looking down into what appeared to be a burnedout warehouse. A young lieutenant commander met us, saluted and cooly, almost smilingly, showed us around. He was careful that we should miss nothing, the flight deck gashed open like a sardine can, the ruined elevators that brought the planes up from the hangar decks below, the lacerated bridge and control tower, the incredible tangle of mangled machinery.

"Yes our losses in personnel were extremely heavy," he said as unwaveringly as if he were reading from the report of an accident that had happened to some other ship. "It was fortunate that we had a third of our planes in the air. Below decks, the engine room crew, not a scratch. We came in under our own power."

A Jap had landed his plane with full bomb bays right on deck. For the first time I heard the word: Kamikaze.

"Don't mind me," said the atoll commander in an unexpectedly gentle voice as the launch staggered back in the teeth of the wind towards Azor. "You'll be hearing that word . . . I thought it might help you interpret the news . . . to see what it meant."

Somehow the sight of that gutted flattop, the thought of the men dead and burned and torn to pieces, relieved me of any appetite to go home for Christmas. Let the magazine editors worry about getting my stuff past the censors. The least I could do was stay in the thick and report what the boys who bore the brunt of it did. I tried to explain that in my next few letters to Grace. That was how it happened that I found myself eating another turkey with my Seabee friends whose barracks occupied most of tiny Azor. Their outfit rejoiced in the name of the Bougainville Bastards.

Not long after Christmas when I was beginning to enquire about ways and means of getting across to MacArthur's freshly established headquarters at Tacloban on Leyte a message came through to me one morning from Guam. My name had been included in a list of correspondents invited for a cruise on a battleship. That meant some action was brewing. A seat on a plane had already been arranged for next morning.

A couple of goodbyes and Ulithi had vanished into the immense Pacific.

Guam was a transformed island. The passenger terminal of gleaming white concrete had been completed at the airport. There were even murals in the waiting room, bare brown chamorritas against a background of blue seascapes. The correspondents' tent was as grubby as ever but the flies and mosquitoes had gone and the food at the mess was easier to eat. Ranks of new quonsets stood up on every hill. Four lane highways of glistening white coral led from airstrip to airstrip.

I saw more of the island than I'd bargained for. My battleship tour kept being postponed from day to day. Days ran into weeks. Time and again I watched the great flights of bombers taking off for Japan and waited through the late night in the tense group beside the doctor and the ambulance and the flak truck for the sight of them coming in. When the first superforts appeared over the field the floodlights would glare into the powdery white haze. Looking like long silver dragonflies they would roar in through the thickening coral dust. Then I would sit in the group of young airmen fidgetting beside their flakvests in the mess shack as they tried to choke down the fried chicken while they waited for the last laggard planes of their mission to be accounted for.

One day I got myself taken along in a flying boat on a

reconnaissance flight—known as the Cook's Tour—up the whole chain of the Marianas, volcanic islands that strung in a huge arc for hundreds of miles to the northward. The Spaniards had first named them the Islands of the Lateen Sails. They found them thickly settled with warlike Chamorros who cruised in huge sailing canoes from island to island. They conquered the Chamorros and settled them in mission settlements on Guam. Now these magnificent islands were empty, except for a few neutralized Jap outposts that still showed flak or machinegun fire from time to time. Our men called them Dunker's Row. They were searched daily for superforts forced to ditch on their way back from bombing Japan.

Some were only steep rocks aflutter with snowy terns. Others were Crusoe's isles with ferny green valleys that spread from narrow glens high up in the purple mountains down to yellow beaches and sapphire bays. The further north we flew the more volcanic they became. The last islands were active bare cones that trailed steam and smoke in the tradewind.

That day there was not a "Mae West" or a life raft to be seen.

As the freckled redhaired pilot circled the last cone and turned his flying boat's nose south he shouted in my ear, "After this there's one more volcano, a big one, and then Iwo Jima."

I had just about decided to give up the battleship cruise and to head on west to the Philippines where the communiqués had MacArthur going great guns, when Junior appeared one afternoon in the press tent with a look of important news on his applecheeked countenance. Within an hour I was jumping for a battleship's gangplank from the heaving deck of a captain's gig. Correspondents, the men kidded us as we roamed dazedly through the great battlewagon's cluttered steel passageways, correspondents meant trouble. The ship had been lucky too long. They guessed they were in for it now.

We spent that first night at anchor between Saipan and Tinian. The admiral had invited us to dinner in his big bare airy cabin. In the formal moment when we stood around waiting for introductions to be made I caught sight of a familiar face.

Roger Thurloe was wearing an officer's uniform without insignia. His face stood out startlingly pale among the bronzed faces around him.

He was not surprised to see me. It came over me right away that he'd had something to do with getting me invited on this junket, whatever it was. He shook hands with me stiffly as if he were meeting me for the first time but immediately his mouth broke into a smile: "Ro it's great to have you along," he said.

All I could think of was: "Roger how's Grace?"

"Why she's wonderful . . . She's perfectly wonderful. I see her every day."

I couldn't seem to phrase another question. My throat stiffened with unaccountable constraint. I wanted to ask about the boys. I only managed to mumble something about how her letters were probably all waiting for me at Pearl.

The admiral had dark slightly curly hair round a high narrow forehead, and a gentle thoughtful face, more a scholar's face than the face of a man of action; he reminded me right away of my favorite Latin teacher in high school. He was watching us with an enquiring smile.

"Admiral," Roger explained, "Ro Lancaster and I are near neighbors at home. We are old fellow-fishermen from Key West days."

"Just a day's fishing with nothing to think about. That would be nice, now wouldn't it?" said the admiral.

We were already being seated. A Filipino steward was bringing in steaks. My head was so full of things I wanted to talk over with Roger that I had a hard time keeping up with the conversation of the men around me. Roger was having the same trouble. Several times he turned towards me as if to say something, but each time he was distracted by some remark from the admiral's end of the table. Over the coffee after dinner I was hoping we'd have a moment—I knew he would be amused by the story of George Elbert shooting the carabao—but we had hardly taken a sip when word came that they were holding the movie for the admiral. He rose abruptly and led Roger off by the arm. The staff followed and the rest of us straggled after.

It was strange sitting there and watching the candy colors of an Arabian Nights movie perched on the bulging steel immensity of the battleship. The central superstructure towered above the screen in front of us to the soaring observation platform and the signal mast and the sky overhead. I couldn't keep my eyes on the picture. I kept looking out at the long dark shapes of the cruisers to the right and left of us and watching the blinkers' stuttering talk and the occasional red and green identification lights of homeward bound bombers moving among the stars.

As soon as the movie was over the Executive Officer politely detailed his assistant to lead us through the metallic maze of ladders and passageways to our quarters. Roger and the admiral had already disappeared.

I stuck my head out on deck a little before dawn next morning. The sky was covered with pearly overcast. The great mountain of steel was swinging out to sea in formation with three cruisers and eight destroyers. As soon as the last contact with the shore was broken an announcement was made over the public address system: "We are leaving on a mission to bombard Iwo Jima, six hundred miles to the northeast. Cruising at a speed of twenty knots we will reach the island day after tomorrow and bombard from thirteen hundred till sixteen thirty."

"This is it," said a lieutenant who had come to pilot me down to breakfast in the wardroom. "How do you like this life?" he asked me as he led me down a steep companionway. "On a battleship"—he answered his own question—"you are dry and comfortable. It's the kids on the cans—you know, destroyers—who take the beating. It's all or nothing on a flattop or a battleship."

I couldn't help wincing when I remembered the gutted flattop in the anchorage at Ulithi.

After breakfast the gunner outfitted us with battle equipment; life preserver, earplugs, a helmet, gloves and a mask against flash burns. Then we trooped into the dispensary for booster shots against tetanus and into the Exec's office for a briefing. Everywhere we found percolators brewing coffee. The morning was punctuated with cups of strong black coffee. Then we were all shown our battle stations. I had managed to find my way back to the wardroom in time to be served hamburgers for lunch when a yeoman tapped me on the shoulder. "Mr. Lancaster," he said, "they are asking for you in the admiral's quarters." I got to my feet still chewing and followed him along a corridor strange to me.

I was following my yeoman through a sort of gallery filled with long lines of men waiting for chow under roaring electric fans when a voice over the public address system barked an order: 'Man the anti-aircraft batteries.' My yeoman vanished in a surge of men scuttling for their battle equipment.

Right after came the merry stinging bugle call of the alert.

I was hopelessly lost. I popped through what was obviously the wrong passage and found all the trapdoors closing behind me as I climbed steep steel ladders which turned out to be inside the central conning tower. I ended up wearing somebody else's helmet on a lofty perch above the bridge. Way below me the broad fishshaped platform of the battleship sheared through rising seas under a gray sky. To the right and left and aft of us the cruisers plowed white furrows, and ahead, half way to the horizon, the low angular destroyers spewed smoke, tacking and doubling like foxhounds on the scent. "Five bogies on the screen," explained a young man with earphones.

A string of flags broke out from the signal halyards overhead. They were echoed in tiny bright specks from ship to ship. "We are observing radio silence," explained the young man. He gave me a wink. "The bogies are friendly bombers returning from a mission."

The all clear sounded and immediately the deck below us was full of men chatting and kidding as they strolled to their ordinary posts.

It was an hour before I found my way to the admiral's cabin. Roger and several men of the admiral's staff were poring over a chart of Iwo marked up with different colors in crayon. Roger looked up at me frowning. "Too bad you couldn't make it sooner," he said in a hurried whisper. "Now I'm all taken up."

"Tomorrow?" I asked.

"Tomorrow promises to be busy," he said with a dry laugh.

Everybody seemed embarrassed by my being there. An intelligence officer said something soothing about a complete briefing in the ward room at twenty hours tonight. When I excused myself Roger followed me to the door. "Look for me at Marine headquarters on Saipan," he said. "I'm just up here for a look see." I made my way as best I could back to my cabin.

Next morning we had hardly sat down to breakfast in the wardroom when the call came to general quarters. Jim Hitchins the Consolidated Press man and I laughed at each other's awkwardness as, encumbered by our life preservers, we shinnied up the ladders. We were still a long way from Sky Aft when we heard the battle stations bugle call go neighing through the ship.

We were up there on Sky Aft all day. There were six of us on our little perch, two officers with small earphones and two lookouts with oversized helmets over their huge earphones and mikes to report into. One of them, a stubby youngster with a hula girl tattoed on his forearm, answered to the name of Ham. We never did find out the other boy's name. Ham had a direct line to the radar report center and kept us up to date on events.

Already they had the first volcano on the screen. Soon we'd spot it through the glasses. Jim Hitchins, whom I had thought of as a rather proper man, developed a fund of smutty stories that everybody tried to laugh at. When they ran out he began to remember limericks. We were all tense. The next volcano was Iwo.

Some time before we came into sight of Iwo the voice over the public address system ordered one man from each station to go below for coffee and sandwiches. The boys brought us out a cot to sit on and Jim and I sat side by side cosily munching ham sandwiches and drinking coffee out of big stoneware cups. Food settles the nerves. The lieutenant even handed around cigars.

We had hardly gotten a sight of two humps the faint gray of cigar ash on the horizon before a set of signal flags broke out forward. "Bombardment postponed one hour," announced Ham in a disgruntled voice. "It's like waitin' to have a tooth pulled."

As Iwo vanished into the mist again we felt on our changed course the full force of the wind in our faces.

There was a lash of cold rain. The sky had become completely overcast. We were glad of the protection of our life preservers against the sudden chill. "It's the damned airforce . . . late again," said Ham. "We're waitin' for our air umbrella."

"Like sittin' ducks if you ask me," hissed the other lookout.

The lieutenant handed around caramels from a tin.

Suddenly they told of a flurry of bogies over the intercom. Each time a new bogie was announced all the antiaircraft batteries beneath us swung around.

"Raids one and two have dropped their bombs on Iwo and are now reforming at a low altitude," came a new warm explanatory voice over the public address system.

Another bogie. All the guns started barking together. Five inch, pompoms, machine guns. The stoneware cups we'd just drunk coffee out of danced frantically in the corners of the deck. Jim and I were busy dodging burning wadding from the fiveinch guns.

A tiny scary cross-shaped thing coming towards us in the path of the sun was now nowhere to be seen.

"A perfect solution," said the voice over the public address system.

Another bogie. Again the guns.

"This plane's a jill," announced Ham in dramatic tones. For our benefit he added an aside: "A torpedo plane with a fish . . . One of the can's bagged him," he shouted.

Trailing a broad sheet of flame the Jap pitched into the ocean.

"All we have on the screen is friendlies," resumed the cozy voice over the public address system.

There were a few minutes of silence. No sound but the whine of the wind through the superstructure.

"All hands man battle stations for bombardment," the

voice spoke up again in measured tones. "Set condition zebra. Five inch batteries loading in preparation for counter battery fire as we go in . . . Prepare for three three-gun salvos from the main battery."

At each salvo from the sixteeninch guns it was like being beaten with a bag of sand.

After fifty minutes we were right in on the island. "Range six thousand yards," announced Ham in one of his dramatic asides.

The lieutenant screwed up his face.

"Mighty damn close," he said.

Jim Hitchens and I were too breathless to speak. We were gasping. Whenever the sixteeninch guns let loose with a ninegun salvo the whole ship seemed to leap sideways out of the water. The breath kept being knocked out of us. The teeth rattled in our jaws.

Iwo Jima was now two brownish gray piles of volcanic ash joined by the light streak of an airstrip. A camel hump. Through the glasses we could make out a tangle of wrecked Jap planes that had been pushed over the edge of the airstrip. Puffs of smoke, then great dirty smudges began to appear over the island. We couldn't see a speck of cover or a green tree on it.

"Damn Nips are holed up in there like ground hogs," said Ham. He spat to leeward in disgust.

As we rounded the point of the island we caught sight of the curve of a beach. Something had blown up behind the nearer volcano. An umbrella of white smoke appeared in the sky and began to swirl and churn above the airstrip. Specks of flame flickered against it.

As my eyes devoured the beach through the glasses I knew how many eyes from the bridge must be fixed on that same fatal curve. I could imagine Roger Thurloe's pale face set in that comical bulldog look of determination.

There it was. That was the beach. Those were the men who had to make the decision.

The destroyers had gone in after three Jap transports anchored off shore. The public address system reported one blown up and two beached and burning. "The can reports he's sorry he can't blow the other two. They won't seem to blow."

Behind the burning ships we could make out quite clearly the long dirty curve and the crumbly mean hillside beyond, and the enfilading volcanic mountains that smoked as if in eruption from our shelling. The mountains spewed pillars of smoke and dust that were merging into a huge pall. The smoke pall sagged down until it blotted the island out.

Our battleship and her escorting cruisers pirouetted majestically.

The voice over the public address system was full of cheer: "Destroyers and spotting planes report everything along the beach wrecked. A cold front from the north, rain and poor visibility make it advisable to discontinue bombardment . . . Retiring at twentyfive knots to Guam."

Now there was quiet except for the swishing crash of seas over the bow and the whining of the wind in our helmets and the hard patter of the rain. We pulled the earplugs out of our ears. It wasn't till the bombardment stopped that we woke up to the fact that we were drenched to the skin.

I made the hop over from Guam to Saipan in a B24 along with part of a submarine crew, officers and men. Not one of them had ever been up in a plane before. They talked about how secure a man felt under water. In the air they were all scared green.

It took hours of telephoning from the office of the PRO

on Saipan to unearth Roger. When I finally got through to him he told me curtly to stay where I was. He would pick me up. It was evening before he appeared in a dusty jeep driven by a taciturn marine sergeant.

"Did you see that beach Ro?" he asked as we drove off.

I nodded. It never occurred to me to ask where he was taking me.

"There's no other way. Iwo's one island we have got to have."

The sergeant evidently had his instructions. He parked the jeep in the crumbly coral at the edge of a ramp leading up to an airstrip on a hill. From the edge we could look out over the dark hills of the island and the ruffled sea deep indigo with twilight and the last fading topaz streak of day on the western horizon.

We were both sweating. Roger seemed a little short of breath. The breeze had dropped. The air steamed with heat.

"You saw the two peaks?" Roger was talking into the west without looking at me. "They are honeycombed with caves. They are sure to have big guns in those caves to enfilade the beach. That's why we went in so close, to smoke out their locations. The bastards were too smart for us. They held their fire."

I mumbled something about how maybe they didn't have any big guns at all. My voice sounded tinny and frivolous.

Roger didn't even hear me.

"We'll find out all right when the amtracks go in . . . And I've got to stand up and tell all these grand guys to go in there and get killed."

He clicked his teeth together as he bit off the word.

Then he said, still without looking at me: "Tell me something Ro . . . I've got to ask somebody. Ro, do you think it would be . . . you know . . . showing off . . . if I went along?"

I said of course not and asked him if he had any room in his pocket for a correspondent.

"No this isn't your style," he said impatiently. "Let George Elbert Warner do the blood and thunder. He sure does lay about him with a meataxe." He let out a short snort of laughter.

I murmured that before our little cruise I had set things up to go on to the Philippines.

"Sure, sure. That's our great experiment . . . Tell me everything about the Filipinos . . ." He snorted again. "I talk like I was your only reader."

We stood silently side by side; the stars were out. It was night.

"Roger tell me—" I stumbled over the words—"about the family . . . You know how mail is out here."

"I told you." He was in a hurry to be gone. "Grace is perfectly wonderful. She runs my office like a quartermaster colonel. You wouldn't think the little girl had it in her."

He turned to me suddenly. I could see his eyes boring through the darkness to search my face.

"You probably don't think I have any business out here in the first place. Maybe I haven't . . . But I felt at least one of the men who helped make this decision had to go along. I've got to know how the boys feel who really get it in the neck. I've got to know how"—his voice faltered. I knew at once he was struggling to pronounce his son's name—"damn it I've got to know how he felt."

He strode back to the jeep. I had trouble keeping up with him.

"Where do you mess Ro?" he was asking in a casual voice. "The sergeant will drop you off there."

Next morning before day I was in the bucket seat of a crowded plane headed for Peleliu on the first lap of my flight to Leyte.

We flew into Tacloban on the heels of a red alert. It was raining. Under sagging inkstained clouds burning oil tanks vomited coils of black smoke. The faces of the muddy men with rifles hunched in a row in front of the operations hut were yellow from the atabrine they had been taking. Over their heads a sign read TACLOBAN THE WORLD'S BUSIEST AIRPORT. One had a little worried gray monkey perched on his shoulder. On the back of a wet jeep, driven by a bareheaded man in a wet poncho, sat two brightgreen parrots.

The truck piled with bulky dripping dunnage that carried us into town took the left side of the road as it slithred through the puttycolored mud. Over the Chinese-looking gate at the entrance to the town the letters USSAFE were spelled out on a wet cloth. In the town all the motley mudcolored traffic was driving to the left. The Southwest Pacific was a different world.

I found the public relations boys quartered in a tall cramped gingerbread house with stained glass windows that looked like a child's drawing of a Swiss chalet. In the dining room clucking popeyed geckos with cupped toes ran back and forth upside down across the ceiling. I'd hardly dropped my duffle in a corner and reached out for a plate of chicken the Chinese houseboy brought in before a red alert sounded.

Bombs and ackack boomed far away behind the bead curtain of rain like offstage noises.

After the alert somebody produced a bottle of whiskey. Nobody had a chance for a drink before the rattletrap chalet began to heave and shake. The timbers creaked like a ship in a high sea. The electric light went off again, for good this time. It was an earthquake.

After the earthquake nobody could find the whiskey bottle. We groped for our cots through the dense sopping darkness.

Another morning I found myself flying before breakfast in a Billy Mitchell bomber across the Visayan Sea between toppling green cloudcapped islands, skimming over polished water along shores engraved with fish weirs in heraldic shapes, catching glimpses of sailboats out of Chinese paintings and of the curved roofs of houses set on stilts in the bottoms of bays.

There was a rasp of danger in the pilot's voice over the intercom when he announced, "Manila in twenty minutes."

When the photographer opened the bombbay hatch to set his camera a smell like scorched rags was sucked into the plane off the burning city.

We had been crossing cultivated lands and tileroofed farms. Now squares of stucco houses raced by under a scrim of smoke between broad thoroughfares full of people, people in lightcolored clothes, people with faces upturned under big hats. A man waved his hat.

There was a roadblock, rifles bristling towards the diving plane, oddlooking trucks, small men in green.

The pilot gave them a burst out of his forward machineguns, banked upwards and immediately dove again so steeply the wingtip seemed to brush the tiled roofs and the chimneypots so like Havana's, of the city within the walls.

An elegantly carved Spanish window whirled past in the amber glare under the smoke pall.

Beside a steel bridge at the water's edge a warehouse burned with a steady flame like a candle. The dirty puddle of the harbor littered with sunk steamers spun into the sky from under us.

There was a light popping noise somewhere in the plane. "Anybody hurt back there?" asked the pilot over the intercom. "Cylinder blew off right hand motor," he explained. His voice remained casual. "Prepare for crash landing!" he added as if this were something that happened every day.

Instead he managed to level off on one motor over the paddy fields to the north of the city. Twentyfive minutes later we were climbing out to stretch our legs on the steel matting of the Lingayen strip. We were babbling about the fine aim of the Jap gunners and our pilot's skillful feathering of his prop on the conkedout motor. We were groggy with excitement. We could feel the living blood coursing under our whole skins. We were hungry as hell for breakfast.

There followed a day that seemed a week, thumbing rides on jeeps and trucks along the invasion route across Luzon into the city in the vast traffic jam of the army advancing. Everyone spoke of the threat of Jap raids from the left. The stream of trucks and jeeps and halftracks poured through jungles and incinerated towns and flooded ricelands where the white herons perched on the backs of drowsy carabao.

At last we were in sight of the city. It was dark. Smoke blotted the western sky. I found a billet in a flower-banked bungalow in the suburb on the hill. Somewhere among the flowers there crouched a battery of howitzers that slammed you on the head every few minutes.

When the guns went silent after midnight I was still roaming dead tired through the dim secluded streets. Pianos tinkled in the shuttered houses. I could feel the approval in the greetings of elderly Filipinos I met walking their lapdogs in the smell of nightblooming jasmine and the sharp tang of exploding dynamite that drifted across the Pagig. An American uniform meant deliverance to them.

My first night in burning Manila was in the dormitory at Santo Tomás where the American civilians had been imprisoned all the years of the war. Santo Tomás was the old Spanish university. Never had I felt such admiring love for my fellow countrymen as before the uncomplaint of these starved skeletons of men and women. They had kept their children well and starved themselves.

They hardly had time to give thanks for their rescue before the Jap counterattack began.

I lay on a cot in the dormitory that night amid the men sick from scurvy and beriberi and starvation and heard their timid breathing while the Jap mortars bracketed the building and heard the punk of shells, the crash of masonry, the stifled moans and the quiet scuttling sounds as the dead and wounded were carried away; and in the morning saw the gaunt mute host of ghosts sitting on the stairs watching with staring comprehension the body of a young soldier who had been killed on the roof being carried out on a stretcher.

They were old and sick, their skin hung in folds, their legs were like broomsticks, they tottered on canes, but they were alive. The soldier was plump and ruddy with smooth youthful cheeks and a curl in his hair and a smile on his lips but he was dead.

And the day on Mindanao. I stood looking out from behind the pilot's head as the transport followed the windings of a snaky river, up between dense slopes where the morning clouds still clung to the huge trees. He finally jumped the plane over a jagged ridge like you would jump a horse and circled into a tawny valley between blue mountains where he found a scrap of an airstrip the guerrillas had cleared. Farm Eight they called it.

Ears ringing from the altitude I let myself down onto the rough red earth and breathed deep of the sparkling upland air. The beatenup bus that shambled up the airstrip to load the ammo the plane had brought had a tiny stars and stripes fluttering from its shattered windshield. Ragged little barefoot men with rifles sprang up cheering from behind every grassy knoll.

There were saddlehorses waiting under the trees. Halfway up the road into the mountains we met the Oklahoma planter, a tall grayeyed grizzlebearded American who walked with a mountaineer's stride over the rough clay road, a stride ahead and a head taller than the smiling squat islanders who crowded affectionately around him.

He was an oldtimer on Mindanao, he told me. He resigned from the constabulary to plant coconuts. A lazy man's life that's why he liked it. When the Japs came he hid out for two months on his own place before he took to the hills. Gradually he'd found himself taking command of the guerrillas. They liked having him run things because they knew he had no family there to do favors for, they thought he was fair. He grinned. Then they knew he couldn't go over to the Japs. If the Japs caught an American they cut him up in very small pieces. That idea made a man light on his feet. Keeping one jump ahead of the Japs kept a man's mind active. Not such a bad life as you'd think.

We had all been served lunch at a table under the pomulo trees beside the Gonzalez family barn. The Gonzalez family was huge, a grayhaired man and woman who presided with old style grace, and uncles, cousins, nephews, daughters. They told us their five sons were in the Army of the Philippines. The Japs had burned their house when they raided and razed the village a few days before.

The Gonzalez girls had beautiful dark eyes and smiles of peculiarly Castilian hospitality as they brought out the palm wine. They made sure the Oklahoma planter used the only glass. He was their colonel. Everybody else had to drink out of segments of bamboo. They brought out chicken and rice and roast suckling pig and pork chops and green beans and squash pie made of cassava flour. They would stuff him to death, the Oklahoma planter demurred smiling. They hung on his every word.

There was something he had that gave them strength, some simple confidence in himself and his own people's way, some code, something fair and measured and humorous, something that was the opposite of selfimportant. Something that made them feel there were other men like him stateside where he came from.

Back at the airstrip we found the little guerrillas struggling to tow one of our Corsair escorts that had damaged its prop in landing off into a hiding place. Children were bringing palm branches to screen the damaged plane from the Jap patrol. "They'll turn that plane into a haystack in no time," said the colonel laughing.

As soon as he showed his bearded face the little guerrillas fell to tugging and heaving twice as hard on their homemade ropes. The children laughed and cheered and crowded round his legs. They felt secure when he was there. Landless men and landowners seemed to feel he stood for a square deal for each of them.

We only spent five hours at Farm Eight, but I felt as if I'd lived half my life there.

There was a young fellow who drove the jeep another day, in Manila, his face had that same mountain look, rusty cornsilk hair and a long twisted comical nose. "This ain't war," he said over his shoulder in his Tennessee twang as he led the way with swinging stride into the broken church. "It's sumpen worse."

The vestibule of the church was black as a crypt. We stood still a moment wiping the sweat off our faces in the cool quiet dark, straightening our backs bowed by the hammering of the noon sun, breathing the stonecooled air.

"Take a looksee pop," the young fellow said and gave me a shove forward through the lowarched inner door.

It was a big barn of a church. The sun poured in blinding through a hole in the roof. Where the shaft of sunlight blasted the shattered marble paving and the broken pews the place looked empty; it was only when our eyes stopped blinking that we began to see that the shadows crawled with wounded. They were heaped like old rags in the corners. On the steps in front of the altar they were laid out on stretchers. To ears bruised by the racket of battle the church seemed very quiet. The ratatat tat tat of machineguns from outside or the occasional crump of a mortar came as a shudder muffled by thick rubble walls. Inside there was only the continual low moaning of hurt people hunched in pews, now and then a tiny whimper from a child.

The church was full of children. Small black eyes looked out from every huddled group.

No uniforms. These were all townspeople, citizens, ordinary people caught in the crossfire. A smell of burning rose from them, the stench of wounds too and of caked blood, but mostly the smell of burning.

From their niches in the walls above saints in blue and pink plaster robes looked down out of unseeing eyes.

A livid little civilian doctor popped up in front of the altar like a clown out of a jackinthebox. He gesticulated wildly in our faces: "Three rolls of gauze bandages, no antiseptics, not a spongeful of ether." His English was warped by some indefinable accent.

"How about our medics, Tennessee?"

"Busy with our own."

"The Red Cross?"

"Trucks ain't come this far up yet."

Tennessee grabbed my elbow and hurried me into the sunny corner of the church. "Let's get out of here."

He pointed up a set of ladders lashed together that led up through the hole in the roof to a tiny door black in the flank of the tower.

"That there's our observation post. Make it snappy mister so that the Jap sniper don't get a bead on you."

It was the longest set of ladders I ever saw. Tennessee shot up out of sight as if hauled by a hoist.

I started slowly, hand over hand. The ladders swayed. My hands gripped the rungs like claws. My feet in their heavy boots groped for the rungs clumsily. The sweat under my drenched shirt dribbled down the small of my back. I could feel the socks sopping wet between my toes. With my head in the sun I clung to the wobbling ladder.

The sun scalded my cheek. The scalding sun made my head swim. My feet were sliding off the slippery rungs. My fingers ached from gripping. Sweat blinded my eyes. I was going to fall.

Painfully with stinging palms, blindly I made my way back down. Every time my foot slipped the rung above bruised my knee. Fighting for breath I stood on the firm paving swabbing off my face with my filthy wet handkerchief.

Out of the dark of the church I could see their eyes looking me over. I could see the scorning grin on the chalk face of the doctor. Look what we have undergone, their eyes said. Look what I have to do, said the doctor's scorning grin.

"I was getting a little dizzy," I explained to nobody in particular.

I started up the ladder again, placing my feet carefully, rung after rung. I topped the wall. I climbed up into the scalding sunlight, clambering against the burning stones of the tower, up until, breath all gone, my feet flailing helplessly on the slippery rungs, I felt hands suddenly grabbing me under the armpits.

The tower was firm and square and safe after the wobbling ladder. Gasping to suck enough air into my lungs I struggled after Tennessee up creaky wooden steps in the dark.

"We was bettin' two to one you wouldn't make it," Tennessee was laughing. The tower was full of chortling GI's.

"Had us worried you took so long," said another voice behind me.

"Jap sniper must be dozin'."

"Keep your head down," they all snarled in unison as I crawled dazed out onto the hot griddle of the roof.

The boys with telescopic sights on their rifles lay in the slivers of shade by the battlement. Through a slit they showed me where the howitzer shells were clobbering the old city, the Manila Hotel still afire against the bay strewn with wreckage, a knockedout tank, machinegun nests, a truck moving down a flameswept avenue, tiny Japs running behind a wall with a mortar.

"Well pop," Tennessee's voice twanged amiably in my ears as we ducked at last into the shade behind the rubble wall of the church on our downward climb, "doggone if you didn't make it."

Back in Leyte on the beach near Tolosa I managed to get myself thrown headfirst out of a jeep. A slight concussion. A few stitches. Somebody suggested Hollandia for quiet and convalescence. Wearing a bandage like a

Sikh's turban I found myself being propped by my doctor friends in a bucket seat on the morning plane.

The flight was cool and quiet. In Hollandia the war was over. There were hospitals, rest camps, outfits spraying the jungle with DDT, all in a landscape out of another planet, razoredged ridges, trees too dense with foliage, grass always higher than your head.

The colonel who commanded an air-transport wing took me in. He had a log cabin tucked away in a little glen that had the look of a camp in the Cascades Mountains. We sat on his screened porch beside the cage where little marsupials that looked like flying squirrels glided from perch to perch in the gloaming. He was showing me by the light of his flashlight the air photos of what he called his secret valley. He was a tense squarefaced man with a thatch of black hair and black gimlet eyes in a circle of wrinkles, navigator's eyes. He neither drank liquor nor coffee nor tea. He held smoking in horror. To myself at least I called him the Flying Mormon. Flying was his drug.

"See, it's a culture much higher than that of any known natives of New Guinea." The colonel's clean finger nail travelled over the glossy prints. "These ponds are artificial. These ditches are either for drainage or irrigation: see the cultivated strips, the wellbuilt oval huts. They have a race of gigantic hogs. If the war ever stopped so that a man could get a leave, I'd be tempted to make a little visit to those folks. Expeditions have tried but they've all had to turn back; no white man has ever managed to cross the ridges. Want to come along? We'll find time to buzz them in the morning, not too far off course to the Torres Strait. We leave at the first crack of day because we have to reach the mountain gap before the overcast clamps its lid down."

Of course I had to go. As soon as we could see

the sleeve at the airstrip we started in his B24, the Flying Mormon at the controls, me in my Sikh's turban sitting in a redleather armchair installed instead of a machinegun in the forward bubble. Ridge after ridge of parboiled green, littered with tatters of mist swept under my feet to pile up in bluish fogstreaked mountain heaps behind.

From that height an occasional valley looked like a smooth green lawn. If you tried to walk on these lawns you would find that the tall grasses closed overhead. Not a path, not a trail, only toppling slopes that gleamed with wet; here and there on some cragged height a speck of trodden earth round a makeshift shelter where a few black men huddled.

"Ahead you'll see the Orange Mountains," the colonel's voice crackled over the intercom. "The peaks to the right rise to sixteen thousand feet. The sun's on them, see. Watch for the waterfall."

The plane was threading a valley between slopes every moment steeper. The plane was skirting high escarpments that reared out of a tangle of mad vegetation. The steaming cliffs closed in under the leaden overcast to form a tunnel of indigo gloom.

Motors growled as the plane climbed into the thinner air.

There was brightness ahead, a porthole of light in the churning clouds.

Now a sheet of falling water.

I felt my stomach drop. The throttle was wide open, my bubble tilted up into a bright cave of clouds. The motors roared. Like some unimaginable canoe shooting the rapids in reverse the plane bounded up over the white water, up into a river valley shaped like a keyhole; glided easily across the slow meanderings of the river; tossed, pitched in the turbulent air as we climbed again into a boiling pass. Crags, jagged rock pinnacles hurtled by and, quickly, all of a sudden, shaking loose from the clouds, we swooped into sunlight over a green and umber valley.

"Look ahead. This is it," came the colonel's tense voice.

I hardly breathed as I looked down on a network of paths between cultivated fields, walled villages, corrals, ditches where water gleamed.

Where white man's foot had never trod, the phrase popped up out of my boyhood.

The Flying Mormon buzzed a village so low I thought he wanted to fly through the great thatched hut's broad door. There were the black pigs on their long legs, tall bronzy colored men, women and children scampering in fright between hedgerows.

On a path between hedgerows we passed a hunting party with spears. The leader raised his spear, aimed carefully, and hurled it up at the plane.

The plane banked and spiralled up to level off into the south. Now the valley was only a map again marked with crisscrossings of ditches and paths, clusters of tiny knobs for villages.

"Can't show you any more now or we'll run out of gas," came the colonel's precise voice over the intercom. "Suppose we come back and visit with these folks some day?" . . .

We ended up in Cairns Australia where the colonel and his crew had promised to set the Australian girls up to a dance. Up every morning before day for his inspection of airfields, up late every night to dance with the Australian girls, the Flying Mormon never got tired.

At Sydney I left him and sank back into civilian life again. When the headaches subsided and I got so that I could go around without my turban I set off for home.

Manila was taken. The last Jap had been blasted out of the last cave on Iwo. I'd been months without mail. It was time I went home.

At the Sydney airport a congenially inebriated Aussie tried to present me with a prettyfaced wallaby. The wallaby was tame and jumped headfirst into a sack when the Aussie called the way it would have jumped into its mother's pouch. The wallaby was an alert deerlike beautifully marked bigeyed creature. "The perfect pet!" the Aussie said.

I begged off by showing the Aussie my dufflebag crammed with a hundred pounds of typescripts and notes. He scrawled out his address. When I got home if I'd write him he'd ship me a prettyfaced wallaby by parcel post.

I tried to explain that I already had pets at home. I'd been neglecting my pets. The Aussie kept rambling on about the charms of the prettyfaced wallaby until the plane took off two hours late for New Caledonia.

Sitting alone and morose through the flight in the half empty plane I kept thinking of Grace and the boys. I didn't need a prettyfaced wallaby. They were my pets. They seemed to fill the vacant seats beside me: little Grace, blonde, curly, blueeyed, chirruping out little pert remarks like some small neat intelligent bird; Chips, redhaired, with his acne and his chewed fingernails and his sullen pout, awkward and shambling the way I had been as a boy; and Louie, much more like Grace with his blue eyes and the light curl to his hair and his graceful posture and the puckish tilt of that ruined conical felt cap with old tin badges around it he used to insist on wearing. It was more than hallucination. Their presence permeated my senses. My nostrils seemed full of the sweaty calfish adolescent smell of the boys. Grace's beloved indefinable perfume was realer than memory.

Noumea. Pearl. Oakland.

A night flight to New York, only it turned out that instead of being La Guardia, the airfield where we landed, bouncing and bumping through a snowstorm, was near Allentown, Pennsylvania.

Several of us chipped in on a taxi to Philadelphia.

From the hotel I called Grace.

"Ro I can't believe it, Ro," she kept saying.

We neither of us knew how to begin to talk to each other.

"Ro, I've got to go now."

She seemed strained and hurried. I had caught her just as she was going out the door. She couldn't be late at the office. "We'll have dinner," she said in a strangely formal tone. Her voice didn't sound as I had remembered it.

The receiver clicked. Her voice was gone. My memory of her was gone. It took me minutes to get my wits together enough to remember how to open the door of the phone booth. She had seemed so close before I called . . .

11

. . . When Ro wakes again the room is full of sun. He is alone in the bed. His head hurts. His nostrils are sickly sensitive to the smell of roasting coffee mixed with the sourness of burnt gasoline that pours in through the open window. The honking and grinding of the traffic through the street below claws at his ears. Water running from the shower in the bathroom sounds like a cataract. It's Elsa in the shower.

Ro sits up with a jerk, puts his feet to the floor, raises himself shakily from the edge of the bed and pulls on his shirt and pants. To have another minute to himself before he has to speak to her, he hurries into his own room.

He comes back after a while shaved and bathed and

wearing a clean linen suit. His bones are made of glass.

"Come in," she calls.

She's sitting in her dressing gown in front of the mirror rubbing cold cream into her face. Her face has a small crunchedup look in the greenish glass. "This sun," she explains twisting her eyes to one side. She is scrutinizing Ro's image in the mirror beside hers. "Ro you sure look like the wrath of God."

"How are you?" he asks with a weak giggle.

"Me? I'm wearing the iron crown."

Ro feels as if his skull were made of a number of illfitting pieces of metal. A remark that he hopes will be funny shoots out of him like a released spring. "Must have been something we ate," he says.

Elsa catches on and answers. "Or else the Coca-Cola." She half grins half frowns into the mirror. "Ouch it hurts me to laugh."

"How about breakfast?"

"Sure," says Elsa. "The first thing I want to do is go see Joe Herkimer," she adds pettishly as if somebody were trying to keep her from going. "He'll be feeling badly I didn't come to see him the first day."

"This is the first day," says Ro. "Yesterday didn't count."

Elsa gets to her feet and turns round to give him a sharp serious look right in the eyes. "Have it your own way," she says.

He starts to say something more but his tongue won't move.

Still their hangover is a sort of bond.

They agree that it will be too bright up on the roofgarden and hurry across the street into the dark restaurant where they ate supper. Ro keeps his eyes to himself for fear of seeing somebody he knows. He couldn't stand talking to anybody yet. He can just manage to be civil to Elsa. It's a relief to find the place empty.

With the orange juice the elderly waiter with ducktails over his ears brings Ro a morning paper open to an inside page and sets it down with a flourish on the marble table beside him.

It is some time before Ro can get his eyes to focus. He finds himself reading an account of his own arrival. They dug up an old photograph. He can't help the selfsatisfied smile that creeps across his face. In the next column he finds the name of Hon. Mortimer Price listed among prominent people checking in at the Nacional.

"You still rate two paragraphs to Mortimer's one," a voice like a parrot's squawks in his head. "Of course in Cuba they are a little behind the times," answers another voice.

"Fulsome," he says aloud as he passes the paper over to Elsa. "Must be the work of our friend at Rancho Boyeros . . . And Mortimer's in town. We'll have to look up the old stickinthemud to see if he's gotten over being mad at me."

Elsa looks at the paper without seeing it.

"I thought it was my friends we were going to see."

She sticks out her chin.

"We got time for everybody's friends," Ro answers blandly.

They are both still extremely jumpy. Their hands shake when they lift the beaded glasses of orange juice to their lips. They say things to each other but nothing they say dovetails into anything else.

"Ham and eggs?" asks Ro as he drains off his second cup of coffee.

She shakes her head.

"What are we waiting here for?" she whines.

On the sidewalk outside they indulge in a little spat

about whether to walk or ride. In the end they climb into a cab, with Ro still insisting that a nice long walk is the best cure for a hangover. At least it isn't the driver with the smile, he thinks, remembering last night with a shudder; this one is a seriousfaced Negro in an immaculate white silk shirt.

When the taxi stops on an empty side street near the Malecon, Ro insists that Elsa must have the wrong address. The street has an uninhabited look.

The day has become overcast. Shivering in the stiff wind off the sea they wander up and down in front of a series of blue wooden doors which open out from the basement of a huge Americanstyle apartment house that fills the block.

"No, this is it." Elsa starts to knock desperately on one of the doors. Ro's head throbs so he doesn't care. The pavement seems to be tipping. The coffee didn't set too well on his stomach.

After a while a little oliveskinned girl with her hair all in pins sticks her head out of a door beyond the one where Elsa is still knocking.

"Senor 'Erkimer?" asks Ro.

"Tell him it's Elsa," Elsa's screech rasps in Ro's ears. "Elsa from last year."

The girl's eyes are black beads of suspicion. She looks from one to the other. Ro repeats the words in Spanish. The girl pulls her head back and is about to close the door behind her.

"Leave that door open," calls a cracked American voice from some inner room.

Ro finds himself blinking in the half darkness of a long vestibule papered with mounted photographs of baseball teams and football teams with here and there a race horse with a jockey on his back.

"Come on in," continues the voice. "I like it here because it's always cool and I can come and go as I please. First time in my life I've found a place where my wife can't check up on me." The sentence ends in a rasping chuckle.

When Ro's eyes get accustomed to the light he finds himself standing in a dim inside room hung with old bull-fight posters from Mexico. Facing him at a deal table marked with rings where glasses have stood sits a man well along in years with a handsome head of wavy white hair and a pink face full of fine wrinkles. There's white stubble on his cheeks and chin. Not looking at anyone in particular he's talking and chuckling over a glass of coffee.

"What do you think of Chiquita? Picked her up off the streets." There's a peevish tremor in the man's flat Down East voice. "A good thing my wife don't know about Chiquita." He lets out a creaky laugh. "I'm sendin' her to school . . . What your wife don't know don't hurt you."

Alcoholic blue eyes popping out between redrimmed lids fasten on Ro's face for the first time. The mouth pouts like a fish's as he lets out a whistle. "You age 'em up fast, girlie."

Elsa laughs a short harsh laugh.

"It's a different boyfriend, Joe you idiot," she says. "Joe Herkimer, meet Roland Lancaster."

"Robbing the old men's home, eh?" His jowls shake with a silent laugh as he looks them both up and down with a leer in his eyes. "Well time has its revenges."

"You needn't talk." Elsa tossed her head in the direction of the door through which Chiquita has just gone bustling out with a selfconscious wiggle of small hips.

Joe Herkimer gives Ro a heavy wink and says in a confidential tone that somehow makes them accomplices in depravity: "That's what we come here for, old timer, to live as we like."

"I must be a whole head taller," Ro hears his own voice querulously insisting, "than Gov Haines, I mean."

"Excuse it, excuse it," mutters Joe Herkimer. "When you're expectin' to see somebody, sometimes you think you see 'em. This last year my eyes ain't been too good."

He grabs hold of the edge of the table and pushes himself back in his chair. ". . . They're good enough to see that Elsa's still wearin' those goddam canvas shoes . . . We 'most lost our minds with those canvas shoes. She lost one one night and Gov had to get a pair flown down from New York by air."

Without paying attention Elsa sits down in a chair and lights a cigarette. She crosses her legs and jiggles one foot in its soft shoe as she leans back to blow a puff of smoke towards the ceiling.

Joe Herkimer goes on with his story: "Rube Mothershead wrote me to take care of the two young hopefuls when they came down last year. Did the best I could for 'em. These tourists ain't too much in my line. All I knew was to get 'em drunk and keep 'em drunk, but I guess it didn't work out. In my day you got married first and repented afterwards. Now they start repentin' even before they get married . . . Elsa what did you say the old timer's name was?"

"Roland Lancaster. Joe you're getting deaf as well as blind."

"Why not? Dumb deaf and blind. At my age a man don't care any more. What did you say his name was?"

Elsa shouts the name again.

"Oh of course . . . Well well, that sure is a coincidence. I was just about to write your publication, Roland, I think I've got a story for 'em. Now you can save me the trouble of writin' it. Got a photographer along?"

"I'm on a vacation," says Ro. "I'm not connected with any particular publication right now."

"A free lance eh," croaked Joe Herkimer. "Sell to the highest bidder, eh?"

"I bet that's the same story Gov was going to angel a play about," Elsa interrupts.

"Just as good today as it ever was, better, because so much has happened since . . . The Haines boy was going to give me an interest in the play on account of me furnishin' the plot. But I can't wait that long to make my fortune." He looks up in Ro's face and wheezes out a laugh.

"He's pulling out of it," says Elsa. "He's all fouled up."

"So you still hear from him? How's he gettin' along? What does he have to say?"

"What do you expect him to say? Just the kind of letter you would expect from that kind of a heel."

Elsa drops her cigarette on the floor and crushes it out with her foot. Joe Herkimer sits staring at her, blinking his redrimmed eyes.

"Aren't you going to give us a cup of coffee, Joe?" she asks.

"Chiquita . . . café," Joe Herkimer calls in his cracked voice. "That's what I like about these countries." He wheezes out a giggle. "They give you service."

Joe Herkimer twists up all the little wrinkles in his face till the sly look becomes the grimace of an oldfashioned vaudeville hick. "I bet I know what you did last night. I bet she took you out to Paco Cortes' rhumba joint . . . I can't stand that stuckup bastard, even if he is black." His face is serious again. "You sure put Gov Haines through hell out in that rhumba joint, Elsa." He shakes his finger at her. Then he addresses himself confidentially to Ro: "He's not a bad guy either for a broker. The only trouble with him was he wasn't man enough to paste her in the jaw at the right time."

"Joe you don't understand anything about it." Elsa sits

with her head bowed staring at the toes of her shoes. "Rube didn't either."

"Was he down here too?" asks Ro in a constrained tone.

He has the feeling of standing in another man's shoes, of being somewhere on false pretenses, of eavesdropping; he isn't too sure of his own identity this morning, anyway. A sad gray haze keeps cutting him off. Inside the haze all he knows is that he is profoundly sorry for himself.

"No." He hears Elsa's bitter voice coming from a great distance. "All he did was send advice by cable and airmail. A regular correspondence course."

"The art of lovin', eh?" Joe Herkimer turns derisive blue eyes from one to the other. He opens his mouth to say something more and stops.

Elsa's gaze has hardened into a blank stone stare.

Little Chiquita comes tapping back into the room on her high heels smiling a cribhouse smile that sits strangely on her childish face. She has shaken the bobbypins out of her hair. She is carrying a tray with two coffeecups and a plate of sugar buns.

"Shut that door," shouts Joe Herkimer in his cracked voice.

The girl freezes in the middle of the floor. Her eyelashes flutter. The coffee begins to slop out of the cups.

"Didn't I tell you not to leave that door open?"

The girl's desperate uncomprehending eyes switch from face to face.

"What does he say?" she asks Ro in Spanish.

Ro gets to his feet and takes the jiggling tray out of her hands. "Just to close the door behind you, that's all," he answers gently.

She gives him that cribhouse smile again. Just for him. He turns his face away.

Elsa jerks her thumb in the direction of the back room. "What you got in there Joe, bootleg liquor?" she asks.

"Pianos on consignment. What do you think of that? These Cubans are mad for pianos."

The little girl walks trembling to a chair in the corner of the room and sits down looking as if she expected to be whipped.

For a moment no one can find anything to say.

"Too bad we have to start out with a norther." Ro finds himself beginning to make conversation.

"Won't last more than a day or two," says Joe Herkimer. "Never knew it to fail when you came down here to try to get warm. How long are you plannin' to stay, Roland?"

Ro stammers that it depends on a number of things.

"It'll take me a while to get hold of these boys." Joe Herkimer looks him confidentially in the eye. "These flyers, they only sober up once a week when their money runs out."

"What's the story?"

"Arms runnin' . . . revolution in a neighborin' republic. It's the same old stuff but now it's got wings. The guys on the team sure are characters. It's the characters make it good. There are special angles too . . . Reds. Ever heard of the Caribbean Legion?"

Ro nods. Inside he is coming to life. He is forgetting his headache, his embarrassment, his awkwardness about Elsa. This guy has a name in the sports world, he's thinking, even if he is an old reprobate. Maybe he does have a story. Ro is imagining an interested letter from the text editor, a check in the mail, funds by cable.

"I'll have to cable New York," he says in a businesslike tone.

"Telegrams leak," says Joe Herkimer. "There's serious dough involved. If certain guys get tipped off they'll see to it that the boys clam up."

"I've got to know what the story is first."

"I'll tell it and you write it and we split fifty fifty. What do you say?"

There's a look of brotherly candor in Joe Herkimer's blue eyes.

Ro doesn't answer. His head is throbbing again.

Elsa puts her cup down and, still munching on a piece of roll, rises to her feet. "Muchas gracias," she says looking down into Chiquita's startled face with a friendly smile. "We want to go to see the nonobjective painter Pinillo. He goes out about noon."

"He won't go out today, not unless you take him . . . Hasn't anythin' to go out with," Joe Herkimer says with his wheezy laugh. "She'll try to get him to take you out to see the voodoo rites," he turns to Ro. "That's a lot of horsefeathers."

Ro's mind has dropped into misty contemplation again. He can hardly hear what the man is saying. He has to force himself to say something. "We just got here. We're just roaming around the town."

He gives a vague wave of his hand. His arm feels much too long. He has a feeling the hand is going to fly away all by itself. "I'll need a little time to think about this proposition, that is . . . after I know what it is." He laughs uneasily.

Joe Herkimer unbends his legs. He looks different standing up. His shoulders are square for his age. He walks on his toes. He steps toward Ro swinging his arms a little, like a prizefighter coming out of his corner, and puts his face close to Ro's to whisper: "I'll meet you half way. I'll put it up to the boys an' see if I can't get 'em to confer with us some place." His voice is hoarse.

Ro backs away from the old man's foul breath.

"How about the Cayo Hueso?"

"Okeydoke . . . Nobody's obligated to anybody for anything until you've heard the proposition."

"Right," says Ro. "Thanks for the coffee."

Elsa has already disappeared down the hall. As Ro follows, he catches a glimpse of Joe Herkimer reaching out a tremulous hand towards Chiquita.

The sight makes him sick at his stomach. There's a spinning sensation in his head.

Outside on the sidewalk he takes a deep breath of the salty wind. The nausea passes off. He has to hurry to catch up with Elsa. His step is firm now. His feet feel lighter.

"It would be fun," he begins breathlessly, "to stumble on an amusing story." He skips to get into step with her. "Latin American stories are notoriously hard to sell . . . This one might be good . . . I could use a little folding money. We could rent a car and really enjoy the island."

"I thought celebrities were always rolling in jack," she says in her teasing tone.

"You'll learn different . . . On this trip I'm taking a calculated risk."

Ro tries to put some spunk in his voice.

"Pinillo only charges fifty bucks for a drawing," she starts to whine like a spoiled child. "Gov wouldn't buy me one. Couldn't make up his mind which. He never would do anything I wanted."

"I could go that much, but you might as well know that when this spree's over, it'll be nip and tuck."

Elsa hooked her arm in his.

"I might like you better if you were broke," she tells him. "I'm more used to guys being broke . . . Isn't that an awful way to be?"

They turn the corner of the gray battered building. Under the broken glass of the fanlight overhead they make their way into a lobby ornamented with marble pilasters. A tattered kite is tangled in the wreckage of a bronze chandelier that hangs from the peeling ceiling. The cracked pavings underfoot are grimed as if they haven't been washed in a dozen years. Flies swarm round a sour-smelling milkcan in one corner. Beside a bag of spilt char-coal two tiny Negro boys are struggling for a ball.

"What does this remind you of?" Elsa asks with a yel-low gleam in her eyes.

"Park Avenue after a bombing?"

"Right," she answers. "I was going to say Park Avenue after the revolution."

The elevator has been stripped to a bare cage. It is crowded with stumpy men who have the look of being out of work, with old women with shawls over their heads bringing home net bags from market, with barefooted chil-dren. They all grumble about how long they have to wait for the operator.

When the operator finally comes limping down the hall he's a whitehaired old Negro with a club foot and a digni-fied manner. It takes him an age to pull the illoiled gate to and to get the lever in the right place to start. The thing moves upwards in a series of jerks. The brown infant in one woman's arms begins to howl. Elsa leans up against Ro. "Oh God suppose it crashes," she whispers.

"When we go down we'll walk," Ro whispers back with his lips against her ear. She doesn't draw away. He gives her ear a little hasty kiss.

At the top they are let out into a long dark hall that smells of laundry boiling and frying fish and brokendown toilets. There's only one dangling bulb at the far end for light because the fixtures have all been torn off the walls.

"Now let's see if I can find the right door," says Elsa compressing her lips. "Isn't this something?"

Walking slowly along they catch glimpses through doors ajar of bedclothes hung out to air, open wardrobes with starred mirrors, chromos of the Virgin with candles in front of them, oddlooking saints in painted niches, paper decorations in watermelon pink festooned from a ceiling.

"Ñañigo," whispers Elsa in an awed tone. "The place is full of ñañigo."

"Bedbugs too I bet," says Ro. "It's a settlement-house worker's nightmare."

"At least it's real." Elsa's scornful tone puts him in his place.

With a look of saying eeny, meeny, miney, mo, to herself she finally picks a door and knocks.

Not a sound.

"Don't tell me he's not in." She knocks again.

After a long time the doorknob turns. The door slowly opens until the head of a sallow young woman with frowsty short hair all on end is thrust in their faces. She's squinting to see who they are in the dim light.

"The nonobjective painter Pinillo," Elsa asks hesitantly.

"Americanos," says the young woman with some faint trace of approval. She pulls the door open for them.

They step into a large bare well lighted room with walls and ceiling of cracked plaster gray with age.

The young woman vanishes behind a screen painted in yellow with black exclamation marks on it that cuts off one corner. As they look about them they hear feet shuffling and a rapid exchange of whispers behind the screen.

The only furniture is an unmade brass bed and a scarred table where the head and backbone of a boiled fish, precariously balanced on a pile of dirty plates, hobnobs with pots of gouache and smeary tubes of paint. There's an easel beside the window. Unframed canvases lean in stacks with their faces to all the walls. A pair of men's socks and a torn brassière dangle from the head of the bed. Under them an ocarina nests in the midst of a dented pillow.

"Montmartre," whispers Ro, trying to get a smile out of Elsa.

"Nonobjective," is all she will say. "His painting is entirely nonobjective."

They wait.

Ro has stepped unsteadily to the window and is looking out at a flock of pigeons tumbling out of the scud that hurries overhead. His head is full of a scurry of torn thoughts. How did he ever get himself into such a predicament?

The boom of a man's voice behind him breaks into his reveries. "Elsa la bienvenida."

Ro turns and finds himself looking into the sharp black eyes of a slender tobaccocolored man of almost any age. A sharply cut aquiline nose divides his oval face into two unequal segments. Under it bristles a black mustache. The full red lips have an illtempered curl to them. He stares Ro in the face for some time without smiling. "Tu papa?" he finally asks Elsa in a scornful tone.

"Talk American," says Elsa. "Pinillo you know you can talk American perfectly well . . . And besides, he knows Spanish as well as you do. He's Roland Lancaster, the wellknown writer and journalist."

As if reluctantly Pinillo thrusts out two fingers of a tobaccocolored hand. When Ro presses them they lie cold and limp in his palm.

"I know well," says Pinillo. "A famous propagandist for Yankee imperialism."

He arches one black eyebrow and gives Ro a disdainful smile.

"What do you do 'ere, my friend? No good for the artists and workers of the Antilles, it is certain. Who knows? Even in America there are honorable men. Perhaps when you have seen my paintings you will write an article to correct the false impression given by your critics."

He makes a fluttering motion with his fingers in front of his face as if brushing off a fly. "Lack of education. Lack of comprehension," he is declaiming.

"But that's what we came for, Pinillo." Elsa can't wait to interrupt. "I want to show him your pictures. Show him the one you did of me."

"I do not do pictures of anybody," Pinillo hisses. His face twists into a sneer. "That is the delusion of the ignorant. My pictures are the expression graphic of the reality."

Abruptly his features lose their spiteful grimace. He throws back his head and stands staring at Elsa with his shoulders squared.

"Qué belleza!" he cries out. "Lolita," he calls over his shoulder in Spanish, "look how pretty the girl is."

The frowsty girl dutifully sticks her head out from behind the screen. She has been washing and is still scrubbing at her face with a towel.

"The hair is an enchantment," she agrees.

Pinillo turns to Ro with an almost agreeable expression on his face: "I hate your inculture, your 'Ollywood, your commerciality, your materialism . . . but I 'ave to admit 'ow beautiful are your women . . . I am not like my countrymen," he goes on. He hunches his shoulders and rubs his hands together and assumes an obsequious expression . . . "Yes sir, at your service sir, quite all right sir." He makes a series of oily little bows. "Eet ees not shocking my frankness?"

"It's wonderful," cries Elsa. "Don't you think so Ro? It's good for us to be told the truth."

Ro doesn't have a chance to reply.

Pinillo is already setting up his pictures one by one on the easel for them to look at. He goes on talking all the time, only pausing enough now and then to let Elsa emit an Oh or an Ah. He talks in a loud didactic tone as if lecturing in a large hall. He's explaining that he leaves the image to the photographers and the advertisers of frozen foods, the painters of hams and strawberry cakes. The image is a bourgeois convention. The artist has to be free to express reality like a workingman swinging a pick. Motion. The instantaneous flash. The sublimation of existentialist reality. Every time he says the word reality his face takes on a ferocious expression and he brings his fist down whack in the palm of his hand.

Elsa is nudging Ro. "That's the one," she whispers.

"Let's see that one again," Ro ventures in a shaky voice. His head aches worse than ever, there are spots before his eyes that mingle with the blurs and shadings and smudged cryptograms on the canvases before him.

"For Elsa," Pinillo cries out. "See what a good memory I 'ave. The poor Meester 'Aines 'ee could not make up 'is mind. It is not Elsa but eet is inspired by the enigma of Elsa."

"Gov worried himself sick about it," mutters Elsa.

"Poor Meester 'Aines 'ee wanted to understand but 'ee lacked the instruction."

Elsa and Pinillo are both looking at Ro in a threatening sort of way as if daring him not to understand.

"How much is it?" Ro stammers.

Pinillo shrugs his shoulders. His thick lips take on a disdainful curl. "To put a price on a work of art is like a slap in the face of the artist," he splutters. "Eet is impossible to explain to the American businessman that art 'as no value." He turns to Ro with the patient condescending expression of a teacher explaining an equation to a backward schoolboy: "It is not possible to put a price on the ultimate reality."

He begins to talk so fast he splutters: Today zero, tomorrow ten thousand dollars . . . His words become a torrent. On this island art is a disaster. The critics are imbeciles. He spits on the Cuban painters. Slaves of Yankee commercialism. In New York there is money but no taste. In Mexico there is taste but no money. In Paris at least an artist can die of hunger with dignity. The month that comes he will go back to Paris, Paris of the artist and the proletarian, Paris on fire with the red banners of workers demonstrating in the streets. Paris will understand. After the next salon the value of his painting will be established. A price now is merely nominal, an accommodation for a friend. A couple of hundred, what did he know?

"But Pinillo last year you told Gov we could have it for fifty." Elsa makes her eyes very round.

"What does it matter? I 'ave no memory for figures." Pinillo flushes and brushes at his mustache with his hand. "Fifty, a hundred, a thousand, what difference does it make? I shall write on it 'Homage à une femme d'ésprit,'" he adds, compressing his lips.

"Pinillo," Elsa breaks in, "I want you to take us over to Guanabacóa, you know where I mean . . . I want to go today."

Pinillo arches his black brows. " 'Ee would not understand . . . It is not the proper time. There will be nothing."

"Yes he would. I want him to see the real Cuba."

Ro is pulling himself out of the painful mist of his reverie. He has lost touch with what they are talking about.

"Suppose we try to eat some lunch," he interrupts in a boisterous voice. "Won't you join us, Pinillo? And the young lady."

At the same time just to show he's not a piker, he pulls the wad of bills out of his back pocket and peels off a fifty. As he does so he catches a gleam in Pinillo's eye, the instantaneous sharp glance of a pokerplayer estimating how much there is in the kitty. Pinillo's black eyes bore through the wad of bills.

Ro, suddenly wide awake, finds himself wishing he hadn't flashed his roll like that. Won't you ever learn? he scolds himself. At the same time his fingers are hurriedly fastening the button on his back pocket.

Meanwhile the young woman has popped out from behind the screen again and has begun to wrap the picture up in tissue paper with the competent movements of an experienced salesgirl. Pinillo watches her with a frown. The deft way she tucks in the ends of the paper seems to annoy him.

"She is engaged. She cannot come," he says.

The young woman makes a small face and slinks out of sight.

"We can leave the picture at the hotel on the way to the ferryboat," Elsa chirrups. "How about the restaurant on the docks you took us all to last year?"

"Nothing but American tourists," groans Pinillo. "Their vulgarity cuts the appetite but no matter."

Ro has picked his panama off the chair and is brushing the smudges of dust off the brim.

"I'll stop at the cable office on the way," he tells Elsa.

As Pinillo makes ready to leave, smoothing the wrinkles out of his light belted jacket with much clearing of his throat, the girl runs out from behind the screen to hand him his dark blue beret. He takes it out of her hand without looking at her.

" 'Ere the poverty is an art," Pinillo begins to talk as they walk down the hall. "Dying of 'unger like getting rich 'as its especial technique."

They are walking down the reeking stairs. "Meester Yankee Moneybags think 'ee was building a fashionable apartment 'ouse for people of means, but 'ere we 'ave dedicated it to a releegion, the releegion of the misery."

"At least the rooms have light and air," Ro finds himself remonstrating as if he accepted the fact that it is all his fault.

"It shocks you?" Pinillo's tone is exultant. "Those who conform to the materialism of the rich are shocked by the materialism of the poor . . . 'ere I live as in a country village. Nobody cares who I am, another poor devil like the rest. It is a lesson in proletarian 'umility. See?"

He points to the hollow place under a turn in the stairs where a skinny little girl in a torn pinafore with great blue circles under her eyes is encouraging a naked yellow baby to deposit a small turd.

"We live in a state of nature," he turns to Ro with a jeering laugh. "The Garden of Eden, eh?"

Elsa hasn't noticed. "Ñañigo," she's saying, "their religion is ñañigo."

Once outside, when they manage to get a cruising taxicab to stop for them, it's Pinillo, leaning back in the seat, who gives the addresses in a sharp barking voice.

The cable office first.

Ro hates to leave Elsa in the cab with Pinillo but he walks in alone.

The office is empty. A big light in the ceiling like a tired moon. Only one man on duty. Electric fans hum. Ro sits down at a typewriter with a couple of blanks. He feels at home in the cable office. He can renew the oldtime pleasure in filing a story. As he slips a carbon between the two long blanks and fits them into the typewriter all the helterskelter painful edges of his thoughts straighten out as if a soft brush had passed over them. His head is clear. He feels himself for the first time that day.

Memories surge up in him of other cable offices, the sugar planter's villa at San Miguel on Luzon, the office downstairs under the Bourse in Paris that was near so many good restaurants, the dim light and the felt curtains and the quaking hands of the censors in the Telefonica in Madrid where Franco's shells furnished the punctuation. Constantinople, Panama, the office off Trafalgar Square in London. There were always friends with him in those days; Mortimer, George Elbert, worried Waring in his idiotic eyeshade, Dick Turbeville with his passion for secondhand bookstores, Joe Grainger explaining that just today he had to have an early drink. How is it that nobody has any friends any more?

He starts to type the address. Sid Baker isn't exactly a friend, but he's friendly. He won't be in the office. He'll give it more attention right at his home in Westport.

Chance to uncover highly colored Caribbean yarn with startling implications in view of our declining prestige in Latin America.

Corny but it wouldn't tip anybody off down here. He suggests expenses and contact with a photographer.

After he has left the cable with the operator and paid—gone are the days when he had a home office to charge cables to—he lingers staring down at the ads under the glass of the counter. He's loath to leave. For an instant he thinks of starting a conversation with the operator.

Elsa's my business today, he reminds himself with a start. He mustn't let her get cross and hungry. He mustn't leave her alone with Pinillo. It was those chance moments of neglect that had started all the trouble stirring in Grace's sweet little head.

He's been such an egotistical bastard. Too late now to take any chances. His mouth puckers ruefully as he remembers the days when they were all tagging after him. He thinks of Emmaline Cowles, brilliant, boring, courageous, unattractive Emmaline. It is years too late to try patching things up with Emmaline. It's Elsa or nothing.

A man has to be patient with women. Like stalking a covey of birds. Beginnings are rocky sometimes but when you least expect it things smooth out. Tracking down this story will keep him busy, will give him a chance to show that the old hand hasn't lost its cunning. Lifting one heavy foot after the other, he forces himself to go back to the car.

Elsa and Pinillo are lounging back in the seat. They are smoking and chattering cheerfully together. It gives Ro a pang to see how well they are getting along.

"We thought you had died in there," her tone's teasing. "Pinillo's been saying New York's horrible and I've been saying it's wonderful . . . He says pernod is what we need for what ails us."

"The opinion of a medical friend," interrupts Pinillo laughing.

"I'm not going to drink anything much," Ro announces gruffly. "I never drink when I'm on a story."

Elsa starts to say something but suddenly closes her mouth tight. Her eyes are hard brown pebbles again.

At the hotel it's Ro's turn to talk to Pinillo while Elsa goes upstairs with her package.

Pinillo clears his throat and puts his hands on Ro's sleeve in a confidential way. "The cable?" he asks eagerly. "It was about my paintings, no? You will write an article? You are impressed?"

Ro's head feels as if it were stuffed with excelsior. "Art criticism," he answers vaguely, "isn't exactly in my line."

He hurries to change the subject. "I suppose it was in New York you learned to speak such good English."

"The most meeserable years of my life." Pinillo's mustache bristles. His face takes on a livid greenish cast. "Slavery," he splutters. There's actually froth on his lips. "I make a 'undred a week making pretty peectures for an advertising firm but a meelion would not be enough. Every day the insult, the 'oomiliation at the theatre, in the 'otel, in the restaurant. Because my skin is a little dark they treat me like a poor Negro . . . Except for the girls . . . You Americans don't like that, eh?" He gives Ro a scornful look. "With the girls I found no prejudice . . . magnificent." He kisses his fingers like a stage Frenchman.

"I'm sure you would find it different now," is all Ro can find to say.

"There are indignities," replies Pinillo in Spanish, "that a man of honor can never forgive."

Elsa is coming out the door. She'd changed to a bronze-colored dress that goes admirably with the color of her hair. She has put on a broadbrimmed straw hat though the day is still overcast. She certainly is a handsome girl. Pinillo jumps out and helps her gallantly into the car. There's an expression of jaunty good humor on his face.

The norther is keeping people under cover. They have the restaurant almost to themselves. They sit silent at first, looking out through a glass partition at the catspaws creeping across the glum harbor, and at the smacks and the battered schooners and the small rusteaten steamers swinging at their anchor lines under the low gray sky, until a few sips of pernod start Pinillo off talking again.

"So Elsa is interested in ñañigo, eh?" His eyes glitter like a snake's. "The American girls are intrigued by the folklore." He lays a finger on the side of his nose. "Especially when it wears a dark skin . . . Lancaster, I was telling you," he turns expansively to Ro, "the experience in New York . . . In Mexico there was an American folklorista, a lady of a certain age. In the villages, in the pulquerias she would throw herself at the poor Indians. Even the Indians had to be very drunk. They called her la gringa indecente . . . What a stupid people! You see I am honest." He gives Ro a black stare. "But 'ere the ñañigo is very secret," he continues in a more friendly and confidential tone. There's growing selfconfidence in his voice. He's puffing himself up like a toad. "What I showed Elsa last year was a program presented for the tourists." He takes a deep swig of his pernod. "Even the Cuban folklorists"—his eyes flash—"have never penetrated. But for me, because I am Pinillo and because I am dark," he draws his fingers affectionately down his cheek, "everything is possible." He pauses and puts his finger to his lips.

The waiter brings a platter of small steaks. Pinillo's eyes roam sharply critical over the meat for a moment. "Bueno," he says to the waiter in offhand approval.

"It is possible for me to introduce you to every mystery," he starts off again in his confidential whisper when the waiter moves out of earshot, "even to be present at the 'ooman sacrifice. This is only very far away, such as in distant parts of Oriente . . . 'ere it is always a . . ." he paused to search for the word. "Lancaster como se dice un gallo?"

"A rooster," says Ro.

"Why not say cock and be done with it?" Elsa says with a snarl in her voice that makes Ro start as if she'd stuck a knife into him.

Pinillo raises his voice to cover her interruption. "A black rooster," he says severely. "They come with offerings of cornmeal and fruit and rum, sometimes in the afternoon like today, sometimes in the midnight . . ."

Ro's trying to listen but his attention flags. All he can think of is how jealous he is. He's taken a few suspicious sips of the pernod, but it seems only to make him more drowsy. Across the table he can see Elsa drawing on her cigarette with a look of utter abstraction in her eyes under the broadbrimmed hat as she stares into Pinillo's face. Fragments of what Pinillo says drone in Ro's ears through the mist that hems him in.

"Rum is a very important part of the religion. The orgy cannot begin without rum. Perhaps that is why they will never tell when the ceremony will begin. It is necessary to bring much rum. Then the drums begin and they dance.

Perhaps it is espontaneous. Always there is a bonfire. It is the espontaneous liberation of rhythm."

Elsa's shoulders sway the least little bit to some imagined rhumba rhythm. In his own ears Ro feels the remembered resonance of last night's lame halting drumbeat.

"They say the gods and spirits from the dark continent take possession of their bodies." All at once Pinillo's voice is clear in Ro's ears. "It is true. It is true they are completely out of themselves."

"That's what I want to be, just for once in my life," cries Elsa.

"It is certain that they suffer very strange personality changes," Pinillo's voice goes on exultantly. "They walk through the fire without pain. They become possessed of gigantic strength. 'Ere is the power of the priest who is also called the ñañigo. When the votaries have fallen into a certain trance he is able completely to transform their personality. A brave man will become a coward. A weak fellow will perform the most reckless deeds. A modest woman will perform indecent acts. A frigid woman will become libidinous."

Elsa sits staring at Pinillo across the table with her eyes round. She looks half hypnotized. Ro shakes off his drowsiness enough to reach for the menu and place it under her nose. No use trying to interest her in dessert. She won't take her eyes off Pinillo's face.

"Tell me . . . Paco Cortes? Is he a ñañigo?" she asks breathlessly.

"Paco Cortes is an artist. Every artist is ñañigo . . ." Pinillo pulls himself up until he sits very straight in his chair. "I, Pinillo," he taps himself with two fingers on his chest. "I am ñañigo." He looks from one to the other with his eyes rolling and his mustache bristling.

"When can we go? I want to see it all. Gov wouldn't let me stay."

"It is very difficult. It is forbidden by the police. It is even dangerous . . . They go completely out of their senses."

"I don't care. I want to see it."

"Perhaps through my eenfluence . . ." Pinillo starts hastily cutting up and swallowing great hunks of the steak. He has been talking too fast to eat. "Perhaps it is not possible . . . It will cost money," he says with a glance at Ro as he chews. In an instant he has cleaned his plate.

"Why can't we go to the place we went before," Elsa pleads. "Come on, be a sport Pinillo. We bought one of your pictures."

"Leandro?" Pinillo frowns. "Perhaps but you must do what I say . . . You must not be Americans. I will say Germans, French, anything. You must leave everything in my 'ands. Perhaps with my eenfluence . . ."

Elsa will hardly let them finish their coffee and the brandies Pinillo requests before she's on her feet. While Ro pays the bill, she hurries Pinillo down the steps to the antique motor launch that serves as a ferry. To join them on the bench in the cabin Ro has to grope his way past a large Cuban family all dressed up for an outing, a stout little man and his stout wife and three little fat children in starched frills. The woman carries a pudgy little white dog wrapped in newspaper so that only his head sticks out.

"What on earth?" Ro's laughing as he sits down beside Elsa.

"You see?" Pinillo leans across her in a familiar way to whisper in Ro's ear. "You have taught us the 'eepocracy. Dogs is forbidden. They wrap him up and take him as a package. The inspector closes his eyes."

The launch is crossing the harbor in the north wind. Short waves curl over the rail. Halfway across, Pinillo points through the splattered window at a red buoy beyond two anchored schooners rolling in the chop.

"See," he hisses indignantly in Ro's ear. " 'Ere is where you sank your battleship Maine . . . The beginning of all our troubles."

"What's that?" asks Elsa. When she gets to her feet a lurch of the launch throws her against Pinillo. She puts her arm round his shoulders to steady herself. "Why it's a little pig."

They all point at the small black bobbing shape.

"Drowned," cackles Pinillo, "like the Americans on the Maine."

Ro jumps up and grabs Elsa's other arm with his left hand. His right hand makes a fist in his pocket. For an instant he sees himself swinging on Pinillo, sees the blows given and taken, the scuttle of the people on the launch, the explanation in Spanish at the police post in Regla.

"Look," Pinillo cries out. He points with a crooked little finger at a jibshaped fin that cuts through the waves near the little bloated black pig. As Ro looks the fin vanishes. The dead pig is drawn gently under the water.

Meanwhile the Cuban family on the opposite bench have huddled together like birds at the sight of a hawk. "Tiburón," they keep saying. The children whimper. The little dog wriggles inside his newspaper.

"You don't have to hold onto me," Elsa's whispering spitefully to Ro. "I'm not going to fall overboard."

She yanks her arm away.

Pinillo is still pointing at the spot where the pig disappeared.

"A shark, he is beautiful. He is the streetcleaner of the harbor . . . Look. We will see him again. No. Too bad."

Ro is expecting a gush of blood to the spot, but already it's out of sight. The launch has veered round an anchored barquentine. The engineer is slowing for the pier.

"That was quite a ride," says Elsa as they step out on the wooden planks of the pier on the other side of the harbor. "Ugh that shark . . . I think it calls for a brandy."

Pinillo orders the brandies at the small standup bar across the street from the landing. Then he orders a bottle of rum and a couple of dozen cigars to take out. He takes the precaution of having the barman pull the cork on the bottle. He's assuming the bustling air of a man in charge of an expedition.

After the electric train has left, carrying off the stout Cubans and their frilly children all still chattering about the tiburón and the little fat dog duly unwrapped from his newspaper, the street in front of the ferry landing is deserted, Pinillo goes on talking to Elsa in a low voice about midnight rites. Ro has long since lost track of what Pinillo is saying. He stands a little off by himself trying to drink the foultasting brandy, looking up at the lugubrious peeling stucco of the housefronts that face the harbor under the low dun sky. The meal has made him sleepy. All he wants is to roll up in a corner somewhere to go to sleep.

When Elsa nudges him he obediently pays for the brandies and the rum and the cigars. They have to run to catch a solitary bus that's preparing to leave from the next corner with a great roaring of the motor and clouds of blue smoke from the exhaust. They are the only passengers.

When Pinillo makes a point of paying their bus fare, Ro feels again like hitting him in the face. He clenches his fists impotently in the pockets of his light jacket.

The little bus heaves and tosses. All its loose nuts and

bolts rattle over the uneven pavement of a long thoroughfare between deserted arcades. Dust rises behind it.

Elsa's hand has clutched Ro's sleeve. She puts her mouth to his ear. It makes him feel better that she's talking to him again. "I hate guaguas," she whispers in a hiss. "Now I'm really scared."

"With me," Pinillo raises his voice to be heard above the clatter, "there is nothing to fear."

All at once he frowns and lurches forward to ask the driver a question. The bus comes to a sudden stop that throws them all off their balance. As soon as they climb out it rumbles off leaving them choking in the smoke of its exhaust.

The corner has a lonesome look. Pinillo points up a hill and leads the way with Elsa on his arm. Ro tags sullenly behind carrying the rum and cigars. They climb the steep sloping street between battened up houses. Not a dog stirs. No face looks out through the barred windows. The houses look to Ro as if people had shuttered themselves up in them against some plague and died there.

At the top of the stony slope Pinillo stops before a blue door in a crumbling wall. He's out of breath. With eyes popping with anxiety he studies the three tin numbers, tacked at odd angles on the door, that spell out 101. He crosses himself quickly and then knocks. When there's no answer he pushes cautiously on the door.

The door swings open.

Elsa and Ro follow him into the littered courtyard of a fallendown house which opens on a grassy open space at the brow of the hill. Across a low stone wall they see the jumbled cubes and parallelograms of houses on the next hill piled against the silvery streak of the harbor, and the domes and the great arcaded buildings of Havana beyond standing up in amber light against indigo smudges of rain. The wind blows hard in their faces.

Elsa's teeth are chattering. Ro tries to put his arm around her but she shakes him off. "It's cold up here," she exclaims.

Pinillo is walking towards a small frame house with a highpitched roof set slightly askew in the middle of the open space. He takes small cautious steps as if he expected a mine to go off under his feet. The door and tall windows are shuttered tight.

Pinillo stops beside the door and points mysteriously to a spreading figbush. Little strips of cloth flutter from the branches. The great scalloped leaves swaying in the wind are ragged and split as if people have been tearing them off.

Elsa lets out a cry when a sudden clucking rises from under their feet. They have startled a couple of dishevelled hens that are pecking among the litter of cigarette butts, broken pottery, fragments of bread, fishbones and torn papers trodden down into the dry grass.

"This is the place," whispers Pinillo. He knocks gently on the shuttered door. Pinillo suddenly looks very small against the house on the hilltop in the buffeting wind under the scudding sky. "Señor Leandro," he calls in a weak pleading voice.

After a long time the shutters shake. Hands are fumbling with the latch on the inside. The shutters are pushed open into their faces revealing a woolyhaired old Negro man in a white turtleneck sweater and grimy white pants.

He stands looking at them sleepily without any expression of greeting on his face. His skin is a light lavender gray color. There are many warts among the wrinkles of his face. His heavylidded eyes are half closed. It's obvious that he's been waked up out of a sound sleep. He folds his arms to look them over more at his leisure.

"Leandro, thou knowest me?" asks Pinillo in rapid Spanish. "Pinillo, the painter Pinillo . . . These are my friends . . . El Señor Leandro,"—he makes a flourish with his hand—"á sus ordenes."

The faint flicker of an eyelid may or may not indicate recognition. Yawning the old man backs away from the door.

"With your permission," asks Pinillo. Obsequiously he ushers Ro and Elsa into a bare dusty room lit only by an occasional crack in the shutter.

As Ro's eyes become accustomed to the dusk he begins to make out chromos of saints on the walls and a cube of some plastercovered material that might be an altar in the middle of the floor. The tiles underfoot are littered with chicken feathers.

Pinillo holds the old man by the hand. He's talking so fast in such a low wheedling tone that Ro can't follow what he's saying. As Pinillo talks the old man backs away from him until he backs into the altar. He sits up on the edge of it looking down drowsily at the big gray toes of his splay feet. He is yawning as if he would burst.

Still grasping the old man's hand, Pinillo beckons to Ro. Ro advances obediently holding out the bottle of rum and the bag of cigars.

Pinillo takes the bottle and carefully pulls the cork. With a ceremonious bow he hands the bottle to the old man. Señor Leandro holds it up to eye level to study the label. Then he wipes his mouth off with his palm and throws back his head to take a good deep swig. "Bueno," he says and reverently places the bottle beside a bowl full of some kind of meal on the altar behind him.

Feeling like an acolyte, with an expression as obsequious as Pinillo's on his face, Ro presents the bag of cigars. Señor Leandro takes one, solemnly sniffs it, then bites off the end and spits it out. Pinillo is ready with a lighted match. Señor Leandro draws on the cigar and puffs out the smoke.

Through the smoke, now that his eyes are accustomed to the half light, Ro can see the glint of the old man's searching monkey eyes as he reaches back to set the paper bag beside the bottle.

"Well," Señor Leandro asks Pinillo, "what dost thou want?"

In the gray light flooding in through the door behind them Ro can follow the roll of yellow eyeballs as the black pinpoints of Leandro's pupils move from one face to the other.

Pinillo motions to Ro to move back. As Ro slouches out the door he can hear Elsa's whining whisper in Pinillo's ear. "Ask him what his charms are for girls who can't love. Ask him." She's yanking at Pinillo's sleeve. Ro catches the selfsatisfied look on Pinillo's face.

Again he imagines himself hauling his fist back and hitting him. Instead he turns his back and sits down on the doorstep.

He hasn't the strength. He's too drowsy. His legs are tired, his back aches, his head weighs him down. All he wants is to crawl off in a corner and sleep.

Ro sits on the doorstep hugging his knees. "For girls who can't love. For girls who can't love. For girls who can't love," Elsa's shrill squeaking spins like a calliope. Pinillo's, the old Negro's voices drone on in whirling singsong behind him. Their voices fade into a faraway whine.

A tiny instantaneous tatter of a dream has filled Ro's head . . . Ro is climbing out of a taxicab. He is arriving at an unfamiliar apartment house on a street that is strange to him. The taxi driver is helping him stow his incongruous gear in the elevator. The bushyhaired elevator man is asking him who he is. "Of course you must let me in. I'm Mrs. Lancaster's husband . . . back from the Southwest Pacific, Mrs. Lancaster's husband," he shouts angrily at the elevator man. The elevator man can't understand English very well. "There is no 'usband there," he keeps saying. He looks at Ro out of suspicious black beads of eyes set too close together. "She must be home by this time," Ro pleads with him. "She must be waiting for me." Reluctantly the elevator man opens the door with a passkey. He puffs terribly as he helps drag in the heavy duffle. Ro strides through rooms full of unfamiliar furniture. He can feel her presence. She must be there. Where can she have gone? The rooms are empty. In his dream he runs breathless after her along a deep street where the lamps glare like the unshaded lamps in the corridor of a jail. He can't remember her name. He can't remember what she looks like . . . His awakening is a wrench out of agony.

There is a confusion of angry voices in his ear. Señor Leandro is shouting, "You are equivocated!" Pinillo is expostulating. Elsa's hysterically shrieking, "Tell him I think he's wonderful. I want to be one of them."

As Ro stumbles to his feet, he catches a glimpse of the old man's angry pupils black and piercing in his bloodshot yellow eyeballs.

"Out!" Señor Leandro shouts as he pulls the shutters in on himself with a clatter.

The latch clicks on the inside.

"What a barbarity," Pinillo grumbles as they shamble through the blue door onto the street. " 'Ee denies 'ee 'as ever seen me. 'Ee says 'ee's just a poor watchman and we interrupted his sleep. 'Ee says 'ee is just the watchman. I know 'ee is Señor Leandro. What can I do? I offered 'im money. I offered 'im everything. 'Ee is suspeecious." Pinillo is out of breath. They are hurrying as if the dogs were after them. "Perhaps," pants Pinillo, " 'ee thinks Meester Lancaster is a policia."

Ro tries to take Elsa's arm. She pulls it away.

"You fouled it all up," she says spitefully. She looks ready to spit in Ro's face. "You foul everything up."

Their progress down the steep street is a rout. Ro is so angry he can't speak.

"Don't pout at me," she says.

Then her voice becomes whining and pathetic. "How are we ever going to get home? You ought to have had a cab meet us up here."

"There will be the guagua," puffs Pinillo. "There is always the guagua."

"But my feet! The stones hurt my feet."

They are hurrying down the street. Elsa pulls away from Ro like a spiteful child and fastens on to Pinillo's arm.

Pinillo shrugs his shoulders and gives Ro a look that says: Can I help it? Without slackening his speed he puts one arm around her to half lift her as she tiptoes painfully among the cobbles.

Now Elsa is walking in step with Pinillo with her hat tipped so that Ro shan't see her face.

Ro's throat is dry. He can't find a word. There is nothing to it but to trot along after them down the stony sloping street . . .

12

. . . It was from the same squat elevator man with bushy gray hair and eyes too close together who tried to keep me out of my own apartment the day I came home from the Southwest Pacific that we learned of the President's death. I had picked Grace up early because we were going to a cocktail party at the Warings'. Grace hadn't been to the office that day. Instead she had been at the Library of Congress looking up a special point for an address Roger was preparing. Roger never was satisfied with any of his speech writers. In the last years it always fell to Grace to root out references for him while he was making his final revision. Nobody else could find the quotes he wanted.

As I followed her into the elevator I was asking her

whether, if the right people were brought in to talk to the President, they mightn't get him to listen to Roger's thesis that we were carrying the unconditional surrender policy too far. Couldn't the President be made to understand the danger of upsetting the balance of power in the world? Grace was shaking her head. "Roger says he's stopped listening."

Neither of us had read a paper or heard a news broadcast since breakfast. I suppose I should have noticed that the elevator man had something on his mind. Grace said when we laughed over it afterwards that he was puffed up like a hoptoad in the spring with the importance of what he had to tell. Anyway he waited until he had opened the door for us on our floor. Then he clicked his heels together, pulled back his shoulders, drew in a gulp of air and announced: "Lady and gentleman, the President of the United States is dead." He looked at me eagerly as if he expected some suitable comment. "My God," was all I could say.

Instinctively Grace grabbed my hand. Her little gesture made me happy because ever since I'd been home from the Pacific theatres there had been a curious constraint between us. It wasn't that she hadn't been trying to make me comfortable. In fact she had overdone it a little. She had been treating me like a long lost relative, a very close relative, but all the time I had felt that most of her was with Roger Thurloe over in his office at the Department. It was nobody's fault. Their minds just had a way of working in unison. When I opened the front door with my latchkey she pulled away from me and hurried into the living room and stood in the center of the floor with her eyes closed as if she were dizzy. "Ro, what are we going to do now?"

When I suggested more coarsely than I really intended that maybe the President had been dead from the neck up for some time, she turned on me. "That's no way to talk," she said. "The elevator man," she added gently in the tone she would use explaining something to one of the boys. She looked at me with eyes swimming in blue. "You mustn't forget what the President means to people."

The boys weren't home from baseball practice yet. Grace laid their supper out for them before we started off to the Warings'. Poor guys, they often had cold suppers that spring. Grace and I both worked long hours and about the only relaxation we had was an occasional cocktail party. We explained to each other that for our work we had to know what people were talking about. What we weren't admitting even to ourselves was that we were a little afraid of being alone together.

The Warings were an awfully nice couple. Fred was a tall sandyhaired man who had been a Paris correspondent for years. Instead of giving him a cosmopolitan polish, his term abroad had made him more middlewestern than ever. You hardly ever saw him without a green eyeshade on his head. He had a disarming way of taking people on their own valuation of themselves. His wife Katrina came of a Russian emigré family. She too was tall and rangy. She had prematurely gray hair. She rejected everything European with loathing. She was one of those Americanized Russians who rather overdid calling a spade a spade.

There were mostly newspaper people at the Warings' that evening. Nobody from government except a few underlings. The Mortimer Prices had been expected but Gertrude Ann had called up to announce, dramatically —overdramatically Katrina Waring claimed—that they were too prostrated to go out. It was an odd gathering. People huddled up. Grace said it was like a henyard with a hawk in the sky. Nobody ate or drank much. People talked in low sad voices as if there were a corpse in the room. Nobody cared to make any prognostications about anything. There weren't even the usual arguments about whether to increase or to cut off our aid to the Russians.

Emmaline Cowles had me cornered most of the time I was there. Emmaline and I had known each other all our lives. We had been high school cronies back in Columbus. There was a time when we even planned to get married. As usual she lectured me for dribbling my life away in journalism. She wanted me to write permanent works for the library shelves.

Emmaline was a journalist herself. She wrote a column. She lectured. She had grown into a large untidy pedantic woman who smoked too many cigarettes and drank too many cocktails and told too many interminable yarns about English literary figures like Keats and Robert Burns and Walter Scott. She specialized in the romantics. Poor Emmaline had become a walking encyclopedia in the worst sense of the word, but I was fond of her and Grace was fond of her.

Grace was always sporting about other women, particularly if they were women of talent.

Nobody could deny that Emmaline had talent but since she had become a radio personality she'd gotten so that she never stopped broadcasting. As I sat beside her, while she talked on and on in those long wellworded overemphatic sentences of hers, I was remembering the big awkward eager pathetically warmhearted girl with a passion for scholarship I'd known in school. I couldn't help feeling a little twinge of conscience about Emmaline.

Grace rescued me. It was barely eight o'clock but people were already slinking off home. Most of us still had that look of whipped dogs we had when we came. We tried to get Emmaline to come home with us to supper but Joe Grainger had just appeared drunk as a grand duke and we discovered with some dismay that she was planning to go out on the town with him.

It was just as well that we didn't bring Emmaline along, because when we got back to the apartment there was Roger sitting in the kitchen eating cold pork with Chips and Louie.

They were laughing and talking and carrying on so all three of them about whether the Dodgers or the Yankees had the best team, that they didn't see us at first as we stood looking in the kitchen door. I couldn't help a chill constriction of envy when I saw how wholeheartedly the boys enjoyed Roger's company. It wasn't that way with me any more. Out alone, canoeing or fishing or something like that with Louie, we could still have a good time, but when Chips was there anything any of us said seemed to rub the others the wrong way. When the boys saw their mother and father walk in the kitchen they made no effort to disguise their chagrin. "Now you'll just talk politics," whined Louie. Chips' voice cracked as he shouted, "Now Roger won't show us how to throw that curve he was talking about."

"We won't talk politics," said Roger getting to his feet.

As soon as we were in the other room he told us hurriedly under his breath that he had just seen the Vice President sworn in at the White House. There was no expression on his face at all. He added that he was horribly hungry, he'd forgotten to eat lunch. Would we mind if he ate up some more of our supper? We chased the boys into their own room to do their home work and sat talking in the kitchen while Grace, who had pulled an apron over her party dress, fried us some chicken she had in the refrigerator. Roger ate with appetite. When I asked him what was going to happen now he brushed the question off with, "All the bats and owls will come back to roost. Unconditional surrender will be the first one . . . Do you know what I do when I can't sleep at night?"

"Are you still having trouble sleeping?" Grace interrupted. The concern in her voice gave me a pang.

Roger grinned. He seemed all at once in high spirits. "I'm thinking of giving the whole idea up . . . How wonderfully Shakespeare writes about sleep. I bet that poor bard didn't sleep very well either. You know I haven't read any Shakespeare since I was about Chips' age. The last few nights I've been reading him about the antique Romans. My, he certainly had a knack for those antique Romans. I know he's supposed to have cribbed it all from Plutarch but I don't care. I mean particularly *Julius Caesar* and *Anthony and Cleopatra* . . . Maybe it's because the times are a little alike . . . but they just seem wonderful to me."

He glanced down at his wristwatch. "My lord I'm late. I've got to get back to the office . . . Ro I sure do miss you walking over from Georgetown in the morning."

As we followed him with his coat and hat to the door he was saying, "Those quotations probably seemed hackneyed to you but I'm not an educated fellow. When I read them it's as if they had just come off the press. Take *The evil that men do lives after them; the good is oft interred with their bones*. I kept thinking of that all through the new President's cabinet meeting. Good night Grace, thanks for that material. I guess I'll have to tear the speech up and begin another . . . Now all bets are off."

We saw a great deal of Roger that summer. Hardly an evening passed without his dropping in for a moment's chat, often on the way to or coming home from some Administration function. As photographs in the newspapers reduced the death agonies of the European dictators to commonplaces of rotogravure, the total defeat of the hostile powers had become certain. "A matter of a few weeks," Roger told us. "But whose will be the victory?" he would ask frowning.

One night, when by playing up a light cold he had managed to get out of enough engagements to stay to supper, he explained to us laughing that our house was the only place where he could think out loud without being labelled for life as an appeaser or an isolationist or a Fascist . . . "Fool labels," he cried out. "Nobody seems to understand they don't mean a damn thing any more. There's a whole generation of New Dealers being ambushed by their own slogans."

He let himself drop into a chair. His face wrinkled up with fatigue. "These are times," he groaned, "when a man feels absolutely worthless."

Roger had insisted we eat in the kitchen. From the time when he was a small boy in Hartford, before his father struck it rich as a contractor during the first world war, he had remembered his mother's kitchen with its huge coal range and how his family used to eat breakfast there cold winter mornings before day. Ours was an apartment house kitchen and it didn't have a range, but Grace had somehow found time to fix it up with checked curtains and shelves to set a plantstand full of potted begonias in the window. Roger used to insist it gave him the cosy feeling his mother's kitchen had.

"We developed the skills we needed to fight the war, we did it pretty easily," he was saying musingly as we sat at the deal table over a spot of Scotch while Grace fried us another of her chickens—chicken wasn't rationed. We lived on chicken in those days. We had been telling over the miracle of production, the amphibious landings, the invention of the floating base, the prodigious solution of the problems of supply. "Out in Hawaii and in Guam and in the Philippines we did something more permanent, something fairly remarkable, something a little different from British empire building at its best."

He struck his fist in his open hand. "That was another

generation," he said, "those were people who believed hard. They believed in God, in freedom of conscience, in free institutions . . . Among the people I see I just don't find that kind of belief . . . Whenever I run up against a considered plan there's a Muscovite somewhere behind it and their plan is to take us to pieces and dump us in Greasy Creek."

"They can't be that good," began Grace.

"It's a question of producing the right abilities at the right time," Roger interrupted tensely. "Take the scrappy little guy in the White House. He means all right but he just doesn't have the education or the intelligence or the breadth of view . . . It's the mind of a precinct captain."

Grace swept between us with a platter of fried chicken and a bowl of salad.

"You two make me tired," she said as she laid out the supper things. "Can't you see? Just the fact that we three are sitting here puzzling about how the country's going to think its way out of this mess means that other people are puzzling about it too."

"But the great ally who wants to cut our throats," cried Roger. "He's got his plans all laid. All he has to do is carry out his blueprint for the future."

I caught up the phrase: blueprint for the future. "Could you find time to get up an article? I sure could get it published. A short book like Willkie's *One World* would be better."

Grace let out one of her comical shrieks. "Not too much like it."

We got to laughing over that.

He shook his head vigorously. "No no. Roland that's your job," he said. "I've got to be in there punching."

We had hardly cleaned our plates before Roger was on his feet.

"It's a delaying action I'm trying to fight . . . If I can

hold off complete disintegration long enough for the country to come to its senses. Every time I turn my head away something important is lost down the drain. Defensive action is like that. You've got to be on your toes every minute."

In spite of himself Roger was feeling better. He was getting back some of the lift of combat. As he stood there with his shoulders thrown back he had that look of almost comic determination on his face Grace used to say reminded her of the rabbit in Alice in Wonderland.

He turned just as he was about to bounce out the door. "Tell me about Metternich," he asked abruptly. "Wasn't it Metternich who stabilized things after the Napoleonic Wars? One of those Englishmen at dinner the other night was saying that what the world needed right now was a Metternich. Lord how I envy those fellows their reading, their general information. I don't know what I was doing all the time I was in college."

Grace and I both started to talk at once.

"No I haven't got the time now," he cut us off laughing. He spread both hands out in front of his face. "I wouldn't remember what you told me . . . Grace you be an angel and get me up a little synopsis on Metternich."

Grace got up her synopsis but Roger never found time to read it. Such a wild cataract of events poured through that summer that we none of us could keep abreast of them. The news was like a river when a logjam bursts in a spring freshet.

When Roger got ready to go abroad to join the President at Potsdam, Grace took two weeks vacation from the office. It was the first she'd had. We had saved up our gas coupons enough for a trip to Maine and back. The boys were in camp on one of the islands below Bath on the Kennebec. We were planning to find a summer boarding house nearby. I drove by Roger's office to pick her up.

When I went in the office the little thing was sitting there tidying up her desk with that demure look of head of the class in a girl's boarding school she sometimes wore. As we were about to leave the phone buzzed. Mr. Thurloe wanted to see us.

He looked desperately tired. "I wish I could go with you," he said. Sure sure he would take a vacation when he got back from this little jaunt, he had promised his sister Jane he would. "If we only had a plan," he said almost mechanically as if reciting a speech he had delivered many times. "If we only had the type of men capable of producing a plan, we still could put it over. Without a plan we are just driven helterskelter by events."

He sat there scratching the back of his head with a strange vacant expression as if he felt the gesture would somehow help him to conjure up the plan he needed. There was something monkeylike about his scratching. He looked so helpless sitting there at his empty neat shining top executive's desk that I felt myself blushing for him.

Grace hurried to break the constraint that had fallen upon us. As usual she tried to make us laugh. "I guess we are like the sorcerer's apprentice," she said. "We've summoned more spooks than we know how to deal with."

Roger stiffened. He clenched his hands on the desk in front of him and gave us each a quick searching stare. "The sorcerer's apprentice," he repeated numbly. "I guess that's it." He seemed to have no fight left in him.

Grace stood looking at him with such loving compassion in her wide blue eyes that I felt sharp jealousy go through me, a jab of pain like when you bite down on a raw nerve in a tooth.

The buzzer on his desk was sounding. That was all the time he had for us. He was flying to Germany next morning. Our scurry out of his office was like a thief's getaway. Going down in the elevator we stood apart from each other, wrapped in our separate misery.

That trip to Maine which we had both been so looking forward to proved a kind of nightmare. When we called up the camp we found that Louie had come down with acute tonsilitis and was in an infirmary in Bath. Chips was in hot water for breaking bounds and going into town without permission. The director asked us please to remove him before he got into worse mischief. Grace couldn't think about anything but the boys and what Roger was doing overseas.

We were more conscious of Roger than we would have been if he had come along with us. We had separate rooms at the boarding house because I needed a room alone to get up a rough draft of a sort of pamphlet I was doing on Roger's suggestion: *Blueprint for the Future*. When Grace and I were alone together we hardly spoke. When I went to her room at night Grace seemed always to find some excuse to send me back to my own bed.

I would lie there alone tossing with heavy thoughts. Had everything come to an end between us? Ought we to separate for a while? Should I stick things out the way they were? I loved her so. I couldn't decide anymore than I could decide about the catastrophic events that blared out of the newspaper headlines every morning. I kept remembering what Roger had said about being driven helterskelter by their flood. I had quite forgotten that to most people these events meant pleasurable victories.

The weather was delicious. We ate blueberry muffins and the finest kind of lobster and bathed on lovely beaches but we were abjectly miserable. It was with relief that we piled the boys into the car to drive home.

We had been invited to stop off at Roger's sister Jane's place on the way home. It was near Farmington Connecticut. We hadn't planned on having the boys with us, so in order not to overload the Yarboroughs with guests we put up at a tourist home in town. When we had gotten the boys settled and outfitted with supper money and movie money, we drove out to the Yarboroughs' beautiful old weathered clapboard house.

We found Jane and her husband sitting out on the terrace between the house and the river. Jane Yarborough was a lean dark thinfaced woman with something of her brother's look of having been a crack athlete in youth.

They jumped to their feet to meet us as we drove up.

"He's back," Jane was saying. "He's taking a shower . . . It's a relief to have you all here" . . . She was out of breath. I'm such a scared cat," she panted. "It's been a terrifying day."

"What happened?" Grace and I asked in unison.

"Haven't you got a radio in your car?" Edwin G. asked sarcastically. Edwin G. was a blustery redfaced overcheerful sixfooter as broad as a barn door, a lawyer with a reputation for shrewdness under his bluster. "Well if you had," he shouted, "you would know the war's over. We dropped some kind of double blockbuster on a Japanese city."

"An atomic bomb . . . a bomb that releases atomic energy . . . It seems to me absolutely horrible," cried Jane. "The place was wiped out in a flash, a hundred thousand innocent people."

Red in the face Edwin G. was scooping up our suitcases. "Hurry up and come out on the terrace," he called through the door of the guest room after he had closed it behind us. "You need a drink to steady your nerves."

Grace and I stood staring at each other.

"Remember Ro, how strangely he took it when I was kidding about the sorcerer's apprentice?" Grace said. "He knew all about it. That was why he looked so strange."

As soon as we stepped out on the terrace Edwin G. pressed drinks into our hands. "I'm going to rout out Roger," he muttered. "We asked some people to dinner before we knew Roger would be here and I'm afraid when they come he'll clam up on us . . . You know how he clams up."

When Roger came out of the house, followed by an alert young man with closecropped sandy hair in the uniform of a full colonel, he was far from clamming up. He introduced the young man approvingly as Lew Haskell. I had never seen Roger so talkative. He talked in a sharp staccato voice. He seemed in a fever of energy. His face was haggard. His eyes had sunken in his head.

He brushed off our exclamations about the atomic bomb with, "We know all about that, we've allowed for all that. The problem is to set things up so that we won't have to use one ever again."

He was walking back and forth on the flagstones talking as he walked. "It's not much worse than those thousand plane raids over Germany . . . We don't want to do that again either . . . not ever . . . That is what Lew and I are worried about. We've just come from Berlin."

He spat out the word as if it disgusted him.

He stopped in his tracks, shook himself like a wet dog and sat down on a small iron chair and stared in a puzzled way at the huge bumper of bourbon Edwin G. pressed into his hand. He took one taste and pushed it impatiently aside.

Lew Haskell wouldn't drink either. If we didn't mind, he said with a sidelong smile, he would smoke his pipe.

Roger and Lew Haskell talked alternately, Roger in machinegun bursts and Lew Haskell with a sharpshooter's sly sharp stinging quips. The disintegration of Europe was the most appalling thing they had ever imagined. The next most appalling was the disintegration of our own army.

" 'Lust liquor and loot are the soldiers' pay' is what they tell you when you try to expostulate with them. The French are . . . well they are just the French . . . what more could you say? The British are behaving as usual with a kind of unimaginative routine decency. The only people with a plan of action are the Russians. They use looting and murder and rape with a purpose. Beat 'em to a pulp before they have a chance to resist. They are carrying off everything movable. Worse than that they are carrying off people, technicians, scientists. They are looting the know-how of Western Europe. They have already got most of the guided missile plants. Lew here managed to shanghai a couple of experts before the sovietskis nabbed them."

"I brought 'em back in my own plane with their families so that they would be happy.

"No money in an unhappy expert. The sovietskis knew that. First they scare them to death and then they feed them off the fat of the land," murmured Lew Haskell.

"They are carrying off entire submarines, piece by piece, repair shops, toolmaking equipment, experimental laboratories. We hope they won't know how to put them together again but we can't be sure. Now what do you want submarines for except to sink our ships? Nobody else has any ships."

Roger's jaw clamped to when he saw his sister's guests were arriving.

Lew Haskell got in one more remark as we rose to our feet. "And our boys don't know any better than to help them," he said with his dry laugh. "They go to quite a lot of trouble to help them."

"I'm going to try to get Lew in to tell his story to the President," I heard Roger whisper hurriedly to Grace.

Grace tried to make him laugh. "Did Stalin really enjoy his piano playing?" she asked. "Tell me honestly."

Roger didn't answer. He shrugged and made his bulldog face and turned with a frozen smile to meet his sister's guests.

There were some insurance people from Hartford and a Yale professor who specialized in Slavonic languages and his wife with two such pretty daughters that Jane cried out oh if only her boys were home from Italy. There was a taciturn crackerbarrel philosopher kind of an elderly uncle of the Thurloes. Very late, just as dinner was being announced Emmaline and Joe Grainger turned up. He was driving her up to her place in New Hampshire. I thought thank heaven they're both sober.

Emmaline had dressed for the occasion in voluminous purple chiffon with big gold balls and spangles dangling from everywhere. She was more than ever the Pythoness. It was no time for small talk. Most of us felt as if we had had the wind knocked out of us. It was almost a relief to have Emmaline reel off a lecture about how this was a return to the age of Greek tragedy. Prometheus snatched fire. Once again man had stolen power from heaven. She read us quotations from Aeschylus she had jotted down to use in her broadcast later in the week off a little pad she carried in her gilt mesh handbag.

I couldn't find a word to say. I had little appetite for food and less for drink. From my seat at the table I looked out across the green river and the midsummer trees at the trim white shipshape beautifully proportioned houses of the early Connecticut settlers. Every detail stood out in sharp relief in the violet gloaming.

When Roger started talking again his words expressed my thought perfectly. He had been wanting to say something for some time. He hurriedly broke the silence when Emmaline stopped lecturing long enough to eat a slice of roast beef. He was saying that these days it always made him feel better to get a glimpse of the neat Connecticut towns. Of course he had been brought up in them, but he had never appreciated the plan of life they represented. The farmers who planned the houses and the carpenters who built them were conscious of the rectitude of their work. They were pitted against odds. They knew they were right. Their passionate religion would have made them better able to cope with the things we had to cope with. We were up against the problem of evil. They believed in sin. They knew what was right and what was wrong. They believed in heaven and they believed in hell. "I don't know about heaven," Roger cried out suddenly, "but since seeing Berlin I know there's hell . . . hell on earth."

I was unhappy enough to be in hell the next few weeks in Washington. Of course Roger never got his vacation. He was so busy I hardly ever saw him. That meant I hardly ever saw Grace. She would work all day in the office and then after hours she would go to the library or the archives to gather material for his testimony before a Congressional committee he was trying to convince of the need to slow up demobilization. When she got home she would be speechless with fatigue.

The couple of times she did sit up and chatter in her old cute way on the edge of the bed before we went to sleep it was Roger said this and Roger said that.

Often he sent me friendly messages. "Tell Ro to write something that will convince people war isn't a baseball game. 'All right' the American public is saying: 'we won, let's all go home.' "

In our home the boys were constantly at loose ends. They moped and sulked. I tried to get them interested in a course of reading. I tried to get them to take swimming lessons at the YMCA. I tried to get them interested in collecting stamps and making ship models, but all they would do was play jazz records and go to the movies. Then they would come home complaining how lousy the picture had been as if it were my fault. Most of the time they just sulked.

It was a relief to take off overseas. Picture Magazine had commissioned me to cover the Nuremburg Trials. I wanted to get a look at the rest of Europe for background before the prosecution of the Nazi leadership began.

An Army transport plane set me down outside of Paris in the dim russet October evening. The city was shabby and subdued and full of troops but as a background it was unchanged. It seemed so far out of the world of industrial plants and airfields and airplanes and quonsets I had been living in it hardly seemed real. More a sort of Fata Morgana. It was as if some time machine had set me back into the past century where the army jeeps and command cars and the American routines would have seemed incongruous inventions out of some story by Jules Verne.

There was no sign of war damage driving in. The Eiffel Tower was still there and the Trocadero and the gilt figures on the Czar Alexander's bridge and the Place de la Concorde so broadly open to the sky and the fluted columns of the Madeleine and the people sitting out at little tables on the boulevards.

As the twilight faded slowly into night it was more like driving past old steel engravings of the city than through the city itself. There were few lights and not many people. We occasionally passed a sort of rickshaw taxi built out of bicycle wheels or an oldfashioned car made grotesque by a mattresslike tank filled with illuminating gas strapped to the top.

The only street we crossed that showed any animation was the Champs-Elysées. There a welldressed crowd milled over the broad sidewalks. The sense of strangeness was enhanced by the full dresses and the great spiralled turbans the women were wearing. Some of them were towering stiff hats a little like the hats you see on the merveilleuses in prints of the Directoire period. The younger women seemed all to be on bicycles. They wore no stockings. Their shoes or sandals had thick wooden soles. Instead of turbans or hats they wore enormous masses of hair piled up in blond or auburn or black jet billows like the topsails of a fullrigged ship. This was the Paris fashion's way of meeting the challenge of the times.

The press was quartered in the Hotel Scribe near the Opera. I'd known the Scribe years ago as the hangout of English businessmen and German travelling salesmen. Fifteen years must have gone by since I had spent a night there but it had hardly changed at all. There was still the same smell of linen closets and waxed parquet floors and of lubricating oil from the old hydraulic elevator. It was odd to find them doling out American rations in the dining room.

After choking down some spam and a glass of villainous vinagery red wine I went out to find an American woman I knew who had stayed through the German occupation. Rosalind Parker was a Cleveland girl who was a crony of Emmaline Cowles'. She was a painter. She had lived in Paris for years on a small income that came to her from her father's estate. The first year of the war she wrote her friends that she couldn't afford to come home and that besides she liked it where she was. Emmaline would never have forgiven me if I hadn't looked her up.

I had known the city pretty well ever since the days of the Peace of Versailles but it wasn't easy finding the rue Gît-le-Coeur on the left bank in the dark. An oil lamp lit the stony vestibule of the towering old narrow dwelling. An old hag of a concièrge glared malevolently at me through a glass partition. Mme. Parkair lived au sixième. I was fumbling around out of breath in the dark on the top landing when an American voice called out in French from behind one of the doors to ask who was there. I shouted "Ro Lancaster" and after a great creaking of bolts and clanking of chains an ancient oak door swung open. Again I had the feeling of stepping back into the past, twenty years this time.

Rosalind Parker was a tall slender woman with a handsome mop of white hair. In the dimness of the candlelit studio I couldn't see that she had changed a bit since she and I and Emmaline had such a time going to the Ballet Russe together in the early twenties. She still dressed in simple colors with a frill of lace at the neck. The candle light played caressingly on the pictures I remembered, the early Braque, the charcoal sketch by Pasquin, a red white and blue Leger. Rosalind still had that way of searching your face inquisitively when she spoke to you as if searching for a clue to some mystery only you and she could understand. Her hand felt unusually light and thin in my hand when I shook it.

"I was expecting you," she said. "Emmaline wrote me."

As my eyes got accustomed to the light I could see that her face had broken into a myriad of tiny wrinkles. She was excessively thin; it was years since she had had a square meal.

I asked jocosely how it felt to be liberated. That depended, she said on whether you survived it. Her manner was dry and sarcastic. Under the Germans life had certain dangers, if you insisted on taking risks, such as hiding escaped prisoners and things like that, but everything was correct. You knew where you stood. Most of the people she frequented preferred it like that.

But hadn't the French wanted their freedom?

"Nobody ever asked them whether they wanted to be

liberated or not," Rosalind cried out passionately. Even I would have to admit that for the people of Normandy liberation came very high. Paris got off more cheaply. If it weren't for the resistance things wouldn't be too bad. The black market was all right. That was the sort of thing the French enjoyed. The resistance was scum, pure scum: she screwed her face up into an expression of patrician disgust. Spite work, shaving the heads of unfortunate women, looting where they could, shooting down men who had been real patriots . . . Look at Henri Cambronne, a man who had risked his life again and again during the occupation, a really honest patriot, they shot him three nights ago on the Boulevard Raspail. Why? Probably because he was a man the Communists found hard to manage. The only protection was to join the Communist Party. People were joining in droves for just that reason. She was thinking of joining herself. They protected their own.

"Haven't the Americans been any protection?" I asked in amazement.

She gave her head a toss and looked at me with flashing eyes. "Something that happened one night somewhat disenchanted me about the protection afforded by American troops," she said, "at least to a lone woman. I was coming home as usual down the narrow pitch dark part of the street where you turn in off the quay when I found myself in the middle of a bunch of American soldiers. Of course they were drunk. They wouldn't let me go. I spoke English to them. I explained that I was old enough to be the grandmother of every one of them. They wouldn't let me go. Their language was indescribably foul. They tore my dress. I finally got away by main force. They were so drunk I ran too fast for them . . . It was the most disagreeable experience I ever had in my life. I came of patriotic American stock. I was brought up to expect something of my fellow citizens. Scum," she spat out the word again.

It was late. When I got up to leave she begged me not to quote her. If I did she might find herself with her head shaved or shot to death on the quay some night. She just wanted me to know what the French were going through. It was a reign of terror. At least in the real Terror they gave their victims the show of a trial. As I left Rosalind Parker she made me feel that I was to blame for it along with the rest.

Walking back across a dark empty Paris only feebly lit along the main avenues, a Paris without effervescence, without traffic, without nocturnal strollers, I understood better the sense of strangeness I'd felt when I first entered the city. It was a city half strangled by fear.

Paris was abject but Vienna was in a still lower circle of hell.

I drove into Austria from Bavaria after visiting, as all the correspondents did, Hitler's villa at Berchtesgaden which seemed to me disappointingly like any other powerful man's villa.

When we first hit the Danube we found ourselves driving through a captured Hungarian division on its way home. They'd been given some old horses and wagons liberated from German farmers and turned loose. The river was jade green. The autumnal trees were almost chocolate color in the rain. The neglected fields were green with grass. The Hungarians, dressed in scraps from every uniform in Europe, jogged along with their feet on the tongues of the sagging wagons. Behind them jounced their women and their holloweyed children hunched under makeshift canvas covers amid a confusion of cradles and bedding and pots and pans. Their heads were tied up with torn red handkerchiefs. They were ragged. They were destitute, but there was a kind of defiant gypsy merriment about them. The war was over for them. Nobody was shouting orders in their ears any more. They were going home. Their cheerfulness was catching. For the first time since landing in Europe I felt less glum seeing their little twinkling campfires among the great beech trees of a ravine beneath us as the road wound up out of the Danube valley into a foothill country.

Across the Linz the Russian zone began. A few red flags fluttered in an empty village at the bridgehead. The rain had turned to sleet. We began to pass grimy soldiers with high slavic cheekbones driving narrow wooden carts. We passed a holloweyed officer with a red band on his cap bowling along in an ancient victoria with a yellow wicker body. Bundled up on the driver's seat sat a flatfaced izvozchik right out of Tchekov.

Where the road zigzagged up a pass into slushy snow we got tangled in a convoy of American lendlease trucks. The markings on them were in the Cyrillic alphabet. They were driven by excited young slavs who had a coltish look of having come straight out of the isba. They didn't seem to know how to drive. Their trucks were slithering all over the road. Every truck that was still running had a conkedout truck in tow. Up in the pass where the snow was deep the tows had jack-knifed in every direction across the road. The drivers in their long coats stood about helplessly in groups shaking their heads and thrashing their arms to keep warm.

The man driving our command car was a skinny young fellow with a hawk nose and a sharp gray eye who came from a small town in Missouri. He delighted in skidding his car through the deep snow round the ends of the stalled trucks. The Russians watched him wideeyed as he neatly cleared each new obstruction. "No use us buyin' them fellers trucks," he said with an Ozarks twang in his voice. "All they know how to do is wreck 'em."

At the bottom of the next valley we drove through a village, after being waved along by a sentry with a tommy-gun. In the Russian zone no local inhabitants showed their faces but we drove through a large group of Russian soldiers in high black boots standing around a handsome arch of fir boughs decorated with green and red paper festoons. Their flat slav faces amid the greenery, against a backdrop of broken down cottages banked with snowdrifts pitted yellow from the rain, made me think of a chorus from Khovanshchina or the fourth act of Boris. All that was missing was the beards. I was amazed to find myself so deep in Russia so soon.

Vienna gave an impression of utter desolation as we drove into it through the rainy night. Pyramids of rubble, ruined buildings drenched with rain. Shivering misery, a gray caved starvation look on every face.

The hotel taken over for the American press was a contrast to the desolation outside. There was steam heat. There were electric lights in the chandeliers of pink Venetian glass. Starched lace curtains hung in the tall windows. There was a smell of food cooking. The head-waiter with his dyed mustaches and his tailcoat who bowed with slightly ironic obsequiousness as you went into the dining room had just a hint of the look of a grand duke.

The first face I saw, surrounded by whiskeybottles and siphons of seltzer at the end of a long table, was George Elbert's. He had been in Vienna two days, already an old hand.

After we had exchanged our customary round of friendly abuse he asked me what I was covering.

"The Nuremburg trials."

"Hell's bells," he said glumly, "so am I."

"There'll be plenty of room for the press," I announced cheerfully. "The more the merrier."

"I don't know about that." There was something sour about his answer.

I was hungry after my long day's drive through the rain and the snow. The dinner was small but the cook had fried the spam up like wiener schnitzel with fairly good results. There was delicious fresh spinach and potato salad. For a wonder the bread was good.

While we ate George Elbert tried to talk me into going down to Yugoslavia to write up the partisans instead of going to Nuremburg. I would hate the courtroom scene, he said. One of the great old fighters of the Spanish Civil war had turned up to lead the Yugoslav partisans. Right now he was busy cleaning out collaborationists. There were collaborationists who had tried to masquerade as partisans. The damn fool British had backed some of them. It had made a bloody mess but this man Tito was a tough hombre. He'd shot 'em up so fast there weren't any collaborationists left for the British to back. "I hate these damn collaborationists, don't you?"

George Elbert was urging me to go right on down to Belgrade right away. Partisans were my kettle of fish. It had almost made him cry what I'd written about the partisans in the Philippines. The partisans were the only real story left in Europe. I couldn't help asking him why he hadn't stayed with it. "What the hell?" he said, "I wrote it . . . I write and I move on."

When we came out of the dining room a lighthaired American captain stepped smiling up to George Elbert. "Mr. Warner," he said, "I've got your Russian for you."

The captain was a State Department man who had been stationed in Moscow through the early part of the war and spoke considerable Russian. He'd been sent to Vienna to interpret for our commanding general. He was saying that we had better hurry before his Russian got the wind up and scrammed. "They are scared to death to be caught talking to an American."

"Come along Ro. He's a literary gent. He's more in your line than mine," shouted George Elbert.

We found the captain's Russian waiting in the little parlor decorated with English hunting prints of another small intact hotel around the corner. He was a short thick-chested man with crinkly light hair. He looked nervous as a witch. It turned out that he was a school teacher in private life. He lectured on American literature at some sort of normal school in the Ukraine. It was to satisfy his curiosity about American writers that he was risking the interview. He read English but he didn't care to speak it. The captain had to interpret. We had to tell him all we knew about Mark Twain and Jack London and Upton Sinclair and Sinclair Lewis and Theodore Dreiser.

How was it that, since American writers were so critical of American capitalism, they weren't all Communists? That was what he couldn't understand. Now the man who wrote *Uncle Tom's Cabin,* that was his favorite American book, he must be a Communist.

When we pointed out laughing that Harriet was a woman's name and that Mrs. Stowe had written the book nearly a hundred years ago, he looked at us out of his little closeset light gray eyes with all the suspicion of a Connecticut farmer beset by a bunch of bookmakers. We were not telling the truth. He shook his head sagely. He tapped his nose with a stubby forefinger. He understood. We were afraid. The F.B.I. might get us. He understood the capitalist repression. At least we couldn't deny that Dreiser was a Communist, or maybe a sympathizer; in Lenin's heartwarming words, a fellow traveller.

When we had to admit that none of us knew whether Dreiser was a Communist or not he jumped to his feet to leave. He waved his short arms indignantly. How could there be cultural relations between allies without frankness on both sides?

George Elbert soothed him down by declaiming that every redblooded American sympathized with the brave Russian people who had routed the Nazi armies. The captain sent for a flask of white wine. We drank to the brave defenders of Stalingrad.

We must explain something to him, the Ukrainian insisted, sitting down gingerly on the edge of his chair; if America claimed to be a democracy how could any American be so base as to sell his vote for two dollars to agents of Wall Street? In the Soviet Union voting was a sacred duty. Selling your vote would be unthinkable.

"Nobody would buy it," cried George Elbert slapping his knee. "It isn't worth anything."

The captain didn't translate that one. Instead we drank to the brave defenders of Leningrad.

The Ukrainian entered into a lengthy disquisition on the philosophy of voting in the Soviet Union. They didn't vote on opinions. Private opinions were a capitalist delusion. Policies were established by the Central Committee, but they did vote on qualifications. Who was the man or woman best equipped? The campaign going on at home right now for nominations to the All Russian Congress of Soviets was the liveliest he remembered. That was real democracy. American democracy was dollar democracy, false, set up to deceive the people. He beamed at us. He knew more about American democracy than we expected, now didn't he?

We drank to the brave defenders of Moscow.

The Ukrainian had run out of topics. The flask was empty. He rose to his feet, saluted without smiling and left us.

"And you say we can't get along with the Russians?"

George Elbert shouted at me after he'd gone—I hadn't said anything of the kind. . . . "It's easy as taking candy from a baby."

"Ever tried it?" asked the captain who had acted as our interpreter. "There's the grasping reflex you know."

During his long experience in the theatres of war George Elbert had acquired a gift for wangling transportation. We set out in a brand new Opel he had talked some car pool into assigning to him. As we crossed the Ring near the scorched and shattered stone filigree of St. Stephen's Cathedral, we heard a band playing. They were changing the guard at the Kommandatura. British troops were drawn up all spit and polish in front of the building. Down the gutted avenue came swinging a column of French Chasseurs led by a tricolor.

That meant that the British brass hat had finished his month's command of the inner city of Vienna and was ceding to a Frenchman. Then there would be a Russian and then an American, in rotation. It was a system of management which even George Elbert, who was all for making life difficult for the enemy, admitted to be hardly more practical than the arrangement by which Berlin and Vienna, the two bastions of Europe against invasion from the east, had been buried deep in zones of Soviet control. "The damn Russkis read history," was how George Elbert put it. "I guess our boys never did."

As our car drove on we saw a sight that amused us. There was an American GI perched on top of the extensible ladder of a red municipal fire engine in front of the Russian military headquarters. He was fixing the wiring on the strings of electric lights that festooned the oversized countenances of Lenin and Stalin that decorated its facade. He was hard at work. Undoubtedly he was doing a good job.

At the police post in the French zone of the outer city we found the inspector who was to show George Elbert the famous air raid shelter the German gauleiter had built for himself in the Wienerwald. This was a curlyhaired young man with the distraught air of a movie director on a bad day. He was desolated, he cried as he shook us warmly by the hand, he was in the throes of an international incident; would we come back in half an hour?

The police post was in an uproar. A pair of towheaded Austrian policemen were holding a young man with a heavy stony countenance against the counter which divided the public part of the office from the bureaucratic sanctuary within. Behind them milled a crowd of frayed and haggard Viennese bystanders. There were local plainclothes men with faces out of an oldfashioned Punch and Judy show. They were all talking German at once. Behind the counter a number of Frenchmen in various uniforms were talking in French and gesticulating round the sawed-off chesty figure of a Russian officer.

We recognized the officer at once as our Ukrainian school teacher. He was pouring forth a torrent of Russian; he was so much in earnest that he had tears in his eyes. In one hand he held some sort of an identification card which he shook from time to time in the faces of the Austrian police. He brandished the other hand aloft with the index finger pointing to the ceiling like Lenin in his statues. The gist of what he was saying seemed to be that the prisoner was a Soviet citizen. If he were to be arrested he must be arrested by his own police. We tried to attract the major's attention by smiling and waving but he looked right through us.

Meanwhile the police inspector had detailed an officer in an enormous blue beret to take us out for a cup of coffee while we waited for the termination of the incident.

"Qu'ils nous emmerdent ces russes," the Frenchman

exploded as we followed him down the unswept stairs. He explained that the prisoner was some kind of a Russian arrested for pillaging, but what kind? Who could differentiate between all the different kinds of Russians? A prisoner of war, a German deportee, a deserter from Vlassov's army, a Communist agent, what did he know? The documents were conflicting, the Russian didn't read itself easily. The life in Vienna was fatiguing. Fatigant, messieurs. Every day, every hour it was the same. A Russian was committing a rape. A Russian had knocked an old woman down in the street and was stealing her clothes. Two of his own detectives had been trussed up in a doorway and stripped to their drawers. Nobody's wristwatch was safe. If some poor Viennese managed to buy himself a bag of beans they would break into his apartment to steal it. When the Russians came in the working people thought they would be safe. They brought out red flags and plaster busts of Karl Marx. A lot of good it did them. The Russians told them they were too well off to be workers, they were bourgeois and must suffer like the rest. It's not funny to be made to stand on a chair at the point of a gun and see your wife raped before your eyes. "C'est fatigant, messieurs."

It had come on to rain again. The café had a look of having been closed up for years. The floors were deep in muddy grime. The springs were bursting through the stained red velvet upholstery of the benches. It seemed almost colder inside than in the icy downpour on the street. The waiter was very polite. A touch of the Hapsburg style. He brought our ersatz coffee on a neat white metal tray with fittings that in the old days had held sugar and cream. In the cream pitcher there was a little extra hot water. George Elbert and the Frenchman made horrible faces when they tasted the coffee. "What is it made of?" they cried almost in unison.

"That is our secret," said the waiter smiling.

When we got back to the police post we found the inspector standing in the center of the floor with both hands desperately clenched in his touseled hair. The Austrians had all thrown up their hands. Two Russian MPs were preparing to march off the prisoner. His face was stony as ever. His mouth was buttoned tight shut. Our friend the Ukrainian school teacher stood triumphantly speeding their departure. We said How do you do? He looked at us without a trace of recognition in his face. He stood with his index finger high above his head in that attitude of a statue of Lenin while he addressed himself to the baffled French and Austrian police. "A Soviet citizen."

"What will they do with the man?" we asked the French inspector. He shrugged. "Shoot him of course. That's all they can ever think of."

We never did get to see the air raid shelter. Somebody had stolen the key off the French police inspector's desk.

Berlin was the bottom. The ruin of the city was so immense that it took on some of the splendor of a natural phenomenon like the Grand Canyon.

I drove in past the hollow shells of the university buildings and the heaps that had been Friedrichstrasse and the empty spaces where a section of the wall of the famous old Hotel Adlon still stood. The Brandenburg gate was incongruously intact. Through it I had a glimpse of the gritty waste, punctuated by shattered statuary and stumps of trees, of what used to be the Tiergarten. Central Park in New York wouldn't have looked much different.

The GI who drove the car pointed out groups of furtive people with bundles under their arms scattered over an area that looked like an American city dump. That was the black market.

"A pack of cigarettes'll buy anythin' in the woild, from

a set of painted china dishes to a Leica camera. Four Luckies'll get you a goil," said the driver, who was obviously an urban type.

He added that he wasn't wasting his cigs, he was buyin' foinishin's for his mudder's home, shippin' 'em back t'rough de Post Exchange.

I asked him to wait for me a moment. Feeling like Dante in hell I walked among them. The only men and women I had ever seen so abject were the black market operators in Moscow. There I had seen the same harassed faces, the same satchels and bundles stuffed with the pathetic debris of a lost way of life. In their faces I read the full depth of defeat. They kept looking back uneasily over their shoulders as they went about their haggling and bartering. I kept filling in the void of their faces with the faces of American businessmen I knew. The Germans too had been brought up to consider trade and business a respectable way of life. A year ago they were honorable German burghers. Today they were criminals. "Ever think," I asked our GI driver, "what it would be like at home if something of the sort happened to us?"

"They ast for it," he said and sounded his claxon to make an old woman scuttle out of his path as he stepped on the gas.

Further on workmen with cables were pulling down broken walls of blocks of brick buildings. Big wellplanned apartment houses that might have been in Chicago or New York. Women were carrying buckets full of bricks out of the crumbling heaps. There were old women and young women, women who looked as if they were accustomed to labor and women who had never wielded a tool heavier than a needle in their lives. American women would not have looked much different. They rubbed the bricks together to clean them and stacked them at the edge of the street. The women were frowsty. Their clothes were dust-colored rags. Their faces were putty-colored with dust. The skin under their eyes was blue with fatigue. Their knuckles were chapped and bleeding. Suppose that happened to Grace? I asked myself. I kept searching their faces for a face like Grace's face among them.

The November day was raw with spats of sleety rain. The women had bundled themselves up in all the clothes they had to keep warm. There was a horrible shapelessness about their misery. "They like to do it," the GI driver assured me. "A heavy labor card means more eats . . . Greedy bitches." All through the ruins long strings of women were passing the heavy buckets of bricks from hand to hand.

I clawed my way out of Berlin like Christian fleeing the City of Destruction. The Russians had fenced their zone off so effectively you had to travel through half of Germany to get from Berlin to Nuremburg. Redeployment made travel impossibly tight on any kind of American transport. I managed to thumb a ride as far as Brunswick with a pinkfaced English schoolboy dressed up as an officer. "I know it's wrong," he told me, "but I found Berlin just topping . . . Think of using cigarettes for money . . . topping." He let his breath out in a long sigh.

We were both nervous till we'd cleared the Russian zone. "You never can tell what those Russians will do," my schoolboy had said as he slipped a clip into his automatic pistol just before we turned into the autobahn. "In case of a breakdown we have orders to defend the car till help comes."

In Brunswick I found a Yorkshireman about to drive off for Goettingen on an RAF lorry. In the old university town on the edge of the Hartz Mountains I got the impression that the defeated population was getting a better break from the British than from the other occupying armies.

The people on the streets looked better dressed and less frightened. There were lights. Stores were open; I even saw a string of sausages hanging in the window of a delicatessen.

The sardonic redbeaked Scot somewhat gone in liquor who was Town Major found me a bed at the British hostel. The Officers' Club was very collegiate. Conversation smacked of the Oxford Union. The young men I talked to were most of them working on the exchange of populations agreement. They said Russian agents were everywhere searching out opponents of the Stalin regime. "You ought to see our Sergeant Pavlov," one of them exclaimed. "What he calls war criminals are his quarry . . . We let him have a few if he can prove his case";—the Britisher laughed his high superior laugh—"but the beggar's greedy. He's particularly savage after Latvians and Ests. His teeth chatter like a bird dog's at the sight of a Baltic intellectual. You know how their teeth chatter when you show them a grouse they can't have. 'No Pavlov, you can't have that one', we say."

The young officers were all very civil but after they'd had a few drinks I could see they were having trouble concealing the bitter scorn they felt for me as a parvenu American. It was a relief to bid them good night.

In Frankfort I found George Elbert storming the car pool. He was draped with liberated cameras, trench telescopes, Lugers of various descriptions. A walking observation post. He had already attached himself to an Isotta Fraschini. We got a great sense of luxury gliding smoothly from Frankfort to Nuremburg. There were whole tracts of country unscarred by the war. Beautifully kept woodlots of pine and fir banded the hills. In the valleys nestled red-tiled villages out of Grimm's fairy tales. Driving into Nuremburg we told each other that something must have gone wrong with the charting of the allied raids. The industrial suburbs were strangely undamaged but the poor old picturebook city of toymakers and meistersingers had been razed to the ground.

Ruthless destruction had ground the ogival magnificence of the old walled town to powder, but the fake gothic schloss put up in suburban Stein by a pencil manufacturer had not suffered a scratch. This schloss had been set aside to house the correspondents assigned to cover the trials. We were supposed to be suitably impressed by the magnificence of our surroundings. We were comfortable there, to be sure. We slept in rows of cots in the great halls. We ate in a vaulted dining room. We drank in a redcarpeted lounge at the head of a great awkward marble staircase ornamented with mosaics colored like picture puzzles and with bronze chandeliers and statues that looked as if they were carved out of soap. George Elbert almost tore the place apart to try to get himself a private room, but other correspondents had arrived before us. All he managed to wangle was an alcove in what seemed to have been some kind of accountant's office.

The morning before the trial was to open we set out together to tour the old city. The ruin was fantastically complete. About the only intact thing we found was a bronze statue of Albrecht Dürer. Amid the debris at its base German women bundled up in coats and sweaters were boiling potatoes in a stove improvised out of a torn sheet of galvanized roofing. A pack of towheaded children watched with greedy eyes the potatoes bubbling in the pot. Bigger children scampering among the rubbish piles threw stones at us as we left. George Elbert showed me frowning a swastika freshly chalked on a stone wall. "See," he said darkly. "These people have got to be crushed."

We visited the big ugly Bavarian palace of justice where the trial was to be held. There were German war prisoners squdging on waterpaint from step ladders in the corridors. Battalions of German scrubwomen swabbed the floors. The court room had been redecorated with sage green curtains and crimson chairs. Behind a glass screen interpreters were practicing with their earphones. GI electricians were testing out the clusters of floodlights that hung from the ceiling. An American sergeant, with the preoccupied look of a theatrical property man, was smoothing the folds of the four flags: American, British, French and Russian, that adorned the dais where the judges were going to sit. MPs with white helmet linings on their heads and white batons and white pistol holsters were being shown their stations. It was like the rehearsal of an amateur play with a very large cast.

The army colonel in charge of the prisoners was giving a press conference. George Elbert and I trooped in with the rest. He certainly didn't look like the warden of a jail. He was a mildmannered man with a crew cut that gave him a naive youthful look in spite of his gray hair. When he spoke of his prisoners it was without a trace of animosity. George Elbert whispered to me behind his hand that the colonel made him think of the keeper of a zoo. He had dangerous but valuable specimens in charge: "He has to keep 'em sleek and fat for the hanging," he wheezed in my ear.

The colonel was apologizing for the illness of one of his prisoners. A hemorrhage, a very slight hemorrhage due to stress of emotion. The man would not be able to appear in court. Otherwise, resumed the colonel, the behavior of the prisoners had been quite correct. They had their little ailments of course. One complained of abdominal cramps. Another had arrived with a partial paralysis of the left wrist caused by a selfinflicted wound. Another complained of a variety of aches and pains thought to be imaginary. A case of lumbago had been cured. An admiral had some difficulty with flat feet which was being eliminated by exercise. Heat treatment had relieved the Foreign Minister's neuralgia. The leader of the Luftwaffe readily admitted that he was in better health than he had been in twenty years. He had taken off forty pounds excess weight. His nervous heart palpitation had disappeared. His drug habit had been eliminated.

The correspondents asked their questions in a tone of hushed awe. We were all a little intimidated by the proceedings we were engaged in.

The representative of one of the wire services cleared his throat. "Colonel, what are they going to wear?" he asked.

Those who had presentable uniforms would wear them but without badges or insignia. The rest had been issued conservative irongray civilian suits and conservative pinstriped shirts.

"Colonel," George Elbert brayed out, "do they act like they had something on their minds?"

Their attitude, answered the colonel gravely, was thoughtful.

He described their routine. At seven o'clock they got up to clean their cells with a broom and a mop. They had cereal for breakfast. For dinner that day they ate soup, hash, spaghetti and coffee. That night they would have bean stew, bread and tea. They ate with a spoon which was immediately taken away after each meal. They were fed U. S. rations. "At first we tried feeding them the corresponding German rations but they did not thrive."

A bus took us from the schloss to the Palace of Justice in the morning.

Hurrying in out of the biting November day and the dripping desolation of the ruined city, the heated courtroom brimming with silky white light from the floodlights in the ceiling had the look of luxury of a scene in a technicolor movie. The prisoners sat in two rows in front of a rank of American MPs. Their faces were spent and worn-out and drab in contrast to the freshness of the motionless young faces framed by pipeclayed helmet linings behind them.

The theatrical leader of the Luftwaffe wore a pearl gray doublebreasted uniform with brass buttons. For all his leaky balloon look of a fat man who had lost weight, he seemed quite at ease, as if he might take over any minute as master of ceremonies. He bowed affably to a newspaper woman he recognized among the serried ranks of correspondents in the press seats. He settled himself comfortably in his chair. He seemed to approve of the decorations.

His face wore a little of the roguish look of a repentant drunkard. It was Nero's face, an actor's face, hard and soft at the same time, genial, spoiled, selfindulgent. Nobody could help feeling his charm.

Beside him was a putty face squeezed into shadow until all you could see was a pinched nose and hollows where the eyes should be. Further along the row the Foreign Minister in his dark glasses had the look of a defaulting bank cashier. The journalist of the onslaught on the Jews had a face of a soiled Foxy Grandpa out of an old time cartoon. Next to him sat a little round man with pendulous jowls and the eyes of a whipped hound. The financier glared like an angry walrus. The professional military men sat erect and impassive.

Here, crumpled by defeat, were the faces that for years had terrorized the front pages of the world.

While the courtroom waited for the entrance of the judges a plump American sailor with a shock of red hair and the manners of a window dresser moved with pursed lips among the prisoners. He was checking on their earphones. Moving from one to another he was taking exaggerated care not to disarrange his mannikins.

The reading of the indictment lasted all day.

Out of the various voices of the prosecutors, out of the tense outofbreath voices of the interpreters a refrain was built up in our ears . . . "shooting starvation and torture . . . tortured and killed . . . shooting, beating and hanging . . . shooting starvation and torture . . ."

The leader of the Luftwaffe kept shaking his head with an air of mock martyrdom. The whitehaired journalist developed a tic in the corner of his mouth. A general with a bucksergeant look woodenly munched on a piece of bread. When the name of the theorist of the master race was mentioned the man sat up and straightened his tie. He was a dapper youngish man who occasionally stripped his teeth with a nervous doglike movement. The puttyfaced madman sat slumped in a coma.

". . . and crimes against humanity and on the high seas . . ."

Every one of them pleaded not guilty.

There was not much conversation on the press bus that trundled us back to the schloss. A sense of oppression weighed on us.

Next day our American prosecutor opened the case against the prisoners. There was an air of good humor about his closecropped round head and his broad forehead and his round glasses. He spoke in an even explanatory tone. He exuded a sort of friendly reasonableness. When he referred to the responsibility imposed on the court by this first trial in history for crimes against the peace of the world we hung breathless on his words.

"In the prisoner's dock sit twenty broken men . . . Reproached by the humiliation of those they have led almost as bitterly as by the desolation of those they have attacked, their personal capacity for evil is forever past . . ."

Hour after hour the American prosecutor unfolded his cases against them. He took the evidence out of their own mouths, out of their own written orders, out of their own secret diaries. The annihilation of the Jews, the slave labor camps . . . "Crimes against humanity and on the high seas."

Through the glass partition I watched the face of the woman who was making the translation. She had wavy dark hair, staring eyes, deep shadows under the cheekbones. Her face seemed taut with horror. At times her throat stiffened so that she could hardly speak the words. The prosecutor was describing the actions of madmen.

There was often a touch of puzzlement in his voice as if he could hardly believe the documents he was reading from. The note of astonishment. He played up the tone of a reasonable man surprised and appalled by the crimes he had discovered.

"You will say I have robbed you of your sleep . . . These are the things that have turned the stomach of the world . . ."

The choked voice of the interpreter hovered shrill as a gadfly over the prisoners' box.

They had begun to stir uneasily in their seats. They gave strange starts and shudders. One man's dark eyes seemed almost to bulge out of his head. Another kept drawing the stiff fingers of one hand down his face. Another's head twisted so far over it seemed ready to fall off his body. Even the debonair leader of the Luftwaffe stared with twisted mouth out into the white light of the courtroom as if for the first time he had seen himself as the world saw him.

Late in the afternoon, his voice firm and loud and confident, the American prosecutor launched into his thesis that aggressive war was in itself a crime under the law of nations. "The real complaining party at your bar is civilization . . . It points to the weariness of flesh, the destruction of what was beautiful and useful in so much of the world . . . Civilization asks whether law is so utterly laggard as to be helpless to deal with crimes of this magnitude by criminals of this order of importance . . ."

When the court rose we American correspondents moved out of our seats as if we were walking on eggs. We repeated to each other in low judicial voices the great courageous phrases we had heard spoken. We couldn't help feeling elated that it was a countryman of ours who had spoken them.

There was much clacking of typewriters and little drinking under the vaulted ceilings of the schloss that night. Even the French journalists, who had been hitherto skeptical of the whole business of trying the Nazis, seemed to feel a new respect for their American colleagues when they spoke to us.

Still as the days of the great trial wore on I found it harder and harder to preserve my first attitude of respectful awe. The Nazi leaders were guilty as hell but it was becoming obvious that many of the professional and technical men accused with them had little direct connection with their crimes. A few of the English correspondents and most of the French were beginning, over their drinks at least, to describe the proceedings as a hypocritical frameup. The Europeans were worried about the precedent that was being set. In any future war were the leaders of the defeated nation to be made a holy show of and wiped out as if they were the worsted faction in intracommunist politics in the Soviet Union?

The French and the Italians and all the middle Europeans had been defeated themselves. They knew how it felt.

The Americans were mostly too busy rooting out headlines to feel much interest in the ethics of the business. These were problems for the United Nations. George Elbert declared himself bored to death.

George Elbert must have read my doubts in my face. Doubt was something George Elbert hated. He began staying away from me. I thought it was one of his grouches coming on. I had managed to stay friends with him all these years by refusing to take his ill temper seriously: to be perfectly honest this time I thought he was worried for fear my story would get a better play than his did. I was laughing to myself about it. Then one evening his grouch came to a head with a vengeance.

I was sitting on a stool at the bar beside a broadfaced little Balkan I'd taken a liking to. I forget his name. He had light brown monkey eyes that looked as if they had seen more misery than they could well support. His eyes were set in deep shrivelled sockets in a countenance ravaged by smallpox. He seemed to me a knowledgeable fellow with a firm grounding in international law. We talked in French. I had taken to asking him each evening how he had been impressed by the events of the day. This particular evening he was deeply depressed.

"There can be no acquittals . . . I had hoped for one or two acquittals . . . It is like Moscow," he was saying.

At that point I heard George Elbert's heavy limping step beside me. I could hear his heavy breathing as I listened to what the Balkan journalist had to say.

The betrayal of Poland, he was pointing out, the sacrifice of the Finns, the failure of the United States, when we had the power, to rescue the Baltic peoples; how would all that look to the world if our leaders instead of the Nazi leaders were on trial?

In imagination as he spoke I was seeing the President's face, the faces of the members of the cabinet I knew, scowling old Herman Boggs, Roger Thurloe's small tight mouth and high forehead, Walker Watson's sallow cheeks . . . they were seated instead of the Nazis under the chins of the freshfaced MPs . . .

Add to that an air raid on Dresden, the Balkan journalist went on, where sixty thousand helpless noncombatants perished, the uprooting of fifteen million Sudeten Germans from lands they had occupied for centuries, the unnecessary destruction of the residential areas of cities, of museums and works of art: Monte Cassino: his voice was relentless. "How sad for civilization," he said, "that you did not come with clean hands."

"We are all criminals," I was saying, "but not all equally criminal."

"That is why there must be acquittals," he was insisting. "Otherwise it is Moscow."

I had to admit that the influence of these people's thinking was overwhelming the west: subtle, underground, deepseated and overwhelming. No our hands were not clean.

George Elbert's French wasn't any too good, but it was good enough to allow him to get the gist of our conversation. I could feel his heavy breathing down my neck. All of a sudden he nudged me roughly. I turned my head. He had a black look in his eye. "I haven't gotten over hating the krauts yet," he said. "And now you are telling me to go hate the Russians."

He looked about ready to haul off and hit me.

"We ought to be trying to find a way to cut down on these hatreds," I answered lamely.

He had already turned his broad back on us and walked stifflegged away.

"Qu'est-ce qu'il dit? . . . Qu'est-ce qu'il dit?" asked the Balkan journalist.

"What he means is that we are trying to establish the rule of law in the world."

The Balkan journalist shrugged. "Law without justice is oppression," he said. "Justice comes with clean hands."

I found the conversation too painful to continue. I took leave of him and walked down the grand staircase of the schloss. The usual cold drizzle was falling outside, but I found it refreshing to walk back and forth in the flagged courtyard among the parked jeeps.

I had not taken more than a couple of turns when George Elbert stepped out of the shadows in front of me. "How do you know that guy's on the up and up?" he asked. It was too dark to see his face.

"I didn't tell him anything I wouldn't tell anybody."

"That's what I was afraid of," he answered sneeringly. "Look here," he went on, "goin' on four years now I've been all over the world seeing grand guys die . . . our guys. Who killed 'em? It wasn't the poor devils who squeezed the triggers on the guns; it was those sonsofbitches we've got lined up in court. And guys like you with your hairsplitting about justice and all that crap, you want 'em to get off scot free. You say the Russians are a shifty lot but they killed more Germans than we did. You know that goddam well."

I mumbled something about the war being over. There was a time to make war and there was a time to make peace. If we went on turning the world over to these people it would mean a third war.

Walking side by side we were careful to keep our distance from each other.

This was not one of the friendly wrangles I'd had so often with George Elbert during all the years I'd known him. There was hatred in his voice. From the way he had nudged my shoulder in the bar I knew that we were no longer friends.

We stood facing one another under the presumptuously elaborate lantern that hung over the great bronze and glass doors of the lower lobby.

His brows were knotted above his big nose. His red fleshy face quivered with anger.

"What are you going to tell the people back home?"

"The truth as best I can."

"You're going home to write a lot of goddam propaganda for the isolationists and the Fascists and the America firsters. Do you know what I think we ought to do? After we've hung the bloody Nazis I think we ought to go home and hang the goddam isolationists."

"We've each got a right to our opinion."

"You shut up about your goddam opinions if you know what's good for you. You take it from me. Or I'll tell you right now what's going to happen. You'll wake up one of these mornings and find yourself a back number."

This time it was I who turned my back. I spun on my heel and left him.

From that day to this there has been no more friendship between us.

It wasn't too long after that I decided I'd had all of the Nuremburg trials I needed for my article. I was full up to the neck with international justice. I'd had a worrisome letter from Grace telling of what seemed to be a concerted movement in the press to discredit Roger Thurloe. He wasn't only fighting for his program. He was fighting for his job. "And I'm afraid," Grace added, "we are getting tangled up in it in spite of ourselves."

Every avenue of travel across the Atlantic was overloaded by the crush of returning troops trying to make it home by Christmas. Redeployment had become a panic.

Priorities kept getting trumped by superior priorities. I gave up trying to wangle a priority by air and accepted a bunk on a small navy flattop about to sail from Brest.

We bucked heavy westerlies during most of the crossing. It was like being afloat on a huge garage. The hangar deck was incumbered with a temporary wooden structure of bunks five tiers high to accommodate the enlisted men. GIs with waxy faces and rumpled hair crawled in and out of it like wasps on a wasps' nest. Everything smelt of sour wool and stuffy bodies and vomit.

Most of the crossing I lay in my bunk in a cabin in the officers' country below decks and read a copy of Chaucer's *Canterbury Tales* I'd found on the boat. After the crowded hell of twentieth century Europe reading Chaucer was like stepping out into the real world again, a world where there was good as well as evil, a world where love was love, and men were men and women were women and food was food. The lines were full of the fragrance of a fine May morning.

When I wasn't reading I was listening to the endless bull session that went on, between bridge games and rummy, among the young men around me. "To hell with the Germans, it's what our men are doing worries me . . ." "If we did the right thing it would be more profitable in the long run . . ." "Everything we've done since the fighting stopped in the ETO has been wrong."

"Lust liquor and loot is the soldiers pay," they would argue on the other side.

I'd heard that one before.

Most of the arguments ended with the conclusion, "Two wrongs don't make a right."

We docked on Staten Island. After saying goodbye to my cabinmates and dragging my overseas bag down the gangplank, I was wandering in search of a taxi about the huge warehouse, crowded with files of troops waiting for travel orders, when a young man in civilian clothes come up to me. He had some kind of passenger list in his hand. He was a pale young man with a crooked nose and slippery eyes behind his glasses.

"You are Roland Lancaster, the returning war correspondent?" he asked. He coughed. "I wonder if you would like to make some comment on this statement in Quint Busby's column."

In an expressionless voice he read a typewritten line off a slip of paper: "Famed newshound Ro Lancaster hurries home to file proceedings for divorce against his wife the former Grace Hogan naming as co-respondent a cabinet member."

"First I've heard of it," I said, and brushed past him. With sinking heart I went into a phone booth to call a taxi . . .

13

. . . Ro comes down from his room at a quarter to six freshened by a half hour's nap. Standing under the cold shower he has been planning cheerfully how to get started on the Caribbean Legion story. He's sharpened some fresh pencils. He has put on a crisp clean suit and slipped a new little blue notebook into his pocket. Going down in the elevator ideas swarm in his head. His temples are cool. He's mastered his hangover. Darting between cars across the narrow street to the café he's telling himself to pay no attention to anything but Joe Herkimer's story for the rest of the day.

Elsa will just have to take care of herself.

Pinillo is still with her in the café. They are sitting just where he left them hunched over their pernod in a dark corner beside the bar. The only change in Elsa is that little beads of sweat have begun to stand out on her white skin. Pinillo's face has turned green. His mustache is awry. His eyes have a large dreamy lustrous look.

It's some time before Ro can get either of them to look up. Elsa won't take her eyes off Pinillo's face.

"Ñañigo is a science," Pinillo declaims in Spanish, half translating as he goes on . . . "a science more profound than all the atomic physics . . . It is the domination of the mind of the masses by the mind of a leader who surges out of the masses . . . That is why a Marxist may be ñañigo and still remain good Marxist . . . the technique is the same only theirs is more profound. It is existentialism in practice."

Ro clears his throat. "We'd better move along," he says more sharply than he intends.

Pinillo's eyes slowly focus on his. "Your American physics that you threaten the world with . . ." Pinillo's tone is condescending— "is all imported from Europe. In the Union Sovietica they move mountains . . . All you Americans will learn besides killing helpless people is how to flush waterclosets with it."

Ro stands looking down at them with a falsefeeling smile on his face. He is determined not to start on an argument. He is desperate to find some way of ditching Pinillo.

"Bueno," Pinillo says as he gets slowly and carefully to his feet. "If you insist, I will come. 'Erkimer is an American boob, but 'ee is a sportif . . . Sport is the obsession of the American masses. The masses in all countries are pure."

Elsa looks up with film over her eyes. Her voice seems to come from a distance. "You'll have to pay the check, Ro . . . I've spent all my money."

Ro beckons to the waiter. It is the same Spanish waiter with ducktails over his ears and the manner of an elderly diplomat who brought him the newspaper that morning. Ro fancies there is a look of concern on his face when he brings the change back as if he wants to say: "What is a famous man like you doing with people like that?"

"Thank you Meester Lancaster," he says in his deep voice and pockets his tip with dignity. "And may things go well with you."

Ro finds Pinillo and Elsa installed in a taxi waiting for him. It is yesterday's royalblue cab. Ro tries to climb in without looking into the driver's yellow face but the know-itall smile seeks him out from under the narrow mustache.

"Good afternoon señor . . . You rested well I hope," the man says in a tone that seems to carry all sorts of hidden meanings. The thought shoots across Ro's mind as he perches uneasily on the edge of the seat beside Elsa: the man's going to blackmail me.

Half way to Central Park they get stuck in a traffic jam. All the cars are honking. No car moves. "Carnival," says the driver turning back to them with a shrug of smiling resignation.

Ro leaps at an excuse to get out of that damned cab.

"I have an engagement," he exclaims. "We'll have to walk."

Elsa carries on about how the hard pavement will hurt her feet. Pinillo gives Ro a look that seems to say: Too stingy to pay the taxi fare, eh?

Shouldering his way through the crowd a little ahead of them Ro begins to feel the holiday excitement gaining on him. Everybody is out for a good time. Everybody is politely cheerful. No matter how densely people are packed nobody bumps into him. Seeing him in a hurry they make way for him smiling.

The central part of the square swarms with vendors of

macaroons and oversized pretzels and colored balloons, masks, false mustaches, bags of confetti, shiny knick knacks on trays. Children in scraps of fancy costumes scamper around underfoot. Here and there is a clown suit or a domino or a false nose or a tin trumpet. The arcades reveberate with the din of rattles and claxons and automobile horns.

Carnival, what a setting for the story, Ro is thinking with a burst of pleasure. He'll open and close on the carnival. The carnival is the classical setting for skulduggery, political intrigue, disguises, assignations, clandestine appointments, pursuits, escapes. He hurries towards the Cayo Hueso.

The police have one side of the square roped off to leave an alley for the parading cars of the paseo to go through. Now and then they stop the cars to let groups of pedestrians cross. As he crosses Ro glances down the line of gleaming new automobiles full of darkeyed girls in mantillas and bright dresses and selfsatisfiedlooking young men. They are all dressed to the teeth. They are all happy to see and be seen.

The faces in the Cayo Hueso are thick as pebbles on the beach. It's some time before Ro finds Joe Herkimer.

Joe Herkimer's lined pink countenance looks surprisingly spruce. He's fresh shaved. He wears a necktie painted with bathing beauties. He jerks his head back to beckon to Ro and gathers his Panama hat and yellow gloves and walking stick up off the chair beside him.

"Thought you'd stood me up," he says when Ro finally reaches him. "Some joker kept tryin' to get this seat . . . They go mad here at carnival time." He gives Ro a heavy wink. "We're not alone."

Ro turns to find Elsa and Pinillo right on his heels.

"What about your flyers?" Ro hurries to ask.

Joe Herkimer points over his shoulder with his thumb. "They're all here," he says.

Ro settles Elsa in the spare seat. She is all eyes for the carnival. She is treating Ro as if she hardly knew him. She refuses a drink and sits smoking a cigarette staring in a trance at the decorated cars that pass outside.

Ro and Pinillo have to stand a long time wedged in beside the table while a sweating waiter edges his way across the room with extra chairs upended over people's heads. Pinillo stands preening his mustache and looking out into the crowded faces as if he expected them to break into applause at any moment.

Ro, jammed up against him, has the uncomfortable feeling of being bracketed with Pinillo by the eyes of the men and women at the surrounding tables that search the features of each newcomer for something absurd to titter over. For an instant he sees himself as they are seeing him, a lanky kind of an Uncle Sam with a protruding adam's apple and a tired red raddled face. After a contemptuous glance at him all eyes switch to Elsa's red head. "Qué rubia."

There are eyes that seem particularly to be searching Ro's face. One pair belong to a tall black man in a white suit with a disdainful hawk nose and very thin tremulous nostrils. Another pair under a bald head stare fixedly at Ro out of rimless glasses above a clipped black beard. A third pair squints out of the smooth squat face of a boy with untidy brown hair. They all seem to be looking him over for a purpose.

"Want to go to the little boys' room?" Joe Herkimer leans over and whispers in Ro's ear as soon as he manages to sit down. Ro nods. "I'll show you where it is . . . You guys keep our seats, hear?" says Joe Herkimer. "Dames always do this," he adds into Ro's ear as they squeeze their way among the packed in chairs towards the back of the restaurant. "Why shouldn't we?"

Reflected in the mirror that fills the rear wall they can see cars festooned and banked with flowers filing by in the twilight outside, girls in white under canopies of roses, the flicker of confetti, paper streamers, serried hats of onlookers filling the sidewalk.

"Funny if they took us for maricones, eh?" Joe Herkimer's laugh wheezes unpleasantly in Ro's ear.

In the narrow passage that leads past the long bar crowded with waiters and busboys they found the man with the beard and the glasses waiting for them. He is heavyset and younger than he looked from a distance.

"Shake hands with Roland Lancaster of Picture Magazine . . . Roland, meet the major." The major's hand is wet with sweat.

"What I don't like about this deal . . . "the major starts right off in a peevish tone. The man has stomach ulcers written all over his face. The anxious type, Ro is telling himself. "What I don't like is how can you write up the story without giving the whole show away?"

"Leave that to me," says Joe Herkimer.

"I don't like it."

"I don't even know whether there is a story yet," says Ro soothingly. "There isn't any deal, I can assure you."

Joe Herkimer turns his redrimmed blue eyes on the major's face. "Tell me one thing, when did you boys get paid last?"

"We haven't been paid for five weeks," the major splutters in their faces. "When I try to see Delgado he's always in conference."

"He's known as Señor Equis," says Joe Herkimer with a snap of his jaws. "You're the one that's talking out of turn."

"You said this guy was all right." The major's voice is

more querulous than ever. His glasses have fogged up. He takes them off to clean them.

The peevish pilot, Ro is telling himself. *Heroes for Hire,* a title flashes through his head.

Somebody is tugging at his sleeve. Ro turns. He is looking down at the smoothfaced youth with the almond-shaped eyes he noticed before. The boy is flatchested. He hardly looks older than fourteen. He wears soiled sneakers and no socks. His arms stick out skinny from a rumpled blue sportshirt too large for him.

The boy puckers his face into an expression of mystery and gestures with a twist of his head. Ro follows him a few steps down the corridor away from the others.

"See here bo," he whispers hoarsely up towards Ro's ear, "de story's all written."

"Who wrote it?"

The boy gives his head a flip to toss the hair off his forehead.

"I did . . . All you need do is get it published, an' slip me some dough to leave town."

Joe Herkimer lets out a short "psst." When Ro turns to step back towards him the boy tags along, padding softly in his sneakers. "Just read it," he's pleading. "If it ain't no good you don't have to buy it."

"Eddy you button up that big yap," Joe Herkimer snarls out of the corner of his mouth. "We can't talk here. Let's go eat somewheres. I'll call up the Occidente. They'll save me a table even if they have to throw some of these jokers out."

He reaches for the telephone on the wall of the passage.

Someone has walked up behind Ro. He turns. The tall black man is holding out his hand. "Very pleased to meet you, Mr. Lancaster. I know we shall agree." He has a velvet cultivated voice with a trace of the Jamaican intonation. An irresistibly cordial expression ripples across his face. His eyes are blue. "The great ones of the earth can always find a communion. That's what the Duke of Windsor said when he was introduced to me." He flashes a magnificent set of white teeth in Ro's face. "You need look no further . . . The story is I."

"Roland, meet Primus Hicks." Joe Herkimer introduces them over his shoulder. Placing his blueveined hand over the mouthpiece of the telephone he explains: "You know about the Black Condor? Well this is it." Joe Herkimer goes back to talking over the phone. He's talking fast and long. The voice at the other end seems hard to convince. "Naw this is a strictly cash proposition, with propina. Plenty propina," Ro hears him say. "Keep the table in my name. We'll be around in three shakes . . . It's a deal? Okeydoke."

Ro's hand reaches nervously towards the wallet in his back pocket. It will be an expensive dinner. These guys look hungry. What the hell? It will all come out of the expense account.

"There is an old man on a neighboring island," Primus Hicks is saying in his bland tones. "Let us call him the old man of the sea . . . You know the Arabian tale?"

"Oxford?" asked Ro.

"Rath*er*. But only a fleeting glimpse. The war intervened," says Primus Hicks with a deprecating smirk. "The RAF and all that sort of thing . . . I have been fortunate in frequenting the better intellects."

"Go on," says Ro.

"This hypothetical old man weighs on the necks of his unfortunate subjects who feel a yearning for the four freedoms and all that sort of thing . . . The appeal to a man of my temperament and convictions is irresistible."

"Let's all shut our traps till we get out of this joint," interrupts Joe Herkimer. "Roland lend me five dollars to settle their checks. These boys are broke."

"There may be some chits," says Primus Hicks rolling his eyes. "These inescapable chits." He parts his lips in a winsome smile.

"Better make it ten," says Joe Herkimer.

Ro's hand lingers on his wallet as he weaves his way back and forth among men's and women's heads close-packed over the tables towards Elsa's red hair.

Elsa looks at him with an absentminded smile when he speaks to her. Her voice seems muffled. She confides in him, as she would to a stranger, that the nonobjective painter Pinillo has consented to stay and tell them about the comparsas as they go past.

"That's bully," Ro hears himself answer in a hollow voice.

Right away he's dutifully reaching for the check while Pinillo, inching himself carefully to his feet, growls something about the step the comparsas dance having that halting shuffle as a relic of slave days when they danced with shackles on their legs. Once on his feet Pinillo stretches himself and clears his throat portentously. As Ro stands with his hand out while the waiter makes change Pinillo gives him a beady look. "The day will come Meester Lancaster," he announces, "when we will throw off the last of these shackles, the shackle of the dollar."

Outside it's already dark. Pinillo takes one of Elsa's arms and Ro tags along on the other. Kicking up her toes she walks humming in a happy daze between them as they drift with the current of the crowd.

At the old Occidente they find every nook packed with diners. No sign of Herkimer in the main dining room. At last after much interrogation of waiters they are shown to a private room on the second floor where Joe Herkimer sits at the head of a long table under an old fashioned ceiling fan. He has taken off his coat and presides in shirt-sleeves and suspenders.

The flyers are making themselves at home. The major has lost his worried look. Eddy seems in ecstasy. Primus Hicks wears a look of reserved condescension. New faces have appeared.

There's a pail of ice and a battery of blue sodawater siphons in the center of the table. Bottles of Scotch whiskey are tipping gaily over glasses. The bottles gurgle. The soda fizzes. Arms reach out toward plates of cold cuts and anchovies. A basket full of French bread lurches from hand to hand.

"The boys are hungry," Joe Herkimer explains with a grin. He beckons hospitably with the fingers of both hands to Ro and Elsa. "Here we've saved seats for you."

It all suddenly strikes Ro as very funny indeed. "Mighty white of you," he cries. He begins to laugh. "Do you suppose you could spare me a drink?"

"Eddy," Primus Hicks intones suavely, "can't you see the gentleman has an empty glass?"

"Let's see," Joe Herkimer's saying. "Where were we? The boys were delivering the cases full of grand pianos."

"Is that what those big boxes were I saw in your back room?" squeals Elsa.

Joe Herkimer closes his jaws tight. "Don't you see too much, daughter." There's a rasp in his voice. All the little wrinkles of his face twist up into his favorite hick expression. "Didn't you know I was musical?"

Ro leans back in his chair and lets his eyes roam round the table. An opening sentence is forming in his head: *While the carefree carnival crowds throng the streets outside, in the back rooms of Havana cafés, cadging drinks and chalking up meals on credit, the mercenaries of a secret army lounge away the time till D-day. . . .*

"The yacht sailed," one of the newcomers says suddenly.

Ro sees a look of attention flash from face to face round the table.

"Who says she did?" The major's frowning and worried again.

"Seen her myself," shouts Eddy in his cracked voice. "Youse guys would too if you hadn't stayed so long in bed widde floosies."

"Amigo cuidado," cautions Primus Hicks in his most velvet tones, "a lady has done us the honor . . ."

"Eddy," Joe Herkimer roars our suddenly in the voice of a coach bawling out a player, "you keep your dirty little trap shut."

"She put out to sea this mornin' about day," a newcomer is repeating the news. It's a Texas voice.

"Roland meet Tex," says Joe Herkimer.

Two square faces under crew cuts turn towards Ro. "Hi," they say.

"We call 'em both Tex," says Joe Herkimer. "To save having to tell 'em apart."

"Ain't dat what we're here for to tell de story?" Eddy is whining.

"If you know what's good for you you little shrimp you'll let me do the talking," scolds Joe Herkimer. He turns to Ro: "You see Roland it's this way. These boys were recruited over in the States and a little bit all around to do this transport work, air freight you know on these grand pianos . . . just in case there might be a little trouble in one of these little republics, see? Operation airfreight passed off very nicely with the cooperation of some local authorities."

"Who's putting up the money?" asks Ro. He has his notebook in his lap.

At that moment waiters file into the room with platters of food. Joe Herkimer lifts his hand for silence.

"See, Roland," he whispers loudly in Ro's ear, "I ordered chicken and rice and plenty of garbanzos . . . Fill 'em up on garbanzos, I say . . ." His laugh wheezes through his bronchial tubes. "You see I have your interests at heart. The Condor here he has to eat steak, doctor's orders."

"Ever since those missions over Germany," says Primus Hicks with his disarming smile, "I have suffered from gastric disturbances."

. . . *While they wait they worry. Stomach ulcers take their toll of the brave legionnaires,* thinks Ro.

Pinillo's black eyes are fixed on Ro's face from the end of the table. "Eet ees a deception," he hisses. "Eet ees an entrapment by the secret services of Yankiland . . . Perhaps with connivance of the old man. He seeks to entrap every leeberal."

Nobody pays the slightest attention to him.

"But who's putting up the money?" Ro asks again. Joe Herkimer slips an arm round Ro's neck, draws his head confidentially towards his, and whispers with wet lips against his ear that these boys came over in good faith. These boys are all right. When they got here this Señor Equis began to let on that there was more to it than just freight. It might be a question of toting some few heavy objects to drop in the old man's back yard at the same time as a group of his old friends were landing by sea. The boys were offered handsome bonuses for the work and being of a liberal frame of mind . . . well they thought it was good Americanism to do something to help the underdog. "Wouldn't you?"

"Suppose we begin at the beginning," Ro interrupts. "When did it start?" His pencil is poised.

Elsa puts in with a yawn that it has been going on for years. Gov meant to angel a play about it. She'll take a fit if she has to hear all about it again. She gets to her feet and strides to the window and leans out over the sill to look down into the square.

Naw, this is the real story, Joe Herkimer insists, that other was peanuts. What would Roland think of a guarantee that the uprising would happen the day his story hit the stands? Would that make for sales or wouldn't it? But they must work quick. That yacht putting to sea is the signal.

Eddy with his glass in one hand stands tugging at Ro's other elbow. He don't even have to write it, don't he see? Eddy has it all written and nicely typed too, double spaced. The goilfriend's a typist. Every writer has to have a goilfriend a typist. He flips the hair up out of his eyes. "Ain't dat de troot, Mister Lancaster?"

The major's tapping with an empty glass to attract Ro's attention.

"Roland, it's this way," he says frowning till his eyes begin to cross behind his glasses. "We figure that Señor Equis, or whatever that bastard's name is, is giving us the old double cross, we do the work, then he turns us over to the federal agents to avoid paying us. There's laws against smuggling arms out of Yankeeland."

"Beat 'em to the draw," Eddy's voice breaks. "At de same time as we deliver de story to a national magazine we go round to de embassy and give 'em de lowdown. Dat cleans our skoits, see?"

Primus Hicks is on his feet saying that the world will expect a statement from him. He has to make his position clear. There are no sordid considerations on his part. Wherever the disinherited of the earth rise against their oppressors there the Black Condor will come gliding through the air to their assistance.

Meanwhile Joe Herkimer whispers in Ro's ear that this revolution business is like big league baseball. A manager will occasionally buy a player right out of the opposing team. That makes it confusing. It calls for a fresh lineup every day.

Ro can hardly hear what he's saying because Eddy is yammering so loud that before he goes one step further he wants his story considered. At the same time the major is pounding on the table and shouting that his name can not be used in any case. Everybody talks at once. Primus Hicks insists above the din, in his charmingly modulated tones, that whoever writes the story, it will have to be cleared by his public relations counsel.

The Texans are leaning back in their chairs and beginning to sing:

A sailor boy came home one night
As drunk as he could be.

Ro and Joe Herkimer sit quiet as a pair of owls at the end of the table. They both notice at the same moment that Pinillo's chair is empty. "Is that painter on the up and up?" Ro asks.

"The question's out of order, Roland. You know politics on this island," Joe Herkimer whispers back, kneading his shoulder confidentially. "Everybody's working for somebody, Roland. Me I'm friends with all of them and they're all friends with me. I don't ask no questions, Roland, that's why they like me. 'Good old 'Erkimer they say, he no sabbe nothing.' We'll throw a little business his way, see?"

"The truth of it is men," the major shouts in his staccato tones, "we've had the old double cross . . . Let's see we don't get it again."

My dear wife my darling wife
My light of my life said he

roar the Texans.

Under the din Ro begins to note the sound of a drum

beat. Through the window amid the growling hum of the crowd comes that lame halting drumbeat, the sound of distant voices singing in unison: the comparsas. He has to twist himself loose from Joe Herkimer's fumbling grasp to turn round to look. Elsa has gone.

Ro strides towards the door.

"No you don't."

Joe Herkimer wheezing hard has hold of his arm. He has a tremendous grip. His fingers dig into the muscle like claws.

"That's the thing about islands, Roland," he goes on in a singsong voice in Ro's ear. "Nobody can play any vanishing acts. We'll go meet my friend the manager. He's a nice fellow but he's hipped on the subject of cash, and propinas, good lord the propinas. He's a fanatic on spot cash." The breath from his wheezing laugh brushes Ro's cheek. "If we tried to walk out on him, he might do something he'd regret, Roland, like calling the paddywagon and hauling us all off to the hoosegow. He and the chief of police are just like that."

He rubs two knotted forefingers together under Ro's nose.

"I was coming right back," Ro says indignantly.

"Of course, of course," murmurs Joe Herkimer, "that's what we always say . . . but the manager might not understand."

In the manager's little office it takes a dreadfully long time. The manager turns out to be a meticulous little man with carefully manicured fingernails. He is enchanted to meet Mr. Lancaster. He is delighted to offer him the hospitality of the hotel. He is desolated for fear the service might not have been up to the usual high standard. So many people. Carnival. One must make allowances.

A boy has to be sent to fetch the waiter. The waiter has to go back for the bill.

Ro stands first on one foot and then on the other while Joe Herkimer and the manager slyly trade jokes about each other's private lives.

Meanwhile the singing and the drumming grow loud and fade outside as fresh groups pass the hotel. In his mind Ro is combing the sidewalks for Elsa. He can spot her anywhere with that red hair.

When the bill is eventually produced on its white metal tray the manager's face buzzes over it like a bee over a flower. He rubs the ends of his manicured fingers together. If Mr. Lancaster would prefer to write a check on New York, Miami, San Francisco, he will be delighted to honor Mr. Lancaster's personal check.

The figures of his bank balance flash up before Ro's eyes: $49.50 he reads with a pang. He answers firmly that he will pay in cash.

The manager's little oval face breaks into dimples as he smiles. His eyes linger lovingly on each green tenspot as it passes into his hand.

Ro breaks roughly away from the thanks, appreciations and farewells. It isn't till the street door that he is able to shake loose from Joe Herkimer: and then he has to leave him a couple of fives in case the boys get thirsty before Ro comes back.

The comparsas are passing on parade. Ro can't decide which way to go. He wanders distractedly back and forth behind the crowds along the curbs, looking over people's heads at the dancing dark groups. They are dressed as French sailors, as Spanish pirates, as sugarcane workers, as lords and ladies at the court of Marie Antoinette. There are baseball teams and tropical safaris. They carry lit transparencies and Venetian-looking lanterns on poles. They drift by always to the same halting drumbeat, dancing singly, in pairs, in quartettes, in figure eights, slow, lame, dragging, belly muscles writhing, arms writhing, not touching, inciting, beckoning, drifting in slow undulating groups through the square. As they dance now and then they sing with quaint voices in unison.

Ro roams behind the backs of the people thronging the curbs searching every group for Elsa's red head. He hardly knows which way he's going.

At a corner under a dense dark tree in the Prado he runs smack into Pinillo.

"Where's Elsa?" Ro asks out of breath.

Pinillo arches his eyebrows. He turns back to finish what he was saying to a pair of sallow individuals beside him. Then he slants his triumphant black glance up into Ro's face; "Como?"

"Elsa? What's happened to her?"

Pinillo shrugs. "Don't worry," he answers in mocking and familiar Spanish. "These American girls they always land on their feet. One should never try to keep up with them."

Then he turns back laughing to his two companions. They seem very much amused by something he has said that Ro didn't catch.

Ro draws himself up and squares his shoulders. "Señor Pinillo," he says in a tone that is not to be trifled with, "you must have seen which way she went."

Pinillo points with his little finger down the Prado.

As Ro hurries off in the direction Pinillo indicated he feels mocking eyes in the small of his back. The thought of the ridiculous figure he cuts makes him stiffen all over. How did he ever get himself into this predicament anyway? As he strides along trying to search every face under the dark trees of the Prado, he goes back in his mind over everything that happened since he and Elsa landed in the lovely morning at Rancho Boyeros. So far as he can see everything he'd done has made sense. He's tried to make it all easy for Elsa. He's tried to keep from worrying by picking himself up some work to do. When a man's luck goes against him it goes against him, that's all.

He has reached the end of the Prado. It's late. The street has already a lonesome air. The crowd has thinned. A group of bullfighters and another of fishermen are still waiting to join the parade. No sign of a red head.

He starts back at full speed towards Central Park. Almost to the square he catches a flash of red hair beyond the heads of the onlookers lining the curb. He pushes his way through. It's a high yaller in a wig. The dancers are made up like American teenagers. The men wear zoot-suits, the girls dungarees and red and blonde wigs. The spectators laugh and applaud.

Ro's on his way back towards the Prado again when all at once he is bumped into from the side. He turns and starts to apologize. After all it might have been his fault. The man is a grayhaired mulatto with a small mustache and a straw hat. He brandishes a cane. Ro is struck by something theatrically truculent about his manner. At the same time he feels hands pushing him from behind. The mulatto is making gestures of false indignation. Ro feels a hand yank at his wallet. When he turns he can see nothing but the serried backs of the people watching the parade. His right backpocket is empty. No sign of anybody running. When he turns again the mulatto has gone.

"My pocket's been picked. Where can I find a policeman?" he asks a man beside him in Spanish. The man looks surprisingly like one of the sallowfaced individuals Pinillo was talking to but there's no recognition in his face. Ro fancies a derisive glint comes into his eye when he answers, "Quien sabe?"

The man adds in an offhand way that there's a police station in the Central Park.

Ro stands panting, looking about him with clenched fists. "Can't someone help? The thief must be standing right here," he cries out.

People glance towards him with polite smiles and edge shrugging away. They are all absorbed in the comparsas.

"Someone must have seen it," Ro addresses the empty air. All he can see is shrugging backs. His voice trails off. He starts towards the police station.

"I've lost a girl too," he says to himself as his fingers drum in his empty pocket, "but I can't tell them that."

At the police station they are very courteous. Ro is introduced to an elegantly attired young man who speaks perfect English. He has read about Mr. Lancaster in the papers. He is distressed. He extends to him the hospitality of the city. He is heartbroken at this distressing incident. Such a considerable sum. Now the wallet he can almost guarantee to get back and private papers, identification cards, etcetera. But currency. He fears it is hopeless. Express checks now could be stopped.

Ro explains ruefully that he meant to buy express checks, but he forgot.

Imprudent, exclaims the young man, the imprudence of genius, he adds. He refuses to be discouraged. A famous man like Mr. Lancaster. Such a loss will mean nothing to him, while to others less fortunate it might have been disastrous.

When Ro gives the name of his hotel a curious look comes over the young man's face. He begins to intimate in the most apologetic sidelong way that perhaps Mr. Lancaster might be relieved to know of the fortunate resolution of a little incident. A tiny little incident. A thing not of the slightest importance. Since he is staying in the same hotel he may perhaps be acquainted with a young lady. The young man indicates red hair with a circular motion of his hand above his head. As beautiful as a motion picture star, what a beautiful young lady.

Ro admits that they are acquainted.

She was dancing in the streets with the comparsas. The sergeant feared she was overexcited. She seemed to have lost her shoes.

Of course he himself understands, says the young police lieutenant attired in plain clothes, he went to school in the States. In the States we understood these schoolgirl pranks but in a Latin country, he's sure that a man who had travelled as widely as Mr. Lancaster will agree, that people are more backward. There's a lack of culture among the masses. People misunderstand.

He and the sergeant invited her into the staff car and drove her to her hotel. They feared she would overtire herself, and without slippers! He hopes she did not feel they were presumptuous. Perhaps Mr. Lancaster will present his apologies, the apologies of the whole police force of the Havana.

Ro refuses the offer of a lift to the hotel. He hurries back to the Occidental. He must try to get one of those flyers away from Joe Herkimer long enough to make a date with him for tomorrow. There must be some way of getting this story straight.

The private room is empty. In the main dining room the waiters are turning the chairs over on the tables. The manager's dimpled smiles are nowhere to be seen.

Ro sets off on foot back to the hotel. He can hardly drag his feet along the pavement. He is dead tired. No money for a cab. A damn fool, he tells himself, not to accept the police lieutenant's lift.

Rain has started. The norther is blowing in great gusts again. By the time he reaches the hotel his clothes are drenched. His toes squdge in water.

Elsa's door is ajar. The radio is playing low. She sits in her dressing gown on the edge of the bed smoking a cigarette.

She makes mean eyes at him the moment he walks in.

"I know you're going to scold me . . . I can tell by that pout on your face."

"Elsa, I'm very wet and very tired. I've been looking all over for you."

He pulls off his wet jacket and throws it in the corner of the room. His necktie is soaked. He yanks it off.

She sits looking at him with round astonished eyes. "Why didn't you take a cab? At least I didn't get wet."

"I got my pocket picked."

"That was clever."

"Wasn't it?"

Ro gets a towel from her bathroom and begins to wipe himself off.

"I hate people who get robbed. They do it on purpose. Al was always getting robbed."

"They told me at the police station they'd brought you home."

"So you sicked the cops on me? A nice way to treat a girl friend you're asking to marry you."

She lights a second cigarette off the butt of the first one.

"We'll have to talk about that," says Ro sharply. "If we could ever just get together on something." The words tumble over each other out of his mouth. "We never seem to be in the same mood at the same time. There's no warmth to you."

"There was but I caught cold," she drawls. "I caught cold out in the streets."

She is yawning.

She looks up at him with a touch of a smile. "We are both of us sleepy as . . . I'm too sleepy to think what's so sleepy."

She yawns again and draws the smoke in with her eyes closed. She forces her eyes open, gives him one of her little straight smiles and says in an almost friendly way: "You go change into some dry pyjamas. If you catch a cold you'll give it to me and I'll carry it back to the twins . . . Come back and we'll talk." She yawns helplessly. "That is if we don't fall asleep first."

When he comes back she is lying flat in the middle of the bed with her face to the ceiling. Her eyes are shut tight. Her breathing is so easy he can hardly hear it. The cigarette is quietly burning a hole in the rug beside the bed. A blue wisp of smoke rises peacefully from it.

He treads the spot out with his slipper. The threatening smell of scorched cloth hangs in his nostrils.

He locks the door, puts out the light, and climbs into bed with her. He tries to draw her to him. With sleepy force she pushes him away. He's too tired to struggle. Making himself as small as he can on the edge of the bed he sinks gradually into a stupid sleep . . .

14

. . . The day I landed from the E.T.O. was a Sunday. The afternoon train to Washington turned out to be packed with returned service men and their families. No way to get a seat. No way to get into the diner. I was far too distracted to read. Naturally the train was late. Five and a half hours had never been so long. The cab I managed to squeeze into at the Union Station circled round block after block to let off other passengers on the way out Connecticut Avenue. The minutes seemed hours. I stood shaking while I listened for some sound of Grace through the outer door of our apartment. It was a while before I dared put my finger to the bell. I had the latchkey in my pocket but somehow I felt timid about using it.

There she was all at once in a dressing gown opening the door for me. She was yawning. One side of her face was creased with sleep. It was as if I had never been away. "Oh Ro what a relief." She yawned again. "I was afraid it was some wretched reporter." The moment she spoke I knew that this idiotic business of the gossip column would make no difference between us; it would draw us closer together. As soon as I'd dragged in my overseas bag and closed the door, she gave one of her little shrieks and threw her arms around me. "Tell me Ro, who's your girl?" she whispered with her head on my chest.

"Who do you think?"

I held her away from me with both hands to look at her. She had stopped touching up her hair. There was much more gray than blonde in her little silky curls. She was very thin. Her skin had a blue transparent look. It squeezed me all up inside to see how pale and tired she looked. She was still the prettiest woman in the world.

"Whose side are you on, Ro?" she was whispering in a tiny little voice.

"Whose side would I be on?"

"Me too I'm on your side." She hugged me again.

"The first thing I'm going to do is take you on a vacation young woman. You've got to be fattened up."

She shook her head. "Not quite yet . . . Roger depends on me so. Oh there's so much to tell. He's so thin-skinned. Wells Hartley is riding him so in his column. Things are absolutely horrible with him. He needs us both."

"We'll talk about that."

Right away she was telling me that the Perkins family was moving out of our Dumbarton Avenue house on January 1. That was a relief. I had always hated this damned apartment. We agreed to move back in immediately.

We had hardly exchanged a few hurried words before the boys, back from the movies, barged in on us.

Chips gave me a funny look as if to say, "You back?" His face had gotten pimply. His voice had gone down into his boots. "So the divorce is off?" he asked.

Louie piped up in his high voice: "Chips kep' sayin' he'd rather have Roger for a father than Dad . . . He said at least Roger would stay home and take us to the ballgames."

Chips gave his shoulders an exaggerated shrug and strode off pouting towards his own room.

"You boys ought to have better sense than to believe everything you read in the newspapers," I said in a tone intended to be cutting. "You can take it from me that there's not a word of truth in it."

"Dad it's only four more days till Christmas," Louie cried out abruptly. "I want a pair of skis and Chips wants a set of golf clubs . . . He'll be disappointed about the divorce because Roger belongs to the Chevy Chase Club. Now that you are back Dad can't we join?"

"Maybe we can when we've moved and pulled ourselves together a little."

"You boys wash up and I'll have supper on the table in a twinkling," said Grace with somewhat mechanical cheerfulness.

"Don't forget Dad," Louie said as he went off whistling towards the bathroom, "it's only four more days till Christmas."

Christmas wasn't our favorite feast but we did try to make this Christmas a good one on account of the boys. The war being over and everybody's sons and brothers trooping home out of the services filled the country with a sense of celebration. We had a huge tree and the boys got their skis and their golfclubs. As my part of the pillage of Germany I'd brought Grace a set of Meissen china and some sparkling crystal wine glasses. In the afternoon we asked everybody we could think of to an eggnog party. It seemed the simplest way of squelching Quint Busby's canard. People came in swarms on account of the notoriety. There were Herman Boggs and his wife and Walker Watson and the Paul Graves and the Warings and the Turbevilles and Mortimer and Gertrude Anne and Emmaline and Joe Grainger. Some people brought friends we hardly knew. Their jaws certainly gaped wide when they saw Roger Thurloe, freshfaced and full of bounce, walk in with Alicia.

Alicia's hair was white with a little bluish tint. She looked gauntly handsome in a squarely cut royalblue dress but she was stiff as a Coldstream Guard on parade. She looked more the titled Englishwoman than ever.

She walked right over to Grace and me and took one of our hands in each of hers. "You darlings I'm so glad to see you," she almost shouted. "If you knew how funny they all looked," she added in a dry little giggling whisper intended for our ears alone, "coming back suddenly into the world like this . . . If you changed the people where I've been for the people at your party," she went on in a loud emphatic voice again, "it wouldn't make the slightest difference. Wouldn't they all just die if they knew it?"

Laughing uproariously, her eyes searched our faces to see if we were laughing too. I couldn't think how to answer. She refused a drink.

"Roger says you've done a lot of painting, Alicia," Grace stammered.

Alicia rolled her eyes up towards the ceiling. "White on white on white" she murmured. "And then black . . . the colors there are in black . . . When I have a show I'm going to call it the psychopathology of everyday life . . . Don't worry about me, I'm all right," she added suddenly.

Relieved that she seemed to have a hold on herself I started to chat around among the guests. You could see that most of them were a little scared of Alicia. I bustled about trying to give the impression that it was perfectly natural to have her behave so strangely.

Herman Boggs wasn't bothered. As usual he had backed into a corner of the room and was drawing an audience by the acid crackle of his remarks about everything and everybody. He had just handed in his resignation to the President. "For the first time in twelve years I'm a free agent," he was saying. "Now I really am going to say what I think."

Joe Grainger was trying to get a rise out of him by bringing up his name as Progressive candidate for the presidency in '48. "He'd have to be a La Follette," growled Herman. "Anyway the Communists will give the Progressives the kiss of death, you mark my words," he said. "No, I'm out of the rat race now." He gave a threatening look around. "I'll probably write my memoirs."

At the sound of the word presidency I saw a frightened flash in Walker Watson's slit eyes looking out from behind their heavy pouches. A twitch stirred the long seams of his face. For an instant he had the guilty look of a man caught with his hand in the till. Every ear in the room seemed to tighten at the word "presidency."

"What does a man have to look like to get elected President?" Roger asked boisterously.

Grace had made the boys a small bowl of eggnog without any liquor. They were swilling it down in a corner of the room when their ears pricked up at Roger's voice. They were both of them devoted to Roger. "Why don't you be President Roger?" Louie called out in his shrill little voice. "We want Roger Thurloe for President," boomed Chips.

Roger strolled over towards them laughing unashamedly. "The trouble is," he said, "I'd have to wait too long for your votes." He filled his mug at their private eggnog bowl. I hustled over to muzzle any further indiscretions; people are so easily embarrassed by a mention of the presidency at Washington gatherings.

"Then we really would be celebrities," Chips was saying.

"That would be keen," piped up Louie. "Even Dad made Quint Busby's hour. I heard him over the radio."

Something in my face made Louie cringe and slink out of the room. Chips soon followed after him. Roger noticed how many people had stopped talking to listen. The smile left his face. His small jaw clamped tight. Soon after he gathered up Alicia and left.

Neither Grace nor I could think of much to say to people. The party was turning into a frost. I could see that Grace was too tired to care. The guests melted away. Even Emmaline left early. "They are all in a hurry to go home and talk about us," Grace said when the last one had gone. She made a face and gave a helpless little shrug.

"What are we going to say to the boys?" I let myself drop into a chair. "Would it help anything if I gave them each a whipping?"

"It's too late," she said. She looked down at me with tears in her eyes. "Ro you know there isn't any situation."

"Of course. Of course."

The business was too painful to go on talking about.

When the spring mornings began after we moved back to Georgetown I found myself walking into the city with Roger just as we had in the old days. He never mentioned the stories about Grace but he did talk a great deal about Wells Hartley's column. Half truths, he kept insisting. He was doing his damndest to keep the country strong; twist that around a little and you could turn him into a warmonger and a militarist. Before he came to Washington he had helped market the securities of various companies that now had government contracts. Twist that around a little and you could say that he would profit personally by his defense program. "After all, that's what the American people hired me for," he added with a childish whine in his voice, "to attend to their national defense."

He turned to me suddenly with his small twisted smile. We were waiting for the traffic light at one of the circles to turn green. "Ro," he pleaded, "this man's an intelligent fellow . . . Now couldn't somebody go to him and explain to him what I'm trying to do."

"I wouldn't be any good." I shook my head hurriedly.

"How about Mortimer Price?"

"I'll talk to Mortimer," I said although even then I knew what Mortimer would say.

We walked the rest of the way in through the park along the river without speaking. Just before he left me to cross the bridge towards the new huge building on the Arlington side, he stopped again.

"They made it easy for the Prime Minister in England," he said. "They threw him out of office . . . But I don't think the American people want to throw me out of office. I think they agree with what I'm trying to do. It's all these busybodies. I think so often of what the grand old fellow said. Do you remember? . . . It scares me sometimes the way I seem to be losing my memory . . . It was something about 'the rut of inertia, the confusion of aim and the craven fear of being great.'" He seemed short of breath and gagged a little over the words as he repeated them but they seemed to make him feel better.

He gave me a sudden wink and went off across the bridge with his bouncy stride.

I made a formal appointment to see Mortimer at his office to make sure of having an uninterrupted talk. When I tried to outline Roger's program to him he heard me through, frowning impatiently.

"The man has become a megalomaniac," he said. "He drove his wife crazy and now he has involved you and Grace . . . If I weren't a good friend of yours, Ro, all this would sound mighty odd coming from you."

I couldn't help losing my temper at that. Flushing red I jumped to my feet.

Mortimer gave me a frightened look and followed me to the door, his thick brows knitted and his jowls drooping with concern. "Feller, you mustn't mind me . . . You know me from of old. If I have something on my mind I spit it out, as the feller said."

He put his arm around my shoulders. "Look here Ro . . . I know Wells better than you do. He feels that Thurloe is trying to undo all the great work of the past administration . . . The union of peace loving nations. The peace of the world will be based on understanding . . . Nations after all are like people. If you meet them half way they will meet you half way."

He folded up his long body into the chair behind his desk, and leaned back and yawned. "We are hanging the war criminals in Germany and Japan, we can't encourage a new breed of them at home," he said in his most pontifical tone. He puffed out his cheeks and fixed his eyes on the ceiling.

I was talking distractedly back and forth across the office trying to think of some phrase that might penetrate to him when the buzzer for his desk sounded. Right away I gave the conversation up as hopeless.

"Take it easy, Ro," he murmured soothingly as he followed me out into the reception room to say goodbye. "I know how upset you must be. Gertrude Ann and I have been concerned about you . . . What you and Grace both need is to get out of this town for a good long vacation."

Grace and I did take a vacation together that summer. We didn't know that it was our last. We had found what seemed to us a really perfect camp for the boys, run by a man who taught manual training on a small lake in northern Vermont. Grace had arranged to take all the leave that had accumulated for her at the department. The night before we drove the boys up there after we were all packed up and ready to go, Grace and I were wearily stretched out on chairs in the narrow yellow parlor of the Georgetown house. The boys had gone to bed.

She got up from her chair and sat down on my lap.

"Ro," she said, "I've got to have a little operation." She tucked her head into the hollow of my neck. "Dr. Andrews says it will probably be a very tiny little operation." She grabbed me by the shoulders and leaned away from me with wide eyes. "But Ro I'm so frightened."

It was a cyst in her breast, a very tiny one. It might be nothing at all, she hurriedly explained. She didn't want me to but I called up Dr. Andrews right away at his home. His deep voice was reassuring. Exploratory, he kept saying. The chances were that he was being unduly cautious, but he couldn't be sure until he saw what was there.

"Then why can't we do it right away?"

It would be three weeks before he could get the use of an operating room, the hospitals hadn't quite recovered from the dislocations of wartime. On general principles anyway he would rather wait until Mrs. Lancaster was a little rested. She had been working too hard. She seemed rundown. He wasn't too happy about her heart. "Take her for a nice little trip, a complete change of scene. We'll be ready for her on July 15. Enjoy yourselves," he added. "Don't you worry and don't let her worry."

"You see," Grace said tearfully after I'd hung up. "I'm not worth the powder and shot to shoot me . . . You know how pigheaded you got about not coming home from the Pacific . . . well I was just as determined I'd stay on and help Roger but I turned out too no-account."

Then she went on spacing her words slowly as if she were explaining something to a foreigner: "Roger is the only great man we have left."

We placed the boys in their Vermont camp and drove north into Canada. It was years since we had been on a motor trip, just the two of us. We stayed in the best hotels in Montreal and Quebec and were extravagant about our meals. Mostly we talked about old trips we had taken years ago, to Florida and Mexico and to Europe and sailing with the Turbevilles that summer round Sicily and to the Grecian islands. We neither of us ever spoke of it but we could not forget for a moment how fast the calendar was ticking off the days.

We drove around the Gaspé Peninsula in a howling northeaster. When the rain and wind let up mountains and rivers were drowned in fog. We loved it all the same: the dark wet spruces and the great gray swift clear rivers and the surf curling white over weedgrown rocks. We took icy dips on raw beaches or in little pools under the cliffs. We lived on salmon and cod and French wine we bought at the provincial liquor stores. It was a wild blustery week. Too soon we had to wake from our dream of the stormy north and turn southward into boring and familiar landscapes again.

Washington looked hideous to us in the July heat. Grace inisisted that we let nobody know we were there. We huddled for a night feeling like fugitives in our closed up house. Eating breakfast in the kitchen next morning, just for a moment, we were happier together than we had ever been in our lives. Then we whiled away the muggy hours somehow and in the afternoon I drove her to the hospital.

Dr. Andrews was a squarefaced heavyhanded man. He talked the great fisherman and scolded us jocosely for not having gone salmon fishing on the Gaspé. Again he assured us that the chances of a malignancy were so slight as to be nonexistent. He was ready to stake his professional reputation on it, he said.

It wasn't such a bad little room. It looked out on some sycamores in the hospital yard. I brought in her suitcase and an armful of books. She had decided to read the first volume of Toynbee's *History,* and I had brought along her favorite Jane Austens and *Wuthering Heights* and a new biography of one of the Brontës. I insisted on their installing an electric fan.

While they were putting her through all the various tests I drove back home to pick up her glasses she had forgotten. On the way back I kept myself busy buying flowers and magazines and the afternoon papers. I even picked up a jar of calvesfoot jelly in a French delicatessen. I'd heard somewhere that calvesfoot jelly was good for convalescents.

When I walked in with my packages from the hospital-smelling corridor Grace was curled up in a chair wearing the pretty pink bed jacket she had bought herself for the occasion. In front of her was the stalelooking hospital supper the nurse had brought in far too soon. She was looking down at the dishes with her nose crinkled up. "You eat it Ro . . . I just can't."

When the nurse came for the tray she announced threateningly that visitors must be out of the hospital by eight. "I guess I might as well go to bed," Grace said.

We neither of us had anything much to tell each other. We just didn't want to be separated. I sat on the edge of the bed holding her hand and we both stared out at the summer twilight fading on the great dusty leaves of the sycamores.

"Ro the time goes so fast," she whispered squeezing my hand hard. "Teach me not to be frightened."

I sat there half lying back against her pillow with my arm around her talking gently in her ear. My face was buried in her silky little graying curls. I don't remember what I said but everything I'd ever felt for her was in it. Somehow I found in myself the strength to make her strong.

"The time goes so fast," she said again. "There's no time left to be anything but brave."

When I came back early in the morning after a sleepless night she was all ready to buck my spirits up. "Weren't we a pair of sillies to go all to pieces over a tiny little cyst," she whispered low so that the nurse shouldn't hear. "I'm such a vain little thing. I couldn't bear the thought . . . Now I don't care . . . It's because we love each other," she added when I had kissed her mouth.

She waved gaily to me when they trundled her off on the flat rolling cot to the operating room.

I sat waiting in a helpless confusion of fears. A nurse's aide came for me. Dr. Andrews wanted to speak to me. Dr. Andrews was standing in the door of the operating room, a square heavy man hidden under the white uniform and the rubber gloves. His gauze mask hung from one ear. There was no expression on his face. The laboratory reported a malignancy he said. He would have to have my permission to continue with the major operation. I waited two hours. The next time I saw her she was dead . . .

15

. . . Ro wakes with a start.

He is horribly and deeply in pain. He lies on his back beside Elsa pressing his arms tightly against his sides for fear some twitch may wake her.

He has to share his pain.

"You must understand the gamble it was," he explains without speaking the words, "getting you to come, gallivanting around with a crazy redhead with three thousand dollars in my jeans."

He has to tell her: "I should have known it was too late. They do it on purpose, you said. What you said was deadly true. At the bottom of every piece of ill luck there's the wrong choice, the slip of the will that opens the door to disaster.

"Disaster. It's not being broke. I've been broke before. It's not failing to make good with a woman, that's happened before. It happens to everybody sooner or later. Casanova thought nothing of it. If at first you don't succeed try try again. But in every love between man and woman there is a moment when a door in the heart opens. When your heart might have opened I didn't have the manhood to push in. Now it is too late. You caught cold you said out on the streets. I know what you meant.

"It's not to make you sorry for me Elsa, it's just that you ought to understand. To understand is to forgive you know. It is more than a man can bear alone.

"When I was a boy growing up somebody told me that if I could stand the unhappiness of adolescence everything else would be easy, but this is worse Elsa, the frustration of defeat when you are a man grown and aged.

"When I was a boy growing up, how I hated the state university and the routine chitchat of the faculty gatherings Dad and Mother had at the house, and the humdrum, and the schoolrooms, and the dust, and the playgrounds, and the stale Scioto sluggish under the bridges, and the pentup inland air, and Dad sitting at his desk with a few pale wisps of hair always untidy over his bald forehead, and that futile smile that never would assert itself under the round glasses that hid his eyes.

"Under it after all he was a true man.

"I hated him and loved him; but now I know, with Dad and Mother so long dead, that it was their picture of what ought to be I tried to find the words to make come true.

"Elsa, it was religion really, a belief that way down under the playacting of daily life in every man a hermit sits in the desert where Jesus was tempted to evil and where Moses received the law in words of fire. There in the fearful inner stillness of conscience a man must choose the good or the bad. One choice only. No question of adjusting there. I chose the right, remember that when you think of me Elsa, I had the nerve not to follow the easy path with the humdrum multitude. I was too weak to make the right prevail."

He stands on his feet beside the bed. His lips move. "Don't think too hardly of me Elsa." He whispers down to her as she lies sullenly asleep. "You are young enough to try other things, other men. I guess I'm not. I can't stand this any more."

He thrusts his head out of the window. No air stirs. The street lamps in the street below glare through a red blur like the unshaded lamps in a jail. He has to break out.

He tiptoes out of the room. He takes a long time carefully to close the door so as not to wake her. In his own room the light burns his eyes. Blinking he gropes for his trousers, pulls on his shoes.

The empty bed drives him out of the hotel.

In trousers and pajamatop he walks down the street between the rotted coral walls. The air is hot. The street is sour. The night smells of sweat. Each light as he passes it glares out of a red star. Miasma, he catches himself thinking. These were the nights in the old days when the yellowjack fluttered feebly above the cobbles, before the men in tan tunics and the cleanup squads. And would again when Pinillo had his way. What an easy way out. The tiny sting you never felt, the headache, the fever, the cramps, the black vomit, and to sink under coverlets of downy fever into everlasting black.

Now a man has to work to make an end of himself.

Ro stands on the edge of the stone dock. There's not even any coolness over the harbor. The still water stinks of bilge. Rowboats moored in clusters stir in a faint swell. Ro stands there remembering the dead pig. "Drowned," he hears Pinillo's hating voice, "like the Americans . . ." The jibshaped fin.

The harbor's full of streetcleaner sharks. Swim out through the reeking water, swim and swim until . . . He'll be too far out when he changes his mind. The streetcleaners will finish him. Turista comido de los tiburones. The papers will never publish that. The Chamber of Commerce doesn't believe in tiburones . . . It starts to strike him funny. His mind is beginning to work. Now's the time before it's too late.

He starts down the stone steps and slips.

Fear zigzags through him like a lightning flash.

He's sliding on his bottom down the slimy steps. He catches himself, digs his nails in fright into the stone through the harbor slime.

Painfully he drags himself up to the level of the dock again.

He sits on the stone curb a long time shaking. He's rubbing the slime off his hands. A watchman with a flashlight advances ambling towards him. You damn fool you don't want to die, Ro tells himself as he picks himself up and walks away . . .

16

. . . When other men found that life was no longer to be supported they never seemed to find it too hard to make an end of themselves. Roger Thurloe never hesitated. When he found there was no way he could go on living he waited for his moment and slipped quickly out through the high hospital window and let himself drop.

There had been a new intimacy between us the few times I saw him during the last year of his life. It was Grace. Among all the people in the world only we two knew what it was like to be without her. It made for a painful sort of brotherhood. In the end even that bond snapped.

After Grace's death Roger's sister Jane and Edwin G. were immensely kind. They invited me and the boys in to spend the winter with them in their big house in Farmington, while Emmaline Cowles took over the business, which I felt utterly unable to cope with, of selling our house in Georgetown and getting the furniture packed up and put into storage.

Jane Yarborough had boys of her own. She had a great deal of her brother's administrative drive. She took over Chips and Louie with a firm friendly hand. Before they knew what had happened she had them chopping firewood and helping with the chores around the barn. Louie even learned to milk the cow. They did all right at the Farmington High. When the Yarborough boys shed their uniforms and came home full of talk of college and of the GI bill of rights and of plans for careers, my two looked up to them like a pair of demigods. I wrote Emmaline that I was living the life of a poor relation and enjoying it, but underneath everything was emptiness and the ache of irreparable loss.

The last time I saw Alicia was at Grace's funeral. She clamped my arm into hers as we walked into the cemetery through the steaming midsummer haze. It was only then I noticed how she had changed. Her teeth stood out yellowed from a face full of haggard lines. She was dressed anyhow. Her gray hair straggled over her forehead from under some kind of flat knitted hat that seemed intentionally unbecoming to her. It was fitting that she had singled me out. We were companions in agony.

I was hoping that she would say something kind about Grace—just to hear Grace's name mentioned seemed to bring her back a little—but she made no reference to the place or the circumstances.

"Therapy," she was saying, "they talk to me all the time about therapy . . . did Jesus have therapy when he hung on the cross?" She gave my ribs a dig with her elbow. "Look at him."

It was only then that I noticed that the small pursefaced man in a morning coat walking ahead of us was Roger.

Since seeing the wild accusing faces of the boys that morning while I struggled to get them breakfast:—"Dad why couldn't you have gotten a good doctor?"—I had only a fleeting knowledge of who was who among the faces familiar and unfamiliar that crowded about me. When Alicia pointed Roger out I remembered that we had stared at each other like strangers when we shook hands outside of the church that morning.

"He's the one needs therapy," Alicia was saying in a tone savage as the whine of a mechanical saw. "He can't stand failure. He can't face it. He's been successful all his life . . . Top of his class at school, won all the scholarships, Phi Beta Kappa and captain of the football team at college. Quarterback, he's a natural quarterback. What's the good of a quarterback without a team? President of his firm. Never made an investment that didn't succeed. Look how successful he was in organizing production and channeling it into the theatres of war. That was organizing for death. Now he thinks he can organize for life. Remedial therapy. What he doesn't know is that there is no life unless the Christ in us is crucified and on the third day rises again." Her voice went on in a singsong whine.

The minister had started reading the burial service. I tried to get Alicia to keep quiet. "I don't need to listen," her voice rasped. "I have it within me. I am the resurrection and the light." Her voice rose to a shriek.

At that point a woman attendant with beefy cheeks came up from behind and led her away.

Somehow Alicia's having been there made it less painful for me to stand before that open grave. The stubborn derangement of her mind filled me with humbleness and respect. I never saw her again.

She wrote me letters. She wrote Roger almost every day.

Roger used to bring her letters to Farmington with him the few times he could steal a couple of days from the fierce battle his life in Washington had become. From her sanatorium Alicia had fallen into correspondence with the members of a revivalist sect. Almost daily she sent Roger thick packets of clippings from the daily papers on which she scrawled references to chapter and verse in the Book of Revelations.

"She's trying to help," he told me. "It's rather wonderful to know that she is trying to help." He gave his little dry laugh. "Almost everybody else is trying to hinder."

It was a prematurely hot spring evening. We were walking back and forth on the Yarboroughs' terrace looking at the smudges of new green on the bare branches that were reflected in the brown river. Roger had a tired hagridden look but his eyes were bright. He was in high spirits. There was the usual bounce to his stride.

"To tell the truth the Book of Revelations is as good a guide as any," he was saying. "What the bomb really means is that Armageddon is here very much as the religious enthusiasts imagined it . . . What I want you to tell the people of this country, Ro, is that we have the power if we only use it positively and sensibly to give ourselves and the world a hundred years of peace . . . It will take us a hundred years to control the new technology. We've got to know what we want to do . . . It's up to fellows like you to spell it out for us . . . Not in detail, but in outline. There ought to be an American democratic theory like there is a Marxist theory."

I told him I had been beating my brains out on the project all winter. I wasn't the only one. Hundreds of other men were trying to put it into words.

Roger grabbed me by the lapel. He began to talk fast. He was breathing hard into my face. He was so youthfully eager that something about his manner struck me as a sort of parody of what his manner must have been years ago when he was just out of college and went out to sell bonds.

"For a couple of centuries, before they went to pieces, the English managed to teach it to their children . . . You must remember what old Wells told you about picking up the burden of empire, you know, the night you had dinner with him not long before he died . . . All this rubbish about imperialism and capitalist exploitation . . . The Philippines are our kind of imperialism, the good kind . . . What the intellectual muddlers who raise such a racket about the common man can't see is that if we let these people conquer the world it will mean the most brutal exploitation of the common man history has ever seen . . . We've got the power in our hands to thwart them. Just for a few years . . . We won't have it for long. All we need is the will to use it."

We were interrupted by Jane's guests arriving for dinner. When the first pair approached us across the terrace we sealed our mouths up guiltily as if we were planning a bank robbery.

The next time I had a private talk with Roger was in New York. Chips was at Dartmouth and Louie was tutoring for his college boards under Jane's vigilant eye at Farmington. I had moved into the old Lafayette in New York to correct proofs on the book I had finally found a publisher for: *Blueprint for the Future.*

Roger was in New York to deliver a speech. When I went to see him up at the Biltmore I took a copy of the proofs along. His drawing room was full of people. I could smell the cigar smoke seeping out from under the door. When I knocked, his secretary stuck her head out and told me to go into the door of his bedroom.

He came out of the bathroom in his shirtsleeves wiping his hands with a towel. He looked small and shrunken though his jaw still wore an aggressive tilt.

"It's good to see you, Ro." He made a gesture with his head towards the other room. "In there it's full of political cigars and confidential shenanigans. They are all talking about how the Democrats may lose this vote or that vote . . . What I feel like telling 'em is suppose we lose the United States."

I congratulated him on his appointment to what was really the highest office in the cabinet. Certainly it was the toughest.

"It's an office that's likely to be the greatest depository for dead cats in history," he said without smiling.

I brought out my packages of proofs. He snatched at the package and laid it on the bed without looking at it.

"I want to read it. I've got to read it carefully. If I only had time to think and work. You know the way it is, Ro. After really cutting out the inessentials, and God knows I'm ruthless about it, I have eight to ten hours of really necessary conferences a day. In all that where an I going to find the time to think anything through? You tell me Ro."

Already there was a knocking at the door that led into the rest of the suite. Someone opened the door a crack and whispered deferentially, "It's Mr. Blakeman, sir. He's brought those people from the manufacturers' association you said you would talk to, sir."

Roger was standing in front of the dressing table scratching the top of his head as he stared unseeingly into the mirror. His face wore a look of unaccustomed puzzlement. "You see how it is," he said in a tired helpless voice.

When I had gathered up my hat and raincoat to leave he called after me with a burst of his old energy, "Have you got in the airlift? Put in plenty about the airlift that saved Berlin . . . That's the sort of thing we know how to do."

He never did get time to read through my proofs. I finally had to send the book to press without his introduction I had been hoping for.

A few days before the book came out in the fall I had a phone call from Jane. She was worried about her brother. She had been begging him to resign before he was forced out of office. He was insisting that he must hold on till after election. "He says he wouldn't know what to do with himself if he resigned." Her voice droned miserably at the end of the line. "He says he couldn't look himself in the glass and call himself a quitter . . . Poor thing he's so worn and tired he's not himself at all. He's got a sore place at the top of his head from scratching it. I've argued and argued with him and so have we all. All he'll answer is that even if it is just egotism as they all say he has to stick to his job. He says he's a victim of the Washington scene."

Before she hung up she had made me give her my word I would go to Washington and talk to him. Next morning, lacerated by the memories of Grace that trip always filled me with, I boarded the Washington train.

It took me several days to get an appointment with Roger. When I did I found him hunched behind his gleaming executive's desk staring at me with hostile eyes. From a drawer he pulled out a clipping of a speech by Herman Boggs, excoriating him in the best Boggsian style.

"I would have thought some of my friends would have answered him by this time," he said bitterly. "Herman certainly messed up plenty of things in his day."

I started to mutter something about having been busy with my book. I tried to explain that it wasn't too easy to find a place to print unpopular ideas.

Without listening to what I was saying he pulled out a

stack of clippings of Wells Hartley's column. "Take 'em along. Study 'em. Do something about 'em," he said harshly.

The buzzer sounded on his desk. He was hardly civil as I left.

With all the clippings in my pocket I called up Wells Hartley and asked him out to lunch. After a good deal of beating about the bush and talk of previous engagements he suddenly changed his tone and said no I'd have to lunch with him, why not tomorrow? He wants to see what he can get out of me, I told myself.

We lunched at Wells Hartley's usual table at the Mayflower. Hartley had uneasy blue eyes and colorless hair and a rather tallowy face. Little half formed expressions kept flitting over it. As he leaned back in his chair to look me over I felt that all he cared for was that feeling of being in the driver's seat. Maybe not, maybe it was the public interest. His manner was mild. He smiled as he spoke: "Naturally his friends will think it is too bad but when a man has outlived his usefulness in this town the only thing for him to do is step down."

I couldn't think of anything to say. I felt my silence was disloyal to Roger, but I couldn't find anything to say. Hartley was so sure of his own righteousness.

"You read Herman's speech?" he went on. "You know Herman's a very kind man under all his bluster . . . He spoke as he did because he felt it was his duty. That's how we all feel in this town."

It was a very unpleasant lunch. When I finally got around to trying to explain Roger's program I had the same nightmare feeling I'd had when I talked to Mortimer. We were using the same words but the words didn't mean the same things to us.

Right after election I had to go out to Chicago to work on that story for Picture Magazine, the story that took up so many months and demanded so many trips and that in the end they never published. The day I read of Roger Thurloe's resignation I called Jane Yarborough long distance from my hotel. I felt a little shy about calling Roger directly.

Jane was consoling. He wasn't as bad as she had feared. Of course he was terribly depressed. There was something physical, she felt, at the bottom of his depression. She was driving him into a New York hospital for a check up, but mostly for the rest. She felt he ought to be under medical supervision for a while. "Ro, I'll let you know as soon as Roger asks to see you . . . I know Roger will when he's himself again," she added in her cheery hostess's voice.

Arriving back at the Grand Central Station I picked up an afternoon paper and read in the headline that Roger had made an end of himself. In some ways it was a deeper blow than Grace's death. It wasn't exactly the personal loss. All that Roger and I had left in common was deeply painful to both of us. It was the failure of everything we had hoped for. It was his defeat I shared with him as I read the sparse and pathetic details of his end. His death seemed to seal that failure for us both forever . . .

17

. . . Ro wakes up alone in his room in the old Spanish hotel. The sun is bright. The sky is blue. The seabreeze shakes the shade in the window. He rings and orders coffee and orangejuice from a pleasantfaced maid. He gets up and starts to shave. It's Monday morning he is telling himself. A new week is beginning.

The memory of yesterday arouses no feeling at all. No money, no girl, he catches himself shrugging at his own old raddled face in the mirror.

Thank God Mortimer's in town. An argument with Mortimer will bring back the feeling of the old days. Kidding Mortimer will tone up his nerve. He may even borrow a grand, or five hundred at least, enough for a breathing spell to let him get this article written. This is the time a man needs a friend.

He hurries through his bread and butter and drinks up all the coffee in the whitemetal pot. Then he starts to walk across town to save taxi fare to the Nacional.

The stone and stucco streets are bright with sun. The breeze smells of the sea. The sunlight glints on the curved enamel and brightwork of cars, on dark leaves of myrtle, on curly hair; the sunlight flashes in women's eyes. The streets clatter with weekday bustle. Everybody seems bound on enlivening business. Only Ro feels holloweyed and numb. His back aches; in his stoop he feels a premonition of the panhandler's cringe. He'll have to ask Mortimer for some money.

As he stands at the desk in the greenish cool of the great hotel lobby asking for Mr. Price he feels suspicion in the clerk's appraising glance. He tries to get back the brisk bearing of a man accustomed to deference, but his legs are weary; his shirt collar is wet with sweat. The clerk points contemptuously to the house phone. Ro imagines surprise on the clerk's face when Mortimer's bass voice answers, "Come on up."

Ro has hardly raised his hand to knock on the outside door of Mortimer's suite when the door opens in his face to let out a slickhaired young man with a briefcase under his arm. The young man's face wears a smirk of pure conceit. There's a slick little wave to his hair.

The wish flashes through Ro's head to be that young man just for a moment, to shake loose just for a moment from his own doomed self.

The door opens into a hallway. Ro forgets himself in the anticipation of a lively give and take with Mortimer. He can feel his lips shaping into the oldtime smile, his stride lengthening to the oldtime rolling confident gait.

"Well, Mortimer, how is the great man today?"

Mortimer is striding up and down in front of the windows in his old dressing gown with a scowl on his dark mastiff's face. He waves Ro peremptorily into a chair and plunks himself down at the desk to go on dictating into a dictaphone something about . . . "sympathetic understanding of the viewpoint of friendly nations . . . patient explanation of the significance of liberal policies at home . . . generous aid in the betterment of local conditions."

Mortimer's old dressing gown with its purple and dun stripes stirs a recollection. Mortimer had that dressing gown with him on that famous frenzied night in Lisbon after they crossed on the clipper together. Free evenings in his room at the Dorchester he used to slip it over his clothes to keep out the London chill while Ro would button up his trenchcoat and they would huddle in the deep-stuffed chairs over a bottle of Scotch and let their talk ramble as it chose. Mortimer in his old striped dressing gown.

He has an affection for the guy, Ro thinks as he watches Mortimer's face grow sodden with selfimportance while he mouths his phrases into the dictaphone. Ro used to call that Mortimer's stuffed shirt expression. There always were things they couldn't talk about; but Mortimer used to be endlessly amusing about speakeasy life with the New York *World,* and ghosting a play for a Tammany sachem, and what he called his hundred days in Hollywood. Ro used to love his deadpan look while he gave a comical turn to a phrase, and the way he scowled into his glass before coming up with a crack.

Mortimer never smoked. His rooms always smelled of toothpaste and listerine. He was a great one to be gargling his throat, always complaining about his tonsils. Right now it gives Ro a sense of reminiscent pleasure to catch that little whiff of listerine in the air in Mortimer's suite at the Nacional.

"Excuse me Roland." Mortimer has turned the dictaphone off and comes striding towards him. "I had a paragraph I had to finish. Ever used one of these gimmicks? Wonderful time saver. My secretary comes in the afternoon. In the mornings I just walk around the room and listen to myself think. Well, well." He pumps Ro's hand up and down. "Still the old rolling stone. What the devil are you doing down here?"

He glares pettishly into Ro's face as if it annoyed him to find Ro in Havana without his permission.

Ro mutters something about an article, about the building up of hostile armies round the Caribbean, about our country's weakening position in the world. In spite of himself his voice has taken on an apologetic tone.

"Why all the melodrama, Roland?" booms Mortimer suddenly thrusting his face close to Ro's. "You guys are suffering from shellshock."

Ro admits that it's possible to exaggerate—he's stuttering like a schoolboy who doesn't know his lesson—but isn't it useful to have a dissenting opinion published now and then?

"If you looked at the map you might notice the shrinking of the western world."

"All the more reason for not rocking the boat," booms Mortimer. "At the time when we need more than anything a broad reasonable bipartisan approach, you fellows come out with your reactionary dirges . . . You insult the administration. You make us ridiculous in the eyes of the world."

Ro bursts out laughing. "Now Mortimer you just sit down and tell me what you mean by reactionary."

Mortimer is striding back and forth behind his desk.

"No use trying to put the clock back," he booms. "We have to reckon with the new forces.

He's working his arms like a man in a walking race.

"That's just what I was saying, but don't you think they ought to be described?"

"By liberalminded forwardlooking men yes, but not by witch hunters. You guys are suffering from shellshock. You see mightmares under every bed. Criticism ought to be constructive. Why all the melodrama?" he repeats insistently.

Melodrama. On a tiny screen inside Ro's head a black little picture flashes of himself in trousers and pyjamatop clinging in the night to the slime of the steps at the edge of the harbor. Could that have been me? Can it be that Mortimer's right?

He lets himself drop back into the armchair.

"Perhaps it is possible to feel too passionately about the future of your country," he says quietly. He tries to change the subject. "Ever see George Elbert?"

Sure Mortimer saw George Elbert in Paris a couple of weeks ago, the same old George only fatter and saucier. The things he'd said about Roland wouldn't bear repeating. His recent articles were magnificent. He was a comer on the air. George Elbert now, he was a shoemaker who stuck to his last without meddling in matters he didn't understand. His new wife was a charmer. Mortimer will be seeing them in Rome. Mortimer is looking forward to that . . . Two weeks in Rome with the Warners.

Ro sits staring at his dusty shoes. "I know he doesn't think much of me any more," he mumbles.

Ro's thinking of Paris, a rosy antediluvian Paris where the streets always smelt of strawberries when young Georgy Warner used to bring his stories round to his hotel for him to revise before he cabled them; how they used to sit together over beers at cheap cafés reading Chronicles and Kings to improve their narrative style; and Georgy's hanger on who had a system that was going to make them all rich at the horseraces—even in those days Georgy always had a hanger on—; and the jumping race where their magnificent dark horse they'd bet on to win bolted and took all the jumps in the wrong direction; they hadn't stopped laughing for a week.

"We always had a good time," Ro adds musingly," "when we were together." He gets to his feet and steps smiling toward Mortimer who sits with pendulous black jowls glooming behind his desk. "And that goes for you too you old stuffed shirt."

Mortimer half smiles but right away he's off again playing the schoolmaster bent on lecturing an erring sixth-former. "Why don't you snap out of it Roland and write a novel about small towns in Ohio when you were a boy. You used to tell funny stories about them. Everybody likes small towns in Ohio."

"That was mostly Grace," says Ro. "And besides Columbus wasn't a small town."

"You and Grace sure were a likely pair," Mortimer sighs. Ro begins to smile back but Mortimer's eyes don't meet his eyes. "That was in the days of Lou," Mortimer says and sighs again. "Poor Lou . . . Lou was my wife in those days, as men have wives . . ." Mortimer goes on booming retrospectively. "Lord, lord . . . One of these days maybe we can get together and catch up on each other again."

Mortimer's looking at his wristwatch. He clears his throat.

"You are probably busy," Ro hears himself stammer. "But how would it be if we broke away for lunch?" His voice is firm now. "Do you remember that lunch, the first time I took you to see the Molloys? It started at the Plaza in New York and we all went out driving in a red Stutz and they ended by buying a house out on Long Island and we took in a carnival and rode on all the rollercoasters; the lunch that lasted twentyfour hours?"

“What made you think of that?” asks Mortimer.

He clears his throat, coughs.

“Damn my throat,” he says and gives Ro an odd searching look. For a moment his face softens but immediately he’s the public figure again. “I’d like nothing better than to lunch with you, but my dear fellow, my time is not my own. I’m all booked up. I’ve got a dinner at the embassy and I’m flying out in the morning. A man isn’t his own master these days, Roland. In fact there are people waiting for me downstairs right now.”

Mortimer gets to his feet and squares his shoulders as if facing an unpleasant duty. He clears his throat again. “But let me tell you, Roland right here and now that I would take a very dim view of any sensational articles on such topics at this time. I don’t understand why a man of your standing, Roland, lends himself to such distortions. Of course I know the magazines have to have sensations and you feel you have to supply yourself with an income that fits your situation in the world, but don’t expect me to read them.”

Ro stands in front of the desk holding his hat and shifting from one foot to the other while he waits for Mortimer to shake hands. He feels like an office boy about to be fired. Searching for a glimpse of the old friendship he looks up and down Mortimer’s long face with its dark dangling jowls. The eyes in their deep sockets never meet his.

All he can find on that face, now, is the determination to be rid of an unwelcome visitor.

“Well maybe another time,” Ro says haltingly, as he turns to go, but he knows in his heart that there will be no other time.

It isn’t until he’s walking along the hotel corridor towards the elevator that he remembers that he intended to touch Mortimer for a loan. Do you suppose he read my mind? he asks himself. Mortimer always was close with his money. Ro can't help smiling at that. He lets himself drop on a bench opposite the elevator. No friend, no loan, no girl; in the old days when things got bad he always used to cook up a trip.

You fool you're on a trip. A hell of a trip. He feels suddenly desperately weary. It isn't that his muscles are tired; it's boredom. It's so damn boring to spend your life worrying about women and money. He is too weary to get to his feet.

The elevator door has opened and closed a dozen times before Ro pulls himself up with an effort. Elsa will be wondering where he is. He mustn't let Mortimer find him sitting there like a dummy.

At the main entrance of the hotel Ro catches himself just as he is about to call a taxi. Instead he walks around the corner and climbs on a streetcar.

There's a sprinkling of people on the seats, middle of the morning people, people with no visible means of support: desultory people. Two housewives bound downtown for shopping, an elderly man in an oldfashioned flat straw hat with a wide black ribbon who doesn't seem to be bound anywhere in particular, an out-of-work shop girl who looks no better than she should be, a couple of Spanish workmen in blue denims off somewhere in search of a job: desultory people, out of work desultory people like himself.

Ro feels at home among them. Outsiders obviously.

What Mortimer has been trying to explain to him in a crude way, he tells himself, is that Roland Lancaster is an outsider now, a fellow the insiders don't care to waste their time with. Next time I try to see him, he'll probably be out.

Clanging with the screech of wheels on rails the streetcar lurches its noisy way round sharp corners on narrow streets.

Suppose Ro finds himself some little job like his friend the sergeant years ago out on the beach and Elsa gets the children down: they'll live as the Cubans do. Pester the boys for handouts, a remittance man. If she gets pregnant I'll marry her no matter what, I promised myself that. A child will draw them together. She understands that too. She's oddly understanding about so many things. But then there'll be Pinillo lurking around to put him in the wrong. Suppose she starts sleeping with Pinillo or the Black Condor, good God!

Ro comes to with a start. A stout woman with an armful of parcels has dug a sharp little heel into his foot as she puffs past him. Apologizing profusely in cooing Cuban she drops into a seat opposite. He takes off his hat and smiles. It is nothing. She makes apologetic noises and smiles back. Her smile gives him a feeling of confidence.

The street car has made its stop in Central Park and started off out towards the Vedado again before he notices where he is. He has to pay the conductor an extra fare. He stumbles off and stands dazed on a corner. He's on the sunny side of the street, out of the breeze. His face runs with sweat.

"What do I do now?" he mumbles to himself vaguely. "Of course Elsa . . . She'll be wondering where I've gone."

Walking down Obispo he remembers the cable office. They are to hold any message. He hesitates a little in front of the door. If Sid answers so soon it will mean no go. He steps into the cool air under the ceiling fan, hears the sound of someone typing, the customary clicking of the teletype. Good news or bad, he likes it there. The man behind the counter has recognized him and is holding out a cable with a smile.

Before he opens the envelope Ro knows what it will say. Mortimer is litmus paper. Mortimer's notions always did forebode the state of mind of the right thinkers. Sorry. Unconvinced. Inadvisable. Sid was embarrassed. He has used too many words. All about a Puerto Rican feature in the works, articles on the Leeward Islands.

Without reading it through Ro crumples the message in his hand and drops it in the wastebasket.

He slogs on down the street to the hotel . . .

18

. . . *Blueprint for the Future*. Nobody read it. What's the use of writing things nobody reads? I guess I couldn't find the right words, the words Roger used to ask me for so pitifully. Maybe if Grace had lived we could have thought them up together. All that was left of our hopes of those days was a nightmare, a nightmare often recurrent. In my dream I was tacking a small sailboat against an ebbing tide. In my dream I was tacking in a light breeze against a tide that poured around a spit of white sand. Beyond that sandspit was the harbor and other boats luffing up to their anchorage. Sunlight on sails. Blue secure coves . . . First on one tack, then on the other; but no matter how smartly I come about, no matter how carefully I trim the mainsail and jib—look she's making speed, she has a bone in her teeth, she's leaving a straight wake behind her—every time I come abreast of the sandspit I'm further out to sea. Tack and tack again. Gulls shriek derision overhead. Not enough wind. Can't beat to windward against this ebbing tide. The whole implacable ocean pours out past that sandspit, sweeping me away, sweeping me to oblivion . . .

19

. . . Elsa's door is ajar. No answer to Ro's knock. He pushes in. She's lying flat on the bed in her nightgown. Peering out of her white face from under the billow of red hair her eyes look dark and dismayed as the eyes of a squirrel caught in a trap. There's a mussed breakfast tray on the night table beside her, a cup half full of cold coffee that has spilt over on the saucer, some tornup scraps of rolls, cigarette butts on the butterplate.

"I've got the curse," she says right at once. "I'm having a bad time. Cramps. Get me a drink of gin."

Ro closes the door behind him and walks to the phone. For a moment he lets himself lean weakly against the wall with his eyes closed, his mouth against the mouthpiece.

There's a spinning in his head. No pregnancy. He feels a surge of relief; then a sudden drop like down an elevator into disappointment.

He unhooks the receiver. A voice answers in polite Spanish at the other end of the wire. Hoarsely he orders two double gins with bitters and hangs up.

When he turns to face her she's looking him over appraisingly but in fairly friendly fashion from the bed. There's even a small smile on her lips. "Ro you look half dead. Had a busy morning about your article?"

Ro stands in the middle of the floor with his hands in his pockets staring out of the open window at the blue glare of noon. The windowsill glows in the sun like a bar of hot metal. From the street below rises the roaring and the honking and the calling and the crying of the traffic. Ro's heart is thumping in his chest. His hands are cold in his pockets. The things he wants to say stick in his throat. At last he does manage to blurt out something about having done some pacing of the streets last night.

He lifts up her crumpled green dress and lets himself drop into the armchair. He closes his eyes for a second. "Need sleep I guess," he says.

He yawns.

He sits in the armchair with his eyes closed while the light glares red through his lids, smelling the burnt gasoline and the coffee roasting and the midday meals cooking and from somewhere a whiff of heavy fragrance that might be tuberoses. This was what he'd planned to enjoy so, the girl, the warmth, the fragrance, the tropic clatter of the city.

He's helplessly tired. His lids scrape his throbbing eyeballs as he opens them.

He reaches for her long hand that lies limp on the edge of the bed. She lets him take her hand. He sits for a while holding her hand looking about the room with compassionate eyes, at the dress she's washed out that hangs from the bathroom door, and the wet stockings draped over a towel on the back of a chair and the torn brassiere dangling from the bureau where an upset jar of cold cream wallows in crumpled tissue amid a dusting of spilt face powder. Her two poor wicker suitcases lie open against the wall under a pile of soiled clothes topped by a downat-theheel canvas sneaker. He finds an endearing pathos in the litter: she isn't having a good time either.

"Elsa," he says, "suppose I went to a doctor and got all hopped up with hormones?"

"Ro, I told you before it's not you, it's me."

Something in her voice makes him rise to his feet. He stands beside the bed holding her hand and looking down into her face. Her eyelids are red as if she has been crying. All the little muscles of her face tremble. Her lips are pressed tight together. "You've got to believe things I tell you," she blurts out.

He tries to shake out a laugh. "Aren't we a couple of wrecks?" He clears his throat. "Elsa, I better tell you right away. Mortimer isn't going to be any help. He thinks I'm a has been and it's no dice about the article. I picked up a cable as I came past the office."

"We got to go home," she whispers. "I understand."

There's a knocking at the door.

Ro pays no attention and goes on. "What we've got to decide right now is whether to cash in our return tickets and stay here and slug it out or whether to take off for home."

She's not listening any more. She's thinking of something else.

There is more knocking.

Before Ro can get to the door, the waiter has burst in with the tray.

It's a young ovalfaced Spanish waiter who has just come

over from some back village in Galicia. His face is pink and yellow and a little fuzzy like a peach. When he smiles he shows a perfect set of teeth. He hurries past Ro with the tray and sets it on the center table. When he catches sight of the girl in the nightgown lying on the bed his face turns a deep red. He leans over the tray and starts to fuss inexpertly with the glasses. There are four jiggers of gin, lemons, an enormous bowl of ice, sugar, the wrong kind of bitters, a siphon of soda. They never could understand Anglo-Saxon drinks at that hotel.

"Let me do it," says Ro sharply.

The young waiter's workgrimed hands seem to be gripping the whitemetal tray harder than need be as he holds it up for Ro to sign the check. Ro notices that the young waiter can't keep his eyes from roaming over the bed. For an instant Ro catches himself seeing the little scene the way the young waiter is seeing it: the lovely redhead, the tumbled bed, the drinks at noon, the American millionaire: just the jacket of a paperbacked novel. As he presses a twenty centavo piece into the young waiter's hard palm and edges him out of the room Ro catches a glint of furious envy in his eye.

"Excuse me," he says in a formal sort of way as he walks back from the door.

Elsa pays no attention. Her face is turned to the wall.

Ro pours the gin on the ice in the two highball glasses, slops in a drop of bitters and squirts in a little water out of the siphon.

"I wanted pink gin, but it turned out a thwarted Martini," he says trying to laugh.

Elsa isn't listening. She sits up in bed and reaches eagerly for the glass.

"You had a cable!" she's saying in a peculiar bantering tone.

After taking two or three deep swigs she begins to talk

in a tiny singsong whine. She knows it's her fault she keeps saying. Everybody always told her it was her fault. Gov used to tell her it was all her fault. Hardly a day passed that Gov didn't tell her it was her fault the miserable little heel.

She begins to snivel a little sitting up on the bed nursing the glass in her two hands. Her eyes big with outrage are fixed on Ro's face. In the motefilled refraction of sunlight through the open window the skin round her eyes takes on a blue look. As she drinks she is talking fast in her whiny little outraged voice telling about how they had made her go to Gov's doctor and how Gov's doctor had told her he could fix everything if she'd let him psychoanalyze her. Of course Gov was being psychoanalyzed himself. That doctor got thousands of dollars of Gov's good money away from him. Every little thing that happened the doctor made Gov call him on the phone. It got so Gov couldn't do the least thing without calling up that doctor. "Naturally in the end the doc had to make a pass at me."

She drinks down the last of her drink.

Ro doesn't know what to say.

The seabreeze pouring in through the window is freshening his face. An airplane flying low roars overhead drowning out the racket of traffic.

"Poor little guy," Ro's tongue starts to rattle, "he must have been having a tough time. I thought I noticed something a little unbalanced. I felt a sort of sympathy for him." Ro manages a laugh. "I didn't expect to find myself in the same boat."

"You men," Elsa says. "All you think of is each other."

"He'll pull through," Ro shouts. "His banker will pull him through."

Elsa is looking in Ro's face with hard round eyes, hard like pebbles. "That shows how much you know about it," she says and presses her shaking lips together. She drops the empty glass and buries her head in the pillow. "I knew something dreadful was going to happen," she moans through the pillow.

While Ro is groping under the bed for the glass the telephone begins to ring.

"If it's Joe Herkimer I don't want to talk to him," Elsa is still talking into her pillow. "He won't have any use for me any more either. You'll none of you have any use for me. I know how men stick together."

With the glass in his hand Ro stands up against the phone on the wall. In his ear a cajoling voice is apologizing for intruding on a busy man's time. It's some time before Ro recognizes the Brooklyn vowels. "It's Eddy," the voice keeps saying, "Dontcher recognize my verse?"

Eddy hopes Mr. Lancaster has a moment because he's right downstairs with a clean copy of his story. He's decided to take a chance and let Mr. Lancaster see it. Time is of the essence. Hell's going to pop any minute now. All Mr. Lancaster needs to do is read it and mail it in, or maybe it's hot enough for the wire. Any old mag will snap it up on Mr. Lancaster's sayso.

The more Ro tries to tell Eddy he can't get anybody's story published, not even his own, the more Eddy insists. At last Ro has to tell him to leave the manuscript for him at the office in a selfaddressed envelope. "I'll be waitin' in the little gin mill acrost the street," Eddy mutters threateningly before he hangs up.

When Ro turns back from the phone, he finds Elsa sitting up on the edge of the bed with his glass in her hand. She is drinking his gin in little sips and looking musingly down at her bare feet that are still grimed with last night's mud.

It was all that doctor's talk about the father image, she is saying, made her think maybe she ought to try to fall for an older man. "My poor old dad, he let my mother henpeck him all his life. I don't believe he ever had an image."

She looks up and tries to grin at Ro through her tears.

"Maybe you oughtn't ever to have left Al," Ro whispers gently.

She pushes herself up into a sitting position. "And spend my life trying to keep that lazy lizard from kicking the gong around? You must be crazy."

The telephone starts ringing again. This time it's Joe Herkimer's voice explaining creakily that somehow things got off on the wrong foot last night. Hadn't they better get together to talk about ways and means? What he really wants is to get those boys off the hook. An article in a magazine of national circulation will do just that. Suppose Ro brings Elsa around to his place for a couple of cold ones that afternoon.

Ro puts his hand over the mouthpiece. The traffic in the street below roars in his ears. "I don't want to go," Elsa calls from the bed. "I don't want to see anybody."

"Suppose I call you later," he says to Joe Herkimer after an agonizing search for words. "I can't hear myself think in here right now."

"All right old timer," Joe Herkimer answers. His voice sounds aggrieved, "if that's the way you want to leave it."

"I'll call you back," says Ro. He pulls the windows to.

"It's going to be just like Gov's play," Elsa's voice rises shrill. "It gets on my nerves. Nobody will ever do anything because they're such heels."

Ro is standing beside the bed trying to stroke her hair off her forehead.

"Let's take it easy and decide what we ought to do."

She rolls over on the bed with the pillow held against her face: "I know how it's all going to turn out," she is talking into the pillow, "with me back in Milwaukee all cooped up in one house with my mother and the kids and all of us driving each other crazy."

A cable in a blue envelope has fallen out on the floor from under the pillow.

"Read it," she screeches. "Read it. If you had the sense to read it you would know what I was talking about."

The cable is dated Chicago.

MY FRIEND GOVERNEUR HAINES KILLED HIMSELF LAST NIGHT JUST THOUGHT YOU OUGHT TO KNOW. Rube.

Ro folds the paper carefully and slips it back in the envelope.

He starts to walk back and forth across the room. He tries to keep from looking at her.

"How strange," he's saying aloud but to himself. "That one too . . . But some of us have to go on living," he adds, talking up towards the ceiling.

Again the telephone.

This time it's Primus Hicks with his velvetsmooth voice asking Roland and Elsa to come to a party that's being given in his honor that night by some prominent citizens of the island republic, he will be honored and pleased if all his celebrated friends would avail themselves of this golden opportunity to affirm their solidarity with his championship of human liberties and all that sort of thing regardless of race or creed. As the oiled phrases roll through Ro's ears he seems to see them engraved in fanciful spencerian on the wall in front of his eyes. Lieutenant Hicks, he answers promptly, he certainly regrets he can not be present at that most memorable occasion but he has received an urgent cable. He has to leave for home. He will be there in spirit, he adds with a flourish.

Elsa is up off the bed in a flash and running towards him in her nightgown. Ro hastens to hang up.

"His voice warms the room," she's saying breathlessly. "Even over the phone. It's the most beautiful voice in the world."

Ro brushes past her and throws the window open and thrusts his face out into the breeze off the sea. He leans out over the hot sill.

He imagines himself a condemned man leaning out through the bars of a cell in one of the old gray fortresses across the harbor, looking out for the last time at the blue of the sky and the white of the sun and the delicious ochre of the tiles nestling against the proud volutes that cap the buttressed walls of the old cathedral and at the endless shimmer of the sea.

The rooster that lives on the next roof has started to crow.

When he turns back he finds that Elsa has already begun shoving the tangle of clothes back into her suitcases. Her broad buttocks stand up under her nightgown as she leans over them. Her hair has fallen over her face.

"It would have been one swell party," she mumbles without looking up.

Ro has gone back to the phone to call the airline.

Elsa is plucking at his sleeve. "Ro," she's pleading. "Could we try it for just one more day so that we could go to that party? Maybe I could act less bitchy."

A voice is already answering from the airline office. "Reservations please," Ro requests firmly.

He puts his hand over the mouthpiece.

"Can't you understand?" Ro whispers weakly back over his shoulder, "that I can't take it any more?"

He takes his hand off the mouthpiece. "Reservations," he goes on in a firm voice, "what's the first plane back to Miami?"

20

The tanned young man behind the counter of the airline office in Miami is only too accommodating. Of course he'll cancel the round trip tickets. A check right away? Of course he'll be delighted to make a cash refund if Mr. Lancaster doesn't mind waiting.

"I can wait," says Ro.

Chanting something cheery about signing a voucher the young man bounds into the back office.

"I've got nothing to hurry about," Ro hears himself say.

He stands with one elbow on the counter staring out through the broad window at the people milling on the sidewalks of Flagler, old couples who look soft and wrinkly as pricked balloons in their illfitting sportclothes, clumps of longnecked adolescents with acne on their cheeks, hill-billy countenances under strawcolored hair with a trickle of tobacco in the corners of their mouths, sallow foxyfaced men in flowered shirts with copies of *Racing Form* under their arms. The lanky mechanic look. The cracker grin. The hick expression. My own people Ro is thinking; for better or worse it's to them I belong.

The newsvendor at the corner is a woman; a youngish crumpled face with a thousand wrinkles in it that looks as if it came straight out of a mountain cabin in the Ozarks; her face speaks brazen independence.

"Here you are, sir." Ro looks up with a start. The tanned young man is looking into Ro's face concernedly as if he noticed something wrong with him. "Sorry I was so long, sir." He begins cheerfully counting out the bills on the counter. "Sorry not to have you with us on the flight, sir," he rattles on. "Don't forget us when you finally do make your reservations, sir. I guess you've decided to stay down for a while."

The tanned young man fastens his eagerbeaver eyes on Ro's face with an almost too personal interest. For an instant Ro has an impulse to tell him; instead he merely mumbles, "For a while," and stuffs the bundle of bills into his trousers' pocket.

"Don't blame you a bit, sir," the tanned young man cheers him on as he yanks himself away from the counter. "Live it up while you can," Ro hears him chant as he hurries out the door.

Waiting in the crowd for the light to cross the street he stands looking up at the rosyedged great billows of Gulf Stream clouds that drift over the city. At the end of the street they bulge purple with rain. He stands remembering again his own slow steps when he climbed for the second time the ladder, the pain of the climbing, the slipping feet, sweat blinding the eyes, the fear swimming in his head.

Again to drag himself up. Again. How many lives does a man have to lead? He stands remembering the grocer's boy dousing the incendiary bomb at Covent Garden with his bay of Brussels sprouts, the Oklahoma planter striding cheerfully down the hill head and shoulders above the crowd of villagers to meet the planes at Farm Eight, the newsvendor at Great Yarmouth going off on his night rounds with that little strut in his walk; he can't remember their names, he can't remember any of their names. Only Grace. Grace's thin little hand fluttering so gallantly from the cot as they rolled her into the operating room.

Here we are, Ro's thinking, as he crosses the street with the crowd when the light changes, the people without names.

In the entrance to the bus station a legless man squatting by a pile of papers drones out the headlines "Rabbit hunter traps rapist. Blizzards in north." A noisy fellow in a lettered cap is barking about round trip all expense tours to Nassau and Havana. "Thanks I've had my trip," Ro hears himself say.

The bus station is thronged. Here we are, Ro tells himself, here in this bus station. There's a scattering of seatanned sailors, sleepy GIs, an old man in a wheelchair pushed by two women carrying pillows, a retired Rotarian in tweeds distractedly studying his watch, a trio of practical midwest matrons past the prime of life, resort women jingling shell necklaces with fancy baskets on their arms, an ample Negro family with pigtailed tots in pink bonnets. A brown bum lies asleep on a bench. Next him sit two tall girls fresh from the beauty parlor who look like stenographers on a holiday, then a steelyhaired man in his shirtsleeves with a long machinist's face, a glossy little Jewish gentleman with a bag of oranges between his knees. There are outofwork people, people changing jobs, people changing lives, people without names.

It's the people whose names you never know who arise in the hour of need, Ro is telling himself. As if from a great distance, as if through the wrong end of a telescope he sees himself as he sits nameless among the people in the bus station.

Looking for Elsa his eyes move from face to face. His eyes linger for a moment on the face of a broadshouldered young man in a houndstooth sports jacket. The face repels him but there's something pathetically unguarded about it, a bristle of brute masculinity just beginning to break through the downy look of youth. Riding to a fall. Ro looks where the young man is looking.

Elsa sits on a bench in the corner between a lank countrywoman with a baby in her arms and a longnosed studious looking old Cuban with his longnosed son, their heads stooped together over a timetable. As Ro walks towards her he looks, as the man in the houndstooth jacket is looking, at her feet in their inadequate sneakers set firm on the grimy floor in the litter of orange peels and candy wrappings and wisps of cellophane adrift on the last puffs of the breeze off the sea, up her long straight legs to the handsome erect torso and the poised head brandishing the uncontrollable hair.

She's reading the afternoon paper. As soon as she catches sight of him she holds up the paper to show him the headlines: STORM SWEEPS CHICAGO. BELOW ZERO COLD. She gives her shoulders a shudder. "And me with my fur coat hocked for the trip."

Ro pulls out the wad of bills and holds it in front of her face.

"Not here in the bus station," she begins to protest, but already her fingers are closing over the bills. "What about yourself Ro? What about that check you paid the bill with at the Havana hotel?"

"I'll worry about that when the time comes." Ro marvels how hard and clear his voice is. "Give me thirty dollars and I'll buy you your ticket."

"Did you ask how long it took?" She looks up at him anxiously when he comes back from the ticket office.

"Fortytwo hours," he says.

"And you know how I feel about buses. I'll be dead."

The woman with the child has left. Elsa makes room for Ro on the bench beside her. They sit side by side a long time without speaking.

"Elsa," he says staring straight in front of him, "there are things in this world you can't help."

"I'll be worried about you Ro." She speaks in a frail timid voice. "I guess you don't think so."

"I'm past worrying about, Elsa," he answers gently, "and for me the worst is over. Life just by itself has its meaning." He forces a grin. "I might have turned out a VIP like Mortimer."

She's looking in his face out of her round pale brown eyes. "Ro I don't know what you mean." She gives him her old time frank straight smile.

"I guess it's because it's only like this that a man can see himself clear."

"I can't see the good if it," she says.

The voice of the loudspeaker has begun to rattle off names: Jacksonville, Atlanta, Knoxville, Cincinnati, Indianapolis and Chicago . . . Chicago Express.

She gets to her feet. He picks up her two wicker suitcases. He is talking on hurriedly. "Maybe something can be made out of failure." If he only had time he could explain. "That's what life's made up of, really." She walks ahead with her fine leisurely stride. "That's why I don't want you to feel too bad about me or Gov or anything." He's talking hurriedly in her ear as he trails after her through the gate. Already the driver is punching her ticket.

"But Ro," she turns on the step of the bus. "What are you going to do?"

She isn't looking at him. She's looking at the man in the houndstooth sportsjacket who stands next in line.

"I'll wait here for a while," Ro says. "Someday I might be needed."

Her lips wear her straight level smile but she isn't really looking at him any more.

"Well, thanks for a wonderful time," she says.

People press in after her. She is lost in the crowd on the bus.